Jacqueline Winspear is the author of the *New York Times* bestselling series featuring Maisie Dobbs. She has won numerous awards for her work, including the Agatha, Alex and Macavity awards for the first book in the series, *Maisie Dobbs*, which was also nominated for the Edgar Award for Best Novel. Originally from Britain, Jacqueline now lives in the United States.

www.jacquelinewinspear.com

By Jacqueline Winspear

Pardonable Lies
Messenger of Truth
An Incomplete Revenge
Among the Mad
The Mapping of Love and Death
A Lesson in Secrets
Elegy for Eddie
Leaving Everything Most Loved
A Dangerous Place
Journey to Munich
In This Grave Hour

The Care and Management of Lies

A Lesson in Secrets

A Maisie Dobbs novel

Jacqueline Winspear

Allison & Busby Limited
12 Fitzroy Mews
London W1T 6DW
www.allisonandbusby.com

First published in Great Britain by Allison & Busby in 2012.
This paperback edition published by Allison & Busby in 2012.

A CIP catalogue record for this book is available from
the British Library.

10 9 8 7 6 5 4 3

ISBN 978-0-7490-4004-8

Typeset in 10.5/16 pt Sabon by
Allison & Busby Ltd.

The paper used for this Allison & Busby publication
has been produced from trees that have been legally sourced
from well-managed and credibly certified forests.

Printed and bound by
CPI Group (UK) Ltd, Croydon, CR0 4YY

For my brother,
JOHN JAMES WINSPEAR,
with much love and admiration.

If you reveal your secrets to the wind you should not blame the wind for revealing them to the trees.
KAHLIL GIBRAN

He who gives up the smallest part of a secret has the rest no longer in his power.
JEAN PAUL RICHTER

PROLOGUE

Maisie Dobbs had been aware of the motor car following her for some time. She contemplated the vehicle, the way in which the driver remained far enough away to avoid detection – or so he thought – and yet close enough not to lose her. Occasionally another motor car would slip between them, but the driver of the black saloon would allow no more than one other car to narrow his view of her crimson MG 14/40. She had noticed the vehicle even before she left the village of Chelstone, but to be fair, almost without conscious thought, she was looking out for it. She had been followed – either on foot, on the underground railway, or by motor vehicle – for over a week now and was waiting for some move to be made by the occupants. This morning, though, as she drove back to London, her mood was not as settled as she might have liked, and the cause of her frustration – indeed, irritation – was not the men who followed her, but her father.

Maisie was now a woman with a good measure of financial independence, having inherited wealth in the form of a considerable property portfolio as well as investments and cash from her late mentor, Dr Maurice Blanche. To the outside observer, the windfall had not changed her character, or her attachment to her work; but those who knew her best could see that it had bestowed upon her a newfound confidence, along with a responsibility she felt to Blanche's memory. Dust was settling on the events of his death, and as she moved through the grief of his passing to acceptance in the process of going through Blanche's personal papers, Maisie wanted – possibly more than anything – to see her father retired, resting, and living at the Dower House. She had not been prepared for her plans to be at odds with his own, and this morning's conversation, over tea at the kitchen table in the Groom's Cottage, capped several months of similar exchanges.

'Dad, you've worked hard all your life, you deserve something better. Come and live at the Dower House. Look, I'm away throughout the week in London, so it's not as if we'll get under each other's feet. I don't see how we could do that anyway – it's a big enough house.'

'Maisie, we've always rubbed along together, you and me. We could be in this cottage and live well enough. You're my own flesh and blood. But this is *my* home – Her Ladyship has always said as much, that this house is mine until the day I die. And I'm not ready to hang up my boots to sit in an armchair and wait for that day to come.'

Frankie Dobbs was now in his early seventies, and though he had suffered a debilitating fall several years earlier, he was in good health once again, if perhaps not quite as light on his feet. His role as head groom – a job that came with the tied cottage – now chiefly comprised advising Lady Rowan Compton on purchases to expand her string of racehorses, along with overseeing the stable of hunters at Chelstone, the Comptons' country seat.

'Well, what about not giving up work and just moving into the Dower House? Mrs Bromley will take care of you – she's such a good cook, every bit as good as—'

Frankie set down his mug with a thump that made Maisie start. 'I can do for myself, Maisie.' He sighed. 'Look, I'm happy for you, love, really I am. The old boy did well by you, and you deserve all that came to you. But I want to stay in my home, and I want to do my work, and I want to go on like I've been going on without any Mrs Bromley putting food on the table for me. Now then . . .'

Maisie stood up and walked to the kitchen sink. She rinsed her mug while looking out of the window and across the garden. 'Dad, I hate to say this, but you're being stubborn.'

'Well then, all I can say is that you know where you get it from, don't you?'

They had parted on good enough terms, with Frankie giving his usual warnings for her to mind how she drove that motor car, and Maisie reminding him to take care. But as she replayed the conversation in her mind – along with those other conversations that had come to nought – she felt her heels dig in when she looked at the vehicle on her tail. She was damned if she would put up with some amateur following her for much longer.

She wound down the window and gave a hand signal to indicate that she was pulling over to the side of the road, thus allowing an Austin Seven behind to pass, followed by the motor car that had been shadowing her for at least half an hour. As soon as they passed, she turned back onto the road again and began to drive as close to the vehicle in front as safety would allow.

'Now you know I know. Let's see what you do with it.'

She noted that there was no number plate on the black motor car, and no other distinguishing marks. Both driver and passenger were wearing hats, and as their silhouettes moved, she could see the passenger looking back every so often. When they turned left, she turned left, and when they turned right, she followed. Soon they were back on the main road again, travelling up River Hill towards Sevenoaks. At the top, the Royal Automobile Club had stationed two men with water cans, ready to help motorists having trouble with overheated vehicles. It was a long hill, and on a hot day in August, many a steaming motor car lurched and rumbled its way to the brow, with the driver as glad to see men from the RAC as a thirsty traveller might reach out towards an oasis in the desert. Allowing the black motor car to continue – she thought it was an Armstrong Siddeley – Maisie pulled in alongside the RAC van.

'Having a bit of trouble, love?'

'Not yet, but I thought I might get the water checked. It's a hot day.'

The man glanced down to the radiator grille and nodded when he saw the distinctive blue-and-silver RAC badge on the front of the MG.

'Right you are, Miss. Don't want to risk burning up a nice little runner like this, do you?'

Maisie smiled while keeping an eye on the road. Soon the Armstrong Siddeley approached the hill again, this time from the opposite direction, and as it passed, both driver and passenger made a point of looking straight ahead. *Police,* thought Maisie, sure of her assessment. *I'm being followed by the police.*

'She didn't need much, but just as well you stopped,' said the RAC man. 'Can't be too careful, not with this weather.'

'Thank you, sir.' She reached into her shoulder bag for her purse and took out a few coins. 'I wonder, could you do me a favour? A black Armstrong Siddeley will presently be coming back up the hill; he's probably turning around at this moment. Could you pull it over for me?'

The man frowned, then smiled as he took the coins and looked in the direction Maisie indicated. 'Is this the one, coming along now?'

'Yes, that's it.'

Maisie thought the man looked quite the authority as he stepped forward into the middle of the road in his blue uniform and peaked cap. He held up his hand as if he were a guard at a border crossing. The Armstrong Siddeley came to a halt, and Maisie stepped forward and tapped on the window. After a second or two, the driver wound down the window and Maisie leant forward just enough to appear friendly, smiling as she affected a cut-glass aristocratic tone.

'Gentlemen, how lovely of you to stop when you must be so terribly busy.' Her smile broadened. 'Would it be too boring of me to ask why you've been following me? I think it might save on petrol and your time to explain your actions, after all, it's been over a week now, hasn't it?'

The men exchanged glances, and the driver cleared his throat as he moved his hand towards his jacket pocket. Maisie reached forward and put her forefinger on his wrist. 'Oh, please, don't ruin a perfectly cordial conversation. Allow me.'

She reached into the man's jacket, took out his wallet, and smiled again. 'Can't be too careful, can we?' The man blushed as she opened the wallet and removed a warrant card. 'Charles Wickham. Ah, I see. So you must be working for Robert MacFarlane. Oh dear, I think you're going to get into horrible trouble when he finds out I've seen you.' She tapped the wallet against the fingers of her left hand before offering it to its owner. 'Tell you what. Inform Detective Chief Superintendent MacFarlane that I'll be at the Yard this afternoon at – let me see – about three o'clock. He can tell me then what this is all about. All right?'

The driver nodded as he reclaimed his wallet. To her surprise, neither man had spoken, though there was little they could say. There would be plenty for them to talk about when they were summoned to explain themselves to Robert MacFarlane.

Maisie and the RAC man watched as the black motor car went on its way towards Sevenoaks and London.

'Funny pair, them.'

'They'll be even funnier when their boss hears about this.'

Maisie waved to the man as she pulled out onto the road again. She was deep in thought for much of the time, to the extent that, when she reached the outskirts of the capital, she could barely remember passing landmarks along the way. Though she had kept the exchange light, she had cause for concern given that the men were reporting to Detective Chief Superintendent Robert MacFarlane of Special Branch. She had worked alongside him at the turn of the year on a case involving a man who had threatened death on a scale of some magnitude. At the close of the case, she hoped never to have to encounter such terror again. But now she suspected that MacFarlane had deliberately sent a pair of neophytes to follow her, and therefore subsequently expected her call. She shook her head. She was not in the mood for Robert MacFarlane's games. After all, Maisie Dobbs was her father's daughter, and any sort of manipulation did not sit well with her.

ONE

'Morning, Miss. Bet that fresh country air did you good for a few days.' Billy Beale, Maisie's assistant, stood up when she entered their one-room office on the first floor of what had once been a grand mansion in Fitzroy Square. The room was neat, tidy, and businesslike, with two desks and a large table by the window at which Maisie and Billy would sit to discuss work in progress while poring over the case map.

'You're right, Billy. There's nothing like a Saturday-to-Monday spent in the heart of the Weald of Kent – and I bet you're looking forward to going down to Kent yourself, for the hop-picking. You're leaving on Saturday morning, aren't you?'

'Bright and early on the Hopper's Special. Truth is, we need to get away, and Doreen's feeling the heat, what with carrying so big – you'd think she's expecting twins, but the doctor reckons it's only the one.'

Maisie laughed as she stepped towards her desk and began leafing through the post. 'As long as the baby doesn't get ahead of itself while you're down there, I'm sure it will do you all a power of good.'

'Nah, she's not due until October, so we'll be all right. Anyway, I'll put the kettle on.'

Maisie shook her head. 'Wait a moment – pull up a chair, Billy.'

'Everything all right, Miss?' Billy positioned a chair in front of Maisie's desk and sat down.

Relaxing into her own chair, Maisie shook her head. 'No, I don't think it is.' She sighed. 'You remember last week, when we noticed a man on the other side of the square, the one who seemed to be watching the building?'

'Shifty sort, if you ask me. Haven't seen him since, though.'

'Oh, he's been there – along with a few others who've been following me.'

'Following you, Miss? Why didn't you say? I mean, you could have been—'

'I didn't say anything because I was waiting to see what happened, and I didn't want them to know they'd been rumbled.'

'But you could have been set upon. I don't know what—' Billy stopped himself.

'You don't know what James Compton would say? Well, he's away in Canada for at least another month, so let's not worry about what he would say.' Maisie paused and seemed to look into the distance as she spoke. 'The truth is, I didn't feel threatened. I suspected they were gathering information, and I wanted to wait until they showed their hand, then base my next move on whatever that hand held.'

'Lucky it wasn't a knife.'

'Billy.'

'I'm sorry, Miss. I just worry, that's all.'

'Thank you. I appreciate your concern; however, I took matters into my own hands today and have discovered that – as far as I know – Special Branch is behind the subterfuge. I'm seeing MacFarlane at three.' Maisie looked at the clock on the mantelpiece. 'In fact, I should leave at about two o'clock. That'll give us just enough time to go through our cases and discuss the week ahead. There's a lot to be done before you go on holiday.'

Billy waited for a second or two before leaning forward. 'Any luck with Mr Dobbs?'

Maisie shook her head. 'He's as stubborn as a mule and will not be moved, so I suppose I will have to wait.'

'He likes his independence, that's what it is. And it's hard to take from your daughter, Miss, even though the Dower House is yours now. After all, it's a father's job to provide for his children.'

'But I'm hardly a child, Billy. I'm thir—'

'Doesn't matter. You're still his daughter. I'm sorry if I've spoken out of turn there, but I'm a father and I know. You'll have a job to get him to move up to the Dower House, no two ways about it.'

'I know,' replied Maisie, with a sigh. 'Anyway, let's get on.'

Billy opened the notebook he had brought with him to Maisie's desk. 'You had a visitor this morning. On the doorstep when I got here, she was.'

'Who?'

'That Sandra. The tall girl who used to work at Ebury Place; the one who stayed with you for a while, just before she got married.'

'Sandra? Sandra came here?'

'Yes, and very unhappy she looked, I can tell you. I would say she was mourning, what with the black costume she was wearing, and her cheeks all sunken.' Billy looked away. 'Put me in mind of Doreen, after we lost our Lizzie.'

'Did she say what she wanted?'

'No, just to let you know she called, and that she'd come back again – sounded like she meant today.'

Maisie capped and uncapped her fountain pen several times as she wondered what might be the reason for Sandra's visit. She looked up. 'Billy, have a look in the card file. Her address is in there under her married name – Tapley. She and Eric live in a bed-sitting-room over the garage where he works. I won't have time to go over today, but I'd like to have it on my desk, just in case.'

'Right you are, Miss.' He made a note and looked down at the clutch of papers in his hand. 'Now, there's the Rackman case. The old lady was on the dog and bone again, just before you walked in the door . . .'

They continued to talk about various cases in progress,

passing files back and forth, and going through client notes one by one until two o'clock, when it was time for Maisie to leave for Scotland Yard. She collected her linen jacket and shoulder bag, but stopped before she reached the door.

'Billy, if Sandra returns while I'm out, tell her she should come to the flat. I have a feeling I'll be at the Yard for a while, so I probably won't be home until about six-ish. Tell her to come then.' She looked from Billy's desk to her own. 'I sometimes think we need a Sandra to help us out – she's taken commercial courses, so she's up on secretarial work. I don't know about you, but I sometimes think we could do with a bit of help.'

As Maisie approached the main entrance to Scotland Yard's ornate redbrick headquarters on Victoria Embankment, a young man wearing overpressed black trousers and a grey jacket with worn elbows came forward to greet her.

'Miss Dobbs?' He held out his hand. 'DC Summers. Delighted to meet you. Come this way, please. Detective Chief Superintendent MacFarlane is waiting for you.'

'Thank you, Detective Constable Summers.'

As Summers led Maisie along a labyrinth of corridors and up stairs, she considered informing her guide that she knew the route to MacFarlane's fiefdom as if it were the back of her hand, so, given the heat of the day, there was no need to meander the hallways in an effort to confuse her sense of direction. Fortunately, they were soon standing outside a door bearing MacFarlane's name. Summers knocked and was met with bellowing. 'The bloody door's open!' He blushed when he looked at Maisie, who shook her head and observed, 'Ah, he's in a good mood. Lovely.' She reached past the detective constable, pushed against the door, and walked into MacFarlane's office.

'Miss Dobbs. A pleasure.' MacFarlane held out his hand to indicate that she should be seated on one of three armchairs clustered around a low table alongside the window.

'Oh, the pleasure is all mine, Detective Chief Superintendent.' She looked around the room. 'I see you've made some changes here.'

'A little more comfort for visiting dignitaries.'

'And I'm a dignitary?' Maisie hung her shoulder bag across the back of the chair as she sat down. She had found that it helped to appear relaxed in all communications with MacFarlane, who was given to flying off the handle at times, and whose wit could be cutting. He was a tall man, and upon first meeting him, Maisie thought he had the frame of a docker. In his mid-fifties now, the detective chief superintendent kept his thinning hair short and made no attempt to cover the scar where a stray bullet had caught him in the war. Apparently he had raised a fist to the enemy and sworn at them over the parapet for daring to put a hole in his tam-o'-shanter.

'You're dignified enough, Miss Dobbs.'

'I shall take that as a compliment.' She took a number of plain index cards and a red pencil from her document case as he opened the door and yelled into the corridor. 'A pot of tea wouldn't go amiss in here, or has the tea boat gone down in high tide on the bloody Thames?'

Maisie pressed her lips together, trying not to laugh. Despite herself, she liked MacFarlane, and she knew he had regard for her – and she rather hoped he might have plans to ask her to work with the Branch again. Such a role was not for the fainthearted, but there was an edge to it that challenged her. And she liked the idea of a new challenge. When she thought about it, her life had softened in the past couple of months, and she realised, while listening to MacFarlane bellow along the corridor, that she needed a sharp edge or two to keep her on her toes. Soft didn't suit her.

'There, that's put a firework under a few rumps. Can't abide that afternoon lull – shake them up a bit, that's what I say.' MacFarlane came back into the room and shut the door behind him before taking a seat opposite Maisie. He said nothing for a moment, and simply looked at her, as if taking her measure. She looked him in the eye without flinching, and without breaking the silence.

'You miss the old boy?'

Maisie nodded. 'Yes, I miss Maurice very much indeed.'

'Hard shoes to fill in anyone's book.' He paused. 'I remember when the man who brought me into the force passed on. Like losing a father it was.' He sighed. 'I started off on the beat in Glasgow, you know. I don't mind admitting I'd been a bit of a tearaway before joining the force; it was a man by the name of Calum Guthrie who sorted me out and set me on the right path. I cried like a wee bairn when he died.' A knock at the door interrupted MacFarlane's reminiscence, and a young policeman entered with a tray. As he set the tray on the table, Maisie noted the fact that it was set for three.

'Ah, so someone's joining us. How delightful.'

MacFarlane nodded and glanced at the wooden schoolhouse clock above the door. 'Any minute now. And as delightful as they come.'

'So we've only a moment or two to chat before he or she gets here.'

'He. And he'll be here on the dot of three – you were early.'

'I'll pour.' Maisie reached forward to pour tea for herself and MacFarlane. As she passed the cup to him, the clock struck the hour, and there was a sharp knock at the door.

MacFarlane stood as the door opened, and Maisie looked up to see a tall man, distinguished in a very English aristocratic way, enter the room. His dark-blue suit had the merest pinstripe, his white shirt still bore a faint scent of starch, and his shoes shone like a just-polished gun barrel. He wore a signet ring on the little finger of his right hand, and his tie bore the insignia of the Household Cavalry. Their eyes met and Maisie stood up and held out her hand – she wanted to stand tall to greet this particular guest.

'Mr Huntley. This is indeed a surprise.'

'Miss Dobbs.' He handed his mackintosh and hat to the constable, and shook her hand. 'We had little time to speak at the funeral. Though expected, Maurice's death came as a shock all the same.'

She nodded as a lump seemed to swell in her throat, preventing an appropriate reply.

Maisie had first met Brian Huntley in France two years earlier. She had travelled to a region of the country to look into the case of a missing wartime aviator, an investigation that had dovetailed with a personal assignment on behalf of her friend, Priscilla Partridge, née Evernden, who had asked her to help solve the lingering question of her brother's death in the war. Maisie discovered that Peter Evernden had been assigned to the Intelligence Corps, and soon after, she realised she was being followed. In Paris she was apprehended by none other than Brian Huntley – a Secret Service agent who was reporting directly to Maurice Blanche. It was a case that revealed to Maisie the extent of her mentor's involvement in matters connected with the defence of the realm; the fact that he had not trusted her with this information drove a wedge in their relationship. It was a fissure that was healed by the time Maurice passed away, and for that Maisie was ever grateful. Now it seemed that Brian Huntley was in an even more senior position, and he wanted to see her.

Maisie looked at the two men and took the initiative. 'Gentlemen, shall we begin? Perhaps you can start by telling me why I have been followed for some ten days now.'

'Robbie, perhaps you'd like to start,' said Huntley.

It seemed to Maisie that Huntley had assumed a certain superiority in the conversation, with his chummy manner towards the detective chief superintendent. She felt ill at ease in Huntley's company, but she remembered how he was well respected by Maurice, and such esteem would have been well earned.

MacFarlane turned towards Maisie. 'Miss Dobbs, would you be so kind as to tell us when you first noted that you were being followed, and recount the instances since that initial realisation that you were under surveillance?'

Maisie looked from MacFarlane to Huntley. She nodded. Ah, so that was the game. She had been tested.

'It was a week ago last Friday. I was in my office and when I looked out of the window, I noticed a man on the other side of the square. I am sure he thought that he was well hidden by foliage, but I noticed him immediately.'

'What made you suspicious?'

'His manner, his way of moving as he walked around the square. He appeared to be looking at the houses, much as one might appraise an area if one were looking to rent a flat. But his carriage revealed him to be a man of secrets – a slight roll of the shoulders inwards, definitely the mark of one who is protective of something; in this case it was his assignment.'

'And then?'

'I decided to test my theory, so I left the office to walk in the direction of Tottenham Court Road – it's invariably busy and wider than most streets, and it has many shop windows in which to see a reflection.' She looked at her inquisitors in turn. 'In my estimation, Mr Huntley, Detective Chief Superintendent MacFarlane—'

'Robbie, please. The title and the name form a veritable mouthful together, and we've only got so much time.'

'Thank you – *Robbie*.' She cleared her throat and went on. 'In my estimation there were two men working

26

together, and one woman, and they were using a method of surveillance that I have always thought of as something like a cat's cradle, in the way that agents move to and fro, zigzagging across the road. Initially I was followed by the man I had already seen in Fitzroy Square; then a man walking in front of me stopped to look in a shop window. At that point a woman crossed from the opposite side of the road as the man behind walked past me, and she took his place. The man who had stopped then took up a position on the opposite side of the road again, and so it went on – one person stopped, and they all changed places. I entered Goodge Street station, bought a ticket, and went through the turnstile, but a group of students – I assume they were students – managed to get into the queue before the people following me. And yet all three were on the platform just seconds behind me, and before the students. I suspect their warrant cards had gained them immediate access to the platform.' Maisie looked from Huntley to MacFarlane. 'Am I right?'

Huntley gave no indication as to the accuracy of Maisie's account. 'And then?'

'On that occasion I simply travelled on the underground for a while, visited a friend's office, just to make it seem as if I had been on a genuine errand, and then returned to Fitzroy Square.'

'Not exactly to Fitzroy Square, though,' said MacFarlane.

'No, I made a detour to Burlington Arcade. My document case was destroyed some months ago and I thought it was about time I bought another, so I went along to the arcade and purchased a new one. And of course, it was interesting, observing the way in which your agents arranged themselves in the arcade.'

'And then?'

'I made my way back to Tottenham Court Road, and before returning to the office I stopped in Heals and bought a—' She held out a hand to Huntley. 'Your turn.'

'Sofa. You bought a sofa. Very nice, too.'

'My flat is somewhat spartan; I felt it needed something a little more welcoming in the drawing room.'

'Did you see the men again?'

'Do you wish me to give you a complete list?' She faced MacFarlane. *'Robbie?'*

'A brief synopsis will do,' interjected Huntley.

Maisie sighed. 'The GPO van outside the block of flats where I live in Pimlico provided a cover for two men working on the connection to the flats. I do hope I don't have to have my new telephone ripped out for fear that you are listening to every call.'

'Go on.' Huntley did not look up as he spoke but continued looking through a dossier that lay open on his knee.

'I was followed to and from work, and down to my house on the edge of the Chelstone Manor estate last Friday. I'd finally had enough during the journey back to London this morning, which was when I intercepted them and gave a message to pass on to Det—to Robbie.'

Huntley looked up, smiling. 'And as I said to Robbie here, I thought taking the driver's wallet from his inside pocket was a little forward.'

Maisie did not return his smile. 'I'm sure you did, Mr Huntley. I catch on fairly quickly. You should have remembered that you did not go undetected in France.'

'Quite right. Very impressive.'

'What's this all about?' asked MacFarlane.

Huntley ignored the question as he folded the dossier, placed it on the table, and leant back in his chair. 'To get right to the point, Miss Dobbs, we have a job for you. This meeting is in absolute confidence, as I am sure you understand. I know I have no need to say that, but I am required to, and I am also required to ask you to sign documents to that effect at the end of this meeting.'

Maisie nodded.

'Special Branch are involved given that this assignment pertains not only to matters of interest to my department, but to the problem of aliens entering Britain for purposes that might not be as described to authorities at the ports of entry – which as you know comes under the purview of Special Branch.' Huntley opened the dossier and handed Maisie a clutch of papers, each stamped with *Official: Top Secret*. 'You will see that this report details the activities of one Greville Liddicote.'

'I've heard of him,' said Maisie. 'Wasn't he a Senior Fellow at Cambridge who made a good deal of money writing children's books in his spare time? I seem to remember he upset the apple cart when he wrote a book which clearly expressed his position against the war, in 1916 or '17.'

'Same man,' interjected MacFarlane.

Huntley continued. 'He resigned his position at Cambridge in late 1917 – it's generally thought he was asked to do so – and he went on to found a college, also in Cambridge, in 1920.'

Maisie nodded.

'The book that got him into so much trouble was an embarrassment for His Majesty's government,' said Huntley. 'It was a controversial story about a group of fatherless children who go to live in the woods, and who decide to journey to France to end the war.'

'That doesn't sound too inflammatory to me, though I haven't read the book,' said Maisie.

'We managed to have most copies confiscated; however, there was an efficient underground acquisition of books by various pacifist organisations – the last decade, as you probably know, has seen a significant rise in the number of such groups. While it appears at first blush to be fairly harmless, the book was written in such a way as to undermine morale both on the home front, and indeed on the battlefield, should it have reached the hands of serving men. The plight of orphaned children will always tug at the heartstrings, so we circumvented distribution to the extent that we could. We did not want the books reaching men in the ranks. Even those with limited literacy would be able to understand a children's book.'

'I understand,' said Maisie. She did not care for Huntley's tone regarding the 'men in the ranks', but made a mental note to see one or two booksellers who she thought might be able to acquire a copy of the offending book.

Huntley glanced at his notes again. 'The College of St Francis was founded by Liddicote on the back of donations made to him by the wealthy parents of several young men who were killed in the war, and who were his students at Cambridge. It is housed in what was once a rather substantial grand house on the outskirts of the city – the property itself was a donation from the grandparent of one of those unfortunate young men – and Liddicote began to recruit students, who come from the seven corners of the world to better their proficiency in the English language and to study English and European literature and the moral sciences. It is no secret that an emphasis on the maintenance of peace in Europe underpins much of the teaching. I should add that proximity to the long-established hallowed halls of learning in Cambridge makes it an attractive proposition to those who wish to have an immersion in the culture of our nation – and as a bonus they can always say they were "educated in Cambridge", without giving details.'

'You were an Oxford man, weren't you, Mr Huntley?'

'Guilty, as charged.'

'It was that slight acidity of the tongue when you spoke of Cambridge.'

'Let it be said that neither of your good seats of learning could be as acid as the school of hard knocks where I come from,' said MacFarlane.

'Quite,' said Huntley.

Maisie leant forward to pour more tea. 'So, how can I help you?'

'We – Special Branch and the office of which I am a

representative – believe that the school and its activities are worthy of more detailed investigation, though we do not wish our enquiries to be transparent to Liddicote or the students. That's where you come in, Miss Dobbs.'

'How?'

'An advertisement has been placed in *The Times Educational Supplement*.' Huntley passed a newspaper cutting to Maisie. 'Liddicote's college is asking for a junior lecturer in philosophy. You clearly have the academic background to meet the demands of such a position – you graduated from Girton having studied the moral sciences – and you have the necessary training to be able to conduct an investigation.'

'But there will be many, many applicants for this job.'

'On a practical level, we are able to control the applications received at the college; of those reaching Liddicote's desk, yours will be the only curriculum vitae to name Dr Maurice Blanche as a personal mentor, teacher, and employer. Maurice ensured that a keen eye was kept on the college, and choreographed a chance meeting with Liddicote that revealed shared interests. This was followed by a "friendship" based on quite entertaining correspondence between the two men.'

'Yes, I remember a letter sent after the funeral, with condolences. I had forgotten until you mentioned it.'

'Of course, a sad time.'

Maisie nodded. 'So, if I am to work under cover of a false occupation, surely my name will give me away.'

Huntley shook his head. 'No, not at all. Liddicote is

not worldly, and a brief look at your recent history would suggest that you have left the life of a private enquiry agent behind. And though you have kept it fairly quiet, a little bit of digging would reveal the depth of your attachment to the scion of the family that once employed you – James Compton is himself a man of great wealth. There are those who assume that any woman involved with him could look forward to a life of comfort, without the need to risk life and limb. In addition, except in certain circumstances, we prefer our . . . *representatives* to use their own name. It will make your story that much more believable.'

Maisie stood up and walked to the window. 'So, you effectively want me to leave my business for an indefinite period of time. I am to seek employment as a lecturer at a private college established and run by a man in whom you have an interest. And, in a nutshell, my brief is to – what?'

'You must report back on any observed activities – by anyone – that are not in the interests of the Crown. Do you understand the implications of the assignment?'

Maisie nodded. Huntley and MacFarlane exchanged glances.

'Do I have time to think about it?'

MacFarlane glanced at the clock above the door. 'About three minutes.'

Maisie turned to look out of the window. Yes, life had become a little soft, and for a woman who had worked almost every day of her life, who had seen war, who had held the dying as she tried to staunch their wounds, that ease prickled against her skin. She remembered the letter

Maurice had left for her, and one sentence in particular came to her as she looked down at the end-of-day traffic.

I have observed your work in recent years and it does not claim the full measure of your skill or intellect. In time there will be a new path for you to follow . . .

She rejoined the men, still seated in armchairs around the low table. 'I fail to see how my suitability for this role was determined by my ability to detect the simple fact that I was being followed, but, that said – I'll do it. You should know, however, that I do not work for His Majesty's gratitude, honour that it is. I prefer my payment to be more tangible.'

'Are you sure you're not a Scot?' MacFarlane smiled as Huntley passed a series of documents to Maisie, each one emblazoned with the same livid red stamp marking it as *Official: Top Secret*.

TWO

As she made her way back to Pimlico, Maisie began to doubt her decision to accept the assignment. At first she had imagined a task both intellectually stimulating and professionally challenging; but what if she were to become mired in the day-to-day tedium of an academic institution, looking for acts of – what? espionage? – that did not exist. But on the other hand, a joint proposal from MacFarlane and Huntley certainly seemed to merit her consideration. And Maurice would have wanted her to accept, of that she was sure.

She imagined sitting with him by the fireplace in his study at the Dower House. At first he would give the impression of leaving the decision up to her, yet as conversation progressed, he would show his hand. She was sure he would counsel her to broaden her horizons and accept a new challenge. So she would take on the persona of a spinster teacher, an educated woman on her own in the halls of academia – even if those halls were seen to be wanting by the standards of the more established Cambridge university community. In any case, it was too late to go back now, for she had signed official forms to the effect that she would not impart any aspect of her work to another, and that she would take anything she learnt – good or bad – to her grave. And even though she was well aware that as one of His Majesty's subjects, the Official Secrets Act touched her whether she signed it or not, her signature was her promise as much as her spoken word.

Entering her flat, she glanced at her watch. It was six o'clock, just enough time to make a cursory check on the new telephone she'd had installed several weeks ago. Tomorrow she would ask Billy – who had once worked as a telephone engineer – to conduct a more thorough investigation. She understood the need for surveillance of even the most trusted person working on a case, but the thought of her private conversations being subject to the ears of a Secret Service minion made her shudder.

At half past six, the doorbell signalled the arrival of her visitor. Maisie guessed that Sandra would be grateful for supper, so had prepared a hot soup with vegetables and pig's knuckle, and brought home a loaf of crusty bread, which she would serve with a rich slab of cheddar.

'Sandra, how lovely to see you again,' said Maisie, as she opened the door and stood back to allow the young woman to enter. 'Come on in, you know the way.'

Sandra nodded, and gave a weak smile. 'Thank you for seeing me, Miss Dobbs. I know you're really busy and—'

'Never too busy for you, Sandra. Just hang your coat on the stand there.'

As the younger woman turned away to remove her coat, Maisie's heart sank. Billy's description of Sandra's appearance was woefully inadequate. The poor girl's black clothes seemed to hang on her, and her face was drawn and pale. Maisie knew the evening would not be an easy one – something serious had come to pass, and Sandra needed her help.

'Sit down, Sandra – here, try out my new sofa. It's really quite comfortable. The evening's cool, yet it was so very close last night, wasn't it? In any case, the gas fire's on, and I've taken the liberty of preparing supper for us.'

'That's very kind of you, Miss Dobbs.' Sandra smoothed her skirt and sat down on the edge of the new sofa. 'I didn't want you to go to any trouble.'

'This was once your home, Sandra. I wanted it to be welcoming for you – and me, actually. I've only just returned to London following a few days in Kent. In fact, I only spend about four nights a week in town these days.'

'Mr Beale said you were down there. I sometimes wish I'd gone with the staff when they closed up Ebury Place, instead of staying in London.'

'Oh, but you had an excellent reason, Sandra – you were engaged to be married, and your husband-to-be had found a good job.' Maisie held up the sherry bottle. 'A small one? I'm going to have a glass before we sit down to eat.'

'That would be very nice, thank you.'

Maisie poured two glasses of sherry, handed one to Sandra, and sat down on the armchair opposite the sofa. She lost no more time in getting to the point.

'There's something terribly wrong, Sandra. What is it, and how can I help you?'

As Sandra sipped the sherry, tears came to her eyes. She brushed them away and sat with both hands clutching the small glass.

'I'm a widow, Miss Dobbs.'

'Oh, Sandra, my dear girl.' Maisie set her glass on the table and came to her side; and though she instinctively wanted to put her arm around the distraught woman's shoulders, instead she remained close enough for Sandra to feel a caring presence, but not so close as to stifle her. Maisie calculated the poor girl was all but twenty-four years of age, if that.

'What happened? I saw Eric only a few weeks ago, when I took my motor car into the garage for some repair work – it couldn't have been more than a month past.' Choked with sudden grief, Maisie could barely finish the sentence.

'I buried him a fortnight ago. There was an accident at the garage. The man he worked for had a new customer with a few cars he wanted looked after – a well-to-do new customer, is all I can say – so he had Eric working all hours. Not that he was complaining, because we wanted to get into a flat on our own, instead of living in the loft above the garage, so we needed the overtime money. Even though it had been converted for living quarters, being up in that loft was still like living in a stable.'

'How did the accident happen?'

'Eric was tired, very tired. He said that if he didn't finish the job on time, then his employer could easily find another bloke to replace him. They were both working hard, him and his boss, Reg Martin.'

'Reg is a good man – diligent and honest. And Eric's work was first class.'

'Anyway, this customer kept coming in and going on, saying he wanted the motors in double-quick time. I'm not sure of the story, but as far as I know, he'd bought them cheap, about six of them to start with, from posh people not being able to keep up because they'd run short of money – so I suppose they sold the motor cars for whatever they could get. So after buying them up and getting them on the road looking nice and shiny, this man was selling them for more money somewhere else – he only wanted enough repairs done so money passed hands with no questions.' She shrugged and wiped her eyes.

Maisie reached out and took Sandra's hand, allowing the stricken young woman to continue.

'It was all a funny business, really, but I know Reg was glad of the work – you can't turn anything down these days.'

'What happened to Eric, Sandra?' asked Maisie.

She looked down, her eyes red-rimmed with tears. 'They'd lifted the engine out of one of the motors, with a block and tackle, and Eric was leaning in under it. Then suddenly one of the chains went and the whole lot gave way. He didn't go quick, either. I was coming down the road when I heard the screams, heard Reg shouting out for help. Someone came running and went for the ambulance. I knew there and then that it was Eric, so I ran as fast as I could, and . . .' She shook her head as if to rid herself of the images in her head. 'All I could do was hold his hand. I was just about able to reach in and . . . hold his hand. He bled to death.' She leant into Maisie's arms, and as Maisie rocked her until the keening subsided, she knew the image of Sandra's young husband's final moments would never leave her.

They were still for some time, before the younger woman sat up and apologised. 'I'm sorry, Miss, I shouldn't—'

'Sandra, you've had a terrible shock. And you are grieving.' Maisie thought quickly. She knew Sandra was in a difficult position. The loft accommodation came with Eric's job, and Sandra had not worked – except for helping Reg with his bookkeeping – since her marriage; there were few opportunities for a married woman to find work.

'What can I do, Sandra? How can I help you?'

Sandra sniffed, and took a final sip of her sherry. 'I need a job, Miss, and I wondered if you knew of anyone who needed an office worker.' She paused. 'Well, anything really – cleaning, housekeeping. I'll do anything, but I don't want to waste the hours I put in at night school. I can do all sorts of secretarial work, you know, but I'll turn my hand to anything, because—' She paused again to take breath, as if the weight of her problems was pressing the air from her body. 'Because I can't stay in the loft, not any more. Reg wants another mechanic soon. That, and, well, as he says, it's not right, a widow living on her own above a garage. He's a good man, but, you know, I can see his point. He's said I can stay for another week, and I just . . . I just don't know what to do. I've been to most of the shops up and down Oxford Street and Regent Street, looking for work, and I've been applying for jobs, and—'

'Shhhh, it's all going to be all right, Sandra. Come on, let's get some hot soup into you, and I'll tell you what I have in mind.'

Over supper, Maisie asked Sandra if she would like to come to work for her, on a part-time basis to begin with. She explained that over the past few months, the task of keeping good records and filing away reports and invoices had fallen by the wayside. She did not share details of her own change in circumstance, though she was sure that Sandra would soon grasp the situation. She explained that she needed a private secretary, someone who could be trusted with confidential matters concerning the business, and who would also support Billy in the day-to-day running of the office. In addition, Maisie said that she would speak to her friend's husband; Douglas Partridge was a busy writer who was currently working on a new book and, due to the fact that he had lost an arm in the war – which hampered his progress – according to his wife, he could do with a secretary. Perhaps they could work out a plan where Sandra worked for Maisie in the mornings, and then went on to assist Mr Partridge in the afternoons.

With two jobs, Sandra would have a reasonable income.

Maisie also extended an invitation for her to live at her flat, moving her belongings back into the small bedroom that Maisie referred to as the 'box room', which had been Sandra's room for some weeks before she was married.

Sandra began weeping again. 'I hope you don't think I came here for you to do this for me, Miss Dobbs. I just thought, well, you know so many people, and you might hear of something.'

'Don't worry, Sandra, it's all right, really it is. I am so very sad that your terrible misfortune brought you to me, however, I think I can help. I need some help in the office, and though I am sure you will get us sorted out very quickly, I also want to render our filing system easier to use. The files and notes go back many years, with a wealth of information that I draw upon to this day, so it is no small task. And fortunately, we have had more work coming in of late – just as Mr Beale is about to leave for Kent and the hop-picking.'

'I'm sure I'll do my best, Miss Dobbs.'

Maisie refilled Sandra's soup bowl, and when she returned from the kitchen, she looked at Sandra directly. 'And there's one more thing, Sandra. Your confidence extends to my visitors here at the flat, and to any aspect of my life to which you are privy.' She paused. 'Though, having said that, I will be away for some weeks, starting at the end of the month. I'll be back on occasion, and I'll keep in touch. You will have a means to contact me; we'll talk about all that when you begin work. Now, perhaps you'd like to move your belongings in on Saturday or Sunday – I'll be in Kent and you'll have some time to yourself. Come to the office on Monday at twelve – I don't generally arrive until later on Mondays – and we'll begin work. I should have more information on the other job by then.'

Sandra swallowed, as if to digest everything Maisie had said. Her flushed cheeks and rounded, tired shoulders revealed a profound sense of relief at having found work and a roof over her head.

'Oh, Miss, that poor girl. I remember him – Eric. Nice bloke, wasn't he? Didn't he work at Ebury Place?'

'Yes, he was a good lad. And if you remember, he came and mended the locks on the doors here, when we were broken into.'

'Gaw, and you say the engine fell on him? Now, that's what I call a freak accident, something like that. Not that you don't hear about these things – look at that bloke who copped it when that horse bolted on Tottenham Court Road last week, frightened by one of those noisy lorries coming up alongside it. Mind you, this town's not made for horses any more, is it? And that's why you've got people like that Eric working in what used to be stables, and poor Sandra now being thrown out of her only home.'

Maisie nodded. She was used to Billy railing against the slightest injustice, and using those events to underline how much better life would be if he could only get his family away from the British Isles. Just a month previously, Maisie had commented on the surge in house building, in what people were increasingly referring to as 'suburbs'. Streets of mock-Tudor houses boasting indoor bathrooms and 'fitted' kitchens, with enough room to raise a family and close enough to both city and country to enjoy fresh air and town life. The spirit of *Metroland* had spread from the north and west of London to the south and east, and Maisie believed she could help Billy and his family improve their living conditions sooner rather than later. Cheap down payments – just one pound – could be made, with additional payments until the property was ready for habitation. The houses seemed like a good investment – at the very least she could provide the down payment as some sort of bonus for Billy. The stumbling block proved to be her assistant's pride.

'I know it sounds all very nice, Miss, but you've done enough for us already. And to tell you the truth, Miss, this government has taken a lot from us blokes; in the war, and now in this slump. The very least the likes of me can do is put a roof over our families' heads.'

Maisie had not pressed the point, but now wondered how it might be received if she were to invest in a house and rent it out – to Billy and his family. She would wait and broach the subject again, perhaps at a time when Billy was more open to accepting such an offer. When Billy and Doreen returned from Kent, they would doubtless be chagrined to be back in Shoreditch, with the added pressure of a baby soon to be born.

'I've invited Sandra to stay at my flat again, which will

help her get on her feet. And it will be a weight off my mind to know that someone is at home when I am away; at least the place will be inhabited.' She paused for a moment. 'And I have some good news for us.'

Billy looked up from his desk. 'Oh – a new job come in?'

Maisie shook her head. 'No, some help for us – she's looking for a job, so I offered her the position of secretary. It'll be part-time as she'll also be working for Douglas Partridge. She can catch up with the filing, type up our invoices and reports properly, and generally keep us in some sort of order. When she's here and clients come to the office, you won't have to miss half the conversation because you're bringing in the tea – Sandra will be able to take care of those . . . those . . . housekeeping details. Plus, when I'm away, it will be company for you, someone to talk to in the office and provide clerical support when you're working on your cases.'

Billy shrugged. 'I thought we were doing quite well here, just the two of us. And it's only lately that the filing's piled up. And where will she sit?'

Maisie thought a stronger, yet equally compassionate tack was needed. 'This is a very spacious room, Billy. You could hold the Cup Final in here. We'll keep the table by the window for the case maps, and for our discussions when we're working on a case. We'll reposition those filing cabinets and the card file against the two walls either side of the bay window. Your desk could be placed at an angle to the wall – very nice with a view to the square – and if I move my desk slightly more towards the fireplace we can fit another desk here – thus the first person to greet visitors will be Sandra.'

'We'll need a desk, Miss.'

'Could you find a suitable desk for Sandra? Have it brought to the office "cash on delivery" and I will settle the bill when it arrives.'

'Right you are, Miss.'

'And I've another job for you.'

'Yes, Miss?'

Maisie picked up the index card that Billy had left on her desk. 'This is where Eric worked – you remember, they always looked after my motor car. Sandra and Eric lived over the garage. I want you to take the MG over there and ask them to check a possible oil leak. There is no oil leak – well, no more than usual – but you can get chatting to the owner. Ask him about the business – you know how to slide it into the conversation. He has a relatively new customer who's been giving him a lot of work. Find out who it is. All I want is a name at this stage.'

'Is this for Sandra?'

'In a way.' Maisie sighed and leant against the back of her chair. 'I have a sense that, when she's settled and the problem of where to live and how to earn money is solved, her thoughts will turn inwards, and she will begin to doubt that her husband's death was an accident.'

'And you want to have proof that it was, so that she can forget it?'

'No.' She chewed the inside of her lip for a second before

continuing. 'No, not exactly. Accidents happen, Billy. The people most likely to make mistakes are the ones who think they know, who consider themselves to be experts. But when she told me about how Eric died – let's just say I had a sense of doubt. I might be completely wrong, and I hope I am; but there are times when a piqued curiosity cannot be ignored, and this is one of them.'

THREE

In her application for the position of lecturer at the College of St Francis, Maisie made much of her academic achievements. She mentioned her work for Maurice, but massaged details of her life over the past several years so that it might seem as if she had been afforded the time to pursue intellectual interests. And while awaiting a reply, she spent more time at the Dower House, immersing herself in the many books on philosophy in Maurice's library. Sitting late into the night, taking notes in a leather-bound book, Maisie at once felt as if she were thirteen years old again in the lowly position of maid in the Comptons' Ebury Place mansion. She had tiptoed into the library in the early hours of the morning several times each week, to work her way through the books and make up for the education she had been forced to abandon when her mother died. Upon being discovered by Lady Rowan Compton, she thought she would lose her job, but instead a new world opened up for her when Maurice Blanche asked to meet the young maid who dared to teach herself Latin in the small hours.

Now, as she sat at the desk, she felt an excitement: the same feeling she experienced as a girl surrounded by books that should have been out of bounds for her. She was about to embark on something completely new, a task that represented a risk, a gamble of sorts. Would it test her skills to the limit? Or would she rue the day she'd stopped the motor car on River Hill? Would she succeed in the eyes of her overseers, or would she fail? And how would that success or failure be measured? Maisie sat back in her chair, pulling a book towards her. She considered it serendipitous when she opened it to lines written by Johann Wolfgang von Goethe: 'A man can stand anything, except a succession of ordinary days.'

As she left the library – she still thought of it as Maurice's library – she stopped as she walked past a looking glass in the hallway. She had never been one to linger over her reflection, but since Maurice's passing she found that she sometimes stopped to check her appearance, as if circumstances had made her something other than she knew herself to be. But there she was, the same. Her black hair, inherited from her mother and grandmother before her, was still worn in the bob she had adopted almost three years ago, and her deep midnight-blue eyes seemed recovered from the weariness of grief. Her clothes had never been ostentatious, and despite her newfound wealth, she still welcomed Priscilla's castoffs, which were often all but new when dismissed as 'old hat' by their owner. And as the months passed, Maisie had felt the dread of having no resources lift from her heart; it was a fear wrought by a childhood spent in poverty, and it had weighed upon her since she was a girl. She traced a few lines along the sides of her eyes and mouth, while repeating to herself, again, the words she had just read. She hoped the days ahead would be extraordinary.

'Good morning, Miss. Lovely morning, isn't it?' Sandra greeted her new employer with a smile; Maisie was glad to see the young woman beginning to look more like herself again, though she often heard Sandra crying herself to sleep at night.

'It certainly is a good morning. There was hardly any traffic on the road from Kent, and the sun was shining all the way.'

'I'll put the kettle on, then. You have a postcard from Mr and Mrs Beale, and he also telephoned this morning to say that he would be back on Monday.' Sandra had set the morning's post on Maisie's desk. 'A postal order and two cheques have come in, and you have two letters that look as if they're from possible new clients.' She paused. 'And one from the College of St Francis – the one you've been waiting for.'

'Thank you, Sandra. My, this office is looking neater than it's looked in a long chalk!'

Maisie went to her desk without taking off her jacket or

hat and opened the letter from the college. Greville Liddicote informed her that he had been in receipt of her application for the position advertised in *The Times Educational Supplement*, and he was pleased to inform her that she had been selected for interview, to take place on September 1st, 1932. He added that the appointment was a late one, in terms of the academic year, and was due to unforeseen circumstances. He hoped that, should she be the candidate selected for the position, she would subsequently be available to take up her post within one week. He added that if there was any doubt on her part regarding the proposed arrangements, perhaps she would be so kind as to let him know, as her candidacy for the job would be affected.

'Interesting,' said Maisie, as she reread the letter. She suspected he intended to make a decision on the day of the interview, which was not unusual in a school or college.

'Did Billy say anything else? He seems to be returning early from hop-picking.' Maisie looked up at Sandra as she brought in the tray with a mug of tea for Maisie and a cup for herself.

'He mentioned that he was a bit worried about Mrs Beale down there, and that he thought they'd all be better at home.'

'Hmmm, I hope everything's all right,' said Maisie.

'They're probably just being on the safe side.' Sandra paused. 'When will you be leaving?'

'I'll go up to Cambridge next week, on the first, and if it all goes to plan, I will be living in digs close to the college soon after – I will need to do a lot of preparation.'

'Funny that, wasn't it? That Dr Blanche wanted to see you in a college for a while, teaching.'

'Not so funny if you knew Maurice.' The lie had come easily when she had first explained her reasons for applying for a teaching job, though Maisie felt guilt at having to deflect the truth from an employee she trusted implicitly. 'Maurice always set stock by the ability to teach, and I am glad the opportunity presented itself. In any case, Billy will be here, and I will be back on occasion to catch up with work – when I get into the swing of things, I expect to be able to drive down at the end of each week. We're doing quite well at the moment, so you'll both have your work cut out for you. In fact, as time goes on, I expect we'll need you here full-time, Sandra, though I expect Mr Partridge might have said the same thing – is everything going well there?'

'Very well, Miss Dobbs. In fact, you're right, Mrs Partridge says that they might like me to come full-time at some point – I've been doing some office work for her, too, you know.'

'Oh, I bet you have – social secretary?'

'Yes, sort of.'

Maisie laughed. 'We'll just have to fight over you, then.'

Sandra smiled and nodded, and went back to sorting through a series of files. She had already developed a new system of cross-referencing the card file and the larger client files, the manila folders filled with notes on each case, and to which the case map was added when an assignment had been brought to a satisfactory conclusion. The new system delighted Maisie, though she thought that Billy might not care for the change – she suspected he had become used to 'business as usual'.

Having arrived in the city with time to spare, Maisie used the opportunity to drive around and indulge her memory of her first days in Cambridge. Though the university students would not begin their Michaelmas term for another few weeks, it seemed that already young people were swarming around on bicycles, much to the consternation of those driving motor cars and omnibuses. She parked the MG and walked to the Clare Bridge; it had been a favourite place to stroll on a Saturday morning in late autumn, when, with a low sun throwing light upon frost-bedecked willow trees, she would linger on the bridge and marvel at her fortune in coming to this place, how fate had stepped in and set her on a path she could never have imagined even a year before. Clare was the oldest bridge in Cambridge, and there was something about standing on the bridge, with her feet on a thoroughfare walked by scholars for almost three centuries, that had filled her with anticipation of what the future might hold. Then the cold would nip at her fingertips and toes, and she would make her way to the market, perhaps to buy fresh bread still bearing the fragrance of warm yeast which she would later spread with an indulgent layer of butter and Mrs Crawford's strawberry jam. And she would consider herself lucky indeed to have such a sweet for tea. She smiled, remembering the hamper of comestibles the cook at Chelstone had sent to her shortly after she arrived at Girton College to begin her studies – homemade apple pie, strawberry jam, a quarter pound of Brooke Bond tea, and a jar of honey from the hives at Chelstone. Priscilla had joined the afternoon feast. 'She probably thinks they starve you here,' she'd said, before tucking into a slice of toast and jam, then wiping crumbs from her lips. 'Do write and tell her how hungry you are, and she'll send us some more – that jar won't last long at this rate, I can tell you!'

The College of St Francis was housed in a grand mansion just off the Trumpington Road, within walking distance of the Cambridge Botanic Garden. Standing in front of the considerable property, Maisie thought it must have been built in the early years of Queen Victoria's reign, testament to the fashion for Gothic Revival architecture, with churchlike windows, the chimneys close together in three clusters, heavy leaded windows, and an oversized spire on the roof above the substantial front door. She suspected that students would doubtless remember it as a place of echoes, of ghosts, of the creaks and wheezes inherent in an old house as nighttime cooled the rafters. Camellias and rhododendrons in bud obscured part of the view, though leafy cherry trees that would be filled with blossom in spring gave visitors cause for cheer, as if the trees and shrubs were assuring them, 'It's not as bad as it looks in here.'

She looked up at the spire once more and walked towards the door, where she pulled the cast-iron bell handle to the right of the entrance. A young woman opened the door and gave an economical smile.

'Are you Miss Dobbs?'

'Yes, to see Dr Liddicote.'

'Follow me.'

The young woman was of average height. Her light-brown hair was cropped into a short bob with not a hair out of place, and Maisie noticed the merest blush of rouge on her cheeks. Her brown shoes clicked against the polished floorboards as she led Maisie along the corridor towards a door with a frame that Maisie thought would have been well-suited to the inner sanctum of a church.

'Please wait in here, Miss Dobbs. I will come for you when Dr Liddicote is ready to see you.'

Maisie chose an armchair close to the window, which looked out on the grounds. Flanked by an assortment of both deciduous and evergreen trees, the lawns were also bordered by rhododendrons and flower beds with dahlias and asters in bloom. She closed her eyes and cleared her mind, in part because this was her practise before an important meeting, but also to marshal the butterflies of anticipation. Reflecting upon her story to Sandra – that Maurice had wanted her to spend time in a teaching capacity – she reminded herself that there was an element of truth in the tale. Maurice had often spoken to her of the importance of passing on knowledge, and of the skill involved in presenting ideas and facts in a manner that was engaging and made a lasting impression – whether the recipient of that knowledge was an employee, a student, or a child. She rubbed her hands and waited, half-wishing she had brought one of Maurice's notebooks to read so that his words could sustain and inspire her in the moments before her meeting with Liddicote.

* * *

'Dr Liddicote will see you now.' The young woman held the door open for Maisie and led the way along the corridor to a room with a carved oak door. She tapped on the door twice, and moved closer, resting the side of her head against the wood to listen for a response. She pulled away and knocked again, this time with more force. 'He's a little hard of hearing,' she whispered.

The second knock had the desired effect, for this time even Maisie could hear Liddicote call, 'Come!' without having her ear to the door.

'Miss Dobbs.' Upon entering the room, the woman announced Maisie's name in a loud voice, and waited for acknowledgement.

Liddicote swivelled his wooden captain's-style chair around to face Maisie, and beckoned her towards the visitor's chair, then he cast his eyes down to refer to the sheaf of papers that she assumed contained both her letters of reference and curriculum vitae. She could see that he had scribbled notes in a small, precise hand underneath several paragraphs, and along the margins.

'Thank you, Miss Linden.'

Maisie noticed that his eyes did not meet those of his secretary, and that as she closed the door behind her, her face was as stone.

Liddicote set the papers on the desk in front of him and clasped his hands under his chin as he leant back in the chair. The swivel chair had clearly seen better days and seemed as if it might give way at any moment. As he looked up at her once again, Maisie thought Liddicote might apply some sort of dye to his hair, for it seemed unnaturally dark brown, like the polished boot of a soldier. The colour was particularly incongruous against his face, which was lined, though no more than one might expect of a man past sixty; she would have thought it more natural if a few wisps of grey were evident. His clothes appeared more expensive than one might expect of a professor, and she thought he might always be prepared for a meeting with a person of importance, one who had the funds to make a bequest to the college.

'I've read your application in some detail, Miss Dobbs. Your references are impressive.'

'Thank you, Dr Liddicote.'

'But why do *you* now want to teach, Miss Dobbs?'

Without preamble, the question felt as if it had been shot from a gun.

'I have long wanted to teach, Dr Liddicote. It was always an ambition, inspired and encouraged by my own beloved teacher, Dr Maurice Blanche.' She paused. 'Dr Blanche began directing my education when I was a girl – at the time I was struggling to teach myself Latin.' She took a deep breath, wondering how much of herself she should reveal. 'My years of formal learning – which could best be described as "limited" – ended when I was twelve, due to my mother's death and my father's circumstances. So I set out to teach myself, and was fortunate when my employer consulted with Dr Blanche regarding my future. It was Maurice Blanche who taught me that the word "education" is rooted in the word *educare* – or *ex ducare* – and the most important aspect of the definition is that it has two meanings; one being to acquire knowledge – from books and study – and the second to explore and understand that which is within us. Dr Blanche underlined that the second is a search, a journey leading to the places where wisdom lies and is crucial to who we might become. In taking up the teaching profession I am not only imparting knowledge but playing a part in each student's personal pilgrimage of learning. It represents a great responsibility, but one that is rewarding, without doubt.'

Liddicote looked at Maisie and held her gaze for longer than was comfortable, though she did not look away. She felt it was as if he were assessing her response and looking for evidence of where *she* might be on that personal pilgrimage.

'And what if the student shows no talent for introspection, Miss Dobbs? How would you deal with such a situation, if your ambition is to lead your students towards a nirvana of personal wisdom?'

His tone verged on sarcasm, though she suspected he was playing devil's advocate.

'I see my role as being instrumental in introducing the study of philosophy in a way that has meaning for my students, rather than regurgitating a series of lectures on modern thought, as if it were biology or chemistry. There is of course a syllabus that must be adhered to for the students to achieve standards set by the college – and those standards represent a promise by any other name. However, in my approach I would hope to teach concepts in a manner which encourages personal introspection and energetic dialogue.'

'And how will you do that?'

'I intend to introduce the important philosophical ideas and the teachings of the masters in such a way that students are turned towards their own personal experience as a path to understanding. I would see my role, ultimately, as one tasked with inculcating a sense of wonder regarding the self.'

'A lofty ambition.'

'I may be an idealist, but I believe that when one enters teaching, one's ambitions should be lofty.' Maisie's eyes met Liddicote's once more, and she wondered if she had not overdone her reply.

Liddicote cleared his throat. 'Something you should know about how we go about education – *educare* – at St Francis: we offer the study of English, both language and literature, European languages and literature, and the moral sciences, which you studied at Girton, though you would have had the benefit of a more scholarly intensity than our students, for whom the study is introductory by comparison. Yet they take it no less seriously. The concept of peace – peace among men, among nations – underpins our work here, which is why we encourage and welcome students from the Continent. There are German and Austrian students here, as well as from France, Italy, Spain, the Netherlands, and Belgium. This blend of cultural origin is reflected in the staff as well. Do you have any objection to working with those with whom this country has been at war in the past?'

'Of course not. I would not have applied for the job if my personal sentiments had leant towards such a position.' Maisie took a deep breath and was aware that her voice trembled a little as she began to speak. 'I do not hold with the idea that we should fight each other towards an end goal of mutual destruction.'

'Go on.' Liddicote leant forward, resting his hands on the desk in front of him. They were the hands of a boy barely out of his teens, as if Liddicote had never lifted anything more heavy than a pen. His nails were manicured and seemed unsullied, except for a smudge against the inside of the top joint of his middle finger, where the ink from his fountain pen had leaked onto his skin. Maisie often bore a stain in exactly the same place.

'And I believe,' said Maisie, 'that the study of philosophy, of the meaning of life itself, helps us to consider the problems that face mankind from a new perspective – from multiple perspectives when all students engage in broad conversation based upon their exposure to both traditional and new works. And if we then know more about ourselves and each other – as I said in response to your earlier question, with that sense of wonder – surely we will be less inclined go to war.'

There was silence as Liddicote leant back and regarded her. He nodded. 'Come, let me show you around the college here; a short meander around the grounds. I'll tell you more about our founding as we walk, and we'll continue discussing your application in the gardens. I'm a great believer in walking, you know.'

Maisie stood up. As they made their way along the corridor to the doors that led into the grounds, she noticed several other candidates waiting in the room to which she had been taken when she arrived at the college, and she wondered if Liddicote had remembered that he had other people to see. She felt there were more specific and challenging questions to come as they walked through the college and around the grounds, though she was now more confident. She had felt a welter of warmth when he'd said, 'I'm a great believer in walking, you know.' Though his tone and presence were quite different, it was a sentiment shared by Maurice, and there was a comfort in that.

A 'short meander' around the college grounds was extended to reveal a larger property than Maisie had at first imagined, and included Greville Liddicote personally accompanying Maisie along a path referred to as 'a Meditation on St Francis'. The path led into woodland and snaked around a stream before emerging close to the opposite side of the property. At points along the way, stones were set into the ground, or hung on a tree, or perhaps placed alongside a wooden seat, each engraved with several lines from the Prayer of St Francis. On a bench adjacent to a stone etched with the words *'to be understood, as to understand; to be loved, as to love'*, Liddicote sat with Maisie, questioning her further on matters of philosophy, before escorting her back to his secretary's office, where Miss Linden informed him that he was now running far behind schedule. Liddicote appeared unfazed by his tardiness and smiled as he introduced his secretary as if the women had never met, though Maisie suspected he was diffusing the young woman's anxiety with humour.

'Miss Dobbs, this is my secretary, Miss Rosemary Linden, without whom the wheels of learning would doubtless grind to a halt and there would not be a pencil or chalk to be found – and, more to the point, our staff would never know where to go or which class they were teaching.'

Maisie smiled and extended a hand to Rosemary Linden, who offered the hint of a smile in return and barely grazed Maisie's fingers by way of a handshake.

'Miss Linden, I would like Miss Dobbs to meet Dr Thomas and Dr Roth.'

The woman nodded. 'Yes, of course, Dr Liddicote. I'll summon them to the library meeting room; that would probably be the best place for them to see Miss Dobbs.' She handed him a folder. 'Mr Shepherd, your second interview. Dr Poole will be your third.'

Miss Linden turned to Maisie. 'Let me take you to the meeting room, then I'll find Dr Thomas and Dr Roth.'

With the new academic year at the College of St Francis already in session, students walking to and from their classes now filled the previously empty corridors. Maisie could see where the house had been altered here and there to accommodate the needs of a learning institution, but thought it still seemed to bear the mark of an intimidating family home designed to be cool in the summer and warm in winter. Sandstone walls were adorned with tapestries, landscapes of the local countryside, and portraits of the masters of knowledge – she suspected the latter had been commissioned especially for the school, as they all appeared to be of the same recent vintage. Maisie took the opportunity to ask a few questions that she had not put to Liddicote.

'Where do the students live, Miss Linden?'

'Those in their first year here live in the dorms over in the east wing. We are a small college, but there are about fifty new students each year – they study at St Francis for between one and three years.'

'So, I take it that after the first year they move into lodgings.'

'We have a roster of landladies who meet our standards at boarding-houses around the city.'

'That must be difficult, when one considers the great number of students here in Cambridge.'

Linden led the way up a broad staircase with a grand banister that curved from top to bottom; at both ends the wood had been carved into a globe cradled in two hands. 'Our students have a good reputation among the landladies, we administer all rents, and we pay well, so accommodation problems are rarely encountered.' She took out a set of keys as they came alongside a door adjacent to the library. 'Here we are. Please make yourself comfortable while I find Drs Thomas and Roth.'

The young woman closed the door before Maisie could thank her. Had she not already known something of the property's history, Maisie might have thought the architecture was Elizabethan. Dark wood panels flanked the walls, with a square diamond-paned bay window looking out on to the grounds. A wooden table was situated in the centre of the room and could easily have done justice to a medieval banquet, though the leather blotter at each place marked it as a table where the school's business was discussed. Armchairs were clustered around the edge of the room, and above the fireplace the crest of the original occupants of the house continued to be displayed. The crest lent an air of gravity and, from the point of view of the college governors, no doubt, underscored a longevity that such a young educational institution could not yet boast.

As she settled on a window seat cushioned with needlepoint pillows, she looked out at the lawns, where a man, wearing brown trousers and a tweed jacket with leather elbow patches, and a young blonde woman were walking along another path that led into woodland. From the manner in which she used her hands to express herself, together with the way she kept turning to her companion, as if for reassurance, Maisie judged the woman to be young, perhaps in her early twenties. The man was older. Maisie watched as he moved alongside the woman; his stance seemed to imply some level of intimacy – perhaps a father visiting his daughter. He placed a hand on the woman's shoulder at one point and they turned towards each other. As Maisie watched, both the man and woman looked around as someone whom she could not yet see approached; they stood apart, with the man lifting his chin slightly in greeting, while the woman began to turn away, half-opening a book – Maisie thought it an attempt to suggest that the page in question was the topic of conversation; a hurried movement borne of momentary panic. Maisie leant forward in time to see Miss Linden approach the man. They spoke for just a moment, then the man bid a hasty farewell to the young woman and followed Liddicote's secretary. It came as no surprise when, ten minutes later, Miss Linden returned to the meeting room with the man, Dr Matthias Roth, and informed them that Dr Francesca Thomas would join them shortly.

'Miss Dobbs,' said Roth, with just a trace of a German accent. 'Welcome to our own League of Nations. The neutral Swiss will be here as soon as she's finished her tutorial.'

'Maisie Dobbs. What have you got for me – you've been a bit quiet, I thought you might have gone off to the Riviera with your friends from Biarritz, or wherever it is.' The fact that MacFarlane had deliberately pronounced it 'Beer-itz' was not lost on Maisie.

Maisie opened the door of the telephone kiosk just enough to allow fresh air to circulate. 'My Beer-itz friends are in London now; their boys are back in school. But you knew that anyway, didn't you, Robbie?'

The detective laughed. 'Too-chay!' His pause was brief. 'Got the job yet?'

'Waiting to hear. I've just had my interviews and the powers that be have sent me off for a walk while they put their heads together. This is the way it's done in colleges –

they see all the candidates on one day, then they meet and discuss and the final decision is made. My sense is that Liddicote goes through the motions of including other members of staff in his deliberations, but when it comes down to it the decision is his alone.'

'Anything out of the ordinary?'

'He gets on his secretary's nerves, but that could be part of his role as the absentminded professor – when he wants to play it. He's a very acute man – despite being genuinely hard of hearing, I think. His stock-in-trade seems to be pressing the unexpected question.'

'Anything you know that I don't know about him?'

'Not yet.' Maisie coiled the telephone cord around her fingers.

'Who else did you meet?'

'Dr Roth. He lectures in philosophy and German literature in translation – and in some quarters that's seen as just one subject, not two. And Dr Francesca Thomas. Roth said she was Swiss, but there is no trace of an accent; she speaks as if she attended Roedean.'

'Have you met anyone else?'

'No.'

'We already had a staff list, so we know about Roth and Thomas – and as far as we know, there's nothing to concern us about either one. But we'll have another look at Roth, just in case. What did you think of them?'

'Both very approachable,' said Maisie, reflecting upon their meeting. 'It was more conversational than an interview for a job at the school. Neither of them seemed out to question my shortcomings, or test me in any way, though they obviously asked about my credentials and queried my experience. Without doubt, Thomas is a highly educated woman; she had nothing to prove. Roth was confident – possibly an overconfident teacher – but pleasant.' She looked at the clock on the outside of a nearby shop. 'I should be getting back.'

'Right you are. Telephone when you know the lay of the land,' said MacFarlane, by way of goodbye.

As Maisie walked along the corridor on her way to the office, she took the liberty of checking the waiting room to see if the other candidates were still on the premises and was hopeful when it appeared they had left. She informed Miss Linden of her return; the secretary said little before escorting her directly to Greville Liddicote's office.

'Miss Dobbs,' said Liddicote, taking her hand in both his own. 'Welcome to St Francis. You've been selected to join us as junior lecturer in philosophy. You are still here, so I take it that you intend to accept our offer.'

'Yes, indeed, I'm delighted.'

'Come now, the staff are waiting to be introduced.'

Miss Linden was offering glasses of sherry to the staff when Greville Liddicote brought Maisie into the library meeting room. Rapping his knuckles against the wooden table, Liddicote brought the twelve or so gathered to order – Maisie noticed that she was one of only three women, and was surprised it was not more, given the number of women who had entered the teaching profession since the war.

Among the staff were a professor of English and American literature visiting from a college in Ohio, a Swedish lecturer in Greek literature and English fairy tales, as well as Matthias Roth and Francesca Thomas. To her surprise, the young blonde woman was introduced as Delphine Lang, a teaching assistant who had recently graduated from the University of Heidelberg, though in Maisie's estimation she spoke English with a Home Counties accent that could cut glass as easily as the voice of Dr Francesca Thomas. And as the welcoming reception went on into the early evening, Maisie noticed Roth making his way towards Delphine Lang, and when she turned to continue her conversation with Francesca Thomas, it was evident that Thomas was following the pair with deep interest.

FOUR

'How are you, Miss Dobbs?' enquired Sandra, when Maisie telephoned the office from Cambridge the following morning.

Maisie worried that Sandra's cheery tone sounded forced but thought it best to answer in the same vein. 'Very well, though I could have chosen a quieter hotel, I must say. The good news is that I have been offered the position – if Dr Blanche were here, he would be thrilled.' Again, the subterfuge came with ease. 'I'll be back in London late this afternoon, after I've found somewhere to live while I'm here. Is everything all right? Did that new client, Mr Trent, call again yesterday?'

'Yes, and Mr Beale spoke to him.'

'Mr Beale?'

'Well, as you know, he came back early from hop-picking. Mrs Beale wasn't feeling very well so they returned on Saturday.'

'How is she now – do you know?'

'I think it's just that it's the last month. They say it's the worst; all you want is for it to be over and done with. Not that I'd know anything about having babies.'

Maisie heard a catch in her voice and it struck her that, of course, she and Eric had expected to start a family; Sandra had probably hoped to have a child soon.

'Is Mr Beale there?'

'No. I expect he's got his hands full.'

'Yes, of course. Well, when he comes in, tell him I'll be back later. Everything else all right?'

'There was a telephone call from Canada. It was very strange, the operator saying she had Mr Compton on the line for Miss Dobbs, but it was as if she was talking through cardboard, and her voice kept coming and going.'

'Yes, that happens on those telephone calls.'

'Anyway, I told her you were out and she said "Thank you" and went.'

'He doesn't know there's a telephone at home yet.'

Maisie was aware that she had referred to James Compton as 'he' – and she knew it was because she did not want to use his title. As the son of a man who had several titles – but who preferred to be known simply as 'Lord Julian Compton' – and a mother who laid claim to her own title, James had been bestowed the title 'Viscount Compton', a form of address that Maisie found both fussy and intimidating. Upon his father's death he would inherit titles and lands, yet she knew that in certain circles – especially in commercial circles, and more particularly when on business in Canada – James was happy to introduce himself as 'Mr Compton', even though those he met knew exactly who he was.

'Oh, speaking of the telephone at home, Mr Beale came round to the flat to check the new line you've had put in. He knows some of the engineers who installed lines around the Pimlico area, so he was able to get into a junction box – or something like that – and check the lines from there.'

'Did they find anything untoward?'

'He said he wasn't one hundred per cent sure, but he thought you should be careful about what you say on the telephone. He had his mate with him, and they said that it looked like someone had been working on that box who wasn't a proper GPO engineer. It was clear enough to see, he said, because you don't have a party line.'

'No, I wanted a private line to my flat – frankly, more for personal telephone calls. Anyway, point taken. I'll speak to Billy about it when I see him.'

Having looked at three vacant rooms, Maisie paid a deposit to the landlady of a boarding house closer to the centre of Cambridge, yet within easy reach of the College of St Francis. Though she could now afford much more comfortable surroundings, she did not want to seem ostentatious. In any case, her room – the front bedroom in a double-fronted Edwardian villa with large bay windows and a staircase that swept up through the centre of the house to the two floors above – was clean and comfortable. There was a double bed with a floral eiderdown and counterpane, an armchair with a slightly worn floral cover – which did not match the counterpane or the eiderdown – and a desk in the corner with an angle-poise lamp. She hoped it would help to throw light on whatever Huntley and MacFarlane suspected might be going on at the College of St Francis that was 'not in the interests of the Crown'.

Her lodgings secured with a deposit and one month's rent, Maisie thought she would meander around Cambridge – a walk down memory lane to some of the places she enjoyed when she was a student at Girton College. Her early days there did not afford her the opportunity to socialise much beyond the college, though Priscilla had certainly accepted every invitation that came her way and seemed to know a great number of people. So many of those young men, including Priscilla's three brothers, had died in the war. Maisie walked along the Backs, watching a younger set larking around on punts. They were just boys, she thought. *All just boys.*

She continued on her walk, looking in shop windows and leafing through magazines in a newsagent's, before deciding it was time to drive back to London. She remembered a short cut between a row of houses, across a bridge, and then a park. It was as she set foot in the park that she noticed a young couple holding hands under a tree. They might not have attracted her attention at all had not Delphine Lang's blonde hair caught her eye. Maisie moved into the shadow of a tree to continue on her way – she did not want Lang to see her, as it was clear that this was an assignation the teaching assistant and her male friend were trying to keep secret by meeting in a park used, for the most part, by local people. She could not avoid noticing, however, that Delphine Lang was weeping and that her friend had drawn her to him to soothe her.

It was on Maisie's final day in the office before her departure for Cambridge, that Geoffrey Tinsley came to Fitzroy Square.

'I thought I would come over with the book you asked me to acquire for you. I was lucky to find a copy, you know.' The bookseller – whom Maisie had first met at his bookshop on Charing Cross Road while working on a case at the end of the previous year – unwrapped a book with a burgundy cloth cover. There was no dust jacket, but the front was embossed with an illustration of three children standing together, looking up at a soldier. Behind the soldier were rows of crosses diminishing in size to suggest a battlefield cemetery.

Maisie took the book from him and ran her hand across the cover.

'Rather startled me, to tell you the truth,' said Tinsley. 'I had heard of Liddicote's children's books – indeed, we have several on our shelves – but this one is very hard to come by. I obtained it from an overseas dealer – quite a stroke of luck – that's why it's taken me a while since your enquiry; almost all copies were taken out of circulation.'

Maisie turned the pages, drawn to the stark illustrations

depicting first a family receiving news of a father lost, then in the next chapter, a gathering of children. Another showed the children sailing for France, with the caption 'Poor little mites – looking for their fathers.'

'Some of the pages are foxed, and there's that damp smell – it will eventually abate if you leave the book where it can get some air, but I would caution you not to leave it exposed to the light. Don't put it out on a table near the window, that sort of thing. I didn't provide a new jacket as I knew you would want to see the embossing, but I can certainly have the cover boards wrapped for you.'

'Not to worry, I can do that.'

'It's an interesting book, considering the trouble it caused.'

Maisie looked up. 'I've heard something about the "trouble", but I wonder what you've heard.'

Tinsley shrugged. 'Well, as you know, copies were withdrawn from distribution under government order, and I understand that there was talk of the author being charged with sedition. It clearly didn't come to that – I think everyone wanted the book's reputation to be swept under the carpet. But there's a rumour attached to the book – a couple, actually.'

'Go on.'

'The first is that Greville Liddicote was not the author. The second rumour is that this book was at the heart of a mutiny on the Western Front, in 1916 or '17.'

'A mutiny?'

'It's just talk – such things are covered up, everyone sworn to secrecy and that sort of thing. If mutinies happened, there will never be any public knowledge of them; well, certainly not in our lifetime.' He looked at the clock on the mantelpiece. 'I must be going. I left a note on the door that I would be back by one o'clock, and if I don't dash now, I will be late. It's not that I'm crushed by customers trying to get into my shop, but I don't want to miss the one customer of the day who is waiting for me to return on time.'

Maisie looked across towards her new secretary. 'Sandra, would you settle Mr Tinsley's bill from petty cash?'

'Right you are, Miss Dobbs.'

When the bookseller had left, Maisie sat down, unable to dismiss the urge to begin reading the book written by Greville Liddicote that had caused so much trouble.

'This envelope was delivered for you while you were talking to Mr Tinsley.' Sandra passed a brown envelope towards Maisie.

'Ah, yes, I think this is what I've been waiting for. By the way, what time will Mr Beale be back in the office?'

'He said by two – he's had to go over to see someone in connection with the Richards case.'

'Good. You should pop out for something to eat, Sandra.'

'Thank you, Miss.' Sandra placed a brown cloth cover over her typewriter, gathered her hat, jacket, and gloves, and left the office. 'I'll see you in half an hour, then. Would you like me to bring you a bite to eat, Miss?'

'No, not to worry – I'll go out myself later; there'll be something at the dairy that takes my fancy.' Maisie smiled at Sandra. 'What time will you be leaving to go to the Partridges?'

'Not until later on today, but he wants me to stay on for a while this evening, if I can. He says he's got a deadline.'

When Sandra had left the office, Maisie picked up the paper knife on her desk and slit open the large envelope. She'd already received similar communication, in plain envelopes at her request, from several building firms – Taylor Woodrow, George Wimpey, and John Laing among them. This one, from a smaller company building new houses in the Borough of Woolwich, *within easy commuting distance of the City*, opened their letter with thanks for her enquiry and stated that the 'show home' on an estate of new family houses in which she had expressed interest – Tudor-style semi-detached properties complete with indoor plumbing and gardens front and back – was now ready for viewing. It went on to add that Eltham was a wonderful town for family life, offering the Eltham Park Lido and numerous parks. Just one pound down and twenty-five pounds at completion of contracts would secure a home for 'today's family'. A personal note added that her specific question regarding a greater deposit to reduce mortgage repayments had been noted, and on a separate sheet she could peruse the figures, which made home ownership a possibility *for almost any modern family*.

'And that's a downright lie!' said Maisie aloud to herself, as she thought of the many men she saw on the streets each day, walking from factory to factory, from the docks to the building sites – men wearing out shoe leather looking for work. But there was only one family she had in mind for a new house, a family about to add one more mouth to feed, a family with a father too proud to accept 'other people's charity'. She had been the recipient of great generosity when her mentor, Dr Maurice Blanche, died; in his will he had left her almost his entire estate. She was now in a position to help her assistant. But until she had worked out how she might open the discussion with Billy once again, she would have to keep her plans to herself.

Settling into her new lodgings and college life came more easily than Maisie expected. Her preparations served her well, and at the end of the first week – during which time she had taught three classes each day, and had been able to reintroduce herself to other members of staff during morning coffee and afternoon tea in the staff room – she was summoned to a meeting with Greville Liddicote. When she arrived at his secretary's office, she could hear Rosemary Linden speaking on the telephone, so she stepped back to wait in the corridor. Sound echoed from the office, which had frosted glass windows atop dark wood wainscoting facing the corridor.

'I am terribly sorry, Professor Larkin, but Dr Liddicote couldn't meet with you this morning after all.' There was a pause. 'Yes, I know it's urgent, and I have conveyed your message that you wish to see him at his earliest convenience . . . Yes . . . yes, indeed, sir, I will most certainly . . . of course . . . Dr Liddicote is completely aware of the urgency of the sit—Thank you, I'll tell him.'

The call having ended, Maisie waited a moment, then knocked on the office door.

'Ah, yes, Miss Dobbs,' said Rosemary Linden. 'Dr Liddicote is in conference at the moment, so you'll have to wait outside – he'll be finished soon, I daresay, and it's the best place to wait to avoid someone else weaselling in before you. Everyone seems to think that what they have to say is urgent today.' The previously dour secretary seemed to have softened somewhat, now that Maisie was a member of staff. Though she wasn't what might be termed 'pally', she appeared more inclined to greet Maisie with a 'Good morning' and a smile.

There was a plain, dark oak settle with needlepoint cushions outside Liddicote's office, and Maisie waited here for his meeting to end. She took four exercise books from her new leather briefcase and began to read through essays submitted by the morning class, but became distracted when the mumble of voices from Liddicote's office became louder and more urgent. She could not make out the cause of the argument, only the harsh tones as two men argued.

'You're a fool, Roth, if you think that—'

'Dr Liddicote, far be it from me to say this, but it is you who are the fool.'

As the voices raised, Miss Linden emerged from her office and walked briskly to Liddicote's door, knocked, and stepped just inside the room. Maisie kept her eyes on her work.

'Miss Dobbs is waiting for you, Dr Liddicote.'

'Yes, of course. Roth, do not do anything until I have considered this further.'

Maisie heard a sound that she thought was Roth snapping his heels as he emerged from the room, ignoring Maisie as he walked along the corridor and out into the grounds. It took no special observation skills to see that Roth held within him both anger and disappointment, for there were tears in his eyes.

'Come in, Miss Dobbs.' Linden waved Maisie into the room, with a brief suggestion of a smile as she closed the door behind her.

'Thank you for your time, Miss Dobbs. Please sit down.' Liddicote nodded towards the visitor's seat.

When they were both seated, Liddicote leant back in his chair, closed his eyes for a moment as if to banish the previous conversation. His face seemed flushed, and he placed a hand against his chest as if to settle his heart. Maisie was about to ask if he felt unwell, when he opened his eyes and gave a forced smile.

'How are you faring?'

'I think the first week has gone well so far.' Maisie offered no more, waiting for Liddicote's lead.

'I've heard on the college grapevine that the response to your lessons is good, and other lecturers have noted your professionalism in your role. We are happy to have you here at St Francis.'

'Thank you, Dr Liddicote.'

'And in case you're wondering, it's customary for me to have a meeting such as this with new members of staff towards the end of their first and second weeks in particular.'

'Yes, of course. I understand.' She was relieved to see that the conversation was calming Liddicote.

He paused, allowing silence to enter the space between them before speaking again.

'Tell me about the existence of God, Miss Dobbs.'

Maisie was taken aback by the abrupt instruction, but countered her surprise with a question.

'In what context, Dr Liddicote?'

He smiled. 'Ah, not one to assume anything.' Another pause before continuing. 'As a college where the concept of peace underpins so much of our curriculum, the nature of God is crucial to our dialogue. We have students of several faiths here; we have those who have seen much in their young lives, and who are inclined to question the existence of God – and of course it is a fundamental question in terms of philosophical discourse. Therefore, Miss Dobbs, speak to me of God. Does he exist?'

Maisie cleared her throat. 'It was Saint Anselm of Canterbury who laid down the question, "Does God exist?" He then gave the example of the artist who has a picture of the not-yet-executed masterpiece in his mind's eye. Can the painting be said to be real because the painter can see it? Or is it only real when the masterpiece is finished for all to see? Anselm gave the argument for supporting the existence of God; however, the essence of his deliberation is in the question itself.'

'Another question, then, and one of particular resonance to your generation. If there is a God, then why does he allow war to continue?'

Maisie inspected her hands as she considered the question, then looked up as she framed a response. Liddicote was waiting for her to speak, his chin resting on his steepled hands.

'With this question,' said Maisie, 'I sense that you have asked for an answer that reflects my personal experience of the world. I confess that during the war – and many times since – I have asked this same question, and to be frank, at times with many tears and a deep pain in my heart. But I have allowed the question to exist, to remain, because there is no answer to satisfy when one has lived through the tumult of war. On a simple level, one can only hope – can only trust – that if there is one single omnipotent God, then he knows what he is doing.' She stopped speaking.

Liddicote did not press her, knowing that she had more to say.

'I think, therefore,' Maisie went on '. . . that it is admissible to say that God exists, even if we have no rational means of proof. But if that is so, we must also assume that evil exists. As far as my teaching is concerned, I believe there to be a richness of debate when we discuss what is meant by good and evil, and how the philosophical dialogue is reflected in the human experience.'

Liddicote nodded. 'Good answers, Miss Dobbs, and thoughtful. I anticipate joining one of your classes next week – I think perhaps on Wednesday afternoon, when you teach the more senior students.'

'I look forward to it, Dr Liddicote.'

'One more thing, Miss Dobbs, then I will release you

to the staff room, for it's almost time for morning coffee.' He took out his pocket watch and checked the hour. 'It has been suggested that we apply to join a debate among students from the Cambridge colleges, on the fragile nature of peace and our position regarding Germany, particularly in light of political developments in that country. Such a debate is bound to attract the attention of a broader audience – not least the press. Certain members of staff are in favour of accepting the invitation, some against. What side of the fence would you choose?' He cupped his hand around his ear and leant forward, as if to ensure he caught every word of her reply.

'I would like to have more information on the two positions suggested for debate – is one for a resumption of conflict? Is this a result of the Peace Conference and the mood in Germany as a result of the outcome of the conference? Or is the debate inspired by the limitations of the League of Nations? In principle, I am in favour of any benign argument that has as its purpose the discovery of a means to sustain peace – but I have some reservations regarding the debate's genesis.'

'Good enough, good enough. Now then, I have another appointment on the hour.'

'Of course.' Maisie gathered her briefcase and papers and left the room. Francesca Thomas was waiting as Maisie emerged from Liddicote's office. Her tailored costume of navy-blue jacket and matching skirt enhanced a natural elegance, and seemed to draw attention to her angular features, her wide eyes set off by high cheekbones. She greeted

Maisie, and as she moved, so the navy-blue-and-magenta silk scarf at her neck shifted and a faint scar was revealed on her neck. Dr Thomas had either undergone a serious surgical procedure, or she had been the victim of an attack. In either event, at some point in her life, a blade had penetrated her delicate skin in a most vulnerable area.

As Maisie continued along the corridor, Miss Linden emerged from her office with Delphine Lang, and sighed when she saw Francesca Thomas close the door behind her as she entered Greville Liddicote's office.

'I'm afraid you'll have to wait now – he's going to be a while, I would say.' She nodded as Maisie passed, turning to the pale teaching assistant to suggest that she come back after morning coffee.

Touching her own neck as she walked up to the staff room, Maisie reflected on the fact that the school's founder seemed particularly busy on that morning; now she had just enough time for a cup of coffee before her next class. Perhaps the warm, though barely palatable, liquid would temper the tingling sensation that seemed to have settled on the skin at her throat.

There were no bells rung to announce the end of a lesson; instead the clocks in corridors and classrooms were synchronised by the caretaker each morning. When she checked the time and brought the first class of the afternoon to an end, Maisie gathered her books and made her way to the staff room. As usual, she was one of the last to arrive; several students had remained to ask questions following the lesson, and she had gladly given of her time. Already she was planning to hold an informal conversation salon on one evening each week, when students could – she hoped – feel more at liberty to ask questions that they might not put to her during the more structured lesson period. Now, as she walked towards the staff room, she relaxed, knowing that her teaching was finished for the day and she could use the final period after tea for marking essays.

The staff room was busy, though the line to be served tea and cake had diminished, and the lecturers now clustered in groups, some discussing classes, others talking about the end of the working week. Maisie joined Matthias Roth, who had just come into the room and was now in conversation with Dr Alan Burnham, the topic being the World Peace Conference in Vienna, which had convened on September 4th. Another group of lecturers was discussing the situation in Germany, where talks had broken down between the Chancellor and Adolf Hitler, who had garnered a significant number of votes and had demanded to be made Chancellor. The conversations buzzed around her, some of matters beyond the college, others in connection with the behaviour of certain students and their performance.

Maisie was about to make a comment on the peace conference when she was distracted by Miss Linden entering the room, clearly in search of someone in particular. No one else seemed to have noticed the young woman, though Maisie sensed immediately that something was wrong. And at that moment she felt as if time itself stood still as she, too, took stock of the room – Matthias Roth expounding on the outcome of the conference, Alan Burnham nodding his head, poised to counter the argument. Delphine Lang was moving towards the window, and Francesca Thomas turned from her conversation with a teacher of world politics, Mr Osbourne – who was discussing the recent Olympic Games in Los Angeles, where an Argentinian had won the marathon – to stare at Miss Linden. Then time righted itself as Greville Liddicote's secretary moved towards Maisie, and motioned her to step aside.

'Would you come with me, please, Miss Dobbs? It's urgent.'

'Of course.'

Maisie set down her cup and saucer, stepping away from Roth and Burnham, neither of whom seemed to take account of her departure.

'Is it Dr Liddicote?' asked Maisie, as she kept pace with Rosemary Linden. Already she felt the weight of foreknowledge across her heart.

The young woman nodded but said nothing. Soon they came alongside Liddicote's office. Linden took a deep breath, unlocked the door, and entered, turning the key again as Maisie stepped across the threshhold.

It was clear to Maisie, even before she pressed the first two fingers of her right hand to his neck, where she should have felt the rhythm of Liddicote's carotid artery, that he was dead.

FIVE

Having established that the young woman was in command of her emotions – as much as could be expected – Maisie instructed Miss Linden to return to her office and to continue as if nothing out of the ordinary had taken place. And if anyone asked, she should inform them that Dr Liddicote had left the college for the day; she didn't want a series of callers waiting on the settle in the corridor.

Maisie took the key and locked the door as Linden left the room. She checked Liddicote's pulse once more, lifted his eyelids, and took note of the narrow threads of blood that had emerged from his mouth and nose. Pulling a clean handkerchief from her shoulder bag, she covered her fingers, picked up the telephone receiver, and asked Miss Linden for a line. She then dialled a number she had learnt by heart.

'Detective Chief Superintendent MacFarlane, please. It's Maisie Dobbs, and it's urgent.'

The wait was short.

'Maisie, tell me the worst – if *you* say it's urgent I know you're not crying wolf!'

'Greville Liddicote has been murdered. I have secured the room where his body was discovered – his office – and thus far the only people who know are his secretary and myself. I have not questioned her as I wanted to call you first.'

'That's all we bloody need! Cause of death?'

'Liddicote's neck has been broken. In my estimation, he's been dead for less than an hour.'

'Silly question, but I have to ask—'

'No, it wasn't an accident, Robbie, and it wasn't natural causes. And more than that, I would say the murderer was a professional – few people can just break someone's neck. This could be the work of an assassin.'

'I'll have to inform Huntley, but expect me there by about half past five. I'll bring Stratton – we could do with a former murder squad man on this one. We'll alert the local constabulary, in our own good time – and don't worry, when we arrive, we'll go about it all very "softly-softly" so as not to alarm the natives. I want that college going about its business, and I want you there as Miss Dobbs, intrepid teacher.'

'Robbie.'

'Yes.'

'The secretary came to me first. She could have gone to

anyone in the staff room, but she came to me – I'm not sure, but my position here could be compromised.'

'Question her.'

'Just you and Stratton to start with, Robbie. I'll find a way to bring in the pathologist and to exit with the body.'

'I'll telephone Huntley now.'

Maisie began her examination of the room. The curtains were partially drawn against the late-afternoon sun, and on one side the drape of material flapped back and forth. She used the handkerchief to pull the French door back towards the frame, securing the lock and closing the curtains before going back to Liddicote's desk. There were two neat piles of papers, one relating to proposed architectural alterations to the college, another concerning catering arrangements. A folder marked 'Debate' was open. Maisie closed the file and placed it to the side to read before MacFarlane arrived.

She left the room, locked the door, and walked towards Miss Linden's office.

'I am terribly sorry, Dr Roth, but Dr Liddicote has left college for the day and I am not sure whether he intended to go directly home or not.' Rosemary Linden was pale and her voice trembled as she spoke to Roth.

'I was supposed to meet with him! How could he forget such a thing?'

Linden shrugged. 'I'll let him know you came – perhaps tomorrow morning?'

'The man is losing his mind!' said Roth, his voice raised, before stepping around Maisie without acknowledging her as he left the office.

Maisie waited until he was out of earshot before meeting the secretary's eyes. The young woman was shaking. 'Are you coping?'

'Yes, Miss Dobbs.'

'I can't let you leave yet – the police are on their way and they'll want to speak to you.'

Linden nodded. 'I know.'

Maisie pulled up a chair until she was close enough to lower her voice so that she would not be heard through the glass panes and wooden wainscoting.

'I have to return to Dr Liddicote's room to await the police – someone should be with the body. Fortunately, in an hour or so many of the students and staff will have left; and the police will – I hope – appear like any other visitors to the college. Bring them to Dr Liddicote's office as soon as they arrive.' Maisie wondered if MacFarlane and Stratton could possibly be taken for 'any other visitors to the college'; she could always tell a plainclothes policeman, even at a good number of paces distant.

'Right you are, Miss Dobbs.'

'Miss Linden,' whispered Maisie. 'Why did you come straight to me, and not to another member of staff?'

The woman shrugged. 'I see all the personal files, Miss Dobbs, so I know you're the only one with any medical training in the whole college – we don't have a matron here, though we summon the district nurse or the doctor if someone's sent to the sick room.' She cleared her throat. 'I knew you were the person I should tell; Dr Liddicote wouldn't have wanted any panic.'

Maisie nodded. 'I'm sure he wouldn't,' she said, then added, 'Dr Liddicote lived alone, didn't he?'

'Yes, not a half mile away, it's an easy enough walk.'

'Did he ever name a next of kin in any documents held here in your office?'

'I've already had a look, Miss Dobbs. He is not close to his children – his son lives in London – he's a solicitor, something like that – and his daughter lives in Dorset.'

'Do you have their addresses?'

'I've written everything down for you.' She passed a folded sheet of paper to Maisie. 'Was it a heart attack, Miss Dobbs?'

'Yes – yes, I believe it was. In any case, a pathologist will be coming with the police. Can you suggest a good entrance and exit for the pathologist and his staff – they'll have to remove Dr Liddicote, though fortunately it will be dark by then.'

'Come with me, I'll show you the best way.'

Maisie regarded the body of Greville Liddicote. She had continued her search of the room, taking care not to disturb belongings as she worked; but she knew that time was of the essence if the dead man was to relinquish his secrets. There was a collection of his own writings, including his children's books, on the shelves to the right of the window, though the book that had caused so much trouble in 1916 was not among them. A stack of manuscript paper revealed that he was in the midst of writing a new book on the world since the war – a cursory sifting through the pages suggested the work might be deemed inflammatory by his peers.

A filing tray on the desk held more recent correspondence. Maisie read quickly, her eyes flashing across each line, searching for a word, a sentence that stood out. One letter was from the local council, with a series of questions regarding the proposed renovations and alterations to the buildings. Another letter came from Dunstan Headley, a benefactor to the college, querying an aspect of the plans he'd seen, and the costs. The letter was cordial, but Maisie detected an undercurrent of dissatisfaction, and a hint that the writer felt that more information should be forthcoming before he parted with his money. He also said that, while he supported the college and its mission to promote peace and understanding along with academic endeavour, he did not wish to deal with Liddicote's deputy, Dr Roth, in the future, given that he was German. 'As much as I support peace, I have not yet come to terms with the death of my eldest son in the war, though I know he would not support my position with regard to our former enemy.'

Liddicote's deputy?

Maisie shook her head. Of course, Greville Liddicote would have established a chain of succession for the college, and would have been required to do so by the Board of Governors and by those who contributed financially to the ongoing work and advancement of the college. She wondered why Brian Huntley had not mentioned this information during their first meeting. And she also wondered how long they could wait before informing Dr Matthias Roth that he was now principal of the College of St Francis.

She discovered various items of limited interest in the desk drawers: a selection of fountain pens, a packet of cigarettes – she had not taken Liddicote to be a smoker – and a double-hinged silver frame designed to accommodate three photographs of about three inches by five inches each. When opened, the frame revealed a posed studio photograph of two children seated together, a portrait of a woman – again, taken in a studio – and another of four children clustered around a woman whom Maisie took to be their mother. This last photograph had been taken outdoors and reminded Maisie of her own attempts at photography when she first purchased her camera. The children squinted against the sunlight, and the woman was shading her eyes. She could not tell whether it was the same woman who had been seated for the demure photograph by a professional or whether this was someone else. The children in the second photograph were not as well turned out, as if they had been playing a rough-and-tumble game in the garden; but that would be understandable – Maisie imagined a mother would fuss over her children prior to a studio photograph, keen to ensure that not a hair was out of place. But all the same, she wondered about the children in the second photograph.

Running a finger down a column of figures in an accounts ledger, Maisie could see that the college was well funded, not only by student fees but by the support of a number of prominent donors, some of them the parents of former students, others students who had no doubt seen their education at St Francis as a pivotal point in their journey to greater things. Maisie was curious about a category of contributor known only by the name 'The Readers', who were listed by initials only, rather than full names.

A personal ledger revealed Liddicote's immediate finances to be in good health, though on the first page the calling card of one Hubert Stone of the firm of Stone, Tupper and Pearce, Cambridge, indicated that a will might be in place, and that there were other investments that likely would be dispersed in the event of Liddicote's death. She took the card and clipped it to a page of rough notes she had taken as her search progressed.

Then she sat back and studied Liddicote's body. Maisie was no stranger to death, whether the body was newly deceased or already well into the process of becoming dust. She heard Maurice's voice in her mind. 'If we are afforded the time, Maisie, those moments of quiet in the company of the dead give the one who has passed an opportunity to tell of their passing – in their position, their belongings, and the obvious causes of death. Allow yourself that moment, if you can.'

Greville Liddicote was seated, not in his usual chair but in the chair set in front of the desk for visitors. It appeared that he had not been moved into that position but rather had taken the seat before being attacked from behind. Though the attack was not brutal – there were no other wounds, there was no sign of struggle – she suspected that death had come quickly, with a deft twist to break his neck. Yes, a very deft twist, by someone for whom such killing came with training, or experience.

Maisie stood up and moved to Liddicote's side. His head was resting on his right hand, which was folded, with fingers pressed against his palm; the left was hanging at his side, almost as if he had fallen asleep after a long midday meal. She leant forward and, using her forefinger, tried to ascertain whether there was anything clutched in his right hand. She felt a piece of paper, and though she knew she should wait for the pathologist, she moved the head – just a touch – to enable her fingertips to tease the paper from Liddicote's grip. As if she were lifting the head of a sleeping child away from the side of a cradle, Maisie returned Liddicote's head to the position in which she had discovered the body. Stepping aside, she turned on the desk lamp and inspected the paper, a crumpled photograph of a woman. As with the photograph of the five children and the woman outdoors, this was not a professional portrait, but a more informal study – taken, Maisie thought, outside, and possibly at the same time as the other photograph. Though the woman had shielded her eyes in the first photograph, the clothing seemed the same; the blouse had a wide shawl collar, and the woman wore a cummerbund-style belt around the waist of an almost ankle-length gored skirt.

The two children in the first frame of the studio photograph were likely Liddicote's son and daughter, for they shared so many features – a slightly snub nose, large eyes, and wavy hair – but she wondered who this woman was, laughing into the sun, with one child on her hip and three others gathered around her skirts, squinting as the light played upon their fair, summer-kissed hair. If she had to guess, she would have taken the woman and her children to be the family of a farmer, and she wondered who they were to Greville Liddicote – she was sure it was not his wife, and that the children were not his. He had gone to his death with this countrywoman's image in his hand, held close to his heart. She wondered why he had taken hold of the photograph in the moments before he died.

Rosemary Linden blushed when Maisie answered her knock on the door.

'Your guests, Miss Dobbs.'

'Thank you, Miss Linden.' She nodded to Robert MacFarlane and Richard Stratton as they entered.

'Would the gentlemen like a pot of tea?' enquired the secretary.

'Got anything stronger, lass?' asked MacFarlane. Maisie and Stratton exchanged glances and smiled. MacFarlane had claimed his turf.

'Um, well – let me show you.' Taking care not to look in the direction of Liddicote's body, Linden crossed the room and opened a cupboard set between two bookcases. She brought a bottle of malt whiskey and two crystal glasses to a table in the corner of the room and pushed aside a pile of books before placing the items on the table.

'Och, he was a man after my own heart, bless him.' MacFarlane looked at Maisie and grinned. 'You'll be having tea, I assume?'

'Oh, I beg your pardon – I didn't think . . . .'

'A cup of tea would suit me well, Miss Linden – thank you.'

'Of course.'

'And, if you don't mind, the gentlemen would like to speak to you as soon as they are finished here. I am sure they will have a driver escort you to your home afterwards.'

'No, that's all right, I've got my bicycle. I'll be in my office, when you're ready.' Linden turned and left the room.

'Poor wee mite, it's not right when a young woman like that has to come across a murder.' MacFarlane shook his head as he moved towards Liddicote's body and peered down into his face.

'She thinks it was a heart attack, and she's kept her head – I dread to think what we would be dealing with now had she not had such a good measure of common sense.'

Stratton had said little beyond greeting Maisie and seemed uncomfortable in her presence, and yet it was clear he was pleased to see her. Since they first met, some three years earlier, Maisie had known that Stratton, who had shown himself to be a shy man in matters of a personal nature, had an affection for her. He was a widower with a young son and a job that demanded work at all hours. And though their exchanges had sometimes become heated when their work brought them into contact with each other, he remained fond of her, and she was sure he had heard she was being courted by James Compton. It was now clear that he was embarrassed at having revealed his emotions in such an obvious manner.

After the pathologist arrived, Maisie took the opportunity

to engage Stratton in conversation, though her attempt at rendering the atmosphere a little easier was not helped by MacFarlane.

'How's your son – he must be, what, eight years old now?'

'Growing fast, eating me out of house and home. But he's doing well at school, though I've thought about sending him to a boarding school – my hours, you see.'

Maisie shook her head. 'No, don't, try to keep him at home – your mother lends a hand, doesn't she?'

'Yes, she's a great help.'

'I was sent away after my mother died – admittedly, I was older, and it wasn't for school – but I missed my father very much, especially having lost my mother.'

'You do know you're speaking to a woman who's affianced, don't you?' MacFarlane interjected, having left the pathologist and his assistant for a moment.

'Take no notice, Richard, he's having you on – I am not engaged.'

'It's only a matter of time, according to my sources.'

'Wouldn't your sources be better employed on police work?' Maisie threw the tease back at MacFarlane, though she was annoyed that he would try to embarrass both her and Stratton.

'And what if it was police work?' replied MacFarlane.

'Sir—' Stratton touched MacFarlane on the arm to let him know the pathologist had begun to put away his instruments and had instructed his assistants to prepare Greville Liddicote's body for removal.

The pathologist, Tom Sarron, joined them. He was a tall man, thin, with a serious look about him that reminded Maisie of other scientists she had met in the course of her work. When he entered the office, he had taken off his jacket to reveal shirtsleeves already rolled up, and the white coat he donned was freshly laundered, still with creases where it had been starched and pressed. Sarron had moved around the body with reverence, and Maisie had heard him talk to Liddicote, even make a light joke, as if the dead man's soul were still present and watching.

'Anything we don't know?' asked MacFarlane.

Sarron shook his head. 'Not really. The deceased seemed in fair condition for his age, but even a twenty-year-old pugilist with a strong neck musculature would have struggled to survive this sort of attack – sudden, immediate severing of spinal cord, severe damage to brain stem, with arterial and vascular damage.'

'Had to be a strong person.'

Again Sarron shook his head. 'No, don't assume strength. It's the technique. If someone is swift, the attack unexpected, the angle just right, and the perpetrator knows exactly where to place their hands and how to do it – it's not in the strength but in the execution.' He looked up and half-smiled. 'Sorry about the pun. I always seem to do that.'

'Aye, you do. We'll be calling you Sorry Sarron before long.' MacFarlane turned to Maisie and Stratton. 'Any immediate questions, before I let this good man and his boys go on their merry way?'

They replied 'No' in unison, though Maisie noticed that

as the pathologist made ready to leave the room, Stratton stepped towards him. 'Oh, just a minute, Tom – got a question for you.' She did not hear the question Stratton put to the pathologist, as MacFarlane chose that moment to ask her if she wouldn't mind bringing Miss Linden in for a few moments.

According to Rosemary Linden, she had been working for Greville Liddicote as college secretary for almost two years, during which she was responsible for matters of college administration, although a bookkeeper, Miss Hawthorne, came in weekly to work on the accounts.

'I know Dr Liddicote saw Dr Roth and Dr Thomas earlier today – and of course I had a short meeting with him – but who else came to see him?' Maisie took care to appear relaxed, not least to set a certain tone for the interview, so MacFarlane did not trample ahead and intimidate the young woman.

'Several students, and Miss Lang.'

'Delphine Lang?' asked MacFarlane, casting his eyes down a list of names.

'Yes, that's right.'

'When did these meetings take place?'

'I generally go to the post office just after lunch, which is when he has student meetings, and Miss Lang went in to see him – but she had wanted to see him in the morning, and when I came back from the post office, I saw her in the corridor and asked if she'd managed to pop in and see him, and she said that everything was all right, so I assume she went in after the students.' Linden looked from Maisie to MacFarlane. 'If you're trying to work out when he had the heart attack, it must have been about three-ish. I come back from doing the post at about a quarter past three, and by the time I went along to see him, it must have been, oh, half past three. I didn't stay long, and just came out of the office straightaway to look for Miss Dobbs in the staff room.'

Maisie nodded. It had been roughly a quarter to four when Linden had arrived in the staff room.

'In these cases,' said MacFarlane, his voice grave, 'we try to ascertain the reason for a heart attack, if some level of anguish or worry had caused the heart to spasm.' He did not look at Maisie, who wondered if Miss Linden would fall for his explanation. 'Do you know of any concerns that might have brought on the heart attack? Or had Dr Liddicote had any arguments with members of staff or the students here?'

Linden shook her head. 'Nothing out of the ordinary.'

'Which is to say – what? That he often had arguments or times of worry? Or there was nothing in his demeanour to suggest that he had any untoward concerns?'

'Nothing out of the ordinary.' Linden looked from Maisie to MacFarlane, and again directed her response to Maisie. 'He and Dr Roth were often rowing about something or another, but that was just the way they were with each other. Dr Roth is Dr Liddicote's right-hand man, and he's also deputy principal. He has lots of new ideas and wants the college to be a bigger, more important, concern.'

'And Dr Liddicote didn't?'

'He did – and he didn't. Dr Roth once said the ship was no bigger than the captain at the helm – and he was ready for a bigger vessel.'

A few more questions were put to Linden, who, when asked, grudgingly agreed to bring the personal files for both teaching and nonacademic staff.

'They're private and confidential, you know,' said Linden.

'We're the police, lass, so di'nae worry y'self. And I'll have one of my men accompany you home.'

'Please don't, I am quite able—'

'It's settled.' He turned in his chair to the plainclothes policeman standing at the door. 'See this young lady gets home in one piece, Harris.'

Linden left the room and returned with Roth's file. 'When will the staff and students be told that Dr Liddicote has passed away?'

'I daresay there will be an announcement tomorrow,' offered Maisie. 'Mr MacFarlane here will be informing Dr Roth as soon as possible.'

As Linden left the room, MacFarlane looked at Maisie. 'Stripping me of my hard-earned title now?'

'I didn't want to scare the wits out of her – how often do senior officers from Special Branch get involved in heart attacks?'

After the body was removed and Miss Linden had left the college, MacFarlane, Stratton, and Maisie planned to leave separately so as not to draw the attention of any students or staff remaining at the college. A police forensic specialist would remain for some time, combing the room – everything from fibres in the carpet to the leather on the desk and the dust on the shelves – to ensure that anything out of the ordinary was captured and logged. The room would be locked overnight, and a policeman would remain on duty – inside the room, so as not to attract attention.

Sitting opposite Maisie in the chair that Liddicote had occupied at the time of his death, MacFarlane sighed before speaking. 'Maisie, I know this will not be welcome news, but you will not be involved directly in the search for Greville Liddicote's murderer. Your position here is as a lecturer in phil-bloody-osophy – and what kind of worker is that supposed to turn out, I wonder?' He looked at Stratton, who had pulled up another chair, then turned back to Maisie. 'Anyway, you are here on behalf of Huntley's department in the first instance, and that position must not be open to doubt or be compromised in any way.'

'But—'

MacFarlane held up his hand. 'Hold your horses, I've not come to the end of my soliloquy.' He sighed, then went on. 'But, on the other hand, you are in the best position to find out what's going on. Stratton will be in charge of finding the killer, so any leads you uncover that will help him will doubtless be gratefully received – so channel everything through him or me. We have a tricky one here, a crossing over of interests, and—'

'It's a web, Detective Chief Superintendent. A web. The death of Liddicote could be inextricably linked to whatever else is going on here, and frankly, I've not even got my feet under the table yet – though I've already learnt that the pacifism-promoting College of St Francis is far from peaceful.'

'Your brief from Huntley was loose – I'll be honest, I think they've got only a wee shadow of a clue that something's amiss here, which is why they wanted someone like you to come in and rake over the coals to see if their suspicions were on target. On our part, as we said at first, there were suspicions based upon an influx of aliens entering the country bound for this college – and the two came together.'

'And what about the mutiny?' Maisie threw in the comment to see if MacFarlane knew about the reputation attached to Liddicote's book.

'What mutiny? What are you talking about, lass?'

'Liddicote's children's book, the one published in 1916, was withdrawn from circulation – as we know – but were you aware that there was talk that it was implicated in a mutiny on the Western Front, later that year?'

'There were no mutinies on the Western Front.' MacFarlane stared at Maisie.

As Stratton cleared his throat and looked away, Maisie remembered that he had been with the military police in the war. *Ah, he knows,* she thought, and pressed her point. 'I have heard it said that there was not just one but several occasions when men downed the tools of war and walked off the job.'

'The boys on the other side might have walked off –

there was a fair bit of mutiny in the German trenches in 1917 and on towards the end; they were starving, most of them – but our boys never mutinied, not the soldiers of the Crown and her colonies.'

'I think, Detective Chief—'

'And *I* think there's a piece of paper with your signature on it, vowing that you will keep the secrets of the Crown. So, continue with your work, find out if there is anything going on here that is not in the best interests of His Majesty's government.'

Maisie stared at MacFarlane. 'Of course.'

He sighed. 'Now then, time for you to go back to your lodgings, it's been a long day for you and you've a big job on your hands. Stratton and I will pay a visit to Dr Roth this evening. Anything else we can do for you?'

'I'd like two of those files, please.' She stood up, went to the desk, and lifted two folders from the pile left by Rosemary Linden. She passed them to MacFarlane to view the names. 'Here's a card I found on Liddicote's desk.' She unclipped the card she'd found earlier. 'I think it's his solicitor, and I didn't want it to get lost. Perhaps tomorrow I could see Dr Roth's personal file for my business here; I appreciate you'll need it this evening.'

It was only as she left the room that she remembered that she had walked to the college in the morning, but she had no intention of going back in to ask for a lift to her lodging house. Her briefcase was quite heavy now as she walked along the corridor, at the end of which she stopped to thank the night watchman as he opened the heavy door for her to leave. She had intended to draw MacFarlane's attention to the photographs she had taken from Liddicote's office; she knew she should have informed him of their existence. But his harsh response to her final question had surprised her. She could not do the job for Huntley if she were effectively banned from seeking the person who had murdered the founder of the college she was investigating.

Tonight she would read through the files she had taken – those of Francesca Thomas and Delphine Lang. One thing had surprised her – or had it? Perhaps it had not taken her aback as much as she might have expected; but all the same, it was interesting to note that the file pertaining to Miss Rosemary Linden was not among those left for the detectives to mull over.

SIX

In her room that evening, with the windows open and the fragrance of night-scented stock rising up from the garden below, Maisie curled her legs under her as she relaxed into the armchair. Her landlady had left a sandwich covered with an extra plate in the kitchen; and now with a cup of tea set on a table alongside her, she flipped open Francesca Thomas' personal file.

Thomas was forty-one years of age, and, although born in Switzerland, she was educated at Oxford University and the Sorbonne, in Paris. There was no mention of her marital situation so one could only assume she was a spinster. There was no notation as to where she had received her doctorate, only that her teaching career – which had begun in 1925 – had taken her from France to Germany, then on to the College of St Francis, where just a year earlier she had become the first woman to join the staff. According to the file, she had published papers on French literature as well as on subjects such as 'The Philosopher and Modern Society'. Her two letters of reference had come from the Sorbonne and from Oxford, the latter provided by Professor Jennifer Penhaligon at Somerville College.

Maisie sighed. 'Nothing much to pick at there,' she said aloud to the empty room, though she made a notation to contact Professor Penhaligon.

Setting the pages to one side, she flipped open the folder for Delphine Lang, who, it transpired, was twenty-six years of age. Following education at Roedean – *No surprise,* thought Maisie – Delphine Lang attended university in London, but in short order went on to Heidelberg to continue her education. Delphine probably didn't need to work – there was a note in Liddicote's hand to the effect that her father was a wealthy man – so the fact that she had sought out a profession was to her credit. Maisie was aware that her own generation of women had set an example to those who followed, and more women were choosing education and a job – with the former only available to those who could afford it.

Without doubt, Delphine Lang was well educated, and her references were 'First Rate!' as Greville Liddicote had noted on the corner of her original enquiry letter. But her contract, which had begun in January, was for only one year and expired at the end of 1932 – unless the contract were renewed, Delphine Lang would be out of a job in three months.

At that point, Maisie realised that she had not even been asked to sign a contract. She wondered if that might affect her job, now that Liddicote was no longer principal – after all, the British Secret Service could not force the college to keep her on, could they? It was late when she put the folders aside and began to review her lesson for the next morning. Her teaching schedule ended after the first period on Friday morning, allowing her to return to London, if she wished – something she had planned to do at the end of each week.

It was past midnight when she made ready for bed, sitting first in quiet meditation for some moments, her legs crossed, her eyelids not quite touching, her breath slowing to still her mind. She had wondered about her relationship with James Compton, and, as it deepened and as time went on – if it went on for them – how he might respond to her claiming a quiet time in the late evening. Though he did not share her need for this period of silence, he knew Khan – Maurice's friend who had taught Maisie that 'seeing is not necessarily something that we do with our eyes alone' – and thus far he had taken care to allow her the moments in solitude each evening when they were together.

With her thoughts on James, she picked up the framed photograph she'd placed on her bedside table. The photograph had been taken during a summer visit to Priscilla's country home. James – tall, fair, and of athletic build – was standing with his arms around Maisie, pulling her close to him. She smiled as she touched the image of him laughing; his wounding in the war had led to a deep depression, and he had eventually been sent to Canada by his parents, ostensibly to oversee the family's business interests, but in truth to find the peace of mind he craved. Maisie had known James for many years, but it was only in the recent spring that they had grown closer, a development that proved something of a surprise for them both.

James had taken over as head of the Compton Corporation in London upon his father's retirement at the beginning of the year, but it became clear that a visit to the Canadian office at some point in the summer would be necessary, so he had left at the end of July, with a return not expected before October. Maisie realised how much she missed James; missed the comfort of his arms around her, her hand in his. She missed the twin aspects of his character she enjoyed – an ability to accept whatever the day had to offer, along with a need for his own quiet interludes, when he rode out on one of his hunters across the lands of the Chelstone estate. She understood only too well that he had struggled to find such lightness in life. But as much as they both enjoyed being at Chelstone Manor, their visits were not without a certain awkwardness. Though an independent woman, Maisie did not want her father to know that when James Compton breakfasted at the Dower House it was because he had remained in her company since dinner. This had led to poor acting; James had commented to her on one occasion, 'Maisie, I'm beginning to feel like a third-tier actor in an Oscar Wilde stage farce, pretending I've just walked in the door – as if I'd crossed the lawns in my dressing gown to say, 'Good morning, Miss Dobbs, might I scrounge a bit of toast and egg?' Imagining such a scene, Maisie found she could not stop laughing. And that was something else she liked about James Compton – they laughed together, with an awareness that there was between them a joy that neither had experienced since the war. Theirs was a laughter fuelled not by pressure from others, nor by alcohol or the whims of a partying crowd, but by a certain optimism that, even in the midst of the difficult times in which they lived, they had grasped a sense of possibility before it slipped through their fingers.

Maisie replaced the photograph and, once in bed, opened the book Tinsley had brought to her office. He'd slipped a note inside, more information on the novel. She ran her fingers across the embossed cover once again and considered the picture of the young children surrounding a soldier, with the crosses in the background. It reminded Maisie of a woodcut, framed as it was by a trellis with ivy growing in and out of the diagonal lines, a Celtic knot at each corner. She began to read Tinsley's note:

THE PEACEFUL LITTLE WARRIORS BY GREVILLE LIDDICOTE

A tale of orphaned children who go to live in the woods, taken care of by animals, birds, fairies, and wood nymphs. They decide to go to London to see their King, to try to stop the war. The King and his Council laugh, so the children march to the battlefields to stand between the great armies, where they lay their woodland flowers at the feet of the soldiers. The war is stopped when the men lay down their arms, and the children of the world come from their towns and villages to bring their fathers home again. Reminiscent of the story of The Pied Piper, but with children taking the adults away.

Miss Dobbs, you will see that the book is written very much in the Victorian tradition (there was a resurrection of fairy stories during the late Queen's reign). In this tale, wood nymphs and fairies and 'otherworldly' beings have been used to bring comfort to children, who in turn bring sense to the world. A traditional story, with an untraditional subject. It was very clever at the time, of course; the cover of the book is both familiar, and a gauntlet thrown down to the war's supporters. For those who buy a book based on the cover alone, the picture could also have suggested a story supporting the war, much as those posters did (if you remember, the ones with women and children telling men to go to war?).

Yes, Maisie did remember, and at that moment was overcome by fatigue. She had read enough for one day.

The following morning, Maisie arrived at the college with only a couple of minutes to spare before the start of classes, but was intercepted by Miss Linden as she half-ran along the main corridor. 'Miss Dobbs! Dr Roth would like to see you in his office and wondered if you could meet him there after your class.'

'Of course. Please tell him I will come directly I've

finished.' Maisie paused. 'How are you this morning, Miss Linden?'

'Managing, all things considered. It's strange not to have Dr Liddicote here.' She pushed her hair back, and as she moved her hand, Maisie could see she was shaking.

'You had a lot to deal with yesterday, and I know being interviewed by the police can be difficult.'

Linden nodded. 'It's funny that they came all the way from London – I thought you would telephone the local police.'

Maisie shook her head, her response framed to stall Linden's curiosity. 'I know that in some circumstances – when the cause of death is not immediately evident – the local police contact Scotland Yard. Something similar happened to me once, and I recalled that valuable time was lost in the to-ing and fro-ing between the police, and it was finally a job for Scotland Yard. I have met Mr MacFarlane before' – Maisie once again did not use his full title, knowing recollection of the man himself could be intimidating enough. 'So I thought he might be the best to contact, to save time. The cause of Dr Liddicote's death wasn't immediately apparent, though we assumed at first that it was a heart attack.'

'I see,' said Linden. 'Was he . . . was he murdered, Miss Dobbs?'

'I am not really at liberty to say, but there were some suspicious circumstances.'

The younger woman nodded and straightened her back. 'Right. I'd better get on with my work.'

Linden continued along the corridor with a ledger under her arm. Maisie noticed she had left her office door unlocked, so with haste she stepped inside and closed the door behind her. She returned the files for Francesca Thomas and Delphine Lang, and ran her fingers across the remaining folders looking for another name, though she knew that some were in MacFarlane's possession. She pulled out the folder for Dr Matthias Roth and discovered that it contained only a copy of the contract he'd signed when he first came to the college – which was before the doors had opened to students. The second file she searched for was not there, or perhaps had never existed, unless it was kept in Greville Liddicote's office. She still could find no folder with Rosemary Linden's name on it.

Following her next class, during which Maisie introduced a discussion on the response of philosophers through the ages to the uncertainty of life, she remained with her students to answer questions for a few moments, and when the last student had left the room, she gathered her books and notes, pushed them into her new briefcase, and made her way up to Dr Matthias Roth's office on the next floor. She knocked twice on the door and stepped in when his resonant baritone voice bellowed, 'Come!'

'Ah, Miss Dobbs, thank you for coming.'

Roth was standing behind his desk, not sitting. He was a tall man of heavy build, and he had the carriage, Maisie thought, of a sergeant-major. She could imagine him telling his students to sit up straight if they wanted to learn properly. A light tweed jacket hung over the back of his chair, and it appeared he had just arrived back in his office following a class, for the sleeves of his pale-blue shirt were rolled up and his fingers were dusted with chalk. She noticed that the skin on his hands was raw in places; she thought he might suffer from a skin ailment – perhaps psoriasis, which was known to be exacerbated by stress. He held his hand out towards the chair in front of his desk and began to roll down his sleeves as he spoke again.

'How are you settling in, Miss Dobbs?'

'Well, thank you. Both staff and students have made me very welcome.'

Roth pulled back his own chair and sat down. 'I wanted to see you with regard to the death of my dear colleague, Dr Liddicote.'

'Of course,' said Maisie. 'Yesterday was a very sad day. I have not been at the college long, but I recognise the implications of his loss, not only on the staff and students, but on the future of the college.'

'Indeed. Though I would not worry about the future of the college, if I were you – we are sufficiently endowed to weather such a storm, and together with new students applying to study at the college, we anticipate going ahead with our renovation plans and expansion. Greville Liddicote's work will continue.' He paused and rubbed his hand against his cheek. Maisie thought he seemed tired, as if he had not slept, and though he had a naturally ruddy complexion, the colour in his cheeks appeared heightened against the blue-grey of the skin under his eyes, clearly visible under wire-rimmed spectacles with round lenses.

'The police came to my house yesterday evening and informed me that there were suspicious circumstances surrounding Greville's death. I was asked many questions, and I wondered if you played a part in their charade.' Roth's hair – which had been brushed back at the front and sides – had fallen down into his eyes when he looked at a page of notes on the desk in front of him. He ran his fingers back through his hair as he looked at Maisie again, reminding her of a schoolboy in his teen years.

'Charade?' Maisie looked at Roth and decided to respond to his words in an equally direct manner. 'In the circumstances, I thought the best person for them to speak to was you – you are, after all, Dr Liddicote's deputy, and it was crucial that you should know what had come to pass.'

'You called the police first, though.'

'Of course. Miss Linden came to find me, knowing I had been a nurse. She did not want to raise an alarm that might cause panic among staff or students. If you remember, you left the college soon after tea. Frankly, I did not think it was a cut-and-dried case of heart attack, so I immediately alerted Scotland Yard and I remained with the body.'

He sighed, shook his head, and looked out of the window, before turning back to Maisie. 'You *knew* that he had been murdered?'

'I suspected the possibility.'

He reached for a file on his desk. 'I see you worked for a Dr Maurice Blanche, as his personal assistant. That's how you know people from Scotland Yard, I assume.'

'Yes, that's correct.'

'Blanche was a friend of Greville's, wasn't he?'

'They were acquainted.'

'Which means that Greville wrote long letters about philosophical matters and your Dr Blanche indulged him; or perhaps it was the other way around.'

'I don't know what you mean.'

'Greville had a responsibility to ensure the financial viability of the college, and to that end he took his acquaintances quite seriously. I am sure your Dr Blanche accommodated a request for a contribution to our cause.'

'And I assure you he did not.' Maisie steadied her breathing; she did not want to rush to Maurice's defence and in doing so make a comment she would regret. 'I have some knowledge of Dr Blanche's philanthropic expenditures – all of which are in favour of the clinics he founded. If he was in contact with Dr Liddicote, it was due to their mutual intellectual interests.'

Roth sighed. 'In any case, the police are treating his death as suspicious – that is their language, as I am sure you are aware – and they will be speaking to staff and students over the next few days. I daresay they have already interviewed you.'

'If they are to interview staff, then I will be included, of that you should have no doubt.' Maisie paused again when she realised that Roth's eyes were filled with tears. 'Are you all right, Dr Roth?'

He nodded. 'It has been a troubling night, Miss Dobbs, and a difficult morning thus far.'

'Dr Roth, may I ask a question of you?'

He waved his hand, as if he had lost all energy. 'I have been answering questions for half the night, so a few more won't do any harm.' In his fatigued state, Roth's accent had become increasingly guttural. Until that point his English pronunciation was almost regal – it was common knowledge that the royal family spoke their native language with more than a hint of Germanic inflection.

'How did you come to know Dr Liddicote? You must have been acquainted when the college was in the early stages of planning.'

Roth removed his spectacles, folded them, and placed them on the desk in front of him. His movements seemed precise and measured. 'Lack of sleep, Miss Dobbs.' He rubbed his eyes. 'And I fear my vision is becoming quite inadequate for my purposes.' He sighed as he replaced the spectacles, blinking as if to refocus. 'In 1916, when I was thirty-two years of age, I was an officer in the German army on the Western Front. It was not my choice to go to war; it had never been my desire to fight. But when I saw my students – fine young men, and not one of them a warrior – conscripted from their classes and sent to France to fight with barely six weeks of training, I could not see them go unless I, too, went forward to do my part. My rise through the ranks was as swift as it was for many of your young men – attrition begets opportunity, if one can call it that. Our leaders, such as they were, were all swept away by a tide of complete and utter stupidity – just a year before I joined the army, my students and I were welcoming our counterparts from France, Austria, Spain, Great Britain, and Sweden for a summer school in which we shared our knowledge and understanding of the great philosophers.' He coughed and removed his spectacles, and rubbed his eyes once more. 'But in 1916, there I was, in this cold, ugly, stench of war. We had just taken a ridge that had been greatly contested – just a small ridge, a few feet for a few thousand French, British, and German lives – and when we went into the trenches, the vision of those boys – boys whom we had killed, boys who looked so much like our boys – all but broke my heart. We moved and buried the bodies as reverently as we could, in the circumstances. I stopped alongside one of them; I had an urge to know more about him, to know who he was, if there was a letter from his mother or a photograph of his girl. Instead I was taken with a book in his pack. It was a children's story by Greville Liddicote. All around me was the . . . the . . . sickness of war, and here in my hands was a children's book. And I sat down in that mud and wept. Not one of my men stared at me, not one stopped what he was doing. They just went about their business, and as soon as I was able to conduct myself as an officer, I went about mine.'

Maisie nodded. 'And after the war you sought out the author.'

'I went back to my teaching position and wrote to his publisher, who passed on the letter. Greville and I began a fruitful correspondence, and when he invited me to visit him, I came as soon as I could.' Roth blinked several times as if to prevent his emotions becoming evident. 'He was something of a hero to me, you see. Plans to open St Francis were under way, and when he asked if I would join as his deputy – he felt he knew me well enough, and also considered it a "message" to have a deputy who came from Germany, the former enemy – I was excited by the offer and jumped at the opportunity to join him. You see, Miss Dobbs, in 1916, shortly after taking that ridge – and keeping that bloodstained copy of Greville's book – I was sent home to Germany with a wound that no one could prove was self-inflicted.' He sighed. 'I am aware of the rumours that accompanied *The Peaceful Little Warriors* and why it was removed from circulation in Britain, but as far as I know, the only mutiny caused by Greville Liddicote's book was mine.'

Maisie had wanted to ask Matthias Roth about the intercollege debate, and why he and Liddicote had been at odds about the issue; however, it was clear that the man was barely in control of his emotions. Such moments were often difficult to gauge – should she take advantage of a person's distress, using it as a moment to press him further? Or would she be better served by patience, by a level of consideration that would encourage the person to be more frank with her, more open, at another time? On this occasion, she decided upon the latter, though she had no doubt that MacFarlane would have expressed an opinion or two on her decision.

Part of her wanted to remain in Cambridge, though she knew she must go to London. As she made her way along the corridor towards Rosemary Linden's office to inform her that she was leaving, she saw the secretary accompanying two visitors towards the stairs; she suspected they were on their way to Matthias Roth's office. One was a man of late middle age, with light-grey hair, a dark suit, white shirt, and black tie. His shoes were polished and he carried a black homburg. A younger man accompanied him, and such was the resemblance between the pair, Maisie assumed they were father and son, though the younger man was taller, and more suitably dressed for a summer's day, wearing light-brown trousers and a cream linen jacket, an open shirt, and a white panama hat that he had not removed. Maisie waved goodbye to Miss Linden, and as they passed, the younger man took off his hat and smiled at Maisie. Her recollection was immediate – he was the man with whom she had seen Delphine Lang in the park.

The day was fine for the drive back to London. As she negotiated her way through the city of Cambridge, Maisie once again reflected upon her good fortune to have been educated in such a place. She remembered her first term at Girton, and the forays into town for tea with Priscilla, who always wanted to go from one shop to another and stay out past their curfew. Every time Maisie lingered to look up at another building with tall spires and noble buttresses, and stained-glass windows in rich hues, Priscilla would roll her eyes and say, 'It's only bricks and bloody mortar!' All about them, more and more young men were in uniform – so different from her return to complete her education after the war, when the distant laughter seemed to echo around those spires and along the Backs, where once a boy Priscilla was seeing had tipped a punt underneath overhanging willows, and they'd splashed onto the grass, drenched to the skin.

With Cambridge behind her, the journey was easy. Clouds scudding across the summer-blue sky threatened only the merest sprinkle of rain, so she stopped once to pull back the roof on the MG and stow her hat. As the road opened up, she considered the events that had unfolded since she arrived at the College of St Francis. She had often thought of the early stages of an investigation as something akin to working a tapestry; at times it was as if she were searching for loose threads so she could unpick the completed image to see what might lie underneath and how a certain play on light or colour was achieved. As with a tapestry, some crimes proved to be true masterpieces of deception. And she knew from experience that when a life had been taken in the act of murder, there were few black and white places, only grey shadows in which the truth lingered – and truth sometimes held only a passing connection to fact.

Her thoughts came back to Billy and Sandra. Her first order of business, she thought, was to broach the subject of the house with Billy. Then there was Sandra, who had settled into Maisie's flat and was a good and quiet guest. In time she would need to find other accommodations, but not before Maisie considered her strong enough; she had suffered a severe emotional blow, and it was important to give her the time she needed to get back on her feet.

And there was something else – Maisie had seen a spark in Sandra, and it had burned brighter since her husband's death. It was as if there was a determination to do something more with herself; in her work she took on more than was asked, and Maisie had noticed that she made several visits to the lending library each week. If she could help her get on in life, she would.

'Good afternoon, Miss. How was your drive from Cambridge?' Sandra stood up when Maisie came into the room, closing the notebook she had been writing in as she welcomed her employer back to the office.

'Hello, Sandra. Where's Billy today?'

Sandra blushed. 'He's out seeing a Mrs Clark – we received an enquiry letter from her yesterday, something to do with her son having left home and she didn't know where he'd gone. Mr Beale went along to see her – Belgrave Square – and he said he had a couple of other appointments and might not be back here today.'

'Oh dear, I wanted to see him – this is my only opportunity to speak to him before I go away again on Sunday evening.'

Sandra collected the teapot and cups from their place on top of the cabinet next to Billy's desk. 'He seemed a bit tired again, Miss, to tell you the truth.'

'I might drive over to Shoreditch this evening. I do hate to just drop in on the family, but I'm a bit concerned.'

'Right you are, Miss. I'll get a cup of tea and we can look at what I've done this week, just so you know. And

I'm in no rush to go to Mr Partridge as he's out on an appointment with his publisher today.'

Maisie removed her gloves and hat, and took a seat at her desk. She opened the large drawer to her right and removed the papers she had been sent from three building firms regarding new properties for sale under what they described as 'terms'. She picked up the telephone and dialled the number on a letter she had already made notes upon, checking the time on the mantelpiece clock as she did so. Three minutes later, she replaced the receiver, having made an appointment to see one of the finished houses on a street within 'reasonable' walking distance of Eltham railway station – according to the Mr Walsh she spoke to about the properties. The appointment was for eleven o'clock the following morning, an hour that would give Billy and Doreen plenty of time to catch the train out to Eltham, and for Billy in particular to gauge the journey, as well as the cost of the train fare. Now all she had to do was get them to agree to view the house, which she knew would be a difficult first step.

Sandra went over the transactions of the past four days, pulling out a ledger so Maisie could see the bills sent out and remittances received. Business was not bad at all. New clients, along with several commercial customers who paid a retainer for their services, had made the year a good one, thus far.

'I think it's time to call it a day,' said Maisie.

'Right you are, Miss.' Sandra pulled the cover across the typewriter.

'I can give you a lift home, Sandra, unless you've other plans.'

'That's all right, I've some shopping to do, so I'll come home on the bus.'

Maisie smiled. 'I'll see you later, then, Sandra.'

She did not leave Fitzroy Square immediately, much as she wanted to go straight home. Instead, she waited until Sandra left the building, and watched her walk across the square. Maisie could not follow her employee – her MG was far too distinctive, and to do so would demonstrate a level of mistrust that should not exist between an employer and her staff. However, when she saw Sandra's colour rise as she said, 'I've some shopping to do . . .' Maisie knew she had been told a lie. Maisie studied Sandra's gait and, when she was out of sight, emulated the same walk for a few yards – the set of Sandra's shoulders, her step narrower than usual. Maisie noticed that even her jaw seemed to be clenched as she walked. It had always intrigued her, how such a method could reveal so much. Sandra was afraid, but was forging on despite the sense of fear that enveloped her. It was as if she had set out to do something – something that challenged her – and she had resolved not to turn back. In that moment, Maisie wished she had suggested accompanying Sandra to the shops – and she wondered what shops, exactly, would be open for Sandra after the working day was done on a Friday afternoon.

The street where Billy lived was not as desperate as some, though in Shoreditch there were still families who had no running water, forcing the women to struggle along to the communal pump several times each day. Those who lived in the two-up-two-down terrace houses fought a never-ending battle against damp, soot, and rats. It was common for more than one family to live in each house, with little food on the table, and no shoes on the feet of children. A motor car was rarely seen on these streets, which, though not far from the wealth of the City of London, might as well have been a thousand miles distant. There was a poverty here that clung to the soul, as if it were the fetid ochre smog that lingered above the dark waters of the River Thames.

Though Billy's mother had previously lived in a cottage along the same street, thanks to a bit of money put by after her husband died – money that was now gone – she had been living with the family for some time, sleeping in a room with the two boys and keeping an eye on Doreen during the day. She was a kindly woman whom Maisie had only once seen without a pinafore, and that was on the day little Lizzie Beale was laid to rest. Maisie had been glad old Mrs Beale was present when she called at the house, and that she remained in the kitchen – though at the sink, washing laundry – while Maisie put her idea to Billy and his wife as the three of them sat at the table. Maisie explained that she had a little money she wanted to invest in property, and had an idea that might help them all; she had seen details of a new house in Eltham that she wanted to put a down payment on, however, she would need to rent it out. She told them she'd already done her sums and the rent she would need to ask was – she believed – probably less than Billy was paying at the moment. Then she'd brought out a sheet describing the house, along with an artist's impression, and pushed it across the table to Billy and Doreen.

'Oh, I don't know, Miss, it's all very nice, but—'

'Billy, it's got an indoor lav, look at this!' Doreen's growing excitement was evident in her voice.

'Hold on, love, what I'm trying to say is this, that—'

'And three bedrooms,' added Doreen. 'A garden for the boys. And I think we'd rather pay rent to Miss Dobbs than that rotten bloke who—'

Maisie interjected. 'And if – when – you want to go to Canada, you won't be tied to the house. But if . . . if you decide not to go, for any reason, we can talk about the arrangements again, because you'll have paid money into the house and I would like you to see a return on it. So, all things being equal, it's an arrangement that works for both of us – I can invest my money, and you can move with no concerns about a higher rent, or being tied. It's an easy ride into Charing Cross on the train, or there's the bus, according to the man I spoke to this afternoon.'

'Miss, this is all very well, but—'

At once, and with soapsuds covering her hands and forearms, Billy's mother turned to the trio, focusing her attention on Billy.

'Here I am, doing a sinkful of bedclothes – for the second time today – that will go out on that line and be black as soot by the time they come in again; your boys have always got snotty noses, your wife is fit to pop, you're working yourself silly doing two jobs and you've got the cheek to sit there and say, "This is all very well." I don't know where you've had your head, Billy Beale, but in case you hadn't noticed, it's not very well – not very well by a long chalk. Miss Dobbs has come here and made you an offer that even to my uneducated mind sounds like a dream come true, and you want to turn it down in case your Canada boat comes in. You've got a nerve, son.' She turned away, muttering under her breath, her wet, reddened hands dragging a scrubbing brush back and forth across a sheet laid out on the draining board.

Billy shrugged, his face reddened. 'I reckon we can look tomorrow.' He turned to his wife. 'You feel up to it, going down there on the train?'

'It's hardly Brighton, Billy – it's not that far.' Doreen rubbed her swollen belly and turned to Maisie, her smile more open than it had been for months. 'I want to see this house. And thank you, Miss Dobbs, for thinking of us – you know, before you went out and talked to anyone else, or put it up for rent in the paper.'

Billy accompanied Maisie to the door. She turned to him before leaving.

'Two jobs, Billy?'

'I was going to talk to you about it, really I was.'

'You can talk to me about it another time, Billy. In the meantime, get a good night's sleep and I'll meet you and Doreen – and your mum – at the building office in Eltham.' She pressed a few coins into his hand. 'And don't let Doreen walk any further than she has to – here's a bit of bonus money for the taxi.'

'What bonus money?'

'For listening to your mother.'

* * *

A letter from James Compton was among those waiting for Maisie at the flat, and as she opened the envelope, she took care not to damage the Canadian stamp – Billy's sons might like it as a keepsake. In the letter James explained that he would be sailing for Southampton later than originally planned, and that it would be a few weeks before he arrived home. She read on, then slipped the letter back in the envelope to read again later. As she slid her fingernail under the edge of the stamp to peel it back, she noticed the franking was smudged, but not enough to hide the fact that the letter had been sent not from Toronto, but from London.

SEVEN

By Saturday afternoon, Maisie had returned to the building company's office to sign the preliminary required letter of intent to purchase a house in Eltham with three bedrooms, one bathroom, one new-look 'fitted' kitchen with an electric cooker, and French doors leading onto a small garden with a shed at the end of a narrow path. The front garden, the builder promised, would be finished with planted flower beds and a willow tree – in fact, on Willow Avenue, all the houses were to have front-garden willow trees as a 'feature', according to the builder's pamphlet. The only drawback was the wait – the house would not be completed for another month, and with Doreen due to give birth at some point in October, Maisie hoped they would be situated in their new home in a timely fashion.

'And you're sure it will be all right to rent only until we go to Canada, Miss?' said Billy. They were lingering in what would become the back garden, while his mother and Doreen remained in the kitchen, opening and closing cupboard doors that were yet to be painted and had no fittings. The family had been lost for words upon entering the house, and when they stepped into the drawing room, Doreen had walked across to the broad bow window, looked out at her boys running around at the front of the property, and burst into tears.

'Yes, I'm sure, Billy,' replied Maisie. 'This is a big step for both of us, but it's your home for as long as you want to live here.'

Billy nodded and blushed, rubbing his hands together in a manner that revealed both his excitement and his nervousness. 'This is good of you, Miss.'

'You're a valuable employee, Billy, and if you're constantly worried about your family, that doesn't serve either of us. Anyway, it was time, and it's a good place for my nest egg, too.'

Having settled the arrangements, Maisie could return to Cambridge, knowing that one concern was off her plate, for the moment. In the meantime, though, she just wanted to go back to the flat – to sit in the quiet of her own home, gather her thoughts, and make plans for her next move. True, she was not supposed to be directly involved in the search for Greville Liddicote's murderer, but she did not see how she could separate one investigation from the other – though she was sure that she, MacFarlane, and Stratton would, at some point, be falling over one another's feet in their quests to unearth the truth.

It was mid-afternoon when she arrived back at the block of flats in Pimlico, parking the MG close to the path that led from the street up to the front door. Her keys in hand, she made her way along the pavement, but at once felt a cold shiver across her neck. She had been wounded in the war when the casualty clearing station where she was working, close to the front, came under enemy fire. The resulting scar, which ran from her neck into her scalp, no longer ached as much as it once had; yet it came alive with her senses, and if it bothered her, she trusted that there was something to be bothered about.

A man was walking towards her, and she knew it was this pedestrian who had tweaked her senses. He seemed an ordinary man. His suit was neither new nor old; his shoes did not shine, though they were not dirty, and though he wore a clean shirt and a tie, the shirt was not as white as it could have been and the tie was of a colour that was not quite black and not quite blue. His face was forgettable, and his hat looked as if it had been steamed over a boiling kettle many times to keep its shape. He was a man who would not be remembered by a passerby. As he approached Maisie he brought out a packet of cigarettes from his pocket, opened the top, and without using his fingers, took one between his lips. He returned the packet of cigarettes to his pocket, then patted up and down his jacket as if searching for matches. He looked up at Maisie at the very point when they would have passed each other, and removed the unlit cigarette from his mouth to speak. 'Trouble you for a light, Miss?'

'I'm sorry, sir, I do not smoke, though you might try the gentleman opposite.'

'He doesn't look like a smoker to me.'

'But sir, he has brown fingertips. Don't all smokers have that stain?'

He nodded, looking down at the pavement as he made to walk on. They had each spoken their lines in a prearranged script, one of several she'd been tasked to memorise following her meeting with Huntley. The man who had asked for a light was now satisfied that she was the person he was looking for.

'Around the corner. Black motor.' The words were spoken without missing a beat. Then he was gone, pushing his hat back on his head as if it would help him find someone with a light for the cheap Woodbine he now held between two fingers.

Maisie stopped, then went back to the MG. She rummaged behind the front seat of the motor car as if she had forgotten something, locked the door again, and this time walked past the block of flats and around the corner, where a black motor car was parked, with engine idling. The passenger door opened as she walked alongside and she stepped in.

'A delight to see you, Miss Dobbs.' Brian Huntley turned to the driver and knocked on the glass partition. 'Scenic tour, if you don't mind, Harry.'

The driver, with his oversteamed hat back in place, pulled away from the curb and set off down the road. Huntley turned back to Maisie.

'Bring me up to date, Miss Dobbs. I've had a full report from Robbie about Liddicote's murder – a spanner in the works, as far as we're concerned, I must say – but I want to know what, if anything, you've observed thus far; and don't worry, I appreciate you've only been on the job a week.'

Maisie gave Huntley an account of her first days at the college, then asked a question.

'Why didn't anyone tell me about the rumours that Greville Liddicote's book caused a mutiny during the war?'

'Not important; the information wasn't required, and it is not exactly true that there was a mutiny – perhaps some rumbling in the ranks, which is why the book's sale was curtailed.'

'Dare I ask who curtailed it?'

Huntley shook his head. 'Classified.'

'I see.' Maisie knew there was little point in pressing Huntley; this was not Scotland Yard, where she could wheedle a piece of information here, a nugget there. This was the Secret Service, and she knew that between walls there were more walls, and every door required a different key – a key held by someone, somewhere, she had never even heard of. And though her association with Huntley's department was still in its infancy, she was gaining an impression that with so many walls, so many doors, and key holders who were not aware of – let alone able to speak to – one another, details could lay undisturbed for years.

Huntley nodded as she spoke, and it occurred to her that he must have worked quite closely with Maurice, perhaps more so than she'd previously thought, for he had some of her mentor's distinctive gestures: the slight incline of his head as he listened, or the habit of closing his eyes when she spoke, as if to bring forth an image of a person or situation she was describing. It made her aware, for the first time, that she, too, had probably absorbed much more of Maurice than she had imagined. She knew she had a habit of leaning her head to one side – just a little – when she replied to a difficult question, or when a thought occurred to her that she had yet to give voice to. She wondered how much of himself Maurice had seen in her.

'Robbie has informed me that you will be playing little or no part in the investigation into Liddicote's death. However, I know you will find it difficult to draw back from the enquiry. Though your work is part of a joint investigation between Special Branch and ourselves, and I have asked you to effectively keep MacFarlane apprised of your progress, do remember that in the first instance, your allegiance is to my department – and if that means keeping an eye on Robbie MacFarlane and his men, then so be it.'

'I can envisage some conflict—'

'Then deal with it in a manner that befits your role.' Huntley turned to Maisie. 'This may seem as if it is a light case – a college in Cambridge, a group of eccentric teachers with pacifist leanings – but there are troubling undercurrents in our institutions of tertiary education. Students from abroad, the political sympathies of the new generation, and among them a fascination with what is happening in Russia – put that together in a place of ideas, and you have a highly volatile cauldron on hot coals.'

Maisie nodded. 'Yes, that much is becoming evident. But what can you tell me about a debate among the Cambridge colleges?'

'That's what you are there to tell us, Miss Dobbs. Debates are a part of university life – you know that from your days at Girton. And an intercollegiate debate would be an event of some proportion, and could be of interest to us – dependent upon the subject to be debated.'

'I'll find out – but you should know that Greville Liddicote was against the idea of his college putting forward a team of students to enter a planned debate. And it was causing some friction with his deputy, Matthias Roth.'

'Oh, yes, the German.'

Maisie regarded Huntley for a second or two, then put another question to him. 'Mr Huntley, how much do you already know about the college? In my briefings, I was given to believe that your current information was limited, yet I feel as if I am giving you intelligence you already have to hand.'

Huntley replied without pause. 'We have the sketch, Miss Dobbs. Your job is to uncover the masterpiece, so to speak. We could only go so far; you had the background to secure an academic post and work from within. We believe something is going on at that college, and we want to know exactly what it is. If it is simply a cover for bringing refugees – albeit wealthy young refugees – into the country, then that is one thing; but we believe there is more there than meets the eye. Consider no information too small or insignificant to report.'

At that point he opened the glass partition again. 'You can double-back now, Harry. Find a suitable point where Miss Dobbs can catch a bus to Pimlico.'

The driver nodded.

'Well, thank you for the consideration, Mr Huntley. At least you didn't ask me to walk the whole way.' Despite the comment, Maisie smiled as she left Huntley, and made her way back to the flat.

Maisie spent Sunday preparing for the week ahead and hardly saw Sandra, who left after breakfast to visit her husband's grave, a weekly pilgrimage of devotion. Maisie left the flat before Sandra emerged from her room on Monday morning, and was grateful for another trouble-free drive on the London–Cambridge road, a route which followed the old coach road, and was marked by ancient milestones at intervals along the way.

Arriving at the college mid-morning, Maisie was informed that an important formal announcement was to be made at noon, when students and staff would gather in the assembly hall – formerly a ballroom in the days when the property was still a private residence. Matthias Roth was to inform the assembly of Greville Liddicote's passing, though she imagined there would be no mention made as to cause of death. Maisie's first class was not until after lunch, so she went directly to the staff room, where refreshments were being served. As she waited in the line for coffee behind other members of staff – she was becoming accustomed to the bitter brew – she learnt another snippet of news: Rosemary

Linden had departed the college without notice, leaving only a list of tasks completed and instructions regarding the efficient execution of her duties. Her stated reason – in a brief note penned in her precise copperplate hand, according to staff-room gossip – was that she did not wish to work at the college without Dr Liddicote at the helm.

Maisie took a cup of coffee and made her way over to speak to Francesca Thomas, who was seated in an armchair, making notes in red pencil on a student's heavily fingered assignment. She held her coffee cup in her right hand and wrote with her left.

'Dr Thomas, may I join you?'

'Ah, Miss Dobbs. Of course, do join me.' She cleared a stack of papers from the chair next to hers. 'There you are. Did you have a restful break from college?'

'Yes, I returned to London. You?'

'Oh, I seldom venture out of Cambridge. I rent a flat in town, just a small bed-sitting-room really. And I belong to a choir, so there is usually a practise to attend. There is always something to do in the city.'

'Yes, I was here as a student – well, you know that, from my interview here.'

'Indeed.'

'It's a shame about Miss Linden leaving – and quite suddenly. She seemed so efficient, I cannot imagine her just going off without a by-your-leave.'

Thomas shrugged. 'She was young, and of course she was the one who discovered Greville – a lot for her to deal with, I think.'

'Do you know where she lived?'

'I believe she came from Suffolk. She was a country girl who had come to Cambridge for some town life, I would imagine. But of course, the academic world is more insular than it might first appear, and if you are not a student at one of the colleges here, you are considered "town" rather than "gown" – and never the twain shall meet.'

'Yes, I see what you mean.' Maisie changed tack. 'The college must be very different for you, coming from a larger university.'

Thomas smiled. It was not a broad smile, not an expression that would welcome a long-lost friend, or accompany joy. Rather, it was measured, a smile of knowing as opposed to celebration. 'I see you have discovered rather a lot about me, Miss Dobbs.'

Maisie was quick to respond. 'I looked up the senior members of staff before I joined the college – it's quite simple to find out – because I assumed I would be interviewed by a committee, and I decided to hazard a guess as to who would be on that committee. Knowing something about you and Dr Roth helped me to anticipate some of your questions when we met in the library.'

'And you did very well, Miss Dobbs.' Thomas looked at her watch. 'Ah, we should make our way down to the assembly hall. Roth is due to speak from on high.'

Maisie gathered her briefcase and books, and followed other members of staff down the oak staircase and along the corridor in the direction of the assembly hall. She did not acknowledge the sarcastic tone of Thomas' last comment, though she noted the inflection in the woman's voice when she referred to her colleague by his surname only, without the respect one might accord the man who was now principal.

There was already a buzz of conversation among the gathered students when they entered, and Maisie was surprised to see how many were there. The student body was larger than she had imagined. They were seated in rows according to the number of years spent at the school. The first-year students were in the front, followed by second and third years, with a few students at the back who were engaged in research studies following tertiary education elsewhere. Many of the students had already completed formal education in other countries, though there were also a good number of British students in the hall. The staff were assigned seats along the side of the main audience. On the stage at the front of the assembly hall, seats had been allocated for the Board of Governors, along with the principal and deputy principal. The event was formal, thus those to be seated on the stage would not enter until the audience of students and staff were settled. At twelve noon a bell rang from beyond the hall – Maisie thought it might have been the first bell she had heard at the college – and the busy chatter subsided to a mumble, then to silence.

The double doors at the back of the hall opened, and Matthias Roth led a procession of ten governors and one other teacher – Maisie recognised him as Dr Alan Burnham, a teacher of classics who, although born in London, had spent his childhood in Greece. To Maisie's surprise, MacFarlane and Stratton walked along, side by side, at the end of the line, and she wondered why MacFarlane had chosen to be part of such a public display.

With the procession seated, Matthias Roth stepped towards the lectern and in his booming baritone addressed the school.

'You will have heard, by now, of the passing of our dear founder and principal, Dr Greville Liddicote.' He stopped speaking to allow time for the collective gasp and whispers of dismay to run through the gathering, as if they were waves drawn to the beach. 'The College of St Francis was the result of his imagination and hard work – he dared to believe that we could create a world of peace, of harmony, and he was not afraid to step forward to set us on a path that would lead to such a world. Every student in this room, every member of staff, every governor is here because of Greville Liddicote. Today we mourn his loss.' Roth paused, cleared his throat, and continued. 'We will give thanks for his life in a service at St Mary's Church – details will be posted on the main notice board. Dr Liddicote will not be laid to rest for some time – I will explain later – but that does not prevent us from giving thanks for his life, his wisdom, and his accomplishments, particularly in the realm of medieval literature and in stories that enchanted children – and adults – the world over. Whatever your religious persuasion, we know that you will come to St Mary's – Greville Liddicote was a Christian, though he never pressed his beliefs, nor ever discredited those of another. With that in mind, we must do what is right when we remember him. Before I ask the chairman of the Board of Governors to speak, I would like to take this opportunity to inform you that the events surrounding Greville Liddicote's death are . . . questionable. So that we might come to know the reason for his passing, I have requested the assistance of two members of the police, whom you will see on the premises over the next week or so. I ask that you give them your full support and attention; that, if asked, you answer their questions truthfully and with respect for Dr Liddicote, and that you endeavour to recall any events that might help them in their enquiries.' He turned to MacFarlane and Stratton, his hand extended, palm up, to ask them to stand. 'Detective Chief Superintendent Robert MacFarlane and Detective Chief Inspector Richard Stratton are here to help us so that we might discover the reason for our beloved founder's untimely passing.'

Maisie cast her gaze along the line of teachers on both sides of the hall. One or two teachers had nodded off, despite the gravity of the meeting; others were listening intently, their interest roused when the presence of detectives was announced. Francesca Thomas was sitting with arms folded, that same half-smile on her face as she watched Matthias Roth speak.

When MacFarlane and Stratton were seated again, Roth invited the chairman of the Board of Governors to speak. The elderly man, who introduced himself as a supporter of trade between nations and an ardent pacifist, was a noted local businessman who repeated much of Roth's speech in his summation of Greville Liddicote's work. He followed his reminiscences of Liddicote's life with the announcement that Dr Matthias Roth had been appointed principal, and that Dr Alan Burnham, 'a classicist without equal', would be his deputy. Matthias Roth was invited to the lectern again, and gave an account of what was to come, now that Greville Liddicote was dead.

'As I have already said,' continued Roth, 'we are all here – staff and students alike – because Greville Liddicote wanted to see a more peaceful world. But he knew that such a world would not come without dialogue, and that for us all to agree, there would be times when we would disagree, and that in the effort to find a common ground upon which to walk forward together there must be compromise and acceptance of one another, with an emphasis on those elements that bind us rather than set us apart.' Roth stopped speaking for a moment, and, taking a handkerchief from his pocket, he lifted his spectacles and pressed the cloth to his eyes. When he continued speaking, his voice cracked, though he forged on, his eyes shining, his words clear. 'To that end, and in our dear founder's memory, I am happy to tell you that the College of St Francis will be taking part in the forthcoming debate between the Cambridge colleges. It was what Greville Liddicote would have wanted – he told me himself that our students must play an important part in such an event. It has just been announced that the subject of our first debate is the political climate in Germany – "Could the Tenets of Herr Adolf Hitler's National Socialist Party Be Adopted in Britain?" He paused as a current of conversation swept through the hall, then cleared his throat and began to speak again, silencing the audience as he went on. 'More than a debate, this is our opportunity to inform, to shine, to tell the academic world here in Cambridge that we at St Francis are an international force of youth to be reckoned with. The debate will draw a "town and gown" audience, and it is expected that various unions will be represented among the spectators.' He looked at the assembly in silence for a moment, his eyes casting back and forth as if looking at every single person seated before him. Once more his voice caught as he began to speak, and again he recovered, and ended with a power and resolve that ignited the students. 'Our commitment to the beliefs of our founder will underpin our arguments; we will not fail him.'

Maisie watched as the gathering broke into applause, and though several of the governors appeared stony-faced, others were beaming with a delight that matched Matthias Roth's. It seemed as if the reason for the assembly had been forgotten. The staff were turning to each other, some showing signs of concern, others shrugging shoulders. It was clear to Maisie that there was a certain knowledge that Greville Liddicote, far from being a supporter of the debate, was against the college taking part. She looked towards Francesca Thomas. The woman sat immobile as the students alongside her were caught up in the applause; she was staring at Roth with a mixture of disbelief and – Maisie could see it now – something akin to hatred. The ever-elegant woman gathered her belongings and left the hall, the rubber-edged double doors swinging back and forth in her wake.

After the meeting Matthias Roth came to the staff room with MacFarlane and Stratton to announce that the visitors would be interviewing all members of staff. He had drawn up a schedule of appointments, posted on the noticeboard, based upon each person's teaching timetable and tutorial commitments; interviews would begin immediately and would take place in the faculty library.

'The first interviewee will be Miss Lang.' All gathered looked around the room, expecting Delphine Lang to step forward, secretly glad that they would not be first. 'Is Miss Lang here?'

'Actually, Dr Roth, I believe she went home with a nasty summer cold – she left after the assembly,' offered the American member of staff.

Roth shrugged. 'This is where we begin to wish Miss Linden were still with us – at least I would know who is in college and who is not.' He peered at the schedule, then more deliberately at Maisie. 'In that case, Miss Dobbs, I believe you're next.'

Maisie took up her briefcase and the pile of student essays that she was by now getting used to having under her arm, and left the room. She made her way along the corridor and up the grand staircase to the landing where the library was situated. She knocked on the door and walked in.

Both MacFarlane and Stratton looked up when Maisie entered, then looked down again at the sheet of paper bearing the staff roster.

'No, I'm not Miss Delphine Lang, she's supposedly at home with a cold. So I'm the first – fire away! Oh and I'm supposed to be at the front of my classroom, ready to teach by two o'clock, so we'd better hurry.'

MacFarlane did not miss a beat. 'What did you think of the dog and pony show in the assembly hall?'

Maisie shook her head. 'Well, you make a lovely couple, though I think some flowers would have brought out your finer points, gentlemen.'

'Very funny, Maisie, very funny indeed. What a charade that was, but we were playing their game.' MacFarlane pushed her file to one side.

'We thought it would be a good idea, seeing as there are so many to interview,' added Stratton. 'Bring it out into the open, rather than having a lot of speculation about who we are, seeing as we're going to be on the premises a fair bit.'

Maisie nodded. 'Do you need to interview me?'

'I can talk to you anytime,' said MacFarlane. 'Rushing off somewhere later?'

Maisie looked around at the grandfather clock in the corner. 'I have one lesson starting in about ten minutes, after which I am not teaching until late morning tomorrow. I have to leave Cambridge, possibly overnight.'

'Going anywhere interesting?'

'I won't know until I get there – but I'll be in touch if I uncover any deeply held secrets.'

EIGHT

Maisie enjoyed the lesson that followed. Knowing the students would be abuzz with speculation about the morning's assembly, she decided to put her prepared lesson to one side and discuss the issue of death and what the great philosophers had to say on the subject of passing from one world to the next, if indeed that is what they believed.

She took the liberty of ending the lesson early and, with homework assigned, and the previous week's work discussed – 'A deeper reading of the assigned texts might have resulted in better marks,' observed Maisie – she hurriedly gathered her belongings and made her way to the station.

Finding a person when there was only a vague starting point was, she thought, rather like finding a pin on a lawn

– there was the occasional glint of possibility when light hit the subject, but that flash often did not last long enough for the pin to be found. If she were able to catch the next train to Ipswich, she would arrive in plenty of time to visit the records office; her starting point would be the town hall, to see if records listed anyone in the region by the name of Linden.

She arrived at the station with just minutes to spare, purchased a ticket, and hurried to the platform to await the train. Soon the train approached, rumbling towards the long platform, steam chuffing out sideways as the locomotive slowed alongside the waiting travellers. Maisie climbed aboard and settled in a seat next to the window. With a whistle and a flag held high, the guard waved to the driver; steam punched the air again and the train began to move. It was as Maisie's carriage began to move away from the station that she saw Francesca Thomas step forward to await the next train. She was opening her handbag to put away her ticket, so did not look up while the train was passing. Maisie craned her neck to look back at Thomas and saw the woman check the time, and then begin to pace the platform. It was the only sign that she might be holding some tension, for her face was devoid of expression or emotion. Maisie recalled that the next train from the platform was bound for London's Liverpool Street station, and she thought about her most recent conversation with Francesca Thomas, during which the older woman maintained that she seldom ventured out of Cambridge.

Though Thomas dominated Maisie's thoughts as the train went on its way, the side-to-side motion of the carriages soon lulled her into a half-sleep. She had hardly slept since the previous Friday; there had been so much to accomplish, so much to consider, with events at the college inviting intense speculation and consideration. But in truth, one thing had kept her from sleeping more than any other; the letter from James. She could not work out how a letter with a Canadian stamp had been franked in London. Admittedly, the postmark was smudged, and it was difficult to read – but no, she was certain it was London, though she had already been informed by James that there was, indeed, a London in Ontario . . . *would you believe it, Maisie?* She considered James and realised she had been doing her best not to think about him since accepting the assignment with MacFarlane and Huntley – to no avail. What might he say if he knew she was working for the Secret Service? Possibly he would be concerned that the job might be more dangerous than that of a private enquiry agent, though to her it seemed as if the risk were minimised with her current assignment. They had become closer as the year progressed, so close that she knew there was already speculation as to what might come next. Priscilla had cornered her on the subject during an unexpected visit to her flat.

'I know that when I don't see much of you, it's because you don't want to talk about something, and I would lay money on that something being James. Come on, what is it?'

'Nothing. I like James. We enjoy each other's company.'

'Oh, for heaven's sake – it's me you're talking to, not your prudish old aunt!'

Maisie shrugged. 'I just don't know where it's all going – I mean, I loved Simon dearly, but there was no destination to the journey, if you know what I mean. And now I don't know about James. In some ways I would like to think there was something in the distance, a place to land. On the other hand, I'm satisfied just going along as we are.'

Priscilla shook her head, pressed a cigarette into the long holder she favoured, held a lighter to the end until it smouldered, and leant back on Maisie's new sofa, snapping the lighter shut as if to punctuate the conversation. 'This is very comfortable, by the way – it softens the room.' She inhaled, blew a smoke ring and regarded Maisie. 'Sometimes, you flummox me, Maisie, really you do. Of course there has to be a destination – of one sort or another, and if I were you I'd go for the known road.'

'Known road?'

'Marry the man! Of course, you can keep ambling, as long as you both understand the pros and cons, the whys and wherefores. You have your house and this flat, and you could live in sin quite merrily. But that's not you, Maisie. And for all the wild ways of my youth, it wasn't me, either. I wanted to know where I stood. I knew I needed a specific garden with a fence around it in which to grow. And I have flourished – haven't I? Admit it.'

'Marriage agrees with you, Pris.'

'I have a fine spouse, my three toads – who of course are in the dog house again, but I love them for it. And I have a good life, which is nothing to be sniffed at.'

'But I don't know if it's me, that sort of life. And for a start, James hasn't asked.'

'Probably too bloody scared to ask, if you want my opinion.'

'What do you mean?'

'Well, a man asks a woman to marry him when he's pretty sure she'll say yes. Getting a *no* isn't exactly an edifying experience, is it?'

Maisie looked out of the window. 'Well, anyway . . .'

'I know that *well anyway*.' Priscilla mimicked Maisie's voice. 'It's the phrase that says, "I really don't want to talk about it any more." Well, *anyway*, Maisie – I do! Now then, the question is, do you want to marry him, regardless of whether he has asked you?'

'I don't know.'

'What, exactly, don't you know?'

'Whether I could relinquish my work. Frankly, I don't think I could.'

'Oh, I hate all this old-fashioned twaddle, you know, that a woman has to do this or that when she's married.' She turned to Maisie. 'Strike out, for heaven's sake! After all, dear old Maurice left you with more than simply his estate. His greatest bequest was a good deal of freedom, don't you think? You now have the wherewithal to please yourself, and to hell with what anyone thinks.' She paused.

'You've got to snap out of it, Maisie – being concerned about what others think of you. It's a bit late now, anyway, to be worrying about that sort of thing, what with your business and the fact that James is a very frequent visitor to your flat.' She inhaled from the cigarette holder, as if for effect. 'I bet his shaving mug is a fixture in your bathroom, for a start. But of course, the real question is more fundamental, isn't it, my friend? The real question is, do you truly love the man?'

Maisie snapped awake as the whistle blew to signal arrival in Ipswich, the county town of Suffolk. There were other records offices in the county, but she had to start somewhere. The afternoon was sunny and warm as she walked towards the address she had been given for the records office. She knew a county records office was sometimes lacking in information, and that parish records often held more of the sort of detail she was looking for. But parish records were all very well if you knew which parish to start your search – otherwise it could be a time-consuming exercise, with no joy at the end.

The clerk assisting her was a man who looked to be in his fifties, and who gave the impression of knowing a great many people in the county.

'Linden . . . Linden. Rosemary, you say? Not a great number of Lindens about, to my knowledge. Approximately twenty-eight years of age? Well, if her birth was registered, then we should know about it, though do bear in mind that not all parents – especially those in agricultural areas – are given to taking the time to register a child. Often there's the wait to see if the child lives past its first month, then if it does, they might register the birth – that's if they can lose a day's pay to come into town. Anyway, let me see if I can find anything.'

Maisie waited for some time, watching the late-afternoon sun waft across the room, highlighting dust motes and flies that buzzed back and forth from window to window.

'Here's a few Lindens for you, but no Rosemary, I'm afraid.' He held out a piece of paper. 'You'll see we've got a Cyril and his wife, Mary; a Stephen and Julia and four children; a Rupert and Jane, plus two, and an Emily – elderly, widowed. There were also three deceaseds: James Christopher – eight months; Margaret, spinster; and Rose, another widow.'

'Do you have addresses?'

'I have last-knowns, though they can change, what with people being out of work, short of money to pay the rent; people have to move to find a decent day's wage, and there's the old people who're having to depend on charity.'

Maisie nodded and thanked the man, looking at the clock on the wall as she departed the office. It was now half past four. If she could secure a room in a guesthouse, she would stay overnight and return to the college the following morning, in time for her class at eleven o'clock. And if she could at least see one or two of the people on her list, she could come back to Ipswich again towards the end of the week to investigate further. It meant she might not be able to return to London on Friday, so she'd have to review the week with Billy and Sandra in a telephone call. Maisie sighed. She had hoped to spend some more time with Sandra – she was worried about her. And she had left her with some pamphlets on evening classes at Birkbeck College – in the hope that her interest might be sufficiently piqued to consider extending her education, which Maisie thought could help her find a way through her grief. She had been planning to ask Sandra what she thought of the idea. And she also wanted to find out if Billy had made any headway in the search for more information on Eric's death.

The Lavender Inn was snuggled along a side street within ten minutes walking distance of the station, which suited Maisie well; fortunately, there was a vacancy. She left a small bag with the few personal belongings she had travelled with in her room and set off to find the first address, which was in the town – in fact, all of the addresses, bar one, were within a reasonable distance by foot or bus. Walking past buildings through which an architectural history of the town could be traced – from the beamed wattle-and-daub hall-houses of medieval times, to the Gothic redbrick Cornhill building, and Victorian terraces – she eventually found the home she was looking for in Saltwater Lane. As she knocked on the door, a dog barked from deep within the small terrace house and was reprimanded for causing a noise. Footsteps moved closer towards the door, which opened to reveal a heavyset man with a handle-bar moustache and oiled hair parted in the centre. His eyes seemed larger than they might have been, due to the thick spectacles on his nose. He held a newspaper in his hand and looked at Maisie over the glasses in order to focus on her face.

'Mr Linden?'

'Who wants him?'

'My name is Maisie Dobbs, and I have come from a college in Cambridge in search of one of our employees. She left due to family matters without collecting her wages, so I thought I would bring them to her – but we don't have an address. Her name is Rosemary Linden, and I thought you might know of her.'

The man shook his head. 'Don't know anyone of that name.'

'Do you know the other Lindens in Ipswich?'

'There's my boy, Stephen, and his family. And my brother's widow, Rose. They didn't have children, so there's no Lindens on that side – in any case, she passed recently, about a month ago. We hadn't seen her for years anyway. And if there are other Lindens, they're not us.'

'I see.' Maisie paused. 'So you wouldn't know a Rosemary Linden, about twenty-eight years of age?'

'No, no Rosemary Linden that I know of.'

A voice came from the back of the house. 'Cy-ril! Cyril, your dinner's getting cold.'

The man began to close the door, but Maisie held out

her hand. 'Please wait. Let me write down my name and my address in Cambridge. I realise it would be most unlikely, but if you come across the name Rosemary Linden, would you be so kind as to send me a postcard? I would really appreciate it.'

Maisie allowed the man to see the cash in her purse as she looked for a pencil. Though she did not offer money, the glimpse would – she hoped – suggest a monetary reward for information. She thanked him for his help, wished him a good evening, and went on her way. She could leave Stephen Linden and his family for now, though she wondered about the newly deceased Rose who, according to Linden, had died about one month before. It was now getting on for seven o'clock, so she decided to catch a bus and walk along to Beet Street – and the small cottage that had been the home of Rose Linden.

The cottage and garden seemed to have been well tended, though the grass was high, the shrubs in need of pruning, and the weeds on the cusp of being out of control. Maisie unlatched the gate and began to walk around the house, following a path of stepping stones that appeared to be homemade, with colourful shards of broken crockery set into the concrete. Deadheading roses as she went, it struck Maisie that the house might once have been built for a farmworker, and it reminded her of her father's cottage at Chelstone – it had a similar cat-slide roof, a gutter running into a water butt, and lead-paned windows. It was another old house built to be cool in summer and warm in winter, and, she thought, probably had an inglenook fireplace inside.

Reaching the back door, Maisie instinctively tried the handle. To her surprise, it turned, and though she had to push with some force against the door, it opened to allow entry into the cottage. She stood for some seconds to become accustomed to the dark interior. It seemed the home had hardly been touched since the day Rose Linden passed away. Feeling rather like Goldilocks in the three bears' house, Maisie began to walk around the kitchen, then the sitting room, stepping lightly so she made little sound. There were no immediate neighbours, and she had seen no one else on the street, but at the same time, she didn't want to give any passerby cause to raise the alarm that a common thief was on the loose in the home of a dead woman.

As she looked about her, Maisie sensed that Rose Linden had been a kindly soul, that she had lived in her house, worked in her garden and accepted her lot with a certain ease. She had most likely lived the seasons of her life with no more and no fewer ups and downs than anyone else, and probably took the blows of sadness with the same equanimity as she received the gift of joy. And without doubt, Rose Linden had friends, if the photographs on top of the sideboard were any indication. She had won prizes for her roses at the local fete, had welcomed schoolchildren to her garden, and was not short of company. Maisie smiled as she considered each image, and hoped that Rose had lived a good life, and lived it well. She suspected that the woman was one who had mourned the lack of children, and in all likelihood had shed the tears of a barren wife. Maisie hoped she had died in peace.

Stepping with as light a foot as she could, Maisie set off up the stairs, and though dusk was approaching, she did not want to use the gas lamps as the glow might attract unwanted attention.

In the main bedroom a lace counterpane covered a bed made for two. Underneath, a pink silk coverlet had been draped over the bed, which had been stripped of sheets. Maisie looked at the lace and pink silk together, and knew that Rose Linden had passed away in her own home, in this bed. She hoped that a loved one was there to hold her hand, and wondered why Cyril and his wife had not paid attention to the house and garden, for surely they would be the primary beneficiaries of her estate. To be sure, the house did not represent a lucrative bequest, but it was something in such times. Then again, the estate could have been left to someone else.

Maisie stepped into the second room, which was smaller, with low beams and whitewashed walls. A single bed was made up, as if ready for an expected visitor. A towel had been placed on the wooden stand alongside the window; and the pitcher inside the china bowl was still filled with water, though there was a greenish ring where some had evaporated in recent weeks. A cupboard close to the door was partially open, and when Maisie looked inside, she discovered it was filled with books. She began to read the titles on the spine of one book after another, then knelt down to better see those on the floor of the cupboard. As she lifted each book, Maisie knew she was searching, that this was no idle curiosity; she recognised the sensation of expectation, the way her fingers tingled as she laid book after book aside, having checked the title, opened the pages, and read the inscription. Then she saw it. The cover was familiar to her now; the children looking up at the soldier and the crosses growing smaller in the distance. She ran her fingers over the embossed board, across the Celtic knot pressed into the dyed cloth, then with care opened the cover, and the first page. The inscription had been penned in a clear copperplate hand: *To our darling Rose, with our love. Ursula.* And with the same pen and ink, the writer had crossed out Greville Liddicote's name.

It was too late to return to Cyril Linden's home, so Maisie decided to wait until the following morning. It was to be an early call, so she would have to take the chance that her visit might be met with some degree of reticence. She also wanted to return to the records office before leaving Ipswich. If all went to plan she would arrive back at the college in the nick of time – not exactly the way in which a new member of staff should conduct herself during a period of probationary service; however, she was not behind in her work as she would use the evening in the guesthouse to mark her students' essays and prepare for the following day's classes.

Though she had read Greville Liddicote's book, she took out her copy once more before going to bed.

Some of the children missed their mothers, but the leaders, Adam and Alice, marched on. 'We're going to find our fathers!' they exclaimed. Then the children set off two by two, little soldiers on their way to stop a war.

'Where are you going?' asked the mayor, with a rope of shining gold coins around his neck, and a red cloak with an ermine collar drawn around his very big middle with a black leather belt.

'We're marching to find our fathers,' said Peter.

A cheer went up and when the mayor turned around to see what had caused such a cacophony of noise, his cheeks became as red as his cloak. From another street a thousand more little children came running.

'We want to find our fathers!' shouted a French boy named Jean. 'We want to march with you!'

'And we're coming too!' said Inge, the little German girl.

At exactly half past eight in the morning, Maisie knocked on the door of Cyril and Mary Linden's house on Saltwater Lane. It was early to call but she suspected the Lindens rose with the sun. Again she heard the barking dog admonished and the heavy clump of footsteps coming towards the door. Cyril Linden did not look pleased to find a visitor on his doorstep.

'Oh, you again.'

Maisie smiled. 'I am so sorry to bother you this early in the morning, but I have to catch a train in an hour and I really wanted to ask you another question or two more, if that's all right.'

The man sighed and shook his head. 'I'm having my breakfast, so you'd better come in. I don't want it to spoil.' He turned and led the way down a dark passageway towards the kitchen at the back of the house, which elicited an odour of fried bacon and eggs, and the musty dander of dog.

'Mary, this is Miss Dobbs – it was "Dobbs", wasn't it?'

Maisie nodded and held out her hand. Mary Linden wiped her damp fingers on her apron and took the proffered hand, smiling, and adding, 'Pleased, I'm sure. Would you like a cup of tea, Miss Dobbs?'

'Oh, that would be lovely, thank you, Mrs Linden.'

Linden pulled out a chair for Maisie, then sat down to finish his breakfast. A fox terrier banished to the garden outside barked and pawed at the door, while another, older, dog with a grey muzzle and glassy eyes lay on a clump of blankets in the corner, only raising her head once to acknowledge Maisie's entrance. She returned to her snoring.

'That dog can send them home when she likes,' said Linden, scraping up egg with a wedge of fried bread. 'Now then, what can we do for you?'

'I wanted to ask you about your sister-in-law, Rose Linden. You said she passed away about a month ago.'

'Yes, as far as we know.'

'As far as you know? Were you not close?'

'I was close enough to my brother, as a boy. But not to her.'

'I take it your brother was older than you.'

Linden nodded. 'Ten years. And she was older than him, though you would never have known it. He passed years ago; his heart.'

'Do you know her family?' asked Maisie.

'Don't really want to know them.' Linden brushed off the question.

'Cyril, don't you speak ill of the dead. It's not right.' Mary Linden had been pushing wet laundry through a wringer. She picked up a wicker basket filled with damp bed linen and opened the back door, whereupon the dog barked again and tried to get into the kitchen. 'And you can get back out there, Midget. I've enough to put up with, without you at my feet.' She closed the door behind her.

'May I ask why you wouldn't want to know Rose's family? I'm enquiring only because I am anxious to find Rosemary Linden and I think there might be some sort of connection.'

He pushed away his plate and leant back in his chair, wiping his mouth with the back of his hand before reaching for a cup of strong brown tea. 'They wouldn't be Lindens, though, would they? She took a good name, Linden, and there's no Rosemarys on our side.'

Maisie nodded. 'Do you know her maiden name?'

Cyril Linden sighed. 'I can't say as I remember, to tell you the truth. But hold on a minute.'

He pushed back his chair, opened the back door, quieted the barking dog, and shouted out to his wife. Maisie listened to the conversation as she sipped her tea.

'Mary – what was her name before she got married? Can't for the life of me remember.'

'Rose?'

'Of *course* I mean Rose. Can you remember her name?'

'Lummy, I don't know.' There was a pause. 'Wasn't she a Thurber? Thur-something?'

'No, no, that was the sister's married name. I thought old Rose was a Gibson.'

'She might've been, Cyril – I can't say as it sounds right to me, though.'

Linden closed the door behind him, and took his seat once again. 'Reckon it might have been either Gibson or Thur-something.'

Maisie gathered her bag as if to leave, and asked another question. 'It seems you didn't care for Rose very much, Mr Linden.'

He shook his head, and shrugged. 'Well, what can you do? My brother was the educated one, a teacher, and he married an educated woman. Came from a funny family, she did; all books, all know-all's they were. They never had any children of their own, my brother and Rose, and if I was to say anything for them, then it would be that it's because of their help that our children got a good education

166

and have managed to do well in life because of it. Pity the same couldn't be said of her sister's boy. They made sure he had a good education, too, but look what he did with his brains.'

'What did he do?'

'Him? Good for nothing conchie, that's what he was. But the less said about that, the better. I don't want talk about a yellow belly in this house.'

'What was—'

He scraped his chair back, stood up and began walking towards the front door. 'And seeing as he's got nothing to do with your Rosemary Linden, and we don't know her, anyway, I reckon you'd best get going – you'll miss your train otherwise.'

Maisie bit her lip and smiled as she shook his hand at the door. 'Thank you, Mr Linden. You have been most kind.'

He nodded and closed the door.

Maisie walked down the path, unlatched the front gate, and was about to continue on towards the station when she heard a whistle from the other side of the street. A black motor car had just come to a halt, and as she looked up, MacFarlane called out to her.

'Come on, get in and we'll give you a lift.'

Maisie crossed the road and stepped into the black Invicta motor car, where MacFarlane and Stratton were already seated.

'I might have bloody well known.' MacFarlane's words were accompanied by a rolling of his eyes. 'So, we can't walk in there now, they'll probably set the dogs on us.'

'There's only one you really have to worry about, Robbie. The other's old and grey.'

MacFarlane turned to face Maisie. 'Which is what I'll be if we don't get the territory sorted out.'

'To be frank, I'm not sure it's possible. I'm not saying that defence of the realm is wrapped up with Liddicote's murder, but it might be.'

'So, what have you got for us, Maisie?' Stratton leant forward, entering the conversation. He seemed subdued. Not for the first time, she wondered if his transfer to Special Branch had lived up to his expectations.

She recounted the items of interest that she had uncovered during her visit to Ipswich, adding, 'I'm interested in Rosemary Linden because of her position – she knew more about what was going on at the college than anyone else there, despite a role that some people looked down upon. I know some members of staff saw her as little more than the maid in the office, even though she was privy to most of the college's official correspondence, and to the records of all staff and students. And no sooner does Liddicote die than she leaves.'

'It would be hard for a woman to wring a man's neck, Maisie,' said MacFarlane.

'I'm not saying she murdered him, but I would like to speak to her all the same. I think there was a connection, somewhere, between Rosemary Linden and Greville Liddicote. I am not at all sure what it was, but I intend to find out. And before you ask – yes, I do think there's an outside chance that it might be connected to our national interests, especially considering the information she might have to hand; information that others might not dream she has. And if they do, we might not be the only ones looking for her.' Maisie paused. 'Have you discovered anything earth-shattering, gentlemen?'

MacFarlane rolled his eyes again. 'Bloody boring, these education types.'

'Careful, Detective Chief Superintendent MacFarlane, you're talking to one of them.'

'Staid, but never boring, Maisie.'

'Staid?'

NINE

MacFarlane and Stratton were returning to London later in the day, but escorted Maisie back to Cambridge, so she had plenty of time for some last-minute preparation before her first class. When they arrived, MacFarlane stopped to speak to the driver, while Maisie and Stratton walked on towards the main entrance.

'Richard, I wonder if I might ask you a quick question.'

Stratton turned to face her. 'Fire away – though I might not answer.'

'We're all in the same boat here, aren't we?'

'No, we're not. But if I can help you, I will.'

Maisie ignored the 'No, we're not' and went on. 'When Tom Sarron had completed his initial examination of Greville Liddicote's body, you called after him as he was leaving. I was just curious to know what you might have seen – if you can tell me.'

Stratton looked towards the Invicta, where MacFarlane was still conversing with the driver, then turned back to Maisie. 'Robbie said that when you initially telephoned him about Liddicote's death, you thought he might have been killed by a professional, someone who knew exactly how to sever the spinal cord with one snap of the neck – instant death. I just wanted to ask him about it. Two things occurred to me: first, given the fact that Liddicote was a man – not a physically strong man, admittedly – I wondered if a woman could have done it. Second, I wanted to know in which direction the neck had been twisted, and whether a reflex – you're killing a person and you want it done quickly – would lead you to twist to the right or left, dependent upon which hand is your dominant hand. So, for example, would a right-handed person twist to the right, and a left-handed person twist to the left?'

'That sounds like a reasonable question.'

'But it's awfully muddy.' He sighed. 'Most people write with their right hands; even those who began writing with their left hands have been taught at school that they should write with the right hand – if you'll excuse the pun, it's what's considered right. However, in the heat of the moment, even if a person who has been forced to use their right hand as the dominant hand, would they turn the head to the left if they were acting under a certain pressure? And even a trained killer is under pressure. By the way, I believe you were correct in your assumption, as it does seem as if the murderer in question was versed in this sort of attack.'

'But the "muddying" hardly helps us, does it?'

'And, of course, we could have a completely ambidextrous killer,' added Stratton.

Maisie nodded. 'Have you seen Liddicote's family yet? I know he lived alone, but didn't he have a couple of children?'

'Yes, and we're interviewing them over the next day or so – they've been informed of his death, of course. The son and daughter are in their mid-twenties and, as far as we know, didn't have much to do with their father. We understand he and his wife lived quite separate lives; she more or less left him when he lost his Cambridge appointment and became obsessed with founding the college, so she took the children back to Oxford, which is where they had met. Apparently she died in 1925, and the children chose to remain with her family – they didn't want to go back to their father.' Stratton kicked at a stone as he spoke. 'We've also discovered that our friend Liddicote was something of a philanderer when he was younger, had an eye for the ladies, especially young students, it seems.'

'Oh dear, family troubles and a wayward eye – more muddying of the waters. I wondered why there was no family at the assembly.'

Stratton went on. 'They were told about it, and according to Roth they've been informed about the memorial service, but we don't know if they'll come. The son is now in London, an architecture student, and the daughter is in Bath, with some relatives.'

'Right then, this will never get the eggs cooked on this little case, will it?' MacFarlane's voice boomed behind them. 'We can't be chatting all day, can we, children? Ricky? Maisie?'

Maisie saw Richard Stratton look away as MacFarlane approached. She knew that Stratton only ever used the name 'Richard' when introducing himself by his Christian name. Any abbreviation without an invitation to do so represented a certain unwelcome familiarity, and Maisie could not imagine Richard Stratton saying to anyone, 'Call me Ricky.' She watched Stratton's expression as he turned back to answer a question put to him by MacFarlane. *Ah, he doesn't like MacFarlane. He doesn't like him at all.*

Maisie was in front of her second-year class, a larger group than usual as apparently Francesca Thomas had to leave the college due to sickness – she was suffering from a very bad cold – and it was felt her students would be best served by joining the junior lecturer's philosophy class. Maisie had written two words on the blackboard with a crisp new stick of chalk: *Good* and *Evil*. Soon the class was in full swing, and, following readings on the nature of the opposing forces, a vibrant discussion ensued in which the nature of those two elements within the human condition was debated. As the class drew to a close, Maisie set homework for the students, and asked whether there were any final questions. A student put up his hand.

'Yes, Daniel.'

'Miss Dobbs, will you be helping the debate team

prepare for the competition?' Daniel, from Sweden, spoke with only a slight accent, testament to several years spent in a British boarding school while his father travelled the world on business, accompanied by his mother.

'I don't believe so, although I know that several of our staff are very involved in the debate, under Dr Roth's leadership. Why do you ask?'

Daniel shrugged as he gathered his books and made his way to the front of the class, while his fellow students began moving towards the door. 'Our discussion today is so connected to the subject of the debate – good and evil; the Oswald Mosleys and Adolf Hitlers of this world – are they for the good or the bad? Are they misguided leaders or prophets? And what about the forces in Spain?'

Maisie nodded and smiled. 'Good questions, Daniel – perhaps to ponder along with your homework. We might well discuss each of these men and their philosophies next time, so come prepared. Are you one of our debaters?'

'I'm a stand-in, in case someone is ill. I might have made it, but they had to make a place for someone who isn't technically a student here.'

'Who's that?'

'The son of one of the board members. He wanted to debate but doesn't belong to a college – I think he's already been to university in London and now works for his father. He's been given an opportunity to stand for the college. Despite the fee my father is paying for my extended education here, it seems the governor's son trumps any skill I might offer.'

'Oh, I see. Well, you never know, perhaps he'll go down with chicken pox – do you know his name?'

Daniel shook his head. 'His father is that man Dunstan – I can't remember the surname. He's been here to the college, oh and—' He looked around as if he were about to reveal a secret. 'I think he's sweet on Miss Lang. I've seen him with her, but I think they don't want anyone to know.'

'Why do you think that?'

'Oh, I'm not sure. When I saw them they seemed as if they were on the lookout for people who might recognise them – which is silly, really. For a start, you can't really avoid looking at Miss Lang – she's so pretty.' He laughed, waved, and hurried to catch up with his classmates.

Maisie scooped up the essays left for her, and pushed them into her briefcase along with her notes and two books she had brought to class. She knew she had to work fast. There were people she wanted to see, and only so much time in which to see them.

As she walked towards the office on the way to the staff room, Maisie was stopped by Miss Hawthorne, the bookkeeper. Miss Hawthorne, who usually came in on a part-time basis, was now at the college every day, helping with administration until a new secretary could be found. A temporary typist had been taken on, and though paperwork was kept in check, it was clear that Miss Hawthorne was having some trouble with her work – she seemed more than a little harried, and rather breathless, as she called out to Maisie.

'Miss Dobbs! A moment, please.'

Maisie turned. 'Hello, Miss Hawthorne – keeping your head above water?'

The woman sighed and shook her head, which seemed to have become even greyer overnight. 'I'm choking on the water, if you must know.' She held out a small sheet of paper towards Maisie. 'Please be advised that I am not a runner of messages; however, a Mrs Partridge telephoned, most insistent, and asked that I inform you immediately' – she pronounced the word *immeejetly* – 'that she needs to speak to you as a matter of some urgency.'

Maisie took the paper. 'Oh dear. I wonder what's wrong.'

'You'll have to walk down to the telephone box on the corner, you know. No staff telephone calls from the office.' She looked at her watch. 'You'll have time before the next period, if you go now.'

Maisie did not reply, but turned and ran to the main door, across the driveway and down the street to the telephone box. Shaking, she pulled out a few coins and pressed them into the slot. *Had something happened to one of the boys? What was so urgent that Priscilla had tracked her down at the college?* The telephone rang just once before Priscilla answered.

'Priscilla, what on earth's the matter? Is everything all right?' She could feel her hands shaking.

'Thank heavens! I thought I would have to wait by this telephone for hours before you called back. And what are you doing at a college? Good Lord, have you lost your senses – a couple of terms at Girton was enough for me, but you are a glutton for punishment.'

'Pris! For goodness sake, what's the matter?'

'Sandra is in police custody.'

'She's *what?*'

'That hurt my ear. She's in police custody; Douglas is on his way to Vine Street police station, where we understand she's being held on suspicion of breaking and entering. We think she'll be moved to Holloway Prison, at some point.'

'Breaking and entering?' Maisie put her hand to her head. 'Breaking and entering? You are sure we are talking about the same young woman – Sandra? Breaking and entering? Holloway Prison?'

'I don't think I have ever heard you panic, Maisie – you're repeating yourself. Anyway, it wasn't one, but two properties, so young Sandra is in a fair bit of bother.'

'Priscilla, I can't get away until Friday – can you and Douglas do what you can to get her out? I will deal with this when I get back.'

'You should know that she broke into the offices of a William Walling. He's quite the businessman, top-notch city contacts, that sort of thing.'

'What on earth would she . . .' Maisie's mind was racing now. 'Where else did she break into?'

'The garage off the Marylebone Road where her husband worked. A policeman on the beat saw a light on in the back office – a window had been smashed and the door unlocked. Clearly the silly girl is no professional, despite working for you. Anyway, when she said she used to live there and had come back for some belongings, he let her off with a warning – she told him her husband had died at work, and the owner wanted her out in such a hurry, she'd left a few things behind. The policeman felt sorry for her, but at the same time, felt duty bound to report it, though she wasn't arrested. It couldn't have scared her much, because she moved on from there.'

'Priscilla, do your best to get her home, to your house – and keep her there even if you have to tie her down. I'll be back on Friday – in fact, I might see if I can get another teacher to take my class, so that I can leave on Thursday evening. By the way, how did you find me?'

'I telephoned your Mr Beale. I just told him he had to trust me in that I needed to be in touch with you soonest. So I wheedled it out of him that you were at this college. By the way, take what class?'

'Nothing, it's nothing.'

'What are you doing, Maisie?'

'I'm teaching philosophy, Pris. And don't you dare say a word about it.'

There was silence for a moment, then, 'We'll get her out – and we'll provide bail if we have to. And, as you know, when I turn up and say a few choice words, they'll want all three of us out of their hair in seconds.'

'Thank you, Pris – I really do appreciate it.'

'I'll keep you posted – I take it the school isn't the best place to send a card or telegram?'

Maisie gave Priscilla the address of her lodging; there was no telephone on the premises. 'And not a word to anyone about my being here, it's extremely secret.'

'Mum's the word. And I suppose that's one thing that Sandra learnt from you. She's clearly harbouring a secret or two of her own; very nice girl, good at her work, well turned-out – but she's a common burglar. Very nice, I'm sure.'

'Look after her.'

'Don't worry – if Douglas is there, she's in the very best hands. He's pure gold.' There was a click as Priscilla ended the call.

Maisie left the telephone kiosk and walked back to the college, her mind awash with speculation as to what Sandra had discovered that had led to the second attempt at burglary, never mind the first. And as she walked, Maisie thought, too, about Priscilla's description of her husband. It was not a lingering thought, but rather a question that seemed to pass by as she filtered her recent conversations with Sandra in her mind. *He's pure gold.* It always touched her when she saw Priscilla demonstrate her affection for her beloved husband, or when she spoke of him in a way that reflected the depth of her feelings. Maisie wondered, briefly, if it would come to pass that she might say such things about a man she had loved for years.

When Maisie arrived back at her lodging house that day – a day when so much had happened, it seemed – she was almost surprised to find it unchanged and quiet, the path bordered by flowers, and on the trees the first leaves beginning to turn. She opened the front door and stepped across the threshold, and was relieved to see two plain postcards in reply to letters she had sent just a couple of days previously. The cards were a useful means of communication for short messages, and were cheaper to post than a letter. The first was from Jennifer Penhaligon, suggesting that Maisie should come to see her on Friday morning, if that would be convenient. *No, it isn't, really,* thought Maisie, considering that she was already planning to miss a lesson in order to go back to London early. But the appointment with the person who had provided an academic reference for Francesca Thomas was an important one; she could not afford to miss the opportunity to learn more about the woman, who, to be frank, intrigued her.

The second card was from the office of Dunstan Headley, suggesting Wednesday afternoon at half past four. Maisie's sigh was one of relief – she could only massage her timetable so many times to account for absence, especially at such an early stage in her teaching appointment at the college. She would miss tea after her last lesson of the day and go straight to Headley's office. In the meantime, using college stationery she had procured from the office in a moment when it had been left unstaffed, Maisie wrote to the Registrar for Births, Marriages, and Deaths in Ipswich. She explained her dilemma – she wanted to contact a former member of staff who had left without receiving wages owed to her – and asked if he might be able to locate records pertaining to the family of Rose Linden, née Gibson – or it might have been a name beginning with 'Thur'. She understood there was a sister, and possibly a nephew. Any help would be most appreciated. She also added her gratitude for the assistance already extended to her.

When she returned to the college, Maisie stopped alongside a noticeboard, situated just inside the main doors, that provided a forum for the many messages staff and students left for one another – a dance in the town, a literary salon, a meeting of the French Conversation and Appreciation Society, a warning about late homework. She had become used to casting her eyes across the many cards and scraps of paper, in case there was something there of interest. A new card with bright-red lettering drew her attention, informing students that there would be an early evening practise session for the debaters, after the final class of the day. She made a note of the time and location.

The room was noisy as the debate team took their seats, with students who were not selected but would be substitutes in case of illness or absence, in the first row of the audience. Other students filled the seats, along with a few members of staff. Roth brought the students to order.

'The debate will be held in a hall that, though old, was made for debating. Expect your voices to carry, and expect to be able to hear almost every shuffle and sneeze in the hall. Your competitors will be familiar with their surroundings, but do not allow distractions to put you off your stride. Do you have any questions, ladies and gentlemen?' Roth looked back and forth across the twelve or so students before him. On the stage of the former ballroom, two tables had been set up at angles facing each other, clearly visible from the audience. Four students would sit at each table with an adjudicator at a lectern in the centre.

'Dr Burnham will moderate the first debate, so will teams one and two please take your seats?' He paused as chairs were scraped back and students made their way towards the stage. 'Now we will see how well prepared you are.'

Among the students in the first team, Maisie noticed Dunstan Headley's son taking his place. As he sat down, he looked up and grinned towards someone at the back of the room. Maisie turned and was not surprised to see him smiling at Delphine Lang, who waved in return; but instead of remaining in the hall, Lang turned and was leaving the room. As much as she wanted to view the proceedings, Maisie followed Lang out of the hall.

'Miss Lang! Miss Lang – do you have a moment?'

Delphine Lang turned to Maisie, then looked at her watch. 'I have a language practise group at half past six.'

'I only need a few moments, if you can spare the time.' Maisie held out her hand towards double doors that led to the grounds. 'Shall we go outside? The weather is really too good to miss.'

Delphine Lang stepped out into the balmy early evening, with the heady fragrance of jasmine on the air. 'I don't know how they get the jasmine to grow here, but it really is quite lovely,' said Lang.

'Yes, it has a lovely sweetness, doesn't it?' said Maisie.

'What would you like to see me about, Miss Dobbs?'

Delphine Lang continued walking, her voice firm but polite.

'I don't know if you are aware, but I was called to Dr Liddicote's office following the discovery of his body by Miss Linden. I was a nurse once and she thought I might be able to help. I have some contacts at Scotland Yard – due to a previous job – so I called them to report the death. I believed they would have been summoned to the college at some point anyway, in the circumstances.'

'Why are you telling me this?'

Lang had stopped walking and was facing Maisie, and it occurred to her, looking at the young woman, that, given her fragile beauty, she was probably seldom countered and rarely questioned as to why she might do this or that. Maisie suspected she had been a precocious, clever child, and might have been indulged by her parents. She seemed like a person to whom the word *no* was unfamiliar.

'I'm curious to know if you heard or saw anything of note when you went to see Dr Liddicote that day. I know you were most insistent upon seeing him, so you came back several times to see if he was available – yet he was not free to see you, which must have been most frustrating. But your repeated attempts put you in the position of being in the corridor outside his office at different times during the day – I wondered if you saw anything unusual?'

Lang seemed to weigh Maisie's words, and began walking again. She took a cursory glance at her watch. 'I saw nothing exceptional. You always expected to see people waiting for Liddicote – he was a dreadful timekeeper and you never knew how long you might have to wait, and chances were that, when you did get in there, it was just before you had to rush off to a class.'

'May I ask why you wanted to see him?'

Lang's blue eyes flashed at Maisie again. 'I suppose it's no secret. I wanted to know if my contract would be renewed. If not, I would have to return to live with my parents, and I really don't want to go.'

'You like it here at the college.'

'It's better than doing nothing at my parents' house.'

'Your father was based overseas with his job, I understand.'

'All over the world. I was born in China, where I was quite the spectacle.' She pointed to her blonde hair. 'And we lived in several different countries, but spent most of the time in China – my father is an expert on the country, the people.'

'That must have been excit—'

At that moment, a cricket ball came flying through the air. In a snap Delphine Lang had reached out and deflected the ball from its trajectory. Without her intervention, it would have hit Maisie squarely on the head.

'Oh, my goodness!' Maisie gasped. 'I didn't even see that until you reached out.' She pressed her hand to her chest. 'Where on earth did you learn to do that?'

Lang smiled. 'Oh, it's nothing really. I was just facing in the right direction to see it coming – you had your back to the ball.'

'But to hit a cricket ball with your hand, and with such dexterity, such speed – that takes a bit of practise.'

Delphine Lang was about to respond when a young man came running towards them, picked up the cricket ball and approached the women.

'I am so sorry, Miss Dobbs, Miss Lang – I didn't mean to hit the ball over here.' He turned to Maisie. 'Are you all right, Miss Dobbs?'

'Yes, thanks to Miss Lang I survived your batting skills!'

The young man apologised again, and ran back to his friends, waving the cricket ball above his head. Maisie turned to Lang, who was checking her watch once more.

'I should be getting back now, Miss Dobbs. Do you have any more questions for me?'

Maisie decided that she had nothing to lose in putting another question to Lang. 'Well, there is one. I don't know if you know this, but it's far from a secret that you are seeing Dunstan Headley's son. I wondered if there was any way he could help you, with regard to your contract.'

Delphine Lang stopped, her blue eyes now ice-like. 'Far from it, Miss Dobbs. I believe Robson's father talked Greville Liddicote into his position. When I first came to St Francis, Dr Liddicote could not have been more impressed with my education and my work here. That changed when I began seeing Robson. Now, if you don't mind, I will be late for my tutorial.'

Lang turned and walked towards the double doors, her step quick and determined. Maisie noticed a fluidity to her movement, a grace that also spoke of strength and fortitude. And she closed her eyes and saw, again, Delphine Lang raise the flat of her hand and deflect the cricket ball.

Nothing in Lang's stance had changed, except her arm and hand, and she'd suffered no discomfort in her palm or fingers afterwards. Maisie knew that such a quick, precise movement was not the result of luck. A swift response is learned, practised, and in order to strike a solid cricket ball in midair with her delicate hand, Delphine Lang must have been the student of a different sort of teacher. She was a far stronger young woman than a first impression suggested.

TEN

Maisie picked some fresh and fragrant late-blooming roses from her landlady's garden, wrapped them in newspaper, and set off towards the address she had for the teacher's flat in town. She had learnt that Dr Thomas was expected back at the college the following day, and wanted to ask if she would be so kind as to take her students on Friday morning, to make up for Maisie accommodating her class. She did not use the MG – she didn't want staff or students to see her driving around in a sporty motor car if she could possibly help it. Instead she borrowed her landlady's bicycle with its large wicker basket on the front, which was perfect for carrying flowers or groceries.

The flat was in a row of Georgian houses built next to the pavement, with no front gardens, though flower-filled boxes brought the windows to life, and lent the granite a less forbidding aspect. Slowing down to look at door numbers, she finally arrived at the correct address, stepped off the bicycle, and pushed down the stand. The front door was ajar, so Maisie walked in and was looking at the list of residents when the landlady came out of her room on the ground floor.

'Can I help you, madam?'

Maisie turned to look at the woman, who had her hair in curling pins, a pinafore over a grey day dress, and soft slippers on her feet. She smiled. 'I'm looking for Francesca Thomas.'

'Dr Thomas isn't here today, probably not until tonight.'

'Oh – I thought she was ill.'

'She didn't look too bad when I last saw her, but you never know, eh? What with all these students mixing with each other and getting up to Lord knows what, you could catch anything.'

'Do you know where she might be? I wanted to speak to her – and I have some roses for her.'

'I'll take them, if you like. Put them in a bit of water – lovely roses, aren't they? I love the scent of a cabbage rose.'

Maisie reframed her question. 'Has she gone to her choir practise, do you think?'

The woman shook her head. 'Choir? No, wrong time of year. She was only with the choir at Christmas. I reckon she might've gone down to London. She goes every now and again.'

'Did she tell you that?'

'No, but I just sort of know. You can tell by the time

she gets back – about twenty minutes after the last London train arrives, so that's what I reckon. I believe she has friends there.'

'Does she?'

'Yes, a big black motor car came up here to pick her up one day. She was waiting on the doorstep for it, and off she went. I wondered what it was, on account of my window looking out onto the street – cast quite the shadow as it drew up, it did. You don't see motors like that around here, so I thought it must've come from London. And the driver spoke with an accent, and I thought perhaps it might be someone from Switzerland, her being from there, you know.'

'I see, well – please give her the flowers, if you don't mind.'

When she returned to her lodgings, Maisie went to her room and removed all books and papers from the desk. She pulled a length of plain wallpaper from her suitcase and drew it across the desk, using brass drawing pins to secure the paper to the wood, pressing the pins to the underside of the desk so as not to incur the wrath of her landlady. With coloured pencils taken from her briefcase, she stood at the table so that she could look directly down upon her work. She wrote 'The College of St Francis' in the centre of the paper and circled her words, followed by the names of all members of staff and some of the students encircled in different colours. Greville Liddicote, Francesca Thomas, Matthias Roth, Delphine Lang . . . everyone she had met or heard of during the past two weeks was listed, with lines linking them, if there was a link. She pinned the photographs found in Greville Liddicote's office to the growing case map – the two children in the professional photograph, and the family in the other, more natural pose. She believed the two children to be Liddicote's children by the wife who divorced him, but who were the children in the second photograph? She circled Rose Linden's name and linked it to Rosemary Linden with a question mark on the red line between the names, and she wrote three more words close to Rose Linden: *Ursula? Conscientious Objector?* Then she sat back and looked at the case map, as a chess master might look at the board. The pawns were in place, but who – or what – was moving them? People, she knew, could be controlled by others, but the controllers were secondary. There was often some weakness, some emotion – an aspect of personal history, a deep love or an abiding hatred – that set a person on a given path, and often into the hands of someone who might then push them to and fro. And, she knew, human beings were quite capable of moving in this or that direction, without interference from another person.

Her thoughts turned to her personal life. What was driving Sandra? Why did she not confide in Maisie? It was clear she was suspicious regarding her husband's death. Then there was James.

'Oh, James,' said Maisie, aloud, to the room. She dropped the red pencil onto the case map and closed her eyes. James had been gone now for over six weeks, and while she missed him, she also felt some confusion. She knew he loved her, though when she tried to distinguish her feelings for him, she felt a knot in her chest. She had loved Simon, the young doctor who had suffered devastating head wounds in the war and then had languished in a home until his death a year earlier. Maisie realised with a start that she had forgotten the day of his death, though she could never forget the day of his wounding, and his last words to her before a shell hit close to the casualty clearing station, where they were working together. But the bittersweet truth of their time together was that she had always known there was no future for them, that she could not 'see' them as a couple beyond the war. And though she was in more control of her innate intuitive gifts, she knew that the only reason she could not readily see herself and James together in the future was that she had deliberately blocked such images – because she was afraid of what a union with him might mean. She had yet to trust happiness, that much she knew. It had been so fleeting with Simon, and she wondered what it might feel like for happiness to be a constant, so that she could rest in its cradle, rather than looking across the parapet for a marching army ready to shoot her contentment down in flames. And letters with Canadian stamps and a smudged London postmark made her uneasy, for it was as if one of her sentinels was asleep at his post and had failed to warn her that James Compton might break her heart.

Maisie did not see Francesca Thomas the following day – she thought she might ask Thomas to cover her class on Friday morning. Thomas was on the premises, that much she knew. She had enquired with Miss Hawthorne if any word had come from Dr Thomas, and asked if she was well again. Miss Hawthorne had looked at Maisie over her spectacles, and replied, 'Miss Dobbs, kind as you are, I really do not have time to answer questions regarding the well-being of a member of staff who cannot see through the common cold to attend to her duties. As far as I can tell, Dr Thomas is now well and in command of her timetable, thank heavens!' She looked down at her work again and, as if remembering that it was Maisie who had stepped in to accommodate the absent teacher's class, added, 'Though I thank you for not succumbing to the plague, and for dealing with the additional students at such short notice yesterday. Very good of you.'

'My pleasure, Miss Hawthorne.'

Teaching invigorated Maisie, and she remembered how much she enjoyed being in a place of learning: the discussion, the back-and-forth of ideas, the delving into books for a quote here, and to substantiate a point there. Soon, though, her day's work had come to an end and she had to rush to her appointment with Dunstan Headley. Once again she would walk to her destination; the office of Headley and Son was situated close to the centre of the city, although she had since learnt that the company also had offices in London and Hong Kong.

The grey building with a low-pitched roof was set in its own grounds, but they were neither so lush nor grand as those surrounding the college. Maisie brushed some lint from the shoulders of a navy-blue jacket, which she wore with a cream linen skirt and blouse. On this occasion, she wore a light straw hat with a wide dark-blue silk band, and with a broader brim than she might usually wear. She clutched her shoulder bag and briefcase, opened the main door, and entered the building. A woman in an office to the right opened a hatch-like window and called to her.

'Are you Miss Dobbs? Mr Headley's four-o'clock meeting?'

'Yes, that's right.'

'Take a seat, if you wouldn't mind, and I'll telephone his secretary.'

'Thank you.'

Maisie listened to the one-sided conversation.

'Valerie? Yes, I've got Mr Headley's four-o'clock here. Right you are – and when you come down we've got your pools coupon here; the Vernons' man will be round on Friday to collect. Yes, I've told her to wait. About five minutes – I'll tell her.'

The woman poked her head out of the window. 'Mr Headley's secretary will be down in about five minutes. Would you like a cup of tea?'

Maisie shook her head. 'No, thank you.'

Five minutes later a woman who was about the same age as Maisie came downstairs to escort her to Dunstan Headley's office.

'We've been very busy today, what with one thing and another. Mr Headley's expecting you now.'

She showed Maisie into a room with bookcases on one wall; however, instead of books, each shelf held a series of ledgers with a year inscribed along the spine, or perhaps another indication of the contents: 'Hong Kong, Supply' or 'Singapore: Accounts' or 'France: Orders'. She had not been completely clear on the type of commerce conducted by Dunstan Headley, but understood it involved purchasing materials in one country, shipping them to another for manufacturing, then to a series of other countries for sale. The actual items manufactured and sold depended upon what was deemed to be in demand by purchasers in that country.

'Miss Dobbs.' Dunstan Headley leant across a large desk of dark wood with a pattern carved into each corner. He held out his hand. 'What a pleasure to welcome you to my office. I'm not used to lecturers from the college going out of their way to see me, so I'm curious as to the purpose of your visit.' Headley did not move from behind his mammoth desk, reminding Maisie of the captain who would rarely leave the wheelhouse of his ship. He was a stocky man, bald but for wisps of brushed and oiled grey hair at the sides of his head. His eyes were pale blue, and he wore a dark-grey suit, white shirt, and a tie the colour of pewter. Beyond a gold pocket watch, there was no indication of his wealth. Indeed, the offices were comfortable but not ostentatious in any way. Maisie recalled seeing Robson Headley, and thought the son must favour the mother, given his height, yet his eyes were the same pale blue, and he had inherited a certain squareness of jaw from his father.

'I wanted to see you about Greville Liddicote. I know this is premature, but I thought that in time people might wish to read more about his work, and I am considering writing a short biography. I thought I would start by talking to those who knew him best, who had some insight into his motives for founding the college.'

'Well, he was certainly an interesting character, to be sure. I must confess that I am still shocked by his death. I've been told that there were some questions regarding the cause.' Headley did not look at her when he spoke, but leafed thought papers in a tray marked 'Urgent'.

'I understand the police are just tying up some loose ends,' said Maisie.

'I see.' Headley tapped a pen on the desk and began to fidget in a way that suggested he was keen to get on with his work. 'And how can I help you?'

'I am curious to know what inspired you to support Dr Liddicote in setting up the college. You have been a most generous supporter, and I understand the new building is to be called Headley Hall, in your honour.' Maisie took out her notebook, as if she were a newspaper reporter on assignment.

Headley tapped the pen for a few more seconds, then reached out towards a silver-framed photograph – it was one of several on the desk, and Maisie could see only the back of each frame. He held out the photograph for Maisie to take.

'That was my eldest son, Martin. He was killed in the war.'

'I am so sorry, I had no idea.' Maisie looked at the photograph of a young man in uniform; he bore a striking resemblance to Robson Headley, but appeared not to have his height.

'He was eighteen when he enlisted. When he came home on his last leave – he was nineteen by then – he showed me Greville's book and told me how much it had touched him. He didn't want to go back, Miss Dobbs; he was sick of the war, sick of what he had seen there, and he was in turmoil.' He took a deep breath, sighed, and then continued. 'I discovered later – though there was nothing I could do about it – that he had been shot for desertion. Killed by his own. With that book in his hand, he had refused to fight.'

'I am so sorry, I never—'

'No, not many know. My son was never the most brave at school, would rarely speak up for himself. He was one of those boys who just wanted to get on with his life in his own way, with as little trouble as possible. My first wife passed away when he was eight years of age – what you might call the very worst kind of unfaithfulness, leaving a husband and small son.' He moved his head as if to shake off a memory, a picture in his mind that troubled him. 'His mother's death changed Martin in some ways – he became a very introspective young chap. I never imagined he would have it in him to join the business here, but when he enlisted, I thought that perhaps being in the army would do him some good. He didn't say much, but what he said – about the war – shook me to the core. I lost my son, and I never wanted to see such a thing happen again. My son Robson was born to my second wife; he's a quite different person. He has some memories of his brother – he looked up to him, as young boys will to a man in uniform. Robson's twenty-four now and – unlike his brother – seems suited to joining the company.'

'So you supported Liddicote because Martin thought so much of his book?'

'In a way, that's how it started. I became disgusted with the war.' He picked up his pen and resumed tapping it on the desk as he leant forward. 'If I have any discord with my suppliers, with my commercial partners overseas – I talk to them. Even if I have to be on a ship for weeks, I will appear in person and I talk to them. I sort it all out – business is too valuable to lose, especially in this day and age. I was disgusted with my country, with my government – that they could do no better than go to war.' He shook his head. 'Never thought I would say that, to tell you the truth. I'm too busy to be a political sort. But they let me down, let my boy down, and let the country down – and they've been doing it ever since.'

'So you helped Liddicote in Martin's memory?'

'Yes, I did. After Martin died, I felt compelled to find this Liddicote man, and when I did I realised that he was a lot more interesting than I thought he would be. You see, I don't really have much time for these college types in town, but Liddicote seemed to talk sense: bring young people together from nations across the globe, teach them and let them go back and spread the word, prove that we don't have to be at war with each other. It was just like his book – send the children among the soldiers to stop the war. It was the sort of thing that Martin would have taken up. He was a sensitive boy – like his mother – and though I always wondered when he would sharpen up a bit, I came to realise how brave he was in sticking to his guns, in refusing to fight. Frankly, Miss Dobbs – I couldn't have done it myself, and I know Robson wouldn't; he's too much like me.'

'You have been most candid, Mr Headley. I confess – if I may in turn be candid – I wondered about your support of the college. You do not seem to be the sort of person who would usually become so involved in such an undertaking – if you don't mind me saying so.'

Headley shook his head. 'I don't mind you saying so – I applaud honesty. And you're right, I'm not the sort of person who would normally get involved in a college, but I looked at Greville Liddicote and I saw someone who could build a place where Martin's . . . Martin's . . .' He seemed to grapple for words. 'Where Martin's character, yes, character, would be honoured. And I have more money than I need, and Robson has been well provided for, so it's as good a place as any to funnel some funds into.'

'And does Robson share your enthusiasm for the college?'

'He is in favour of his brother's memory being honoured in such a way.'

Maisie felt a coolness in his response, as if a breeze had blown across the conversation.

'I understand that your son will be joining the debating team at the college.'

'My son is an educated man – he attended King's College in London – and I believe he misses that sort of intellectual argument.'

'Do you approve?'

'I neither approve nor disapprove.'

'I see.'

Headley, who had barely met Maisie's eyes throughout the conversation, now looked up at her for a brief moment. 'Your questions have deviated away from Greville's memory, haven't they, Miss Dobbs?'

'You talked about your son and the war, and I confess, I became taken with your story. I served in the war myself – I was a nurse.'

Headley nodded. 'And now you are a lecturer at the college?'

'I gave up a place at Girton to enlist for nursing service, though I returned later.'

'Brave girl.'

'There were many.'

Headley looked at Maisie again, as if gauging whether to share a confidence. He sighed, then spoke as he looked away, fingering his papers again. 'I don't suppose you know much about Miss Delphine Lang, do you?'

'She's a teaching assistant. I know her parents travelled considerably when she was younger – her father was a diplomat, Austrian, I believe. She spent some time in China.'

'Yes, as did Robson – well, Hong Kong. That's how it started, with them seeing each other.'

'I take it you do not approve.'

'She'll be gone soon, that's all I care about.'

'Liddicote liked her, at first.'

'She came with a good education behind her, but he didn't know about her activities, did he?'

'Activities?'

'She belongs to a group – they meet in London – they're supporters of the German National Socialist Party. They're all younger people, for the most part. Some at university in this country, some working in commerce, a journalist here and there. She travels down to these meetings regularly, and now Robson is going with her.'

'You told Liddicote about the group?'

'Yes, and he thought it was nothing to worry about – said that it was a good thing that they felt enough freedom in our country to be able to conduct the meetings.'

'But you didn't.'

'Martin would have said the same thing, and I would like to have that sort of confidence in the situation, but I am afraid I do not. I paid attention to the outcome of Versailles, Miss Dobbs, and I felt grave errors had been made, errors that would lead to a deep resentment among the German people. I am a man of commerce, it is my job to assess the mood in the countries in which I do business – buying this, selling that – because I cannot afford local politics to get in the way of what I set out to do. I do business in Germany, and I have been paying attention. I do not care for some of the rhetoric I have been hearing.'

'You think that Britain is vulnerable?'

'Not the ordinary people – the common man, as you

philosophers might say. No, the common man is too busy trying to make ends meet, or to feed his children. In this country, for the most part, the people who are taken by politics of the German sort are those of some wealth, especially the younger set. I hate to say it, but people like Robson, who has been rather spoilt in his life, by his mother especially.'

'You asked Greville Liddicote not to renew Delphine Lang's contract, so that she would have to return to her parents' home in Austria.'

'It would make it more difficult for her to remain here, certainly. Robson is young, he would get over the liaison.'

'Are you sure about that?

'Martin wouldn't have, but Robson – no, Robson will be taken with the next new attraction that comes along.' Headley looked at his watch as he spoke, and raised an eyebrow. 'Oh, dear, I really must call an end to our meeting, Miss Dobbs. Do you have any more questions?'

'Could you tell me more about the group that Delphine Lang belongs to?'

'It's called an *Ortsgruppe.*' He spelt out the word, letter by letter for Maisie to note in her book. 'They are local groups of Germans here in Britain, and they are all members of the *Nationalsozialistische Deutsche Arbeiterpartei* – the National Socialist German Workers Party. They're doing nothing wrong, I suppose – and I daresay there are British people overseas who get together in groups to discuss this or that, drink copious amounts of tea together, and so on. I'm sure the authorities know about it.'

'Yes, I'm sure they do.' Maisie gathered her belongings. 'Thank you for your time, Mr Headley – may I call again, if I have some questions for you?'

'For your biography, you mean.' Headley looked at Maisie with just a trace of a smile.

'Yes, for the biography. I'd like to know more about Greville Liddicote's books, if you have any knowledge you can impart.'

'I've read them all. His first children's books were written before the war, but he really hit his stride with *The Peaceful Little Warriors*. There was a certain passion to it that was not there in his earlier stories. He published a couple more that were well up to that standard – they seemed to have more to them than simply a tale for children; an ethical dilemma, perhaps. Then there was a bit of a gap, and the standard went down again.'

'I see. Well, thank you, again, for seeing me. I appreciate it.'

Headley saw Maisie to the door. 'They break ground on the new building soon. You'll see the sign go up – it will actually be called "Martin Headley Hall". It will be a mix of dormitory residences and lecture rooms, and we expect to launch it with a public lecture on the nature of sustaining peace in this century – in Martin's memory.'

As Maisie walked along the road in the direction of her lodgings, it seemed there were more young people on bicycles than pedestrians. She continued on through a series of narrower streets until she reached the Backs, an area that extended from Magdalene Street down to Silver Street, where the backs of the University's most famous colleges met the River Cam. She stopped and took off her jacket, laying it down on the grass so she might sit and watch the water slip along. She was not alone – students were out punting, many with a lack of dexterity, and others were enjoying evening picnics in the fine weather. She laughed as two young men fell into the water while trying to impress a group of girls picnicking nearby, while another drifted along and brought his punt up on the bank close to the girls, taunting the waterlogged men as he went.

Maisie wondered about Dunstan Headley. She had been honest with him; she had found it hard to equate the man she had observed on a couple of occasions with the image she held of a benevolent businessman. He had used his resources to discover information that was new to her – about the groups of German immigrants meeting in British cities. She was sure that Huntley must know about this, but wondered if they knew about the connection to the college via Delphine Lang. Were there links with British Fascist supporters? Headley showed a certain astuteness in identifying Robson's vulnerability to the influence of such groups, and she wondered whether all was well between father and son. Headley had skimmed over the subject, though he *had* brought it up, which was more than many would have done in his position – such would be the embarrassment. But he had not discussed it at length, either, and Maisie took into account the fact that she had met with him on the pretext of writing a biography of Greville Liddicote, and she had certainly pushed her questions beyond the boundary of the dead man's life and work.

She wanted to know more about the *Ortsgruppe*, and she wanted to know whether Huntley was already aware of the meetings, and if so, why she wasn't told. It occurred to her that, of the staff, already two – Delphine Lang and Francesca Thomas – seemed to be making their way into London with some regularity. Maisie closed her eyes, and though at the perimeter of her consciousness she was aware of the shouts of students splashing around at the edge of the river, the sounds receded as she meditated, focusing her thoughts on the many threads of information she now held. And reflecting upon what had come to pass since her first visit to the College of St Francis, she remembered waiting in the staff library on the day of her interview: she had looked out the window across the grounds, and seen the young woman whom she now knew to be Delphine Lang in the embrace of Dr Matthias Roth. It did not strike her as a romantic assignation, but rather as a daughter might be comforted by her father.

ELEVEN

Maisie planned to drive to Oxford for her meeting at Somerville College, and from there she would go straight to London – hopefully to find Sandra released from police custody. Though the day was overcast, Maisie drove with the roof drawn back and hoped it would not rain. Having left Cambridge early, she intended to stop at a telephone kiosk on the way so she could place a call to Brian Huntley; she also thought it would be a good idea to stop for a cup of tea, as she had departed her lodgings without breakfast, much to the consternation of her landlady.

Maisie spotted a telephone kiosk as she approached a crossroads. The kiosk looked as if it had just been cleaned by local GPO workers, but Maisie still held the door ajar with her foot – such a small enclosed space always made her feel uncomfortable.

'Is the doctor there? I have an emergency and want to speak to the doctor.'

'Will the nurse do? We have a nurse available,' said the woman who answered.

'It's a laceration on the palm of the hand, and I believe it may cause lockjaw. I have to speak to the doctor.'

'And your name is?'

'Dobbs. I am a patient.'

'Hold the line, please. I'll see if the doctor's in.'

She waited for a moment, then Huntley came on the line.

'Good morning. Maisie.'

'Yes. Good morning.' She was never quite sure whether she should call him 'Brian' or 'Mr Huntley'. He had assumed a certain familiarity with her, and she knew that Maurice would have addressed him by his Christian name. She took a deep breath. 'Brian, I wanted to ask you what you know about a group – well, "groups" might be more in order – known as the *Ortsgruppe*. They're essentially men and women from Germany or of German extraction – immigrants, workers here for a short time, that sort of thing – who have sworn some sort of allegiance to the NSDAP – the Nazi Party in Germany.'

'Yes, we know a bit about them, and I've asked for reports on their activities, but we're not worried about them.'

'You're not worried about them?'

'No. Chap called Hans Wilhelm Thost is the leader of the group in London – journalist, can't see a problem with him at all. They're all ardent followers of Adolf Hitler, but we only get truly worried when groups of this sort start doing things such as publishing literature critical of Britain and her Empire. There has been no evidence of seditious material from the group, and we have taken advice from the Home Office that any move by authorities to limit their activities would do more harm than good.'

'May I ask how?' Maisie felt the skin around her neck prickle.

'Our political and commercial relationship with Germany cannot be muddied at this point by anything that smacks of disregard for German citizens in our country.'

'I see.' Maisie ran the telephone cord through her fingers. 'Delphine Lang, a teaching assistant at the college is, apparently, a member of the *Ortsgruppe*. She travels to their meetings in London, and brings her young man with her. He is British.'

'Probably nothing to worry about, to tell you the truth. MacFarlane's men and Section 5 are keeping their eyes on our homegrown Fascists, but so far they don't seem to be making too much hay – the conservatives won't have much to do with them, and they seem a lot more of a threat than they really are.'

Maisie sighed. 'So, you're not really worried about these developments.'

'Not until I get a memorandum telling me I should be.' He paused. 'You seem worried, though.'

'It occurred to me, Brian, that infiltration of our venerable seats of learning would be something that might be on the agenda for these groups – impressionable young people, perhaps, waiting for a cause to support. And I've been reading about the NSDAP; their rhetoric has become increasingly inflammatory, to say nothing of anti-Semitic. They have gained considerable ground in Germany, especially when most of the population feels it was not served well by the Peace Conference.'

'Good points, Maisie, but not quite your bailiwick. Find out what, if anything, is going on at the college. An association with the *Ortsgruppe* is certainly of interest, but as I said, we've been kept up to date, and they've done nothing to alarm us yet. All a bit run-of-the-mill, actually.' He paused. 'I'm looking at your teaching timetable now – shouldn't you have a class this morning, *Miss Dobbs?*'

Maisie was surprised that Huntley seemed to be making a joke, so she answered in kind. 'I'm playing truant. I'll telephone you again soon, Brian.'

'One thing, Maisie.'

'Yes?' She heard him shuffle papers, as if looking for something specific.

'There's a meeting of the London *Ortsgruppe* this evening. An address in Cleveland Terrace. I'll have the details delivered to your office – I take it you'll be in London later today?'

'Yes.'

'And don't worry about your secretary, Maisie. She's been released from police custody, into the safekeeping of Mr Douglas Partridge.'

'How?'

'We really don't want complications or unnecessary attention drawn to you or your activities. Do try to keep her thoughts on her work, whether that work is for you or Mr Partridge. Goodbye for now.'

As Maisie had no opportunity to end the call with a 'Goodbye' in return, she set down the receiver and stepped out of the telephone kiosk. She expected Brian Huntley to be keeping tabs on her, but was surprised at his knowledge of Sandra's dilemma. She was relieved to hear that the young woman had been released from police custody, but also understood that such a release came with strings attached, and hoped that Sandra would abide by the restrictions of those strings. It seemed she had become blindly headstrong since her widowhood, and though Maisie knew she might have good reason, she was determined to sit down with her new employee and find out exactly what was on her mind. Only then could she help her.

The sun was shining again now; a gentle breeze had blown up and she hoped for a pleasant journey. It would be a good deal more enjoyable, she thought, if she did not feel a deep concern about the *Ortsgruppe*, and about Delphine Lang's involvement in the organisation. And she was becoming increasingly perturbed whenever her thoughts turned to Robson Headley, a wilful young man who appeared to have been rather indulged by a father who had already lost a beloved first son. Maisie wondered, again, about Greville Liddicote's book. Already she knew of two people who had been touched by the book – touched enough, each in their own way, to lay down arms. One had lost his life, charged with desertion and shot at dawn, the other risking the same outcome with a self-inflicted wound. One British, one German. How many more young men – and women – might have been moved to some action by Greville Liddicote's simple tale of children who tried to stop a war? And having read the story, how many might have chosen not to fight, brave enough to step forward in conscientious objection to the war – and then borne the brutal consequences of that decision?

'I've asked for tea – I am sure you'd like a cup, having come all the way from Cambridge to see me.' Jennifer Penhaligon's smile was warm, which seemed in contrast to movements that were quick, precise, and which, with a sharper tongue, might seem almost confrontational. She was of medium height, in her seventies, and the shine in her eyes seemed to indicate a still-sparkling intellect. Her silver-grey hair was cut in a fashionable short bob, and she wore a light linen skirt and blouse under her black gown. A gold wristwatch with a delicate safety chain slid down her wrist as she reached for Maisie's letter; her only other jewellery was a pair of pearl earrings, and a wedding ring that seemed to have worked a groove into her finger. Her nails were short – Maisie had discovered that long nails were neither practical or appropriate for a teacher using chalk on a blackboard – and skin that might once have been fair was marked by liver spots, indicating, Maisie thought, that Jennifer Penhaligon loved to garden when not at her desk.

'Thank you – I do believe I drink far too much tea, but another cup is always welcome.'

'Well, let's get down to business—' A young woman came in with a tea tray, and there was a hiatus in the conversation while she poured cups for the professor and Maisie. When she left the room, Penhaligon sipped from her cup of tea, set the cup down, clasped her hands in front of her, and looked at Maisie. 'As I was saying, let's get down to business. You said in your letter that you were writing an account of the College of St Francis, in memory of Greville Liddicote – and you intend to include some sort of biography on each of the senior staff.'

'Yes, I thought it would be an important addition to the history of the college.'

'And you're interested in Francesca Thomas?'

'Yes, Dr Thomas is one of our most admired staff at the college.'

'I can imagine. I remember Miss Thomas very well indeed. First-class languages, excellent student – diligent, and thoughtful. Passionate, is how I would describe her.'

'In what way, would you say, was she passionate?'

'About the things she believed in. Of course, such ideals sound like empty words – freedom, for example, to think, to have a voice – but she had done her reading, her research, and she knew exactly what she meant when she backed up her ideals with solid thought and good, good writing. Very able, when it came to expressing herself on paper, which is not always the case with those who are born overseas and for whom English is not their first language. Mind you, had

213

she not been so gifted, she would not have been accepted here at Somerville.'

'I see, and she was here for three years?'

'Yes, and went straight to London in 1914, to take up a job.'

'In London? I'm surprised.'

'Don't be – with her exposure to languages and so on, she was ideal for her role.'

'What sort of work was it?'

'Something or other in the War Office, or one of the other services where they needed bright young women with linguistic abilities – I'm not really sure, to tell you the truth. She came back to see me once after she'd left, and she said she couldn't really speak about her job – hush-hush, apparently. But if you remember, everything was hush-hush in the war. You would have thought there were German spies in every tea shop.'

'And you didn't see her again until – when?'

'Oh, I haven't seen her since that last visit. I had an idea she'd gone overseas – and you say she earned her doctorate somewhere in Europe? Doesn't surprise me at all, you know, very bright girl, determined. Did she never marry?'

'I don't know,' said Maisie. 'I know she lives alone in Cambridge, so if she was married once, she isn't now.'

'Yes, one doesn't like to ask, but it's easy to assume that a young husband or fiancé was lost – there are so many widows, aren't there?' Jennifer Penhaligon cleared her throat. 'Well, if you have no more questions, Miss Dobbs, I should be getting on.'

'Yes, of course. You've been most kind.' Maisie stood and held out her hand to Penhaligon. 'Dr Thomas was born in Switzerland, wasn't she? I wonder if she went back there during the war – after all, it was a neutral country.'

'Possibly. I wish I knew. But Francesca was what I would call a real European – mind you, if you look back, I am sure we all have a bit of this and a bit of that. My grandmother came from the Netherlands, and another ancestor from Sweden, and we British all have something of our invaders, don't we – some Norman, here, a bit of Viking there, a spoonful of Saxon, perhaps.'

Maisie laughed. 'Oh, yes, you're absolutely right there!'

'But Francesca was rather careful, in terms of her name.'

'In what way?'

'Well, when war seemed imminent, she changed her name – it was originally Seifert, and she thought it sounded too Germanic, so she took "precautionary action", as she put it. The authorities obviously knew she was a British subject through her mother, but she took the name Thomas. Apparently it was her grandmother's maiden name.'

'I see. Well, I think I might have done the same in the circumstances.'

'Yes, so might I. Fortunately, neither of us had to do anything of the sort. Now then, Miss Dobbs, do try to take a walk around our gardens before you leave – the Somerville gardens are known for their beauty, and they really are quite lovely at the moment.'

'Thank you, Professor Penhaligon. I'll go for a walk now.'

* * *

Maisie's stroll through the grounds was brief, but productive; she wanted to breathe in some fresh air before driving down to London, and it gave her time to think. So, Francesca Thomas had worked in something 'hush-hush' during the war. Did she then return to Europe and her education? Certainly, with her background she could have continued her education in Switzerland, gaining a doctorate at a university there. Maisie wondered about her change of name. One could hardly be surprised at her wanting to take her grandmother's name, and 'Thomas' did sound so very English. She would make enquiries in any case.

It was early afternoon when Maisie parked outside the home in Holland Park where Priscilla lived with her husband and sons. The property had once been the home of Margaret Lynch – the mother of Simon Lynch, the young doctor whom Maisie had loved. With both her husband and son now dead, Margaret had no need of the mansion, with its sweeping staircase and many rooms, so it had been leased to Priscilla and her husband, and had once more become a house filled with laughter. On Fridays, Douglas and Priscilla usually took the boys to Priscilla's family estate in the country, but in the present circumstances, Maisie thought they would be staying in London.

'Maisie, thank goodness – you're here.'

'Where's Sandra?'

Priscilla closed the door as Maisie stepped into the entrance hall. 'I really don't know how to tell you this, but she's gone.'

'Gone? Gone where?'

'We don't know. After we brought her home yesterday afternoon, I made sure she went straight to bed – she had been living in the most awful cell, terrible. I took her to the guest room, and came back with something light to eat – soft-boiled egg, a slice of toast, tea – but she wouldn't take anything, just curled up on the bed and closed her eyes. Poor dear, she just wept. I remained with her for a while, and then thought it best to just leave her to sleep it off.'

'When did you know she'd gone?'

'This morning. I asked Mrs Hawkins to go in with some tea and toast – didn't want to push food down her if she didn't want it. They'd tried that while she was in custody. When she wouldn't eat – and I am sure it was from nerves, rather than being bloody-minded – they sent in a woman to literally shove the food down her throat, which of course she just brought up again.' Priscilla paused, and shook her head. 'I thought I would have the devil's own job in getting her out of there, you know. When I arrived at the police station, Douglas was going back and forth with the policeman in charge, when another policeman came out and said that she could be released. His exact words were, "Voices from on high have spoken," as if a pointed finger had plunged through the ceiling and a deep voice had said, "Thou shalt let Sandra go!" So, we didn't ask questions; just bundled her into the motor car and whisked her home – with strict instruction to the effect that she must remain in either our custody or yours. So this is a fine state of affairs.'

'It's not your fault, Priscilla – who would have believed that you might need to chain her to the bed.'

'Let's have a cup of coffee and talk about what we'll do next.'

'We'll have the coffee, but finding Sandra is my job – I'm not entirely sure it's completely safe for anyone else.'

Priscilla led Maisie to the kitchen, where the cook seemed surprised when the two women walked in and Priscilla went straight to a coffee pot set on the stove. 'I'm making coffee, Mrs Hawkins, not tea. And I need it very French and very, very strong.'

The cook shook her head and turned away to continue preparing vegetables.

Priscilla winked at Maisie and said aloud, 'Mrs Hawkins is convinced that I will take the lining off my stomach with the way I make coffee – aren't you, Mrs Hawkins?'

'Not my business to say, Mrs Partridge.'

Priscilla made two large cups of strong coffee with frothy hot milk, and they went through to the drawing room.

'There, put your feet up while we talk.'

'I really must get going, Priscilla, but I needed this – I haven't stopped all morning.'

'And you could do without this little spanner in the works.'

'I'm not sure it's little.' She sipped her coffee, shook her head and sighed. 'Sandra was never like this. When she was at Ebury Place, she was such a diligent girl, very sympathetic to the needs of others. She did things in the way they should be done – you would never imagine her breaking into a building, even in the most pressing circumstances.'

'But the circumstances are probably beyond pressing.

218

She's like a good many women, Maisie; they toe the line very well until someone they love – a child, a spouse – is threatened or harmed, and then you see a completely different side to them. Had that not been so, then this country would never have come through the war. Wars are fought by men, Maisie – but the winning is down to women who are prepared to break windows for their own.' She paused. 'You've got that distant look in your eyes – you're miles away, aren't you?'

'Just wondering where she might have gone. I doubt she would go to family – no, she wouldn't want them to see her in such a state. Do you know if she had any money?'

Priscilla flushed. 'Well, Douglas paid her just before she got herself into this situation, and I confess that when she came out, I tucked a few pounds into her pocket, just in case.'

'Then she could stay at a hotel, a boarding house; she would be safe for quite a while, because I also paid her last time I was in London, and, knowing Sandra, she has savings; as I said, she's a diligent girl.'

'Would she have gone to her in-laws?'

'That's a thought. I'll get Billy onto it. And I'll go back to the flat, to see if she has left her belongings in her room.'

'What if the police want to know where she is?'

'I doubt they'll be contacting you. She's free with no strings – except the ones attaching her to you and me. But having said that, I may contact them – I know someone who I think might help out without the balloon going up.'

They sat in silence for a moment. 'They don't want

Sandra's actions to get in the way of your work, do they?'

'I really can't talk about it, Pris. You know that.'

'And the thing is, I have no idea who "they" are, but you are working on something hush-hush, aren't you?'

Maisie smiled. It was the second time in one day she'd heard the term. 'I'm always working on something I have to keep quiet about, it's the nature of my work. My clients come to me for that very reason – they have a secret and they don't want anyone to know. So if I go chatting about it, the game's up – you know rumours spread like wildfire on a hot and windy day.'

'Since I discovered how Peter died, I've always equated working in intelligence as being a bit of a risky business.'

Maisie smiled and touched Priscilla on the arm at the mention of her brother. She sipped the last of her coffee. 'I'd better get going, Pris. I have to see Billy as soon as possible. If Sandra had gone to the trouble to break into the premises of her husband's employer, and then summon the courage to do the same at the office of a man she didn't know, you can be assured she acted with good reason.'

'Take care, Maisie, with this Cambridge business.'

'It's perfectly all right, I promise you would not believe how very safe I am. It's a college, it's slow, quiet, and deliberate.'

'And a man was murdered there – I saw it in the newspaper, about the College of St Francis. That's where you are, isn't it?'

'Oh dear – I promise you, I am safe. The college is not half as exciting as the press might have you believe. If you were there, you would be snoozing in the corner within minutes.'

'I'll take your word for it.'

Maisie and Priscilla held each other for two or three seconds, then Maisie left, calling out to her friend as she walked down the front steps. 'Keep me informed – let me know if she turns up, or if you happen to have an idea of where she might have gone.'

Maisie parked the MG in Fitzroy Street, turned off the engine, and sighed. Thoughts of Sandra extinguished all other concerns from her mind. *Where is she? Is she safe?* She closed her eyes. Not for the first time, the plight of the wounded animal came to mind. She knew that instinct would always take the wounded creature to its lair. But where was Sandra's lair? As far as she knew, Sandra had left home at the age of twelve, when she was sent to work in service. Her father and mother both worked on the land, and with four daughters and no sons, there was little more they could do for the girls beyond school age, so they were sent to work in service. Like many young girls before her, Sandra had come to London alone, to knock on doors until someone offered her a job. Fortunately, she had not wandered far when she turned up at the door of 15 Ebury Place. She hardly knew her parents now, and had travelled down to Dorset only once or twice a year to visit them. Sandra had done well; considering it important to 'better herself', she had gone to the lending library once a week to collect three or four books that she would read when the day's work was done, and before the light was turned out for the night. She had grown from a quiet but diligent girl into a young woman who, through hard work, intended to make life better for herself – and Maisie knew that for Sandra, life took on a sunnier hue when she became attached to Eric, who also worked for the Compton family before leaving their employ to become a full-time mechanic. How could anyone have known it was a job that was to kill him, and leave Sandra a widow at twenty-four? *Where has she gone?*

Billy looked up from his work when Maisie walked into the office.

'Afternoon, Miss.'

'Billy, how are you?'

'Not so bad. Had a nice drive down?'

'The road was fairly clear, and it's a fine day, so I made good time.' Maisie set her briefcase on her desk and looped the handle of her shoulder bag over the back of her chair. She looked at the stack of papers on Sandra's desk awaiting her attention.

Billy nodded towards the desk. 'I don't know where she's got to, I'm sure. I don't know if I should tell you this, but she's missed a morning or two this week.'

'I know.'

Billy blushed.

Maisie drew up a chair to sit in front of his desk.

Billy shifted in his chair and nodded. 'Miss, I've got to admit, I've been a bit worried, you know, in case you didn't need me here, what with Sandra having done those commercial courses.'

'I didn't take you on to type letters, Billy.'

He shrugged. 'But I was thinking that since I've been working for you, you've had to get me out of trouble a few times, and look at Sandra, she's no trouble at all.'

'She's in dreadful trouble, Billy. She's become a case, and I want you to take it on, for now. Let me explain.'

Maisie recounted the events of the past week, from Priscilla's telephone call to Sandra's release, and her subsequent flight from the home of Douglas and Priscilla Partridge, into whose care she had been entrusted.

'She broke into the garage, then into this other bloke's offices in the City?'

Maisie nodded.

'I had a feeling she was on to something. I don't know what she might've found in our files over there, but she was looking for something that had nothing to do with her work, and that's a fact.'

'We're in possession of a very comprehensive history of many of the most notorious crimes in London and the Home Counties, and we've records that name powerful people in Westminster, in the City, and – as it happens – what could be termed, the "underworld". Even if they haven't been directly implicated in a case, you can bet that anyone of importance is in those files somewhere, even if it's only a name on a card.'

'Blimey.' Billy shook his head. 'She's got some nerve, that Sandra, I'll say that for her.'

'The stronger the emotions, the more they will lead people to carry a burden well beyond their weight – you know that. She's as grief-stricken as anyone I have ever seen, and she's been rolling a rock up a hill.'

'I feel bad, Miss.' Billy picked at the rough skin along the edge of his thumb. 'I thought her being suspicious was all to do with her feelings, that it would pass with time.'

'I know. But it's no good looking back – there's work to be done, Billy. First of all, see if you can find out where her in-laws live. Visit the house, keep an eye on it, see who comes and goes – you know the drill. I don't want you to question them, because I don't want them worried – I daresay they are still burdened by the death of their son. I believe they live near Whitstable. Here's Eric's full name – shouldn't be too difficult to find them. You could even go over to the garage, find out if Reg Martin knows where they live. And while you're there, just talk to the man, see what he has to say about what happened. I don't want you to scare him – in fact, you can tell him you're there on my behalf, that I want to visit Eric's parents to pay my respects. Don't let him know that Sandra has been released, or that we have no idea where she is.'

Billy nodded, scribbled in his notebook, and reached for his jacket. 'I'll go over there now. Anything else, Miss?'

'Yes, find out all you can about a man called William Walling.'

Billy frowned. 'That rings a bell.' He draped his jacket across the desk and went to the card file, where he pulled out a drawer. 'Too bloody tidy, that's the trouble . . . oh, here it is.' He brought the card to Maisie. 'I knew where to find it because I came in one day and Sandra was going through the cards. She left the card sticking up so she knew where to go back to, then went to put the kettle on, so I had a quick look at what she was doing.'

Maisie took the card. 'This is an old card. Maurice's handwriting . . . always a challenge to the eye – oh dear.'

'Uh-oh, I don't like the sound of that.'

'Of course. This goes back over twenty years now. It's just a record of the fact that, when Maurice opened his first clinic in the east end, Walling sent an employee to ask if the premises needed looking after – protection, if you will. Maurice declined, but thereafter ensured that the clinic became a useful tea-stop for the policeman on the beat, so it went around that there was a "presence" there, even at night, with the clinic open around the clock.' She tapped the card against her hand. 'This could be another of our more devious brethren, Billy, so find out all you can about him. I should add that he's now a respected businessman.'

'Aren't they all when they want to be? Seems that the big boys like Walling, and that Alfie Mantle – you remember, who was put away a few months ago – all dress like lords and mix in the right places, so you've got your city gents and your politicians hobnobbing with these men who're right villains.' Billy looked at Maisie. 'What will we do if we can't find her? I mean, she's out there, a woman alone, and with that dark cloud over her – she could do anything.'

Maisie looked at Billy, and saw in his eyes an empathy for Sandra – his own losses were still so close to the surface.

'I'll call the police.'

'But won't that make things worse for her?'

'I think Detective Inspector Caldwell owes me a favour or two, don't you?'

'You reckon he'll agree to look for her, then?'

'He will when I tell him that there's a chance Eric was murdered.' She pushed back her chair, and walked back to her desk. 'Sandra has been in the abyss, but she's no fool. Find out what happened, Billy. Uncover enough for me to go to Caldwell with. This is your case. Make sure you do right by Sandra.'

TWELVE

With Billy gone, the office was silent, the square quiet on a Friday afternoon. At once, Maisie felt a fatigue set into her bones, as if there were no marrow, no fuel for what had to be done next. True enough, she had been intent upon her work, trying to be a good teacher to her students. She had been balancing the demands of her assignment for Huntley and MacFarlane with deep concerns about Sandra, and in the back of her mind there was still a certain worry regarding her father's wellbeing; and on top of that, a nagging thought – it had begun as if it were a scratch on the skin, a minor irritation, but was now a deep discomfort – a sense that James Compton might not be true to her. It was a question she tried to banish, but at the same time, it was as if a few threads had loosened in the fabric of her heart and now a tear was creeping across, in the way that a crack might appear at the edge of a crystal glass, and spread until at once the glass shatters in a thousand pieces. Might she become as bereft as Sandra again – a woman who had rebuilt her heart, only to see it broken once more?

Tears welled up in her eyes, tears she brushed aside with the back of her hand while picking at a needle of splintered wood along the edge of the desk with the fingers of the other. She imagined Sandra, hurt and alone, channelling anger at losing Eric into discovering the true circumstances of his death. Oh, how she wished she could wave her hand and dispel the dark stone of doubt, of unknowing, that had enveloped Sandra. *She had nothing to lose,* thought Maisie. And she knew that, though Sandra had shed tears, though she had come to Maisie for help, and though she had established a soothing routine to her days and seemed to be recovering, in her deepest soul the widow had a sense that there was no more to lose, so any risk was worth her quest for truth. Sandra was in a sort of limbo, where a past with meaning and promise was gone, and the future as yet held nothing she truly wanted. It was a feeling that demanded to be controlled, otherwise it would wreak havoc in the soul, a sense of angry pointlessness. Hadn't that been why Maisie herself leant on her work to bring a meaning that would ground her days? Her relationship with James, the intimacy of connection was a spark that caught fire – could it all be gone, now that she doubted him? Priscilla was right – and wrong. Yes, she controlled her feelings, keeping the dragon at bay with a carefully self-chaperoned life, a protected heart. But Priscilla made letting go sound like a simple task, as easy as a yacht slipping away from the harbour with the wind in her sails. Yet there was always a rock upon which to run aground, and Maisie knew it was her habit to keep a keen eye out for the rocks. And what was the smudged London postmark if not a rock scraping her bow?

Maisie pushed the folders she had intended to work on back into her briefcase, put on her linen jacket once more, along with her light felt hat of pale ivory with a matching band, and left the office, locking the door on her way out. She remembered Eric replacing the lock for her after her office had been broken into, remembered the way in which Sandra had brought her then fiancé to the office, knowing he could help, knowing that no job would be beyond him. They had made a good and happy match, Eric and Sandra, already walking together as if they were meant to grow old entwined in each other's thoughts, knowing all there was to be known about each other. *Where are you, Sandra? If we do not find you soon, I will have to call the police.* And as she started the MG and pulled away from Warren Street on her way back to the flat in Pimlico, Maisie asked another question, aloud, as she drove. *'And where are you, James Compton?'*

Her flat was quiet, the windows closed against a stale air that sometimes wafted up from the river on a warm day. Usually Maisie might not have noticed – it was, after all, something she had grown up with, and though not pleasant, did not disturb her unduly, though she did not want to invite it into her home. She set down her bags, placing the post she had collected onto the hall table before going to the kitchen to put the kettle on. She walked back to the box room – Sandra's room. It was empty. The bed was made. Clothing and personal effects had been removed, but an envelope with her name had been left upon the counterpane.

Dear Miss Dobbs,

By the time you find this letter you will have discovered that I am not as reliable as you thought. I have left Mr and Mrs Partridge because I didn't think it was right. They have three young boys and it is not fair on them to have a criminal under their roof.

I am sorry for embarrassing you and sorry for letting you down, especially with you being so kind to me. But I am not sorry for what I did. I had no choice. I won't say any more, but I thought it best to leave your flat. I don't want to be bringing shame upon you, Miss Dobbs. You've been so generous already, it wouldn't be right at all.

Don't worry about me. I will be all right. I am quite determined to know what happened to Eric, and why he was killed. I am his wife, and I vowed to be his helpmeet in sickness and in health. I know I must look out for him in death, too. It was not an accident, Miss Dobbs. I'm sure of it.

Yours sincerely,
Sandra

Mrs Sandra Tapley

Maisie turned over the page, then turned it back again. It had been prepared with care; not one error, not one misplaced letter typed over. She had signed her name with a flourish – her handwriting seemed larger, stronger, as if she had a purpose from which she would not draw back. There was something about the typeface that seemed familiar to Maisie, but it wasn't from the new typewriter at the office in Fitzroy Square. She walked back into the hallway, where she picked up the post from the small table and took it into the kitchen. With a cup of tea in hand, she sat down to go through her letters. Michael Klein, her solicitor, confirmed that he had the conveyancing in hand in connection with the purchase of a semi-detached house in Eltham and would have contracts for her to sign within another week. As he had advised her, a mortgage might not be in her best interests at the present time, so he had taken the liberty of arranging for funds to be placed in an account pending contract exchange, so that the house could be purchased in its entirety. She nodded to herself; in matters of finance, Maisie had learnt in a short time to trust Klein's instincts. In a letter Maurice had written: '*I am not a person who has ever had a talent for economics, and though I am not one to make terrible errors either, I have found it best to leave matters of finance to Michael. He will rarely make a move without consulting you, and he will listen if your desires run counter to his advice, but at the same time, Maisie, he knows more than you or I – and I have a feeling that you do not have a kinship with the finer points of mathematics and finance any more than I.*' Maisie had laughed when she first read those words – she was more than happy to leave management of the estate to Michael Klein, though she was learning more each time they met.

There was a letter from the building company, confirming conversations with Klein's office, and informing her that the house would be ready for her to take possession in one month. *I hope the baby can wait,* thought Maisie. The next was a letter from James. Usually, she would have torn open the envelope, anxious to read his news, but this time she looked carefully at the postmark, again smudged across the Canadian stamp. Was it London? It was barely legible. She went to her bedroom and gathered other letters from Canada that she kept in a cabinet alongside her bed; she laid them out on the dining room table along with the newest letter and inspected the postmarks. She could not be sure; if James were duping her – *if James were duping her,* she could barely think it without the tear across her heart growing – there would definitely be something amiss in the letters. She took up the new letter, tore open the envelope and unfurled the pages. James wrote in a deliberate hand, the pen pressed so deeply onto the page you could detect where the two halves of the nib had separated by a hair's width. The ink was indigo black, and the fountain pen had required refilling halfway through.

He spoke of missing her, of completing his work, and of how much he looked forward to being home in England. '*I never thought I would say that, Maisie. Canada has always been the place that lifted me. I felt free of so much weight whenever I came back here and dreaded returning*

232

to London, even Chelstone. But now I ache to be home, ache to hold you in my arms again, Darling Maisie.' She caught her breath. Tears filled her eyes again. How she despised herself, how she wished she did not doubt him so; it was her fault, she knew. In truth, what had he done to cause her to have such feelings? She looked at the postmark again, then went back to the letter. *'I think some letters might have gone astray, so in case you have not received one or two along the way, I have also sent a letter for you in the bag that is sent to our office – it was shipped last week. There's something else for you there, though you will have to collect it from our office. You can telephone Miss Robinson, my secretary. She'll have it for you when you come in, though she must know when to expect you.'*

Something was amiss. No, no, she would not let imagination run wild. Surely she was dealing with enough subterfuge at the moment.

She woke with a start at six o'clock, her head sore from resting on the table in front of her, her hand, cramped, still holding James' most recent letter. She wiped moisture from her mouth and rubbed her eyes. The meeting. She would be late. Scrambling to her feet, she gathered the letters, and returned them to the cabinet alongside her bed. In her bathroom, she splashed water on her face, brushed her hair, patted some powdered rouge on her cheeks and ran lipstick across her top lip before pressing her lips together and checking her appearance in the looking glass above the sink. She opened the window, felt the air outside, and pulled a heavier black linen jacket from the wardrobe, then removed her cream shoes in favour of a black leather pair. The cream skirt and blouse would do. Whenever Maisie dressed, it was hard not to hear Priscilla's voice in her head. Her friend could have been a couturier's mannequin; she spent a good deal on her stylish clothes, and always had an opinion on whatever Maisie was wearing. *'Ivory and black, Maisie? Tell me, do you really have that much of an aversion to colour? For heaven's sake – you're not a nurse any more! And what happened to that red dress?'* She grabbed a red silk scarf from a drawer and tied it around her neck. *Oh dear, I look like a bus conductress,* thought Maisie. But she would be late, so banished the voice of her fashion-plate friend from her head and left the flat. All being well, she would be at the address in Cleveland Terrace in time to observe the comings and goings of members of the *Ortsgruppe.*

She drove past the address and parked along the street. The Georgian terrace comprised flats with shops below, with the entrance to the flats a doorway between two of the shop fronts. There were some pedestrians on the street, but Maisie did not want to be conspicuous, so moved the motor car closer to the building, so she could observe the comings and goings of members from inside the MG. Men and women began to arrive, though the latter were far outnumbered by the former. A taxi-cab pulled up outside the address and Robson Headley alighted the vehicle. He held out a hand to Delphine Lang as she stepped out. Headley paid the driver, and they turned towards the doorway. Lang looked around her, as did Headley, and at once Maisie hoped they did not spot her distinctive MG, though given the care she'd taken to avoid using it in Cambridge, they might not recognise it as hers in any case. As they walked forward, Lang dropped a book she was carrying and Headley bent down to retrieve it for her. Maisie watched as he handed her the book, the way he smiled, placed an arm around her shoulder and escorted her into the building. They must have been among the last to arrive; Maisie cast her glance along and across the street. It was then that she noticed a man on the other side of the road. He was slender and wore a suit that despite being well tailored seemed to hang just a little. A broad-brimmed hat was pulled down in such a way as to obscure the face. The man waited for a while, then took out a packet of cigarettes, lit one with a match, and looked up to the first-floor window, where silhouettes of those gathered could be seen in the diminishing light. Maisie continued to watch as the man then turned and began to walk along the street. There was something in that walk, something that intrigued her – the way the man moved, how he continued to draw on the cigarette. She felt sure she had seen him before, and as she slipped the MG into gear and moved away from the kerb, it occurred to her that she knew exactly who it was, though the thought would seem quite absurd if she chose to share it with Huntley or MacFarlane.

Maisie rose as early as she could to drive down to Chelstone. She thought it might be time to press her father again regarding a move up to the Dower House, and at the same time there were several boxes of Maurice's notes that she wanted to read through.

Maurice might be gone now, his counsel not immediately available, but he had left boxes of papers and journals for her, all clearly marked, all catalogued. It was as if his voice were still with her, guiding her, leaving something of his knowledge, his wisdom, in every word, on every page. How she had drawn upon those words in the early days following his death. It was as if she couldn't quite let go, even though she had held his hand as he passed and had mourned his loss in a way that she had not mourned since her mother died. Admittedly, the fledgling relationship with James Compton had done much to gentle her heart, though sometimes she felt as if there would never be an end to the sorrow of losing Maurice.

As always, driving seemed to clear her mind. There was something in the rhythm of changing gear, slowing for corners, accelerating on the straight, that seemed to help her sort through the many concerns that vied for attention when she was working on a case, especially when personal matters also claimed her attention. It was as if her mind comprised a flight of birds swooping and wheeling across the sky – an observation here, an ah-ha there, a question, an answer, a clue, a surprise; they never collided, but wove a web all the same – but driving gathered her thoughts into formation, and set a course. And as she continued on her way, turning onto the Chelstone road just before Tonbridge, the smell of freshly picked hops in the air, the reek of sulphur from the oast-houses as they dried the county's most famous crop, Maisie knew that if only certain pieces in the puzzle could be found, a coherent picture would emerge from the images before her. Hopefully there would be a letter from the Ipswich County Records Office next week. There was still Greville Liddicote's former colleagues at the university to see, if she could gain an interview with any of them. And several more questions had come to mind, questions that would demand time and footwork – MacFarlane would be impressed; he liked footwork. She wondered how MacFarlane and Stratton were getting on. It was as if MacFarlane had put her at arm's length now, not wanting their paths to cross too much. She made a note to ensure they spoke on Monday.

And then there was Stratton. Stratton who had burnt a torch for Maisie at one point, had shown interest again when she parted from Andrew Dene, but who now seemed subdued in her company since it was known she was walking out with James Compton. MacFarlane had seen Stratton looking at Maisie and had known of his hidden affection. As far as Maisie could see, MacFarlane exploited that knowledge, with a comment here, a prod there. He was not an unkind man, but he was not above using another person as a source of fun – as Maisie knew only too well. *'Staid, indeed,'* she said aloud.

Parking outside the Groom's Cottage, Maisie was surprised when her father did not immediately appear at the door. Though she had not telephoned in advance – she had thought to surprise him – Frankie was always there at the door when she arrived, as if he had one ear to the wind, waiting to hear the crunch of the MG's tyres on the gravelled lane that extended from the main driveway to his cottage. There was no sound of a bark from Jook, his dog, so she wondered if he was at the stables. She went to open the door, and was surprised to find that she felt as if she should knock. *But this is my father's house,* she thought. Instead she walked around the house, towards the back door. The sound of laughter caught her ears even before she came alongside the kitchen window. She stopped. There was her father's throaty laugh, the laugh she remembered from her childhood. *Has it been so long? Surely he has laughed like that since mum died.* It was the laugh she'd heard as a girl, after he'd told a story of something that had happened at the market. She could see him now, sitting at the kitchen table at the little house in Lambeth, she and her mother listening, waiting for the next tale. *'What do you think of that, my Maisie, what do you think of that one?'* And he would tickle her ribs, then lean across and pull her mother to him. *'My girls, my girls . . .'* And he would laugh and laugh, a man who loved and was loved in return by wife and daughter both. How much it had changed them both when her mother died. Was that when the dragon first raised his head, was subdued, controlled so that he could not cause havoc? Maisie felt she might weep when the hearty laugh echoed from the kitchen again.

'And you should have seen that horse take off with him, Brenda, I tell you, he fair launched himself around that track, took the stable boy right across the road. Well, I'd never seen the like of it. Bill Webber, the trainer, he just walked up to that horse when he was done – munching away in a field while the jockey tried to get himself out of the hedge – he took that bridle and I swear, he got that horse by the end of the nose and looked as if he would twist it off. "Do that again, my lad, and it's the glue factory for you," he said. And I saw him wait there like that, him and the horse, standing there, looking at each other, until the horse dropped its head. Old Bill let go, and rubbed the horse's neck. Followed him all the way back like a pup, did that stallion. And the jockey was still stuck in the hedge.' He laughed again.

'More tea, Frank?'

Maisie felt her eyes widen. *Mrs Bromley.* Her housekeeper. *Brenda?* She stepped back to the gate, unsure of what to do, then shrugged. She'd come down from London to visit her father, a drive of almost an hour and a half. This was no time to turn back. She coughed twice, then again for good measure as she approached the back door. She cleared her throat again before reaching for the handle. *I cannot believe I am doing this,* she thought. As she was about to turn the handle, the door opened. Her father stood in front of her, his cheeks bearing a faint pink blush.

'Maisie, what a surprise – a lovely surprise, mind.'

'It was a good morning for a drive, so I thought I'd come down – where's Jook?'

'Oh, sleeping under the table. Mrs Bromley's here – she came with some leftovers for Jook, and then – well, come on in, love.'

Mrs Bromley was clearing the table when Maisie entered. It seemed to Maisie that colour was heightened all around

239

when Mrs Bromley turned to greet her – after all, Maisie was now her employer.

'Miss Dobbs, I thought I'd bring down a spot of cottage pie for Mr Dobbs – I made it fresh this morning, and it was too much for one. I really didn't expect you today.'

'I should have telephoned, I'm sorry.' Maisie smiled, anxious to bring a sense of calm to what was obviously a very pleasant lunch – until she arrived. She reached down and ruffled Jook's ear; the dog had emerged from slumber to greet her. 'Well, if there's any left, I wouldn't mind some myself – though if it puts me to sleep like Jook, I will be out for the count for the rest of the day.'

'Here you are, love.' Frankie pulled out a chair. 'Bren—Mrs Bromley made a fair old pie there, and even though I came back for more, there's plenty for another helping or two.'

Mrs Bromley put a plate of cottage pie and vegetables in front of Maisie, while Frankie poured tea from a large brown teapot.

'I suppose I'd better be off now—' Mrs Bromley untied her apron and reached for her basket.

'Oh, no, don't go – I'm sure you've already got a pudding ready, Mrs Bromley, I know you too well. My father will not wish to miss a sweet. Come on, sit down.'

Frankie poured again, fresh cups of tea for himself and Mrs Bromley, while the housekeeper placed a bowl with a slice of apple pie with custard in front of Frankie, and the same in the place where she had been sitting before Maisie arrived.

'This is lovely, Mrs Bromley, just what the doctor ordered.'

'You look a bit drawn, love,' Frankie spoke up, as he often did when he was worried about his daughter.

'Oh, busy, Dad. Busy. Driving a lot, too.' Maisie pushed another piece of pie onto her fork. 'Did you tell Mrs Bromley about the time you caught the stable boy from another trainer putting something in your horse's feed?'

'Oh, that was a fine to-do. It was the third race of the day at Newmarket . . .' Frankie leant forward, and as Maisie tucked into the pie, she smiled, watching him look from her back to Mrs Bromley as he told the story of a day's racing when he was a stable lad at Newmarket in the years before he'd met her mother, before he'd become a costermonger, and before the much-wanted child had been born. And as he spoke, Maisie felt a tear in her heart – one she had become so very used to accommodating – begin to mend again, as the glue of her father's intermittent laughter sealed the jagged edges of unspoken grief.

Later, Maisie returned to the Dower House, excusing herself while Mrs Bromley assured her that she would be up at the house as soon as she'd finished with Frankie's kitchen. She'd asked if Frankie might be joining her for supper, to which Maisie replied that of course he would – in fact, why didn't they take supper together, all three of them, in the kitchen. In truth, she was still trying to get used to being at the Dower House, and was now quite thrown when she considered the unusual nature of her domestic arrangements. She had often spent the day at the house, only to return to her father's cottage in the evening, except when James was at home.

She had, eventually, arranged for the large bedroom at the back of the house to be redecorated in a colour that reminded her of smooth buttermilk, and had pale-yellow curtains made to add light to the room. She and Mrs Bromley had moved the furniture around, though they had summoned a couple of the gardeners from Chelstone Manor to help with the bed and an armoire of some girth that had been brought from Maurice's house in Paris several years before. The housekeeper had made a skirt of the same yellow silk as the curtains, to surround the dressing table, and soon the room was rendered more feminine, without resorting to frippery.

Now Maisie lay down on her bed for a few minutes' rest before going down to the library, where many of the boxes containing Maurice's papers had been consigned. There were still more boxes in the cellar.

In all, the Dower House had four upper rooms: three bedrooms on the first floor, then another large attic room on the second floor. Maurice had chosen the large bedroom at the back of the house to be his own, as it overlooked the land he had come to love. There was another room of equal dimensions at the front of the house, and smaller rooms along the shorter sides of the house; one of those rooms had been converted to a spacious bathroom some years before, at the same time as part of the large bedroom had been sectioned off to form an en-suite bathroom for the Dowager Lady Jane Compton, when she was an invalid. When Maisie lived at the house as a girl, she had been assigned the smaller bedroom to the side of the house, so that she could attend to the Dowager – Lord Julian's mother – if she called in the night. Now, lying on her bed for a few moments, Maisie could hardly believe that such a house was hers; it was a thought she pushed to the back of her mind, for when she considered all that she now owned, she became overwhelmed. She had learnt to take each day as it came. Though her wealth was considerable, she knew that Maurice had intended her to be a responsible steward of that wealth, so already she had begun to consider the financial arrangements Maurice had made to support the less fortunate, not only through his clinics in impoverished areas, but in providing educational opportunity for young people with talent who might otherwise languish, caught within the boundary of a life with limitations.

'This will never do,' said Maisie to herself as she swung her legs off the bed. She slipped on her shoes and went downstairs to the library, where she switched on the light above a mound of boxes she had left there on her last visit. With her head inclined to one side, she perused the outside label on each box until she finally came to the one she wanted to start with: *London, 1914-1916*.

Maisie had known Maurice since she was thirteen years of age, and for some nine years, until his retirement in early 1929, she had been his assistant. She was well aware of his connections before, throughout, and following the war; however, it was during work on a case that had taken her to

Paris in 1930 that she realised how deep and broad his reach into matters of security among the Allies had been. Maurice had received commendations and medals from Belgium, France, and Britain for services rendered, and she knew his influence extended from the Secret Service to the army's Intelligence Corps. He had contacts in Naval Intelligence, and was called upon to advise on the recruitment of agents working in clandestine roles overseas. And he had been involved in liaising with the brave civilians involved in underground resistance to the enemy occupiers in France and Belgium. He had also spent some time in the Netherlands, and she had been aware of the important role that the Dutch had played in intelligence during the war. But little of this had ever been discussed between them, and it was only now that many of his secrets were being offered up. She could never have read through the many papers except as she now approached the task – either on a 'need-to-know' basis, or on a quiet Sunday afternoon, when the stillness inside the house seemed to bring him into sharper focus in her mind's eye. It gave her a sense that she only had to call and he would be there with her, advising her, prompting her, or bringing insight and clarity to a case that had become more opaque as facts, clues, and suppositions clouded the way ahead.

She opened the box, lifted a good handful of papers onto the desk, and began to read, thinking that if there were ever a market for a review of intelligence in the early years of the war, she would have enough background material to write a worthwhile tome. Page after page catalogued meetings, interviews with prospective employees – many of whom,

Maisie thought, would have gone on to become agents working on behalf of His Majesty's government. Then a few sentences took her attention.

> To Whitehall again, this time to see Giles Sheffield. I was taken aback to see so many young women working in the offices, and at all levels of seniority. Girl Guides have been brought in to run messages – apparently the Boy Scouts had been tried out but were found wanting when they put play before work. In walking about the building I came upon a room where the Guides awaited the summons to take a message here or there. Some were called upon to go across London, and all had to swear to the greatest levels of secrecy, for they were in possession of the addresses of every secure building used in the array of intelligence services during a time of war. In the waiting room, the girls read or diligently completed their homework. There was no idle chatter, but a clear-headed willingness to wait until called upon, then to execute their duties as befits the uniform of a Girl Guide.

Maisie went on to the next paragraph, where Maurice remained on the subject.

> Women and girls are employed in all aspects of intelligence. In observing their work I am convinced

they are the most loyal of workers. Not for them a long lunch at Simpsons, or drinks at their club. They remain at their posts until the job is done and it is clear they understand the gravity of their responsibility, from the most lowly girl at a typewriter, to the woman who is charged with breaking a code. Increasing numbers of women are being brought into the service, in particular as more men are required to bear arms on the battlefield. However, I have concerns, which I have voiced in my capacity as an advisor, on the temperament and character required for intelligence work, though the concern is not directly in connection with the traits necessary to be a holder of secrets, or the ability to withhold the truth of one's origins when assigned a duty that requires one to live under the enemy's nose. There has traditionally been a tendency for the recruitment of agents and intelligence staff to be done at random; there is little investigation into the background of a person; indeed, it seems to me that the club a man belongs to has more bearing upon his employment in the service than other, more significant, traits.

I have suggested that there should be deeper investigation into the origins of a person, and therein will be found something of their sensibilities and loyalties. Does the fact that a young woman has a German great-grandmother have bearing on her work? It might. The women and girls recruited are loyal and hardworking, but we cannot rule out the risk of enemy approaches towards an impressionable young person – man or woman. I have also advised that there should be a comprehensive record of the skills of those who work in the service, women in particular. I have discovered a tendency among the men to assume that a woman knows only that which she has revealed in her interview; however, I have pointed out that a man might tell everything, recount every success and any skill, but a woman will not necessarily share her worth. A brief conversation with one young woman revealed that she was fluent in several languages, given her education overseas. Her supervisor was surprised, as were the men who interviewed her for her clerical position. Now she has been placed in a department where her linguistic ability can be put to better use. My prediction is that the Secret Service will be built upon the work of these women and girls – they should be taken on with great care and deep attention to the many abilities they bring to our remit.

Maisie straightened the pile of papers, then leant back in the chair and rubbed her neck. The afternoon sun had moved across the land, and she thought she might walk around the garden before tea. She realised her throat was dry. There were other boxes to go through today, but for now she wanted to think about the girls and women who had worked in secret throughout the war. And she thought back to the conversation with Jennifer Penhaligon, and her comments about Francesca Thomas:

. . . First-class languages, excellent student – diligent, and thoughtful. Passionate, is how I would describe her . . . about the things she believed in . . . she came back to see me once after she'd left . . . she said she couldn't really speak about her job – hush-hush, apparently . . . .

Maisie wondered what Francesca Thomas was passionate about now, and whether there was still much in her world that was *hush-hush*.

THIRTEEN

Maisie returned to Cambridge on Sunday afternoon. She wanted time to prepare for her lessons in the coming week, and welcomed the extra hours she would have in the morning, before her classes started. Of more urgency, she wanted to see if a letter from the Records Office in Ipswich had been delivered to her lodgings.

It was nine o'clock in the evening when she stood up from her writing desk and stretched her arms. Her back was sore from driving and sitting bent over papers, and now there was another line of investigation to follow. She wanted to know more about Robson Headley. How invested was he in Delphine Lang's politics? Had he become interested in the *Ortsgruppe* simply because she was a member? Hans Wilhelm Thost was known to have links with Oxford, and it seemed there was a real attempt to spread the word regarding their leader's political message. Among the aristocracy and landed gentry, there was support for, indeed a fascination with, the tenets of Fascism. Maisie wondered if it was simply a new political game to play along the sidelines of government. Clearly Huntley already knew about the group's activities throughout the British Isles, especially in London, yet his advisors were informing him that the group presented no cause for concern; on the contrary, they were welcomed in certain quarters and asked to speak publicly of the rise of the Nazi Party in Germany, presenting their leader as one with a good deal of charisma. Maisie shook her head, recalling the frustrating conversation with Huntley. Yes, she would have to find out a little more about Robson Headley. And she wanted to speak to Matthias Roth again, to ask him why he countered Greville Liddicote's decision to take an active part in the Cambridge debates.

The letter from Ipswich did not arrive until Monday morning. The clerk who responded to her questions about Rose Linden's family invited her to return to the county offices, as he had some names that might be of interest to her. He indicated that there had been two nephews, though both were now dead. The name of the family was not Linden, however, but Thurlow, owing to Rose Linden's sister's marriage to John Thurlow. One son, also John, died in 1914, at Mons. The other, David, died early in 1915; no other details were listed. The clerk said he would give her more information when she came in.

Maisie borrowed her landlady's bicycle again on

Monday, arriving at the college at lunchtime. She set the bicycle in a rack set at the side of the main building and made her way to the staff dining room, but was stopped on the way by Miss Hawthorne, who was as flustered as ever.

'Miss Dobbs, just a quick word to let you know that there's a meeting of the college – all staff and students – in the assembly hall at two; everyone else knows as the message went round at coffee, so I'm glad I caught you.'

Maisie thanked the woman, then continued on to the staff dining room. Lunch was not a formal affair at the College of St Francis, usually a buffet with one hot dish and vegetables, and a sweet course. A coffee urn was placed at the end of the table, though Maisie would have loved a cup of the rich, dark coffee Maurice had preferred – and which was still delivered to the Dower House from an importing company in Tunbridge Wells. She helped herself to the baked cod and vegetables, and a glass of water, then walked across to the table where Francesca Thomas sat looking out at the gardens.

'May I join you, Dr Thomas?'

Thomas pressed a half-smoked cigarette into the ashtray on the table, giving the fleeting smile that Maisie was becoming used to. 'Of course – do sit down.' She waited until Maisie set her lunch down on the table. 'You've heard that our esteemed leader will be speaking after lunch?'

'Yes, I was told when I arrived this morning. Do you know what it's about?'

'Apparently, the college will be closing from Wednesday until next Monday. Those dreadful policemen – the Scot and the other one – have been making it rather difficult to continue teaching while they conduct their enquiries. So, staff will be expected to furnish classes with sufficient homework to last until next week, though I am sure our students will welcome the opportunity to enjoy the last of the summer.'

'Isn't the memorial service for Dr Liddicote on Sunday?'

'Yes, it is. And the debate team will continue to practise in the interim.'

Maisie looked for some sort of reaction, something that revealed how Thomas felt about the debate. There was none, so she continued.

'I don't think Dr Liddicote liked the idea of the debate.'

'Did he tell you that?'

Lifting a forkful of the milky cod, Maisie feigned indifference. 'I was waiting outside his office and heard him talking about it. He seemed far from enthusiastic to me – but then, I didn't know him as well as other members of staff.' She thought her words must sound as bland as the cod tasted.

'Greville Liddicote *hated* the idea of the debate, Miss Dobbs. He did *not* want our college to be involved.'

Maisie set down her knife and fork and reached for her glass of water. 'Why do you think he didn't want us to take part? He wanted the college to be taken seriously by the Cambridge academic establishment, and the debate would have been the ideal opportunity. I'm a bit confused on that score.'

Francesca Thomas sat back and looked at Maisie.

'Greville was no fool, Miss Dobbs. The topic is one that will bring out a lot of spectators – the debates usually draw a goodly number, in any case. But this is one that he didn't want to take part in, did not want the college to be involved with, because he did not want to support any gathering where the name of our college would be allied with an issue he found controversial. The university is a powerful academic institution and can weather the storms of speculation – indeed, it thrives on having the cat among the pigeons. But this is a small college, a college dependent upon funds brought in from people – wealthy benefactors – who share our ethos. The party of Herr Adolf Hitler is not an ideal representative of peace and inclusion.'

'But surely our team's performance will reflect what the College of St Francis stands for.'

Thomas shook her head. 'I do believe you are playing devil's advocate with me, Miss Dobbs. If not, I can only say that you are pressing a naïve point of view. If anything negative is allied to our institution, then we stand to lose donations. This college will not survive without a healthy stream of money coming in.'

Maisie felt her colour rise. 'But isn't Dunstan Headley one of the main funders? And his son is on the debating team.'

'Another huge error.'

'Because it smacks of nepotism?'

'No, Miss Dobbs.' Francesca Thomas stood up and collected the pile of books sitting alongside her place at the table. 'Because Robson Headley is a Nazi, and while it may

253

seem fashionable at the present time, I believe it will prove to demonstrate very, very poor judgement in years to come. And young Headley has his father wrapped around his little finger, even though he knows what's going on, and does not like it at all. Now, if you will excuse me, I'd like to get a breath of fresh air before the assembly.'

Maisie pushed her plate away as Thomas left the room, and took a sip from her glass of water.

'Did one of Medusa's snakes just have a snap at you?' Alan Burnham drew back a chair and sat down in front of Maisie. 'Don't let Francesca Thomas ruin your lunch, though given that tasteless cod, it seems to me there wasn't much to ruin. Dr Thomas is a forceful woman and can be strong when she's voicing an opinion, but she's one of the very best teachers here.'

'Thank you. She was simply explaining why she thought the debate was a poor idea, especially as Dr Liddicote did not want it to go ahead.'

'Nonsense. Of course he did, otherwise why would Matthias continue? He would never sully Greville's memory in such a way – they may have had the odd spat, but he was always the most faithful supporter of everything Greville stood for. No, Miss Dobbs, you're mistaken. Greville Liddicote was very much in favour of the debate.'

'Was he in favour of Robson Headley taking part?'

Burnham shook his head. 'He wouldn't have known. That was Matthias. Dunstan Headley said his son wanted to join the college team, and given his connections to the college – Robson is charged with continuing Dunstan

Headley's philanthropy when his father is gone – his standing matters to our future. Matthias does not want to rock the boat, especially with the new building work starting soon.'

'I see, so—'

'And Robson is a harmless enough chap. He has a fine sense of his own intellectual ability – which is wanting, if you care for my opinion – but as I said, a harmless young man, if a bit full of himself.'

Maisie saw members of the faculty begin to move towards the door. 'We'd better go down; the meeting is about to start.'

Matthias Roth waited to take the podium until students and staff were seated. Maisie looked for MacFarlane and Stratton, and noticed that they were standing at the back of the room. Maisie caught Stratton's eye and waved; he waved in return and, pointing to his watch and the door, signalled that they would talk to her after Roth had spoken. She nodded.

'I have brought the entire college together to announce that we will be closing for the rest of the week, though you are reminded that a memorial service for Dr Greville Liddicote will be held at St Mary's on Sunday afternoon. I am sure you will all wish to attend.' He cleared his throat. 'I have made the decision to suspend teaching not – as many of you might have hoped – to give our students and staff a well-earned holiday . . .' There was some muffled laughter, and Roth smiled before continuing. 'The days off will allow the police to bring their work to a close regarding any outstanding information in connection with Dr Liddicote's death. With everyone on their own personal timetable, it's been rather difficult for enquiries to be completed; and I know that I, for one, would like to do all that I can to assist in the execution of police work so that we can get on with the job of being a college again, and our students continue with their studies. We have the legacy of Greville Liddicote to honour when we come back next week with the slate clean.' He paused. 'Are there any questions?'

When no one spoke up, Roth invited MacFarlane to join him to go through the schedule of interviews that would take place over the next several days. Maisie turned again; Stratton nodded towards the doors. She left her place and made her way into the corridor.

'What's going on?' Maisie let the door close behind her.

'Robbie was about to flip his lid, so it had to come to this – he insisted upon it. Roth hadn't wanted classes to be disturbed, so he asked us to work around the student timetables – and they're all on some sort of individual curriculum, so it was hard to keep up with who had been interviewed and who hadn't.' Stratton shook his head. 'It's not that we think a student here was Liddicote's murderer, but we certainly want to know if anyone saw anything.'

'You're still interviewing staff as well?'

'Yes, but your name has a big red tick alongside it – you're off the hook.'

'Shame, I might have had a thing or two to talk about.'

'Do you?'

Maisie sighed. 'Probably nothing you don't already

know about.' She looked at Stratton. 'Do you know about the *Ortsgruppe*?'

Stratton nodded. 'All reports have come back that it's really nothing to worry about.'

'Miss Delphine Lang is a member, and she has taken her amour – Robson Headley – along to meetings.'

'Didn't know that. I'll tell MacFarlane, just in case he thinks it has bearing on the case. Probably more in line with *your* investigation – not that I am completely privy to your remit.'

Maisie smiled. 'Tell Robbie I asked after him. I'll be in touch.'

'Where will you be over the next few days?'

Maisie stepped towards the entrance to the assembly hall, but was almost knocked off balance when the door opened to reveal Francesca Thomas leaving. She did not notice Maisie, continuing on her way at a brisk pace. Maisie saw Stratton's eyes follow the woman as she strode purposefully away from them. He looked back at Maisie. 'So, um, where was I – oh yes, where will you be . . . while the college is closed?'

She raised her finger to her lips. 'Sorry, Richard, keeping it to myself, for now.'

Having walked as quickly along the corridor as Francesca Thomas had before her, Maisie tapped on the door of the college office and walked in.

'Miss Dobbs, what do you want?' Miss Hawthorne was standing over a desk bearing mounds of paper and a series of open manila folders. 'Can't you see my hands are full?'

'I have my students' marked assignments here, and their homework for this week, along with readings they must complete before we return next Monday. I'd already prepared the sheets, and I thought they could get on with the work during the next few days while classes are suspended – I wouldn't want them to fall behind.'

'Of course not. Here, I can post them in the students' common room, and I will leave a note to the effect that work handed in last week can be collected here. Well, Miss Dobbs, I'm glad that someone is organised. I just had Dr Thomas in here telling me she would be using the days to complete research for a paper, and that she would be leaving as soon as she could. Had me take dictation for a message to her students – the cheek of it! The sooner Miss Linden is replaced, the better. No wonder the young woman ran off like that – who wouldn't want to vanish into thin air with all this to deal with?'

'Who indeed?' said Maisie. 'I'll see you soon, Miss Hawthorne. You know where my lodgings are, if you need to contact me.'

'It's the police who'll want to know.'

'Oh, I've already been interviewed.'

With that, Maisie ran to the bicycle rack and sped back to her lodgings, where she collected the MG and drove directly to Francesca Thomas' flat. A taxi-cab had drawn up outside, and soon Thomas emerged from the front door and stepped into the vehicle, which moved slowly down the street, before accelerating as it merged onto the main road. Maisie followed, close enough to see where the motor car was going, but not so near as to be identified. The taxi-cab stopped at the railway station, where Thomas stepped out and made her way quickly to the ticket office.

'Damn!' said Maisie to herself. She pulled the MG around and parked on the street, then ran back to the station. Thomas had been in a hurry, so the train she expected to catch would be coming in soon.

'When's the next train going?' Maisie asked the clerk.

'Where to?'

'Just the next train, anywhere.'

The man looked at her as if she were half mad.

'It's about my husband,' she added, leaving the reason hanging.

'Oh, right you are, see what you mean. You'll be looking at the London train, leaves in two minutes.'

'Return, third class.' Maisie set down the money, and ran towards the platform, though she stepped into the shadows as the train pulled in, belching steam and punching out specks of soot.

In the distance, she saw Francesca Thomas step into a first-class compartment, so Maisie joined the travellers in the nearest third-class carriage. She would have to make sure she was first off the train when it arrived in London. The train rocked from side to side, lulling some of the passengers to sleep. Maisie picked up a newspaper discarded by a departing passenger; it was just what she needed to shield her face, should Thomas decide to leave her seat to walk along the narrow corridor in search of the WC. It was getting on for five o'clock when they arrived in London.

Maisie stepped off the train and walked towards the ticket collector. She kept to the side of the stream of passengers, looking out for Thomas. She soon caught sight of her, walking with a purposeful stride. Maisie remained several yards behind, and followed Thomas outside, where she hailed a taxi-cab. Maisie signalled a driver and boarded another taxi-cab.

'Could you follow that taxi-cab, please? The lady dropped her purse; she was walking so quickly, I couldn't catch up with her – and what with the noise, she didn't hear me when I called.'

'You're a right Samaritan, that you are, Miss. Not to worry, I'll make sure we keep up with them!'

Maisie soon realised the taxi-cab in front of them was travelling in the direction of Belgravia – she knew it well from her days living at the Comptons' Ebury Place mansion. With traffic increasing as London's workers rushed home, the taxi-cab carrying Francesca Thomas vanished from sight.

'Sorry, love, I reckon I lost them. From the turn he took, it looks like he went around that side of Eaton Square.'

'Oh dear.'

'She's probably a foreigner, anyway.'

'What makes you think that?'

'Well, a fair bit of the street there is taken up with the Belgian Embassy. Consulate, or whatever they call it. It's all foreigners. Mind you, I'd rather have the Belgians than some of 'em, eh?'

'Could you drive around the square for me?'

'Just in case you see her? Right you are.'

The driver brought the motor car to a crawl as Maisie studied the buildings around the square. Francesca Thomas might have gone into any one of the mansions; she could have a friend with a flat there – indeed, she could have a lover. Perhaps that's why there was something that Maisie doubted about her; she was a striking woman, the sort who rarely seemed to marry, but who never want for male company, though they give the impression of having little time for the rituals of courtship. Thomas was not a woman whom one thought might want to be married, or indeed one who was wrapped up in an affair of the heart, though she did seem to be a woman of controlled passions. Maisie wondered about the phrase – it had just slipped into her mind. *Controlled passions*.

'Look, I don't mind taking your money, but if you like, I'll run you back to the station – you can give the purse to the railway police.'

'Very good idea – thank you.' She sighed and leant back in the taxi-cab. *What a waste of time*. A wild goose chase when the last thing she needed was to run around chasing her tail like a demented dog. She couldn't face going back to Cambridge at that moment, so she leant forward and tapped on the window.

'Yes, Miss?'

'Could you take me to Limehouse?'

'Limehouse, Miss? With that purse on you, to say nothing of your own belongings and my takings?'

'Don't worry, we'll be safe enough. I can go to the station later, but I need to see someone in Limehouse – and perhaps you'd be so kind as to wait for me?'

'If you don't mind paying, I'll wait for ten minutes.'

'Right you are. I'll tell you where to go when we reach Limehouse Causeway.'

Following another stop-start journey, Maisie directed the driver to an address she had remembered from a visit almost twenty years earlier.

'I won't be long – and don't worry, it's not as bad as it looks; I thought a taxi-cab driver would know that half the myths about Limehouse and Chinese slave traders are just that.'

'Never mind the bleedin' myths, hurry up and do your business or whatever it is you're doing, and I'll be waiting here.'

To be sure, Limehouse was a slum, a dark maze of streets and alleys overhung with a listless mouldering smog that seemed to lift only slightly in spring and summer. Soon coal fires would seed the yellow pea-soupers that tested the navigation skills of any sailor emerging from one of the bars or opium dens, many of which were suffering the economic depression as much as West End shops. Maisie looked up at the double-fronted warehouse-like building facing the street and knocked at the wooden door. There was a hatch in the door, embellished with the owner's chop. Within a moment, the hatch was slipped back with a snap, and a pair of dark almond-shaped eyes gazed out at Maisie.

'I'm here to see Mr Clarence. He may not remember me, but tell him my name is Maisie Dobbs, and that I am a friend of Dr Maurice Blanche.'

The hatch was closed, and within three or four minutes the door opened and Maisie was led along a dimly lit passageway, and from there to another door. The young Chinese man who had been sent to accompany her was dressed in a well-made suit with a clean white shirt, his jet-black hair combed back from a wide forehead. He bowed to Maisie, and opened the door. She had not heard a summons to enter, but walked in to greet the man she had come to see.

The spacious room was lined with bookshelves, and at one end, a man of average height stepped from behind a desk. About sixty years of age, he was slender of build and his movements were precise, measured. He wore an expensive suit – Maisie could tell by the cut and fabric – and his shoes shone. His black hair was threaded with grey, and his pallor and features revealed him to be Anglo-Chinese. His name was Clarence Chen.

'Mr Clarence. How kind of you to see me.'

Chen approached Maisie, clasped her hand, and bowed.

'I was most grieved to hear of Dr Blanche's death. You have my condolences.'

Maisie nodded. 'Thank you. I miss him very much.'

'Of course. He was your teacher, wasn't he? Therefore he cannot be replaced. But he left you the legacy of his lessons.'

'Do you remember me, Mr Clarence? It was a long time ago.'

'Of course – please sit down, Miss Dobbs.' He invited her to sit at the desk. A woman dressed in a cheongsam stepped from the shadows and poured tea. She bowed, then left. Chen went on. 'Maurice brought you to see me – you must have been only fourteen, fifteen. He wanted you to be introduced to *wushu*. To the ways of defending the body from attack.'

'It was a brief introduction – I was simply a spectator.'

'You can always come back to learn more – I have a good teacher here.' His accent was such that, if blindfolded, a stranger might think him the son of a well-to-do English merchant, or a banker.

Maisie thanked Chen for the invitation, but returned to the business at hand. 'I wonder if you could help me, Mr Clarence?' Maurice had introduced Chen as 'Mr Clarence', the name by which he was known throughout Limehouse and Pennyfields. She used the name now to honour their first meeting. 'I want to know if a person knowledgeable in *wushu*, in the martial arts, could use his . . . his *skills* to break a person's neck. I know that with sleight of hand much damage can be caused to the human body, but would twisting the head to break the neck be something that a *wushu* expert might do? And if a woman were a *wushu* master, would she have the strength to kill a man in this way?'

'The Chinese methods of combat use *chi*, the flow of energy within the body, in a way that provides great strength

264

without effort. If a mouse were a *wushu* master, he could kill by taking a man's head in his tiny paws and breaking his neck. The practise of *wushu* affords the student stealth, gives him cunning, a way of moving that expends only the energy required to move from one foot to another. It also provides mental acuity; and a cleared mind can accomplish anything – and leave anything in its wake.'

'Do you know of many women who have learnt to kill in this way?'

Chen looked at the table and smiled. 'You are a modern young woman, yet you ask if a woman can learn *wushu?* Of course she can – but do you mean a Chinese woman, or one of your kind?'

'A white woman.'

Chen shrugged. 'She could study *wushu,* and could excel. But where would she learn? Even you would not come to Limehouse as many times as would be required to learn from a master.'

'True. But what if the woman were brought up in China?'

'Ah, then anything is possible. It depends upon the amount her father might pay. In fact, he would be a wise man to do such a thing; after all, a woman is never protected unless she can protect herself. And the principal purpose of any martial art is defence.'

Maisie gathered her bag, and stood; Chen came to his feet at the same time.

'Thank you, Mr Clarence. I have been told by experts that a woman could not kill a grown man by twisting his neck.'

Chen nodded. 'I would ask, Miss Dobbs, what gave the woman the *chi,* the force within, to murder a man in such a way. Anyone can learn to kill, but it takes a certain tipping of the scales to stir the fire inside that ignites heat in the hands. Did the killer leave in a state of calm?'

'There was little disturbance.'

He nodded. 'There are other explanations, other means of committing the act of murder than by snapping the neck. But if it is a woman, and the circumstances are as you describe, then she might well have used a form of *wushu* to defend herself. I assume that is what you came to hear.'

'Thank you, Mr Clarence.'

Clarence Chen bowed deeply, then turned and walked to his desk. The man who had escorted her to the room returned to her side and signalled for her to follow him.

'Blimey, I nearly left,' said the taxi-cab driver, as she stepped into his motor car. 'I thought you were never going to come out of there.'

'I was perfectly safe.'

'I've heard about him, the fellow what lives in there. Chen, ain't it? They reckon he's a right one – bit of both, ain't he? Mother was English, they say, came from some sort of missionary family, and was only young when she had him. I've heard she came back from over there with the boy when her husband died.'

'That's true.'

'I heard no one wanted to know her, so the poor woman had to make her way alone, and did a good job of it, all things considered. And then when the son was old enough, he went off and looked for his own kind – well, he found 'em in this swill pit, didn't he? And they say he's got the opium dens, the smuggling, running all sorts of rackets with the Lascars, and the Chinese and Japanese sailors what come through here – and done up like two penn'orth of hambone, enough to do business in Mayfair, if you please.' He shook his head. 'Nice young lady like you, going in there – I'm surprised you came out again – mind you, you'll probably tell me that half those stories about him are like them myths you were talking about, eh? Can't see a half-caste getting on in there, when all's said and done.'

Maisie looked out at the grim spectacle of Limehouse Causeway. 'Oh, all the stories about Mr Clarence Chen are true; every word. His mother was a friend of a very dear friend of mine. Could you take me to Pimlico now, please?'

Before leaving Pimlico the next morning, Maisie placed a telephone call to Billy at the office.

'Have you been in touch with Sandra's in-laws?'

'Mr and Mrs Tapley. I never saw two people look so ill with losing someone, really I haven't. Not since just after the war, when I went to see some of the families of my mates who were killed over there. Anyway, I asked them if they'd seen Sandra, and they said not since the funeral. They were right worried about her, you know. Said they'd told her she was welcome to live with them in Whitstable until she got herself sorted out, but she said no. They said she was like a wraith at the funeral, couldn't put two words together that sounded right.'

'What about her parents?'

'They live out a bit, well, her father does – mother died a few years ago, according to what I've found out. Father lives in Essex now – apparently that's where he'd come from as a boy before he went to Dorset – so I thought I'd go on the train tomorrow, see if she's there. Mind you, I don't want to cause trouble, so I thought I'd just look around, see if I can spot her coming and going.'

'And remember Reg, who Eric worked for. See what he has to say for himself – lean a bit harder on him.'

'Right you are. Leave it to me, Miss.'

'Thank you, Billy. Oh, and by the way – you can tell Doreen that the house will be ready to move in soon, about three weeks, all being well.'

'Oh, that is good news. You just let me know what I have to pay, and when.'

'Don't worry about that, Billy. They have some sort of special contractual offer at the moment – I didn't want to tell you until I sorted it out, but there's nothing for you to pay for six months.'

The line was quiet. 'You sure, Miss?'

'Perfectly. Came as a surprise to me, so I'm very pleased all around.'

Maisie ended the call and left for the station. She wondered how she had become so much more adept at telling lies since she signed the Official Secrets Act. But then, secrets and lies always went together.

FOURTEEN

It took a while for Maisie to locate the administration office at King's College in the Strand. The grand Georgian building overlooked the Thames on one side, and proved to be something of a maze for the new visitor. Following a wait of over half an hour in the records office, she made her way to the room of Dr Trevor Pollard, lecturer in politics and history. Pollard was tall and thin, with silver hair; he wore a grey jacket and trousers, though they did not match and could not be referred to as a suit. A collar stud had come loose, and he kept touching his neck to stop the starched collar riding up towards his ear while she introduced herself and informed him that she wanted to find out more about a young man called Robson Headley. Maisie explained that he was representing the College of St Francis in a debate, and she was endeavouring to assess the potential for success. Pollard did not seem to doubt her story, though she suspected he might think twice about the reason for her questions after she had left his office.

'I'd like to know what he was like as a student – I understand he left the university only three years ago, so you'd probably remember him.'

'That's right; I remember him quite clearly.' Pollard pressed his collar down and straightened his tie. He looked at Maisie. 'May I be candid, though I would not care for these thoughts to be attributed back to me.'

'Of course. My visit is informal; anything you tell me is in absolute confidence.'

Pollard nodded, and folded his arms. 'I couldn't stand the chap. Opinionated, unable to engage in constructive debate – bear that in mind, Miss Dobbs – and something of a trouble-maker, despite those baby-faced looks.'

'How did he cause trouble?'

'He seemed quite unable to stand back and demonstrate intellectual curiosity without extreme involvement. If he joined a team of any sort – he was a runner, for a while – he would go at it tooth and nail. There was no middle ground, and that extended to his politics. He could not simply argue a point in tutorial, for example. With most students, there might be argument or dissent in the classroom, then when the class is over, it's off to the common room and they're still talking about it, but not necessarily arguing with a venomous ferocity. Well, Headley wasn't like that – he would harangue people. I had heard that on one occasion, he was so intent upon continuing an argument that he woke up a fellow student by throwing stones at his window at night, trying to get him to come down and finish the row outside. The police were called.'

'Oh dear, he does seem rather passionate.'

'I call it being spoilt. His family have indulged him, and I cannot see him changing overnight, though I would hope he has mellowed.'

'Did he become involved in any particular political groups?'

'I can't think of anything off hand, though he did try to start something himself. It was a group that countered the stance of pacifists – there's quite a pacifist movement among students, you know. He was maintaining that an inability and unwillingness to take up arms, along with peaceful overtures towards our enemies, would lead to a disease of weakness. He would hold meetings outside, try to get other students to join him in challenging the man on the street to be part of the cause – and at a time when the man in the street is probably more interested in making a day's living. Passionate? Yes. And misguided. And he isn't quite as bright as he thinks he is; quite a mediocre student, actually.'

'You have been most forthcoming, Dr Pollard. I wonder if your fellow lecturers would share your opinion.'

'Granted, I didn't like Headley, but I think he offended other members of staff, too – it was talked about, especially when he started holding meetings, trying to be a leader, talking about entering politics, and so on. He was giving off a lot of hot air – though I have to admit, when I learnt his older brother was killed in the war, I wondered if that might account for his behaviour. I daresay he was pandered to as a child, and is used to getting his own way. And of course he is quick to show temper.'

'You said he was mediocre, but did he try, did he work hard?'

'He *thought* he worked hard and was surprised when his marks did not meet his expectations. I think he was easily distracted by his ambitions and things that would suddenly take his attention – starting a political interest group, for example, or campaigning for a member of Parliament he suddenly supported – so he found settling down to complete a piece of academic work quite difficult.'

'Did he have friends here?'

'People were drawn to him, then turned away. He wasn't above getting into a fistfight in support of his beliefs, or at least challenging another student physically.'

'Really?' Maisie was trying to reconcile this picture of Robson Headley with the young man she had met, and whom she had seen being solicitous towards Delphine Lang.

'In fact, I saw him once, having a go at another chap after classes. I don't know what he did exactly, but that lad was on the ground in a second – and he was a young man of some heft, not easily caught off guard. But Headley just whipped him up off his feet and was standing over him, calling him all sorts of names – and all due to some argument about the way in which the British defeated the Boers.'

'Well, this is very interesting, Dr Pollard, I—'

'Personally, I put it down to the fact that he's spent a few years overseas – apparently his father had business in the Orient – something of that order, anyway – but he came back here to attend university. In my position, you don't always remember your students – too many of them – but some stand out, and as you've probably gathered, Headley was one of them. I recall thinking that it was as if he didn't really know how to communicate with people his own age and kind any more. Of course, he looks very friendly, almost debonair, but he is a young man who has a fair bit of nasty bottled up inside him. Mind you, he'll be an energetic debater, if he can hold his temper – and perhaps he's grown up since I last saw him. What's the subject of the debate?'

'The title might have been changed again in my absence, but it's to do with whether the emerging politics in Germany – national socialism – could be accepted here in Britain.'

'Then just watch him. I could imagine him being quite a vehement supporter of the motion to accept something along the lines of Herr Hitler's Nazi Party. They've garnered considerable support in Germany and they're very well organised in groups in other countries, to ensure that German citizens abroad are brought into the fold. Wouldn't surprise me if Headley isn't a Fascist – mind you, the corridors of power are littered with Fascist leanings; anything to save the upper classes through disenfranchisement of the common man while allowing the common man to think you're on his side.'

Maisie thanked Dr Pollard for his time. After leaving his office she referred to a rough map of the building scribbled by the administrative clerk, then made her way to the Strand. She would have liked to speak to another of Headley's tutors, as Pollard had been so vociferous in his dislike of Headley – perhaps as passionate as Headley himself; thus she cautioned herself not to take his summing-up as the last word regarding the young man's performance as a student. However, it gave her food for thought. Robson Headley and Delphine Lang might have more in common than time spent in the Orient and membership of the *Ortsgruppe*. She remembered the way in which Lang had deflected the cricket ball as if it were no more than an errant feather in her hand, and she paid attention to Dr Pollard's description of Headley taking down another student during an argument. She did not want to jump to conclusions, but it seemed they both possessed a certain level of control and strength; a physical self-possession that Clarence Chen would recognise.

Upon reaching the railway station in Cambridge, Maisie went straight to a telephone kiosk and placed a call to The Old Fenland Mill, the inn where she knew MacFarlane and Stratton had taken rooms. She left a message for MacFarlane, and said that she would meet them at seven o'clock in the private bar.

Now she was on her way to see Professor Arthur Henderson. Although he was retired, she had managed to find out his address from a porter at Trinity College – again, lies came easily when she was in search of more colour to add to her picture of Greville Liddicote.

Professor Henderson answered the door of the Edwardian villa himself. He wore olive-green corduroy trousers, a pale-green shirt, a green polka-dot bow tie, and a dark-green knitted pullover. Although the professor's clothing seemed more suited to early autumn, Maisie felt over-warm and had taken off her jacket, which she now carried across one arm. She could feel perspiration on her forehead and she welcomed the cool interior of Henderson's study when he invited her in. She explained that she was looking into Greville Liddicote's work with a view to possibly writing an article about his children's books, and she thought he might be able to assist her in her research, seeing as he and Liddicote were colleagues as well as friends.

'Well, I don't know about *friends,* Miss Dobbs.' A knock on the door distracted Henderson, who smiled as his housekeeper entered. 'Ah, Mrs Mills, would you be so kind as to bring two glasses of your delicious lemonade – thank you.'

Maisie was relieved. A cold drink was just what she needed, with the Indian summer weather leaving her parched.

'Now, where was I?'

'You were saying that you didn't know whether Greville Liddicote was really a friend.'

'Yes, yes, of course. But no, he wasn't what you would call a friend, though I was brutally honest with him, I must say.'

'About his work?'

'Well, yes. You see, he would insist on publishing that

damn book, the one about the children going off to find their fathers in the war. I'm not saying it wasn't a good book – as children's books go, it was excellent, which rather surprised everyone, actually – but it caused so much trouble.'

Maisie nodded, and was about to ask another question when there was another knock on the door and the housekeeper came in. She placed two tumblers of lemonade on the table in front of Henderson and Maisie, and at the sight of the pale-yellow liquid, with a slice of lemon and sprig of mint on top, she felt her mouth water with anticipation. She reached for a glass and took a sip.

'Oh, that really is lovely – definitely wakes you up,' said Maisie, setting down her glass again.

'It's certainly a pick-me-up, and she won't divulge her recipe, either, much to the chagrin of many a caller on a hot day.'

'Professor Henderson, regarding the book, why did it surprise you? I know you had read Dr Liddicote's children's books in the past, so you must have been familiar with his storytelling.'

'I was, very much so; I was always his first reader, followed by my grandchildren. But this one was different, in style, tone and – frankly – his ability. It was far more nuanced than anything he had written before; it had layers of meaning not demonstrated in previous books. It was the work of a true storyteller rather than a jobbing writer, which was what Greville was, really, before this one. He wrote to bring in a bit of extra money, and – again, to be frank – saw himself as another Grimm.'

'There was some talk, I understand, regarding the origin of the book; it's suggested he might not have been the true writer.'

Henderson sighed, fiddling with his bow tie before taking another sip of lemonade, setting the glass down once again and then clearing his throat to speak. 'I would hate to comment on the provenance of the book, and of one or two others that followed. But they were not like those he'd published before – or since. There were two more after the banned book, with similar ground covered though the stories were tempered. Then he published another book, must have been in about 1920, and it was just like his pre-war books – very light, silly little stories. Those three that were written during the war – and which, overall, he did very well with financially, despite the first one being effectively banned – were gems in a rather run-of-the-mill body of work.'

Maisie nodded again, and waited a moment before putting forward her next question.

'And were the books – the three written during the war – so controversial that they would have led to his dismissal?'

'He tendered his resignation to follow other pursuits, one of which was to found a college to promote peace, as you know.'

Maisie reached for her lemonade again, taking one or two sips before she pressed Henderson. 'But do you think it might have come to it that Dr Liddicote felt he had to leave, given that feelings were running high regarding his work?'

As Henderson looked down at his hands, the folds of

skin on his face seemed to concertina into a soft place for his chin to rest. He sighed and looked up at Maisie. 'If you're asking whether he was pushed or whether he fell, let us simply say that he fell, but there was a heavy hand at his back.'

'Ah, I see.'

'Indeed.'

'And if – in confidence, I assure you – you had to make a considered guess regarding the three books at the heart of this controversy, would you say that they could have been written by someone else?'

Henderson sighed again. 'How I hate the feeling of being cornered. Makes me feel a bit like I've been ambushed.'

'I'm sorry, Professor Henderson. I beg your pardon, it was just that I wondered, in your opinion, whether—'

'The answer is yes, Miss Dobbs. Greville Liddicote had a very pedestrian writing style, whether we are talking about the task of composing an academic paper or the art of storytelling. Those books, especially the first, were not written by an author with a pedestrian style.'

'I see, so Greville Liddicote did not leave his teaching position simply because of what he wrote, but because you did not believe he had written it.'

'I think I've said more than enough, Miss Dobbs.' Henderson reached for a bell on his desk. 'More lemonade before you depart?'

Maisie declined, and Henderson accompanied her to the door, at which point she decided to press her luck. 'You've been so generous with your time, Professor Henderson, I

278

wonder if I might put just one more question to you?'

'Well, if it's not—'

'There's talk that Dr Liddicote's book caused what amounted to a mutiny in the war, that the book went around the soldiers and the effect of the story caught on like fire in a tinderbox – I've heard they just put down their weapons and started walking off the battlefield. Do you know if there's any truth to the story? Certainly Dr Roth was affected by reading the book while in the German trenches.'

Henderson seemed tired as he answered; his voice had deepened, and he spoke slowly. 'Miss Dobbs, no one will ever know about the subject of mutiny in a time of war – well, not for years, in any case. There will be rumour, conjecture, a word from an old soldier here or there, but those stories will be quashed, they will die a quiet death, and any official reports kept under lock and key, so it will be generations before any truths are known about such things. I am an old man now, but in my time I have seen all sorts of books taken from circulation on the instructions of "official sources", so I know what I'm talking about. There were rumours of a mutiny – there are some who maintain that it was just a few of our men, and a few on the other side. And there are those who say they saw what happened – a full-scale mutiny involving hundreds of soldiers from both sides. All it took was for the book to be thrown into no-man's-land for a German soldier to find and the effects of the story multiplied. It is believed in some quarters that more than just one or two men were executed, and that there was something of a massacre – all because men in uniform were touched by a story of innocents on the battlefield. I suppose, if there is a grain of truth in the stories, the book touched a nerve regarding the futility of the whole mess. But that is only my opinion. Of course, it makes one man shine out, in my opinion.'

'And who is that?'

'Dunstan Headley. He lost his son in the melodrama, a son who read a book and lay down his gun. A good young man who was true to beliefs he came to hold while in the thick of war. Headley must have felt such anger towards Greville Liddicote, and then managed – through sheer will, I would imagine – to transmute that fury into something quite worthwhile on behalf of his son, when he stepped forward to channel funds into the founding of Greville's peace school. That's what my colleagues and I called the College of St Francis in the early days, "Greville's Peace School". He has gone to his grave with the last laugh – the student body is accomplished and the staff roster enviable. I hope his work can continue without him.'

'Professor, I wonder if I might put one more question to you.'

'I'll try to answer it.'

'You seem to know something about the founding of the college – I wonder if you have any idea who "the Readers" might be?'

'The Readers? Yes, of course. As soon as he realised that *The Peaceful Little Warriors* had had something of an effect on people, beyond being a book for children, Greville kept a list of people who had been in touch with him, with the intention of approaching them for donations to get his college going. Dunstan Headley is obviously a Reader; so are many people who read the book and who lost sons to the war. And there are former soldiers on the list, too, and various people who have since served on the faculty – in fact, Matthias Roth is a Reader, as far as I know. I seem to remember Greville telling me that he had made him deputy principal not least because he had put his life savings into the college, such was his belief in what the institution stood for. And I confess, I suspect I am on the list – I made a small contribution after Greville resigned; I thought it was the least I could do. Mind you, you should remember, though the book was withdrawn from circulation, Greville kept a few copies for himself, which he was able to put onto the market at an inflated rate, and the subsequent escalation of his reputation rendered all his other books very successful indeed. He was a wealthy man, you know. And he was clever too – his desire to leave a legacy came from an unexpected quarter.'

'His books or the college?'

'Both. You see, that's what Greville wanted – a sort of fame, if truth be told. I think we've all come across people who want recognition on a broader scale than might otherwise be available to them. As a senior fellow at the university, I might have expected a level of acclaim, but that would be due to the very small pond in which I swim. Greville wanted something bigger, and the notoriety *The Peaceful Little Warriors* gave him presented a perfect opportunity. You see, prior to writing that book, I had never heard him voice any opinion regarding the worthiness – or otherwise – of the war. He had never claimed to be a pacifist, but the book, its reputation, and then his resignation from the university, gave him an impetus to find something new – and so the College of St Francis was born. Greville Liddicote was reinvented, if you will, as a man of peace for the students of the world. And money flowed in from those who had been so pained by their losses, and who wanted to see something better come of it all.' He sighed, as if breathless after speaking for so long. 'And, Miss Dobbs, I have to say this – good for him, because ultimately I do not doubt his commitment to the maintenance of peace so actively championed by his work at the College of St Francis.'

At the door, Maisie slipped on her jacket, and, holding out her hand to the elderly man, decided to push on with a final question. 'Professor Henderson, can you think of anyone who would want to see Greville Liddicote dead?'

'I suppose I could think of a few – though none who would ever do anything about it. I understand police enquiries are in progress, but I would venture to guess it is just a formality. I am sure he must have died from some natural cause or another.'

The church clock was striking seven as she passed on her way to meet the two policemen.

'What'll it be for you, Miss Dobbs?' asked MacFarlane, who had been about to raise a pint of beer to his lips in the private bar when she entered. He had commandeered the small bar for the evening.

'A half of cider would be lovely, thank you.'

As soon as she was seated at a table with the two men, MacFarlane spoke first. 'Been busy, Maisie?'

'Yes, I have been fairly busy. Not only teaching, but I've had a few trips back and forth to London.'

'Never thought I'd be looking forward to getting back myself, but I'm fed up to the gills with this place. I'm not one for your university types – bloody know-alls, every one of them, even the students, still wet behind the ears. Half of them can't even speak the language properly.'

'They're unfamiliar with the language of a police investigation, and perhaps a little nervous – after all, they are guests in this country, and now they're being questioned as part of a murder enquiry.'

'I think you've got a point there,' said Stratton. 'We're trying to take that into account. They're all very bright, actually.'

'Most have already attended university in their own country,' said Maisie. 'Their work at the college represents additional academic endeavour intended to bolster their intellect and the number of opportunities that might come their way in the future. And of course, there is the small matter of spreading peace.'

'Who have you been seeing?' asked MacFarlane, ignoring her comments.

'Academic staff at other universities, actually. A lecturer

who taught Robson Headley, and another who knew Liddicote when he taught at the university here.'

'Why Headley?'

'He's been attending meetings of the *Ortsgruppe* with Delphine Lang. They are a courting couple, as you know; however, it is quite a big step for a British man to attend one of those meetings; I am sure he was accepted on the weight of his liaison with Lang.'

'Do you suspect him of anything?'

'First of all, I don't believe the *Ortsgruppe* are as innocent as you and Huntley might think – and if they are at present, they won't be for long. Secondly, both Headley and Lang have the ability and, I believe, the training, to kill a man instantly.'

'Maisie, have you ever tried to kill someone by breaking their neck? I mean, it really is a job.' Stratton seemed somewhat exasperated with her.

'Aye, lass, it would be a job for a big, strong man,' added MacFarlane.

'But not if a person were able to make an approach that was all but silent, and then move with speed and skill. And remember, Liddicote was likely hard of hearing.'

'Apart from anything else,' said Stratton, 'they both have alibis.'

'Stratton, would you mind getting me a whisky?' MacFarlane winced and held his beer up to the light as if to consider its purity, then set the glass down. 'This beer is not agreeing with me at all.'

Stratton left the table and walked to the bar. MacFarlane turned to Maisie.

'You are keeping to your assigned task for the dark ones, aren't you?'

'Is that what you call the Secret Service?' She smiled, then looked at Stratton waiting by the bar; he raised his hand to summon the landlord and Maisie turned back to MacFarlane. 'As I've said before, the threads of investigation here are intertwined; however, I'm keeping to my end of things. Have you questioned Francesca Thomas?'

'The tall dark-haired woman; got a touch of the Greta Garbo about her?'

'I'm not sure that I would use that description,' said Maisie, 'but I suppose she's the only one in the college whom it would fit.'

'We've spoken to her, and it seems she was teaching around the time of Liddicote's death, so we can rule her out.' MacFarlane glanced in Stratton's direction. 'I take it she's of interest to you.'

'To some extent. She certainly seems to make frequent trips to London.'

'There you are, sir. I bought a malt, not a blended.' Stratton reached forward to place the tot glass of amber liquid in front of MacFarlane, who, in spite of his earlier claim, had made a good dent in his pint of beer.

'Good man, good man. Now then, will you join us for a spot of supper, Maisie? They do a very good fish-and-chips here.'

Maisie agreed, and was soon enjoying a companionable meal with the two policemen, though their conversation was focused on the matter of Greville Liddicote's death.

* * *

285

Maisie was on the road to Ipswich early the following morning, with the intention of being at the door of the county offices as soon as they opened. The letter she had received on Monday had been written by a Mr Smart, and within a short time of the doors being unlocked, she had found his office and was speaking to him about the contents of his letter, and what he had discovered about Rose Linden's family. The documents he had gathered indicated that a family living in a small hamlet some two miles outside the town were related by marriage to Linden's nephew. The man shook his head and gave a deep sigh.

'What is it?' asked Maisie.

'The older nephew, David Thurlow, died in Wandsworth Prison.'

Maisie leant forward, to look at the register in front of Smart. 'Have you any idea what he'd done to warrant incarceration?'

'Doesn't say here, but I can guess. During the war Wandsworth was used as a military prison. I reckon your man here was a conscientious objector. Some of them were given hard labour, but a lot ended up in Wandsworth, or Wormwood Scrubs; it all depended upon your tribunal, and how they felt about you and what you had to say for yourself. People look upon it a bit differently now, seeing as we know a lot more about what went on over there, and of course, all them peace organisations that have popped up in the last ten years. But during the war, you had to be brave to even say you were a pacifist – nigh on got yourself stoned in the street for not wanting to do your bit.'

'Do you have an address for the family?'

'I poked around and found this.' He handed a piece of paper to Maisie. 'It's out in Knowsley, a bit off the beaten track – I looked it up for you, the directions are on the back. I think those cottages are tied to the farm, so one of the family must be a worker there. There's no Rosemary Linden listed, but they may know something, or I might be sending you on a wild-goose chase.'

'I'll soon find out. Thank you very much for your help.'

A light but warm rain that had dampened the drive to Ipswich had now lifted, leaving wisps of mist across flat fields of crops newly harvested. The road was narrow, and soon woodland on either side diminished the view, but offered shade from the bright sunshine breaking through. Once out of the canopy of trees, Maisie entered a hamlet of a few cottages, some thatched and all built in the mid-fifteenth century, with oak beams and roofs that were bowed in the middle. She slowed the car so that she barely rumbled through Knowsley, looking again at her directions. Soon she came to a cottage on the right and pulled up alongside a hedge that in May would be blooming with bright white syringa. She stepped out of the motor car and looked across the front garden. Someone had tied off the last of the summer flowers, though canes were still wrapped with multicoloured late sweet peas. The hedge was high enough so when the door opened and laughter could be heard, Maisie stepped back to watch without being seen. A young man – possibly in his early twenties and with the bearing of a farm labourer – carried an older woman outside. She laughed as he accidentally knocked her head against the doorjamb.

'Leave me with a mind, Adam, whatever you do!'

'Oh, sorry, Mum. Are you all right?'

'I'm well enough. But watch where you're going, would you? Now, if Alice and Amber just put the chair over there, then I'll tell you where to put my things.'

Two girls struggled to bring out a wheelchair and another, younger, lad carried a tray with books and writing paper; he had draped a blanket around his shoulder like a cape. When the mother was seated in her chair, the older girl took the blanket from the boy and wrapped it round the woman's knees, then placed the tray on her lap. The son who had carried her out returned to the house, and the second daughter, whom Maisie judged to be about nineteen or twenty, said she would bring a cup of tea for her mother. The younger boy was tasked with not forgetting to feed the rabbits, and the older daughter remained with her mother, kneeling at her feet as the woman breathed the sigh of one who is exhausted by even the slightest exertion. The mother put her arm around her daughter's shoulder and rested her head against hers. 'I'm so glad you're home, Alice. You were gone a long time, and I missed you.'

'But we needed the money.'

'We certainly did, and now look at us – getting on our feet again. It's Alfie who worries me now, though. He's doing so well in school – he'll go to the university, if we can get the money.'

Maisie stepped back. She closed her eyes and framed

288

words of introduction. It would be a difficult conversation, which is why she wanted just a moment or two to compose herself, to hold her hand to her heart so that she might speak from that place. There was fragility in this household, a lingering sickness that each member of the family worked hard to counter each day – Maisie could see it in the way they had clustered around a much-adored mother. But, of more urgency, Maisie knew she had found Rosemary Linden, for she still knelt alongside her mother, and was held in her arms. And there had been a greater recognition, as the children – now grown – brought the chair, then the blankets and writing materials. Maisie could see in her mind's eye the photograph she had taken from the room in which Greville Liddicote had died. A woman surrounded by her children, the youngest on her outswung hip with the older ones close by, all smiling into the camera. Except one, as Maisie now remembered. The eldest girl stood just behind her sister and brother, and she was frowning at the camera, or more likely the man who was trying to capture that moment.

FIFTEEN

The woman and her daughter did not see Maisie at first. Her approach was part hidden by the sweet peas, their multicoloured pastel blooms bobbing in a warm breeze, while white cumulus clouds seemed to linger above, before moving on to cast a shadow across another garden. Soon she was close enough to offer a greeting, but wanted to do so in a manner that gave the daughter time to gather her thoughts.

'Hello there, Alice – at last I've found you!' Maisie smiled at the young woman she had known as Rosemary Linden, who now stood before her in a sensible brown cotton skirt and a white blouse with a lace-edged sailor collar. She wore sturdy lace-up shoes on her feet, and an apron over the skirt. She gasped when she first saw Maisie standing before her. Yet it seemed that Maisie's open smile had indeed helped Alice collect herself, for she smiled in return, and her reply was composed.

'Miss Dobbs – Maisie – how lovely to see you here.' She turned to her mother, and though her colour heightened the second she called Maisie by her Christian name, she was quick with a story to mask the truth. 'Mother, I met Miss Maisie Dobbs while I was working in Cambridge; we were both members of a readers' club.'

'Mrs Thurlow, I am so pleased to meet you. I was in Ipswich seeing a friend, and I thought I would take a jaunt out here to see Alice. We quite miss her opinion on the latest books.'

'Please, do call me Ursula. Any friend of my children is welcome at our house – especially lovers of literature. One always has riches when one has a book to read.' She turned to her daughter. 'Alice, go and get Alfie to bring a couple of chairs out, so we can sit together, and tell Amber to bring another cup. Then I am sure you and Maisie have things to talk about.'

Alice went into the cottage and soon the younger boy brought the chairs, one held in each hand, bumping the door frame as he came out.

'Careful, Alfie, I think I've already taken a chip or two out of that wood with my head this morning!'

The boy was on the cusp of manhood, with a fluff of beard almost ready for the razor, and a way of walking as if he had grown too fast for his limbs to take account of themselves. He set down chairs for both his sister and her guest, and informed his mother that Amber had put the kettle on for a fresh pot of tea and Alice would be back out in a moment.

'If it weren't for my children, I don't know what I would do, Maisie.' Ursula Thurlow's manner was inclusive and open, as if she had known Maisie for a long time.

'Alice only mentioned that you were dependent upon the wheelchair – she didn't really tell me about your condition. Have you not found a doctor to help you at all?'

'The expense of going to the doctor has prevented me from seeing more than just one or two physicians, though there was a doctor in Ipswich who referred me to a colleague in Cambridge who was interested in my case for "research" purposes. I went to see him once, but I didn't want to go again. It was exhausting, just getting there, and the symptoms did not seem to be deteriorating at any great rate – it has taken since 1917 for me to be so crippled, and at least I still have my mind and my hands, though they wobble at times.' She paused, and sipped her tea. Alice joined them, bringing a tray with more tea and a cake. Amber followed and made as if to remain with them, but when she realised the subject of their conversation, she left to go back into the house, informing them that Adam had gone back to the farm.

Ursula Thurlow reached out for her older daughter's hand, and continued with her story. 'It all started with tingling in my fingers, and a sort of giddiness – the room would spin, then come back into place. I had young children then, so I could not allow it to hamper me. And I was alone; my husband had died, and I believed the shock of his death had likely set off the symptoms, and they would go in time. But they didn't.' She reached out to touch the petals on one of the sweet peas. 'Sometimes I can feel the soft touch of a flower, and sometimes I can't, which tells me that this hand might be the next to go.'

Maisie nodded. 'I know you only spent a short time with the consultant in Cambridge, but did he mention anything to do with myelin? There was some research a few years ago that won a Nobel award; it was to do with the way in which our nerves use something called myelin; lack of the substance leads to the sort of sclerosis that you describe.' She looked at Alice, then at Ursula once again. 'I should have mentioned – I was once a nurse, so these things interest me.'

The woman shrugged. 'Myelin? It sounds familiar, Miss Dobbs, but I have ceased to pay attention. Much as I would like to think that one day someone will say, "Take up your bed and walk," I have come to realise that, each day, I have only that day. I live for the present, Miss Dobbs, and the joy I can leech out of every moment with my children, in my garden, with my books and in my writing.' She reached out towards Alice, pulling her close so that she might kiss her forehead.

'I think you are perfectly right to live each day as you choose, Ursula. I can understand how wearing endless visits to the doctor can be.'

'It was bad enough when Alice chose to go to work with the family in Cambridge, but she's back now. It was a few years in which I would love to have seen more of her, but she insisted upon working to bring more money into the household.' The woman seemed to tire. 'I think I might just sit in the sun here while you two young women go off for a chat.' She paused and looked up at Maisie, who was now standing. 'I am sure we will speak again before you leave, Maisie. May I ask what it is you do, for you are a working woman, that much is clear to me, though you are no longer a nurse.'

'No, I am no longer a nurse. I am a teacher, and I have another job as well, though that is more difficult to describe.'

The woman smiled, and then closed her eyes, her hands resting on the tray with her books and writing materials.

'Let's walk down to the stream,' offered Alice Thurlow.

The two women walked for a while without speaking, then Maisie took the lead. 'Tell me why you lied, Alice. Tell me why you have lived a lie while working for Greville Liddicote.'

'I didn't kill him.'

'I know. But you wanted to, didn't you?'

Alice laughed. It was a short laugh. 'I don't know how I thought I would harm him, though I wanted to see him as deeply wounded as he left my family – and we were already in so much pain, every one of us, especially Mother.'

'Would you tell me what happened?'

'My mother could tell you what happened before my father was taken away. I was not a child, but probably not quite old enough to see anything but the black and white of it all.' She sighed. 'Sometimes, it makes me so tired, so exhausted, just thinking back over those years.'

'Let's sit over here, on this bank.'

Maisie took off her jacket and laid it on the ground. She sat down on one side, patting the remaining fabric for Alice to sit next to her. 'There, that works very well.'

'It won't do your jacket any good, though, will it, Miss Dobbs?'

'Maisie. Please continue to call me Maisie. Now, tell me about your father.'

Tears came into the young woman's eyes, tears that she brushed away with the back of her hand.

'They were very happy, my parents. Very much in love. But if I was to look back on it, I think they were very idealistic. I didn't realise how different we all were until I started seeing my friends' parents, who seemed so ordinary. My parents were always involved in something, and even before the war they had become quite vocal about their support of peace among nations. My father went to a peace march in 1912, and we all went along, too. If one of us couldn't walk, then they carried us.' Alice stopped speaking. She pinched at the grass, pulling up small clumps and throwing them aside. 'My parents truly believed in what they saw as an increasingly aggressive tone in government. To tell you the truth, we – my brother and I – picked up the arguments, the discussion we heard around the table, and took it to school, which made us stand out a bit. So, later, Mother started teaching us at home. And she told stories. Both Mother and Father told stories for us, and they said that if you could teach children about peace, there would be no more wars. We were taught never to fight, never to raise a hand towards another, and to turn the other cheek. I think that was especially hard for Adam, because he was such a big lad for his age – every boy in school wanted to pick on him for a fight, but he just walked away. I think we were all relieved when we came home for school, and my mother had quite a row with the school board man.'

'I'm sure she did,' offered Maisie. 'What happened to your father, in the war?'

'He protested against conscription, and he registered as a conscientious objector.' She swallowed, and rivulets of tears ran down either side of her face. 'My father was a very, very clever man, Miss Dobbs. He had been a teacher, and a writer of political essays, all of which were published. He was firm in his resolve, and he could argue his point with clarity and without resorting to rancour or sarcasm; he didn't need to be disrespectful. Even though I was young, I remember that listening to him argue a point was like watching a concert pianist dance his fingers across the keyboard, or a ballerina execute her steps to perfection. The men at his hearing clearly despised him. I am sure he angered them simply by the way he expressed himself – he was quite imperturbable. So instead of being sent to do hard labour, such was the vehemence – and, I think, the sense – of his argument, that he was sent to Wandsworth Prison, which had a terrible reputation. And we had no means of support in the family. We were living in a cottage close to the school where he taught at the time, and after his hearing, my mother was given notice to leave. She was very worried, so for a short time we went to live with my father's aunt.'

'Rose Linden.'

The drying tears had left water marks across Alice Thurlow's skin, and her eyes were red-rimmed. 'Oh, yes, of course, that's how you found us. Rose was so kind, and so was her husband, though they ended up losing the regard of her husband's family. We were like the unclean, you see – the family of a conchie. My mother told me she would have to get us away as soon as she could, as it wasn't fair on Aunt Rose.'

Maisie allowed a silence to descend before asking another question. 'How did Greville Liddicote come into your lives?'

'My mother had a book – actually she had a couple of books – that she and my father had written together. They had a way of working that really seemed to be fruitful for them, and they took so much joy in the process. They would talk about a story idea, then my father would set to and write the first draft, after which he would give the pages to my mother; then she would go through them and write the story again – and she'd paint little pictures with her watercolours along the way. Then when my father was sent to prison, she wrote a story for us – it was called *The Peaceful Little Warriors*. We loved that story, and she illustrated it.' She sighed. 'We needed money, so Mother thought she would try to get the stories published. She was naïve, Maisie. She asked her friends, one of whom vaguely knew Greville Liddicote, and that he had written some children's books. So she wrote to him and enclosed one chapter of the first book. He came to visit and began paying attention to my mother. She was a striking woman, Maisie. Though she can barely move now, you should have seen her before this wicked disease claimed her.'

'What did your aunt and uncle think of him, calling on a married woman?'

'Liddicote was circumspect, and soon he helped us out – well, it seemed as if he was helping us out. Mother was about to give birth to Alfie, and I think, even though she was pregnant, he seemed to be drawn to her like a moth to a light – even in the worst of times, she had such laughter about her. He found us a cottage to live in, and he offered to purchase the manuscripts – five pounds each for three, which was a fortune to my mother. She was so grateful. He had already paid the rent for several months – he stayed at the house as often as he liked – and the extra money would help out even more. And, to be fair, we needed that sort of support, especially after my father was murdered.'

'Murdered?'

'Yes, he was murdered, Miss Dobbs, though the men who took his life will never stand trial, for they were protected by the war and their position. We heard the truth a few years later, when one of his fellow prisoners came to visit and told us what he understood had happened. The conscientious objectors were treated as if they were the worst of common criminals. If thirsty, they were made to drink their own urine. If hungry, they were starved. If they cried, they were kicked. A man who stands up for what he believes in instead of fighting for what someone else believes in is a threat – people cannot bear someone who has that sort of strength and fortitude.'

Alice Thurlow's passionate description of her father took Maisie by surprise. The woman beside her bore little resemblance to the Rosemary Linden who had diligently gone about her duties at the College of St Francis.

'And I take it that Greville Liddicote not only published *The Peaceful Little Warriors,* but the two other books written by your parents – and all under his own name. He took all the royalties for himself – and the renown – leaving your family with only enough to pay the rent, if you were lucky.'

'Yes. And he never came back again after the first book was published. In truth, I don't think it was out of spite, but embarrassment. He was probably afraid that someone would find out and he would lose everything, so he didn't even send a penny more. My mother made an attempt to press her claim after she'd realised what had happened, but due to her beliefs, she didn't exactly fight for what was hers – and no one really wanted to listen, anyway. You see, Greville Liddicote had left my mother with a reputation – she was the wife of a conchie who had been kept by another man. But she was pressed to that point by a country that saw a true conscientious objection to the war as a reason to cast a family aside with no support. It would have been so easy for my father to take the King's shilling, to offer to drive ambulances, for example. But if he was to be true to his beliefs – and the values my mother held with him – he could not support men killing each other in any way. How might that have seemed to his children? Especially when he and Mother believed that the future of a peaceful world lay with those who were not yet grown.'

Maisie sighed. She wondered how the power of such a worthy conviction could lead to so much desolation, so much pain. And Greville Liddicote had died with a photograph of Ursula Thurlow in his hand.

'Do you think Liddicote loved your mother?'

At first Alice seemed angered – a dull chill seemed reflected in her eyes – but she said nothing, composing her thoughts before speaking again. 'I was a child, Maisie, though I confess, I have asked myself the same question time and again, and I have come to the conclusion that he was a confused – and rather selfish – man who chose the easier option.' She picked at the grass again, then brushed off her hands and looked at Maisie. 'Here's what I think. I believe he was enchanted by my mother, and I believe he loved her, in his way. She did not love him – she loved my father too much – but she was grateful, and I think she was probably scared. I have tried to imagine how she must have felt, having lost the love of her life, the man who shared everything she believed in. I think she would have married Liddicote, had he asked – for the security, if nothing else. But he did not ask, and having worked for him, I can imagine why. He was an ambitious man, and I think he probably saw how marriage to the widow of a conscientious objector – and remember, he didn't really lean towards pacifism until the success of *The Peaceful Little Warriors* – might stand between him and the recognition he craved. She was a liability.' She paused and caught her breath. 'And I think he probably regretted his decision for the rest of his life, though he was not the sort of man who would have taken action to make amends.'

'Yes, I can see that,' said Maisie. 'So you waited until your brothers and sister were mature enough to care for your mother, and you left to seek work with Greville Liddicote. And he didn't recognise you?'

'I would be amazed if he ever even really noticed me.'

'I would be amazed if he didn't, to tell you the truth.'

Alice shrugged.

'Did you think you could kill him?'

'I had anger enough, but when it came to it, there was no will in my heart. My parents had done a good job. I was a child on a mission to avenge a wrong, almost like in a fairy tale, but I don't know what I thought I could do. I don't know at all. I imagined hitting him over the head with a poker, or a vase, or putting poison in his tea.' She laughed, then tears came again. 'How stupid of me. But I earned money to send back to my family, and I came home once a month or so; if I was in service, they might not have seen me quite as much.' She picked at some grass alongside the sleeve of Maisie's jacket. 'And someone else did it, anyway. I think that, if I discovered anything, it was that Greville Liddicote was a very lonely man. I believe I almost felt sorry for him. All that passion for peace, and he was alone.'

Maisie allowed the silence to linger once again, and instead listened to the wheeling seagulls above, whose cry she suspected was a warning that stormy weather was moving in from the sea.

'Do you know who might have murdered Liddicote? You know, of course, that he did not die from a heart attack.'

Alice pulled a handkerchief from her pocket and wiped her eyes. 'There were people in and out all day, but I think he might have had one visitor who was not originally on his list of appointments, though I did not see him arrive.'

'Who was that?'

'Well, Dunstan Headley telephoned to ask if Dr Liddicote was in his office that day.' She looked away, as if gauging how fast the clouds were moving, and seemed distracted as she continued speaking. 'I said he was, and would he like me to make an appointment. He said no, that wasn't necessary, but he might send his son around with a message, or he might come himself. Then he told me not to worry, that he realised Dr Liddicote was busy – and he hung up the telephone without saying goodbye. I still don't know if he came or he didn't – and I wasn't in my office much that day; I seemed to be running all over the place with messages.'

Maisie felt the first large drops of rain splatter across her face and arms. She stood up, and looked at the dark clouds lumbering towards them. 'Come on, we'd better be off, and at a clip – look at those clouds!'

As they walked back towards the house, Maisie asked another question, though she knew she would doubtless have more later. It was clear that, as Rosemary Linden, the woman who strode alongside her had seen a lot more than she might have imagined while working as Greville Liddicote's secretary.

'Alice, what do you think of Dr Thomas?'

'Ah, the woman with the best-cut costumes in the college!' She smiled, and looked at Maisie. They had both broken into a run as the sky lit up with lightning. Alice began to count. 'One, two, three, four—' The clap of thunder followed, loud enough, Maisie thought, to crack the heavens. 'Oh dear,' said Alice, 'it's less than a mile behind us. Come on!'

As they ran into the house through the back door, Alice called out to her sister to ensure all their mother's belongings had been brought in. Ursula Thurlow was now sitting in an armchair in the low-beamed kitchen, and a kettle had been put on to boil. Maisie was thankful she had not pulled down the MG's cloth roof for the drive, for the motor car would have been drenched by now.

'There are warm towels hanging up there, Alice. Make sure you and Maisie dry your hair properly. We don't want you catching a cold this time of year, or you'll never shake it.'

They each took a towel to their wet hair and rubbed the rain away.

'Now you'll have to stay a while, Miss Dobbs. You can't be driving along our lanes in that little motor of yours.'

'Thank you, I would love to stay. In fact, I wanted to talk to you, Ursula, on two matters, actually. I have a very dear friend – Andrew Dene – he's an orthopaedic surgeon of some note and works closely with neurologists, given his standing and the nature of his speciality. I know he would be more than happy to see you. It would not cost a penny. I could arrange for you to go to London, it would be my pleasure.' Before Ursula could reply, Maisie added, 'I know it would take valuable energy, but we could make it a family affair, a trip to London for you and your children, perhaps a few days away to remember.'

The chair-bound woman looked at Maisie with her open face and wide deep brown eyes. 'What is it that you do, Miss Dobbs?'

Maisie smiled. She had half-expected the question. 'I am a teacher, Ursula. And I also work for the government. That is all I can say, and that is between us. Now, perhaps I can ask my second question.'

'You might as well.'

'I'd love to read more of your work – may I?'

When the storm had passed and taken with it the humidity of the previous week, Maisie left the Thurlows' cottage home. Alice accompanied her to the MG, though she had to answer several questions from Alfie, who had been hanging around, waiting to look inside the motor car. She thanked Alice for being so honest with her, for answering her questions, and they made a pact that each would keep the details of their conversation a secret between them, for she guessed it was now clear to Alice Thurlow that Maisie was not simply the junior lecturer in philosophy.

'Before I go, Alice, I want to remind you about the question I asked, just as the rain came.'

'Oh, yes, about Dr Thomas. You were asking what I thought of her.'

'That's right.'

'She's a dark horse, and I wonder if she doesn't have a life in London that none of us are aware of – she might be a dancer or something.'

'What makes you say that?'

'As soon as she leaves the college on a Friday, she goes straight to London, generally on the four-o'clock train. She sometimes misses a week here and there.'

'How do you know?'

'By paying attention, Maisie. If you pay attention, everyone has something they want to hide, even if it's going shopping in London.'

Maisie laughed. 'You're a very dark horse yourself, Rosemary Linden. And that reminds me – the police are aware that your personal file is missing. If it contains anything to inspire them to come to find this house, I'll allow you to remove it, but I'd like to take it back with me. Now go and tell your brother to hurry up, and I'll take him for a spin up to the crossroads.'

With Rosemary Linden's personal file in her briefcase, Maisie dropped Alfie at the crossroads. She noticed a telephone kiosk on the corner, so took the opportunity to place a call to Billy. She gazed out across fields of golden barley swaying in the breeze as she listened to his account of his work since they last spoke.

'I think I'm getting a bit closer, Miss. Reg Martin

wasn't there, but there was a new mechanic, taken on to replace Eric Tapley. I asked him when Reg would be back, but he said he'd gone off with a customer, that William Walling. I tried to get friendly with him, but he was being a bit careful, because he'd not long had the job. Mind you, he did say that he'd known Reg for a while, and that he wasn't as easygoing as he used to be. He put it down to the shock of Eric's accident, but Reg keeps telling him to check everything he works on: the tools, the block and tackle – everything.'

'Have you found out anything about this man, Walling?'

'He's in the shipping business, and he's apparently buying motor cars to send somewhere else. Mind you, if you asked five different people what he did, you'd get a different answer every time. I don't know, it all sounds fishy to me. He could be getting them cars checked so that they can be used on jobs where they don't want anything going wrong. Nothing like trying to get away from a jewellers you've just robbed and the motor won't start.'

Maisie didn't say anything for a moment. She had wanted Billy to take this case on his own, to build his confidence in his work. 'Billy, do you have a sense about it? If you had to guess, what do you think is happening?'

Billy wasted no time. 'Someone is leaning on Reg, and it's this man, Walling, the same one whose office young Sandra broke into. I reckon she put two and two together somewhere, and though she might've come up with the wrong number, I don't think she was entirely out of order. I reckon Reg is being squeezed, and there's a lot of it going on – remember, the villains over in the East End were quite happy about it when Alfie Mantle was put away; it opened up a lot of opportunities if you were running a racket. If I had to guess, I reckon that Reg was threatened, told that something would happen to his premises if he didn't toe the line in a certain way, and the accident with Eric was a warning that they meant business. Now, I don't know that he was meant to die, probably they did something to the block and tackle so that someone was hurt, but it didn't come off like that.'

'I think you're right. And about Sandra, have you found out any more about where she might be?'

'I've gone to all sorts of places, Miss. She mentioned that she used the lending library down Charing Cross Road, so I went there, and I dropped in at a couple of places she'd mentioned – that caff down on Oxford Street, the one you sometimes go to. No one'd seen her at all.'

'Right, we can't take any more chances. Here's what I want you to do – telephone Scotland Yard and speak to Detective Inspector Caldwell, and—'

'Aw, gawd, not him.'

'He's improved, Billy. If you remember, he was quite accommodating last time we had to work with him. As I said, now he's out from under Stratton's shadow, he's much better to liaise with. Tell him everything – and tell him I believe Sandra was on to something, and that there was a murder committed. But tell him he must find Sandra first. Be careful about how you tell him of our suspicions about Walling – the last thing we need is him throwing his weight around; I think he's had a quiet few months, so he'll probably jump on the opportunity to go after someone important.'

'Right you are, I'll do it now.'

'Good. And if you haven't done so already, telephone Mr Carter at Chelstone Manor – tell him you're calling for me – and ask if any of the staff who knew Sandra have any idea where she might be. I didn't ask before, because I know she lost touch, and of course I think there's only one or two who knew her left working there – the domestic staff don't seem to be staying on as much as they used to once upon a time.'

'Will do, Miss. When will I hear from you again?'

'Tomorrow morning. Before I go, how's Doreen?'

'Aching back, aching feet, aching head, fed up, bored, and wanting the baby to be born. Last weeks are always like that, according to the womenfolk.'

'Look after her, Billy – no need to stay later than you have to at the office.'

'I'll telephone Caldwell now.'

'And I'm off to find MacFarlane and Stratton.'

'Rather you than me.'

SIXTEEN

'Ah, Miss Dobbs, glad I've caught you.' Miss Hawthorne puffed into the office where Maisie was standing alongside the bank of pigeonholes, most of them bulging with papers from students as well as mail from outside the college. 'Yes, your students seem a keen lot, don't they? Looks like they've all been timely with their homework. Anyway, I digress – Dr Roth said to send you along to his office if you came into the college today. He wants to talk to you.'

'Me?'

'Yes, something about the debate, I think. Mind you, the only things anyone seems to be talking about at the moment are the debate and Dr Liddicote's death. Not a lot of joy there, eh?'

'I'll go along to his office now.'

'Right you are. That's one thing I can tick off my list of things to remember.'

Maisie could see the cleaners had been at work while the students were absent. Fragrant lavender polish had brought the oak floors and wainscoting along the corridors to a looking-glass shine, and she was careful not to slip as she made her way straight to Matthias Roth's office. She knocked, and entered when she heard his booming voice call out, 'Come!'

'Dr Roth. Miss Hawthorne said you wanted to speak to me.'

'Yes, indeed, do sit down.'

As he held out his hand to indicate that she should be seated, he removed his round spectacles and tapped his teeth with them, then, as was his habit, flicked back hair that had fallen forward and almost obscured his vision. Maisie realised that, apart from an intense regard for Liddicote – though they had crossed swords when it came to the debate – she had not garnered a sense of the man, other than observing his youthful mannerisms: the flicking back of an overlong lock of hair, and the way he walked along the corridors with a heel-to-toe bounce to his step.

'Miss Dobbs.' He paused, as if to frame his words with care. 'Miss Dobbs, I have been looking through staff files over the past few days.' He put on his spectacles again.

'Are you dissatisfied with my work?'

'No, not at all, not at all. Quite the contrary. Your students have come along well, and you are a popular teacher. You have taken part in extracurricular activities and have become part of our community here in a short time.' He rubbed his chin. 'Miss Dobbs, I realise you are acquainted with the two detectives through your former work, and that you telephoned them immediately Dr Liddicote's body was discovered. I have since read through your file, and I have to enquire as to whether you are here at the college in your professional capacity – you were the principal in a successful enquiry agency.' Another pause. 'Are you working with the police to get to the bottom of Greville Liddicote's death?'

Maisie shook her head. 'No.' Technically it was the truth. She had been told that she had her own brief, and that MacFarlane was in charge of the murder investigation. 'I know the chief superintendent, but I am not working for him with regard to his enquiries here.'

'I see. But you're interested in Greville Liddicote, aren't you?'

'Yes, I am.' Maisie did not need to feign an honest interest in her subject. 'What he did in building this college, bringing his dream to fruition is inspiring. I have read some of his work, specifically his children's books, so the whole story is quite compelling – a man who is cast out of Cambridge University, given the controversial nature of his work, which may or may not have caused men to mutiny on the Western Front. The "peace" college he has envisioned grows with the help of parents of men who went to war but who later read his book and were persuaded to lay down arms.' She sighed. 'If nothing else,

Greville Liddicote could sell an idea; however, he drew back from support of the debate, which one would think represents a certain pinnacle of achievement – not to mention the achievement of acceptance by the university establishment when they extended an invitation for a young college to present a team at an annual debate that always draws the attentions of the press.' She looked at Roth, her line of questioning clearly unsettling him. 'Why do you think he was against the idea, Dr Roth? And, more to the point, why have you maintained that he supported it as much as you – and please do not deny my assertion; I was outside the door of his office and heard the argument.'

'He was wrong to want to decline the invitation.'

'Why?'

'Because the debate will be the making of the college. We wouldn't be the first college to gladly relinquish our independence when asked to join the university – and inclusion in the debate, as well as other collaborations, promised a move in the right direction. Greville allowed his fears to overwhelm him.'

'What fears?' Maisie was leaning forward now, her body relaxed just enough to suggest empathy for Roth's position.

'The subject matter is controversial, because it begs the question as to whether Germany's Nazi Party should receive our support when it comes to power – as it surely will. On the one hand, the university's colleges can better weather the storms that might come from supporting such a motion, if that is the outcome of the debate. On the other, Greville was concerned about the effect the debate might have on our very diverse student community. We all get along very well, but he thought it would drive a wedge between the cultures represented here. If you are familiar with Herr Hitler's book, *Mein Kampf*, you will know that he has a particularly vociferous position when it comes to what he describes as "the Jewish peril". Greville was concerned that the debate might be offensive to our students who are Jewish.'

'Those fears seem grounded to me, Dr Roth,' said Maisie.

'But we must not draw back, especially if our team is on the side of peace, of reconciliation, of going forward with an olive branch.'

Maisie sat back in the chair again, wondering how to couch her words. 'You have Robson Headley on the team, and—'

'Miss Dobbs, you are a junior member of staff, and if you have not realised this already, I will tell you. The college depends upon the support of those who believe in our mission here, especially in terms of monies with which to build for the future. We have to prepare for challenges to our curriculum. Many of our students, though graduates in their own countries, are still young and impressionable – they have come here, or been sent by parents, in the belief that they will play a part in maintaining what is a fragile peace, much like a stone thrown into the lake, sending out ripples, only we hope those ripples become waves.' He cleared his throat, removed the spectacles a second time, and cleaned the lenses with his handkerchief, replacing the spectacles as he continued. 'Robson Headley expressed a desire to be part of the team, and will lead our students in their debates. I concede that he may be the indulged son of a wealthy man, but his father has in turn indulged us and never questioned how his money is spent in this college, only that we continue our work.'

Maisie bit her lip. Did Roth know of Headley's connection to the *Ortsgruppe*? If she told him, he might deduce not only that she was making enquiries, but that they were quite separate from the police investigation led by MacFarlane. Should she ask about Delphine Lang? She was not sure how to proceed and retain the integrity of her work, but she knew she had to take the conversation further.

'Are you aware that Mr Headley is involved romantically with Miss Lang?'

Roth raised an eyebrow. 'I am. However, they seem to have conducted their liaison away from the college premises, so I am not concerned unduly. I might if it comes to a sticky end, as these things often do.'

'Are you concerned that Headley might put some pressure on you to reinstate Miss Lang's contract, so that his son is not upset by her departure?'

Roth smiled and shook his head. 'Not at all, Miss Dobbs. In confidence – and I must insist that you keep this knowledge under your hat – Miss Lang is leaving the college because Mr Dunstan Headley did *not* want her contract renewed. It is the only time he has ever stepped forward with a request, which was put to Greville before he died. Of course, he agreed.'

'Do you know the reason for his request?'

'He did not like her. Personally, I believe he did not care for the fact that she is Austrian by birth, but I am sure you understand the implications of my observation; it could render my own position here somewhat tenuous, though I believe I have enjoyed a cordial relationship with Mr Headley thus far. Miss Lang has been very upset, and I can understand why.'

Maisie nodded. She came back to another subject, one that had continued to nip at her heels since she began the investigation. 'Dr Roth, we've talked about Dr Liddicote's book inciting men to mutiny in France, and I wondered if you'd had any more . . . recollections. I have become interested in his work, and when I speak to others about it – I know a few booksellers, for example – there are always mutterings about a mutiny.'

Roth sighed. 'I will tell you this, and then let that be the end of it.' He scraped his chair back across the polished wood floor, stood up, and began to pace, his arms folded across his chest. As he spoke, he looked up occasionally to meet Maisie's eyes with his own. 'Greville Liddicote's book caused a massive mutiny – however, it was not limited to the British line. As you may know, in places, the distance between the German and British front lines was mere yards. There was often some sort of fraternisation across the lines, though when battle commenced it was terrible, terrible. But there was a knowledge that we were all in it at the behest of our betters, so sometimes a word went back and forth, a "*Guten Morgen*" or a "Mornin', all." The book was read by soldiers, and even those who could not read knew the story. Then a copy of the book made its way across, and one day someone attached a note saying that it was about time the fathers went home to their children. Of course, many young men did not have children, but it was as if they suddenly envisioned the children they might have if the war were over. So the few soldiers who walked away from the war were just the beginning; it turned into a massive mutiny on both sides, and at once that few yards of no man's land became a great distance as troops drew back. I was one of those soldiers, Miss Dobbs, though my wound saved me from the fate of execution. In truth, very few were executed, on either side – there were too many to lose – but Dunstan Headley's son lost his life. So, we were all joined, you see, by this event, which was initiated by one very brave man with a pen and paper. Such men do not come along very often, Miss Dobbs, and they are the true heroes. Greville Liddicote was my hero.' He stopped in front of her. 'Your government and my government will never admit this happened. It will be held secret, and if revealed, it will be long after you and I are gone from this world. So, it would be as well if what I have said remains between us, held within the walls of this room.'

Maisie promised discretion on her part, but she had

another question. 'Dunstan Headley is a remarkable man, to have managed to forgive Dr Liddicote for the story that effectively killed his son – don't you think?'

Roth shrugged. 'I'm not sure that he ever really forgave him. I think he has had to work hard at rising above his grief to contribute in such a way. And he knew, I am sure, that Dr Liddicote struggled with his responsibility.'

'Are you saying he disliked Dr Liddicote?'

'Oh, I am sure that in the deep recesses of his soul he hated him.'

They were both silent for a moment. Then Maisie spoke again.

'And you don't think Robson Headley might be a risk, given that he is something of a headstrong young man?'

Roth smiled and shook his head. 'Miss Dobbs, I really cannot see—'

'He is a Nazi, Dr Roth. Robson Headley and Delphine Lang are members of a group who support the National Socialist Party in Germany. That may seem rather innocuous at the present time, but I believe—'

'And how do you know this?' Roth's cheeks were now flushed with colour.

'I happened to overhear them talking.'

He regained his composure and appeared to brush off the news. 'Well, it will make for an interesting debate, I am sure. Now, if you will excuse me, Miss Dobbs. I would imagine you are using your free time this week to plan your tutorials for the coming weeks. I expect to join one of your classes next week.'

'Thank you, Dr Roth. I look forward to it.'

'And remember, Miss Dobbs, I have asked you not to reveal any aspect of our conversation to anyone. Even your friends at Scotland Yard.'

Walking back to her lodgings, Maisie found she could hardly remain focused on one element of her work, without another coming to the fore. She wanted to talk to Billy, so waited by the telephone kiosk while an elderly man shouted into the receiver at whoever it was he had called. Instead of pressing in more coins to extend the call and then pressing button A, the man shoved the coins home and then thumped the button, followed by a clout to the side of the coin box, as if an assault on the inner workings of telephony would yield more minutes for his money. Eventually he ended the call, whereupon he replaced the receiver, took out his handkerchief, and gave his nose a good blow before leaving the kiosk.

'All yours,' he said to Maisie, as he held the door open for her to enter.

She kept the door ajar with her foot to allow fresh air to circulate, pulled her own handkerchief from her shoulder bag, and wiped the receiver from top to bottom. It was still sticky from the man's heated grasp. She dialled the number and waited, pressing button A as soon as the telephone was answered on the other end.

'Miss?'

'Billy, so glad I've caught you – but you're at the office late.'

'I thought you'd be on the dog and bone to me soon, and I wanted to be here. I'll leave soon enough. I don't like to be too late, on account of Doreen being so close to her time.'

'Yes, you should get home as soon as we've finished. Not long now before you'll be in that house in Eltham.'

'Can't wait, to tell you the truth. Anyway, I've spoken to Caldwell.'

'How was he?'

'Not bad, bit of an edge to him, but he softened up when he realised I was calling because we needed help, and that there might be a case in it for him – he's still on the lookout to make his mark.'

'I would've thought he had plenty to be getting on with.'

'He has, but, like I said, he wants to be as well known and regarded as Stratton.'

'Well, I reckon Stratton might be having second thoughts about his move. In any case, what did he say?'

'He's going to sniff around, but he said something interesting before he even started. Apparently, this bloke who Reg has been doing that work for, the one whose office Sandra broke into, has been kept under surveillance by the watchful eye of the CID for a while – the fraud boys and the flying squad up until now. But word's gone around at the Yard, mainly because he's got a finger in so many pies, all cooked up by these supposedly clean businesses of his.'

'Why are they keeping an eye on him?'

'Because he's been moving in on other manors, and there's been some – what did Caldwell call it? Something official-sounding, like "villain on villain aggravation".'

'I see, but that doesn't explain what Sandra might have found out about him, except that he might have been trying to make a point with Reg, and it went wrong when Eric was killed. Or perhaps it went right.'

'There's a bit more than that to it all. Apparently, his mother is Spanish, name of Mendoza, which accounts for the fact that he had a touch of the Rudolph Valentino about him when he was younger. He's got family over there in Spain. I've been talking to a few people, and there's word on the street that he's putting the screws on his runners to do more business, and he's asking more for protection, that sort of thing. They say he's sending money over there, for something or another.'

'Have you told Caldwell?'

'I've told him everything I know, and in return, he's got people out looking for our Sandra.'

'Do you know how he's doing it?'

'Well, he's got informers, friends, if you like, among the ladies of the night, and—'

'Oh, I don't think Sandra would—'

'You don't know what someone might do who was desperate, Miss. Especially a young woman who can't feel anything any more. But that's not it. It's a case of scratching each other's backs – they look out for someone wanted by the police, or they hear of something, and then they get left alone for a while, no moving on or that sort of thing. And I've been asking around the hostels, but nothing yet.'

322

'Oh, dear.'

'Caldwell listened to everything I had to say, Miss. He said that there's no smoke without a fire, and that he'll look into matters at Reg Martin's garage and have a word with Reg himself. To be honest, Miss, I saw Reg and he don't half look pale, not the man he was. He told me that, if he could, he would pack it in and go back to working on coaches and carts, but that there was no business in it now, what with the number of motors on the road and everyone saying there won't be any horses left in London in ten years' time.'

'I wish she'd just get in touch with us. I wish she would come out of hiding.'

'On another matter, Miss.'

'What's that, Billy?'

'That secretary woman at the Compton Corporation telephoned – Miss Robinson; she said to tell you that you should come over to pick up some mail that's been sent from Canada for you. She said you're expected.'

'That's a funny way of putting it.' Maisie sighed. 'Oh well, I'll drop by on Friday, I can't leave Cambridge until the debate is over.'

'The what?'

'Debate. It's part of a series of debates with the Cambridge colleges that the College of St Francis has been asked to join. Our team will be on the spot tomorrow. Then I'll come down on Friday.'

'Right you are, Miss. I'll keep in touch. Don't mind me telling you, I wouldn't be surprised if our family weren't bigger by one sooner rather than later.'

'Oh, I hoped the baby would wait until you were in the new house.'

'I doubt if it will wait when it comes – after all, it's our fourth.'

Maisie heard the words catch as Billy spoke. Their third child had been Lizzie, now buried in the local churchyard.

'Take care of Doreen, Billy. I'll be in touch.'

As Maisie left the telephone kiosk, a black motor car drew up alongside her, the door swung open, and Stratton stepped out.

'You were looking for us?'

'Oh, yes. I'm glad you stopped.'

Maisie seated herself in the back, next to MacFarlane. Stratton pulled down a seat opposite them and tapped on the window for the driver to continue on.

'The sun's over the yardarm somewhere in the Empire, so we thought we'd drop in for a swift one at the local – join us?'

Maisie smiled at MacFarlane. 'Thank you for asking, but I really must be getting back to my lodgings.'

'Making progress?'

'Putting the pieces into place. You?'

'No, not really. Can't seem to get any purchase on the mountain of interviews and who saw this and who saw that. You would have thought the whole college was comatose while Greville Liddicote was murdered.'

'Colleges can be fairly soporific places in the afternoons – and I am being absolutely serious. Whoever walked in with the intention of taking Liddicote's life chose the right time. Classes were in progress, the secretary was out and about in the building somewhere, and a sort of daze comes over the place, no matter how hard one tries to chivvy students along in their work.'

'That much is obvious,' Stratton interjected, looking at Maisie. 'Have you discovered anything that might help us?'

Maisie nodded. 'Yes, I have, I think. Both Delphine Lang and Robson Headley were familiar with Chinese methods of martial art. I know I should have mentioned this before, but I discovered that they have both spent time in the Orient: Lang in China when her father was assigned a position there, and Headley when his father chose to situate the family in Hong Kong after the war. His company had a lot of business there, so when Dunstan wanted to try to put the older son's death behind them, that's where he took his wife and son.'

'Would you consider them suspects?' asked Stratton.

'At this point I wouldn't rule them out.'

'Anyone else?' MacFarlane asked, then he leant forward and tapped on the window. They had arrived at the pub where the detective chief superintendent would have his 'swift one'.

'Not yet, but perhaps by Saturday I might have a name or two for you.' Maisie noticed that MacFarlane had not admonished her again for looking into the issue of Liddicote's death.

'You don't want to give us an inkling – or is this

something else you're going to keep to yourself?' Stratton raised his eyebrows as he asked the question.

'I don't want to implicate someone who might be far from a murderer.'

MacFarlane instructed the driver to take Maisie to her lodgings, where she went straight to her room and spread the case map across the desk. She drew a line between several names, jotted in another, and stood back to consider her work. She noted information she had gleaned from the young woman known as Rosemary Linden, and added a line under Francesca Thomas' name. Tomorrow she would attend the debate, and on Friday she would drive to London. A conversation with Miss Hawthorne revealed that Dr Thomas had mentioned arriving in London mid-morning to conduct research for her paper at the British Library. Knowing that the best liars often disguise their tales with an element of truth, Maisie planned to be outside Liverpool Street station by mid-morning at the latest. And this time she was determined not to lose her.

Maisie left her landlady's bicycle tethered to a tree some yards from the Cambridge Union, then stood to watch the audience of students and academic staff file into the venue for the first debate. She noticed a couple of men she thought to be journalists, and then saw a deep-maroon motor car draw up outside.

Dunstan Headley emerged from the vehicle, followed by his son and Matthias Roth. Some of the onlookers were craning their heads to see who the important guests might be, and as Maisie scanned the line of people, she saw Delphine Lang, alone, waiting along with everyone else.

A contingent of supporters from the College of St Francis waved their green scarves in the air, and soon Maisie caught sight of Francesca Thomas. She was not queuing with the students but had drawn back as if to watch the opening salvo of a battle. She was smoking a cigarette, and when she was ready to enter the building, she threw it to the ground to extinguish the smouldering tobacco. Maisie smiled as she watched her deftly flick the half-smoked cigarette to the ground.

Offering apologies to those already seated, Maisie squeezed into a place close to the end of one of the long red-leather seats, some rows back from the benches where the debating teams were situated. She had a fair view of the lectern, and, in her estimation, the debate teams seemed as comfortable as they would be while anticipating victory for their college. The hall was full; other debates would soon be under way at other university locations, but in the draw the College of St Francis had been fortunate in being selected to present their case in the home of debate at the University of Cambridge.

Soon the Union's president stood to introduce the teams and the motion, and invited the first speaker from the College of St Francis to speak. Maisie was surprised to see that it was one of her own students, and she leant forward to better hear his arguments for the adoption of a national socialism in Britain, based upon the tenets of the National Socialist Party in Germany. She thought his reasoning, while somewhat idealistic, showed a good deal of preparation, and he presented his points in a manner that was succinct and accessible to an audience comprising quite a few people from outside the many colleges in the city. And she would have been disappointed if he had not demonstrated such idealism, for he was yet to reach twenty-one; youth without optimism, without a strong sense of the possible, would represent a very sad state of affairs. As she listened, she realised how much she had invested in her work at the college – on behalf of her students, and in the service of His Majesty's government. She was enjoying the former more than she might have imagined, despite the distractions of her remit.

The young man spent some twenty minutes making his argument, and ended with a statement that brought with it a round of enthusiastic applause. 'National Socialism is the way. There is no other political philosophy that will deliver us from the social stranglehold of our system of lords and serfs, and there is no other party that would protect our shores, while bringing prosperity and security to those of Anglo-Saxon stock.' He bowed to the audience, some of whom were on their feet before being called to order.

The student representing the opposition took his turn at the lectern, and proceeded to press the beliefs his team represented, that National Socialism was Fascism by any other name, with a sole purpose to undermine British life as it had been lived for centuries. Again the student spoke for twenty minutes, and seemed distracted as he pushed his spectacles back up towards the bridge of his nose, then fiddled with them as they slipped down again. He thumped the lectern at one point, and looked directly at the next speaker, Robson Headley, who seemed relaxed as he lounged with one leg crossed over the other, a hand resting on the back of the leather-backed bench. Maisie was surprised to notice that Delphine Lang had managed to sit behind Headley. Dunstan Headley was at the end of the same row, and did not seem pleased – he was glaring at Lang.

Robson Headley was invited to the lectern to give a closing argument on behalf of his team. He stood as if he had all the time in the world, and moved to the place vacated by the opposition's first representative. He opened a paper that Maisie supposed he might refer to, and at that moment she felt a tremor of foreboding. She looked into his eyes and saw a flash of something she could not have put into words. Was it a look of resolution, of vehemence, of blind adherence to his beliefs? Was it defiance? She sensed that he was not about to give a speech with a view to winning the debate with honour, but instead had stepped up with an intention to set the hall afire with his rhetoric – and she hoped that she was wrong. It was as if that foreboding had leeched under her skin and into her bones, because as Headley began to speak, she felt fear grip her heart.

While he repeated many of the main arguments that his

fellow team member had put forward, there was a passion to his words that both attracted and repelled the audience over the course of his allotted twenty minutes. As he spoke, repeatedly hitting his fist against the lectern with every point made, Maisie saw people sitting on the edge of their seats, leaning forward over the balcony; many appeared intimidated, glancing at exits, as if ready to run. Robson Headley thumped the lectern again.

'My argument, gentlemen, is that our country deserves nothing less than national socialism, and that if we had the opportunity we would be well served by a man such as Herr Adolf Hitler standing for our nation as our leader.' He paused, his eyes roaming up to the balcony, and then to the gallery behind him. 'I can make no more forthright statement on behalf of the motion than the following.' He stood to one side, snapped his heels and raised his right hand in a straight-armed salute. 'Heil Hitler!'

Maisie put her head in her hands, but looked up again when a female voice echoed Robson Headley. 'Heil Hitler!' Delphine Lang stood to attention. And Dunstan Headley stared at his son with a deep disdain, and then at Lang with a hatred so fierce, Maisie thought Lang must feel as if she had been burnt. The elder Headley turned and left the hall, which had erupted in a mixture of boos and cheers. Maisie looked along the row of seats to Matthias Roth, who sat motionless. She could see he was in a state of shock. And then he, too, left the hall, though in his eyes there was not hatred, but tears of deep sorrow.

Maisie left her seat and walked to the exit, turning once to look upon Robson Headley as he swaggered back to his seat. She did not care if the motion was carried or not, whether the opposing team's second speaker made a good argument or failed to carry the day. She had already seen much that she thought was not in the interests of the country she had served in a war still too easily remembered.

SEVENTEEN

Maisie had walked for some time following her departure from the Union. She meandered along the grassy verges of the Backs and had eventually found her way to a vantage point from which she could look out upon the spires and towers of the city and be soothed by their silhouettes, bathed in the deep-orange glow of the setting sun. And later, having collected the bicycle, and returned to her lodgings, she sat by her window in darkness, staring out into a purplish-black night sky embellished as if someone had thrown jewels to the heavens with abandon. She could not remember many starry nights as a child, but occasionally the coverlet of fog seemed to draw back and her father would point out the constellations. 'There's the Plough, Maisie – see?' And his hand would sweep across her line of vision, tracing the outline of a cluster of stars so she could see the shape. Now she tried to make sense of all that had come to pass since she arrived at the College of St Francis.

She had read parts of the book written by the leader of Germany's National Socialist Party, but was disturbed by so much of what he had laid down under the title *Mein Kampf.* And when she saw again, in her mind's eye, the vision of Robson Headley standing with his hand held high in salute, and the light in his eyes as he shouted his allegiance, she remembered a line that she had marked in the book. *The broad masses of the people are more amenable to the appeal of rhetoric than to any other force.* Huntley had seemed almost indifferent to her concerns regarding the activities of Nazi supporters in Britain, though she understood that at least one person in his midst had also raised an alarm. There were those who were impressed by the leader, not least Britain's own advocates of Fascism, and she was dismayed that so many of those people seemed to be in positions of some influence.

But what about Dunstan Headley? She doodled his name on the case map in front of her, then tapped her pencil on the paper, absently creating a cluster of grey dots spiralling in and out, in and out, as if following the pattern of a snail shell. Dunstan Headley was an angry man. Robson was almost entirely dependent upon his father for financial support, and she had little doubt that Headley Senior might choose to turn the screw on his son by withholding money unless he agreed to toe a particular line.

Maisie rubbed her eyes and stood up; it was the early

hours of the morning and she finally felt ready to go to bed. When she looked down at the case map, she realised that she had, without thinking, been inscribing the names *Robson Headley – Dunstan Headley – Delphine Lang* time and again in circles across a section of the paper.

The following morning – Friday – Maisie arrived at Liverpool Street station at half past nine, drove into the gate marked 'Way in for Cabs', and parked the MG. She hurried inside to check the arrival times of trains from Cambridge, then returned and moved the vehicle along so that she was not obstructing the cabbies, and that afforded her a view of people exiting the station and setting off again in taxi-cabs. The day was cool and there was a light rain beyond the canopy of the station, for which she was somewhat glad. Waiting in the heat of the day would not be comfortable, though this kind of surveillance always seemed to hurt somewhere in her body. She changed her position frequently, once or twice getting out of the motor car to walk up and down for a few steps, until she noticed a surge of passengers exiting the station, and took her place behind the wheel again. At one point a policeman came to ask why she was waiting for so long, and she explained that she was expecting a friend who'd had an accident and was using crutches. The constable laughed and made a comment to the effect that he wished her good luck getting the friend in the two-seater tourer. The exchange was light, but Maisie knew he might come along again and move her on. Another hour passed and another surge of passengers streamed out, then thinned, and at once she saw a woman whom she believed to be Francesca Thomas. The woman stopped for a second to survey the line of people waiting outside, then walked to a taxi-cab and climbed in. Maisie could not be completely sure it was her, but she knew she had to take a chance. She was slipping the MG into gear when the constable knocked on the window again.

'Still waiting, Miss? You've been here a bit now.'

'I think she must have missed her train, constable. Not to worry, I'll get my motor out of the way and telephone her mother.'

'I'll keep an eye on your motor if you want to run in—'

'Oh, I'm sure she should have been here by now. Thank you! I'll be off now.'

And with that, Maisie stepped on the accelerator pedal, anxious to catch up with the taxi-cab carrying the woman she believed to be Thomas.

'Blast! Where *are* you?'

People were crossing the road, and traffic seemed to be converging on the station from all directions. 'Blast!' she said again, striking the steering wheel with her hand. Then the crowd parted for a horse and cart to come through, and she realised that the taxi cab had stopped not far in front of her. A coster had tipped his barrow and was hurrying to load up the fallen fruit and vegetables. Some people stopped to help, for traffic was snarling up, and Maisie saw the cabbie lean out and shake his fist at the coster.

'You shouldn't be on the bleeding road with that old nag.'

'Don't you call this 'orse a nag, you and that filthy thing you're driving there. Scum of the earth on the streets, you are.'

The taxi driver was about to get out, when Maisie saw the silhouette of the passenger inside lean forward, as if to caution him. In time, the horse and cart moved on, the coster shaking his fist back at the cabbie, and traffic began to snake along once more. Maisie's doubts about following the right taxi-cab and whether indeed the passenger was Francesca Thomas were laid to rest when the journey took them closer to Belgravia. They soon approached Eaton Square, at the same point at which the driver she was with before had lost her quarry. Now she realised why. The taxi-cab's route was circuitous, along smaller parallel streets and cutting back and forth. With traffic easing as they moved into the maze of thoroughfares, Maisie drew back, but kept the black vehicle in sight as it returned to Eaton Place. The driver stopped, and Maisie pulled over at a distance, in the shade of a tree in the square. Francesca Thomas alighted the taxi-cab, paid the fare, then walked along the street and entered one of the grand mansions. Maisie watched and waited for the taxi-cab to be on its way again before slipping the MG into gear and parking on the other side of the square. Pulling her cloche hat down close to her eyes, she walked back to the mansion Francesca Thomas had entered. She looked up at the building, then back and forth along the street, and at that point a man wearing a black suit, white shirt, and bowler hat, and carrying an umbrella, walked towards her. When he was just a couple of steps away, Maisie smiled in his direction.

'Excuse me, sir – may I trouble you for a moment? Do you know this area?'

The man nodded. 'Yes. I work here.'

'You work here?' Maisie had detected a slight accent.

'Yes, many of the buildings along here are leased; this is the Belgian Embassy – though of course we haven't quite taken over the whole square.'

'I see.' Maisie looked up at the building again.

'Can I help you, or did you simply want to know who resided in the square?'

'Oh, no. No, I wanted to know how to get to Victoria station.'

The man proceeded to give precise directions to Victoria, and then with a doffing of his bowler hat, went on his way. With a final look at the building – and an overwhelming sense that she was a fly in a spider's web – Maisie turned to walk away.

'Miss Dobbs!'

Francesca Thomas was standing between the two columns that flanked the mansion's entrance. A man was standing behind her, as if to protect the building and its occupants.

'Dr Thomas.' Maisie pushed up her cloche a little so their eyes could meet, and approached the woman whom she had followed from Liverpool Street station.

Francesca Thomas smiled. It was a wry smile, as if she had seen the funny side of a quip that no one else had quite

338

picked up on. 'Having made such a determined effort to follow me, I think the least we can do is to offer some sort of refreshment. Would you care to join me?'

Maisie nodded. 'Thank you, Dr Thomas. That's very kind of you.'

She led Maisie past the threshold, nodding to the man at the door, who stepped out to look up and down the street before closing the door behind him. They continued across the expansive hallway, up the wide staircase, then along a corridor and into a small room. As they walked along, Maisie noticed that the interior of the mansion bore few comforts. It was, without doubt, a place of work, with plain cream paintwork and no decoration but for portraits of Albert I, King of the Belgians, and his wife, Elisabeth of Bavaria.

'This is the office I use when I am here.' Francesca Thomas held out her hand to one of the beige damask-covered armchairs set in front of a fireplace masked by a needlepoint screen for the summer – the only colour in a room that was as plain as the hall, staircase, and corridor. Maisie thought the office might be more welcoming in winter, with a fire in the grate.

'It seems I have been rather careless, that you have managed to find me here.'

'You had no need to come to the door, Dr Thomas. I may have discovered that the embassy is a frequent destination for your sorties into London, but I confess, I did not quite know what to do with that knowledge – not yet, anyway.'

'But you have an idea of what I am doing here, don't you?'

Maisie took off her hat and ran a hand through her hair. 'I know this much, that you worked for the British Secret Service during the war. I know that you left after a time, and you did not surface in England again until you applied for the job at the College of St Francis.'

Thomas nodded slowly. 'And why are *you* at the college, Miss Dobbs? Oh, and do credit me with some sense – please do not tell me it's for the love of teaching philosophy.'

Maisie regarded the woman seated before her. She was at ease, confident. Her dress was stylish, yet simple – a tailored black skirt and jacket, a white blouse. She was a striking woman, and Maisie could see that she was also one who would brook no subterfuge and would recognise a lie if she heard it.

'I have found that I really do like teaching – but I came to the college to identify any activities not in the interests of the British government.'

'Don't forget the Crown. You have to look out for the Crown, you know.'

'Yes, of course, *not in the interests of the Crown.*' Maisie maintained eye contact with her interrogator. 'And you? In whose interests are you at the college?'

'Belgium. Among others, of course. Our country suffered occupation in the war and we do not want it to happen again, if we can possibly help it. I have been charged with keeping an eye on developments in this country with regard to our former enemies.'

'Developments in *this* country?'

'Let's not start by being naïve, Miss Dobbs, unless you really are without a clue as to what is happening here. You are aware of the *Ortsgruppe*, for example, and their London meetings at Cleveland Terrace.'

'I saw you there, too, Dr Thomas. Only you were dressed as a man.'

'What gave me away, if I may ask?'

'Your cigarette; the way you held it and discarded the remains after barely smoking half.'

'You're an observant one, after all. I'll give you that.' She leant forward, her elbows on her knees, her hands clasped, as if she wanted to let Maisie in on a tightly held secret. 'The infiltration of universities and other such institutions is only one stream of the threat. Your aristocracy, members of your government, indeed, the heir to your throne – they are all quite taken with this man Adolf Hitler. But we know better, we—'

'Dr Thomas, why do you say we? I was informed at the college that you were of Anglo-Swiss parentage.'

'My maternal grandmother was Belgian. I adored her, and I was close to my family there.' She sighed. 'I am willing to brief you on my involvement in the security of my country; however, I must have your word that you will not divulge any detail – not a single crumb of information – of what you will hear to another. Even Brian Huntley.'

Maisie looked into the woman's eyes, her surprise upon hearing Huntley's name masked by an outer calm. And at that moment she saw a shadow of deep sorrow and remembered a conversation with Maurice about the old proverb 'Eyes are the windows to the soul.' She thought, now, that if it were indeed so, then Francesca Thomas had chosen this time to slip the lock on her past and allow memories to escape. Instinct told her that what had come to pass in this woman's earlier years would chill her to the bone.

'You have my word.'

'As you know, I worked for the Secret Intelligence Service here in London. There were many departments that fell under the auspices of the broader security organisation, and I worked in several different ones. I don't know if this will surprise you, but many, many women worked for the Secret Service – tens of thousands in London alone.'

'I was not aware that such numbers were involved.'

'The men were off fighting; and if they weren't, and they happened to be able-bodied, they were under suspicion anyway. Of course there were some rather tedious jobs there – intercepting mail from overseas, breaking codes, and so on; but at the same time, women were working on matters of great significance.' Thomas paused. 'The interesting thing is that one wasn't heavily interrogated prior to being offered a job. They were more interested in where you were educated, who your father was, and what you could do for them. In any case, as time went on, and more and more intelligence was coming through about the situation in Belgium, I realised I wanted to be with my family there. I wanted to save them.' She gave a half-laugh and looked away for a few seconds before continuing. 'There were intelligence groups working all over the Low Countries and northern France, and I thought I would make a good soldier – I was young, I speak several languages fluently, and I was filled with a desire to do more than sit at a desk and go through letters that might be coded.'

'How did you get to Belgium?'

'By parting with some money – a good deal of money, actually. I resigned my position and was smuggled into the country and to my grandmother's house. I speak both Dutch and French Flemish, so I could easily blend into the community. And it didn't take me long to make contact with a group of what you might call resistance agents. Then in 1917 I joined a somewhat new organisation called *La Dame Blanche* – The White Lady. It was a highly structured movement – we were organised along military lines – and we were financed by the British government.'

Maisie nodded. She remembered seeing a folder labelled '*La Dame Blanche*' inside a box in the cellar of the Dower House. She had assumed it was something to do with Maurice's family.

'You might be interested to know that women of all ages were part of *La Dame Blanche* – our leaders were aware that the men could all be captured, rounded up, so there was a plan in place for the work to continue if that happened.'

'What did you do?'

'As soldiers – for that is what we were, what we

considered ourselves to be – we were responsible for almost every kind of intelligence work, up to and including assassination, if that was what the job required.' She leant forward again. 'You must understand, Miss Dobbs, many of our number also held down jobs; they were teachers, doctors, farm workers, shop assistants. Children as young as eight or nine, and elders in their eighties all played a part. Intelligence was filtered via British contacts, or through the Netherlands in particular.' She paused, picking a speck of lint from her cuff with perfectly manicured nails. 'Our agents hardly slept – they reported on troop movements, they committed acts of sabotage, and they consorted with the enemy, if they had to. They gave their lives so thousands could be spared.'

Maisie nodded, waiting for the words to come with which to frame a question or make a comment. 'Such bravery is often forgotten when peace is restored and lives and communities are rebuilt.'

'Those who gave their lives are never forgotten, though. We have, both of us, experienced death in wartime, Miss Dobbs, and I am determined to do all I can to see that it does not happen again. The shadow of The White Lady lingers, ready to be reconstituted and put into service if necessary. My job, at the moment, is to coordinate intelligence from our people around Europe regarding the activities of various groups who threaten a fragile peace – and, of course, I am a lecturer at the College of St Francis, which is certainly an interesting place to be at the moment.'

'You were at the debate last night.'

'Yes, and what a debacle for Matthias! Poor Matthias – he wants so much to be an instrument of peace, to live by the Prayer of St Francis, but he is somewhat misguided when it comes to the motivations of certain people.'

'Robson Headley?'

She shook her head. 'Headstrong Headley and his lover, the very spoilt Miss Lang.'

'You think they're dangerous?'

'They are dangerous with their rhetoric, and they are dangerous in who they know and consort with – which is why they came to my attention. But you must realise, Miss Dobbs, that the college was of interest to me not because of some of the people within the establishment, but due to its placement. It's a good viewing platform for a town of many colleges, and, through academic affiliations, has also given me access to other such places around the country.'

'Do you have any idea who murdered Greville Liddicote?'

'I know he wasn't universally liked, though he tried his best – and he did very well, in fact, if you look at the college – to overcome past mistakes.' She leant back in her chair. 'Liddicote was a man of contradictions. He was not in favour of the war – we discussed this on several occasions – and he thought there should have been a more concerted effort on the part of our government to bring an end to the conflict; it was so bloody pointless. And at the same time, he was an expert on medieval literature, and he wrote his children's books. He was drawn to some artistically inclined people who are quite well known, Miss Dobbs, and he wanted recognition. So even though his motivations were true enough, that desire led to him making more than a few errors of judgement – and ultimately, he lied.'

'Who do you think hated him?'

'His secretary, for a start. Miss Rosemary Linden – though we both know that's not her real name. She would have liked to see him dead.'

'Anyone else?'

'Dunstan Headley – but then Dunstan Headley doesn't care for many people, especially women. In fact, Headley is something of a woman-hater.'

'A woman-hater?'

'Yes. He hates the idea of women in any position of responsibility. He is so filled with hatred and anger over the death of his eldest son, he doesn't know how to live with himself. He blamed his first wife for his son enlisting in the army – don't believe what you might have heard about her dying, she left him for an army officer when their son was young. Apparently the boy joined the army to make his mother proud, something of that order. It was his second wife who committed the sin of dying on him, hence the complete indulgence you see in Robson. He hates Delphine Lang, given her Austrian parentage; I would like to be a fly on the wall in the Headley household today.'

'Yes, he seemed about to explode at the debate yesterday.'

'And he'll definitely explode if he discovers that she was only offered the job in the first place because she's Roth's niece – his sister's daughter. Roth can't be happy about having to send her home to her parents, and I bet he's none too pleased about Robson Headley, either.'

Maisie nodded. 'Oh, of course! That explains Roth's affection for Lang,' said Maisie.

Thomas inclined her head to acknowledge the piece of information clicking into the puzzle for Maisie. She said nothing for a while, then went on. 'You've found Miss Linden, I take it?'

'Caring for her rather ill mother, along with her brothers and sister.'

'You may wish to talk to her again. The last time I saw her before Greville was murdered, she was conversing at great length with Dunstan Headley, in the grounds, along the meditation walk.'

Thomas requested sandwiches and glasses of water to be brought to her office, and over this simple lunch they talked about the clouds that seemed to be forming over Germany, clouds that appeared to have been observed with some indifference by those in power. When coffee was brought to the room, Maisie sipped from her cup and felt she knew Thomas well enough to ask a personal question.

'Were you ever married, Dr Thomas?'

The woman smiled. 'Yes, I was. I was married to one of my fellow agents, a very brave young man. His name was Dietger. I loved him dearly, but love in the midst of war is always more urgent, more undiluted by the ordinary responsibilities of marriage which most couples encounter. I was widowed when he was captured by the German army.'

'I am so sorry.'

She rubbed her upper arms, as if cold. 'It is something we all lived with. He gave his life and it made me an even more determined fighter.' She untied the scarf at her neck to reveal the scar Maisie had seen when she first came to the college. 'I sought my revenge, and won – but I have this to show for my trouble. I found out who was responsible for my husband's death, and I lured him to his end. I killed him with my bare hands, and almost lost my life in return. I buried him with the strength I had left, and I went back to work.'

Maisie realised that the woman before her would continue to seek her revenge; what she had seen and done in the war had all but hollowed her heart. It was evident that Francesca Thomas would not hesitate to kill again to save the countrymen she considered her people.

'You will remember that all we have discussed must be very tightly held,' said Thomas, as Maisie departed in the late afternoon.

'I gave you my word.'

'Good.' She smiled, and whispered, 'You know, the propaganda men would have everyone believe that women agents were little more than Mata Haris who gave their bodies for information. Now you know we gave our hearts – and we worked as hard and took as many chances as our men.'

Maisie walked back to her motor car, having pulled down her cloche again. She had just unlocked the MG, when, as if on cue, a black vehicle pulled up alongside. The driver stepped out and opened the back door with haste.

'Miss Dobbs – step in, please.'

Maisie locked the MG, then took a seat in the motor car, next to Brian Huntley.

'Having me followed, Mr Huntley?'

'A fortuitous sighting as I was leaving a colleague's office.'

'Of course it was. I was looking forward to seeing you this evening – does this mean that I won't have the pleasure of supper with you, Mr Huntley?'

'Sadly, it does. But I am sure you can spare some time now to assure me that you haven't done or said anything that might run counter to your signing of the Official Secrets Act.'

'Absolutely not.'

'Good.' He paused. 'Any news, Miss Dobbs?'

Maisie recounted the events of the previous evening, and Robson Headley's display of support for a regime that had not come to power in Germany but seemed to be stoking a fierce mood among the people, which, she thought, was of grave concern.

'Are you sure it's not just youthful support for something new? Young people are wont to see the world in black and white, and to be taken with revolutionary ideas.'

'He is almost twenty-five years old! He is not just out of short trousers, and knows very well what he is doing. Men younger than he were laying down their lives in the war – and I am sure they saw a good deal of grey amid the black and white—' Maisie stopped herself, concerned that she had spoken out of turn.

'Point very well taken, Miss Dobbs. You have done exactly as I asked.' He ruffled through some papers as the motor car swung around Buckingham Palace. 'Have you observed any activities that might give rise to suspicion that there is Bolshevik activity at the college, or any other college in Cambridge?'

'I have seen nothing to suggest there is a "red menace" at the College of St Francis – yet. However, in my opinion your department must be on the alert and not simply focus your concern on one strand of political belief. I realise the Communist threat is uppermost in the minds of the Secret Service, but you cannot rule out Fascism as the greater threat to peace in the short term.' She turned to face Huntley. 'You see, I believe the two go together. There will be those who see the likes of Robson Headley – and, further up the scale, of Adolf Hitler and Oswald Mosley – and they will be angered or scared by their rhetoric, so they will look to support what they believe to be the opposite, which is Communism. And I'm not only talking about the young and impressionable, though they are the subject of our investigation at the moment.'

'I see. Well, you've made your point in no uncertain terms, Miss Dobbs.' He cleared his throat. 'I realise MacFarlane and Stratton are still engaged in the investigation into Greville Liddicote's death, and of course you were instructed not to become involved, but I know you a little better, I think – do you know who murdered Liddicote?'

Maisie looked at Huntley. 'Ah, now that is a good question. I need to uncover some sort of proof, but I do believe I have a good idea of who took Liddicote's life. However, there are others who are equally culpable.'

'In what way?'

'I don't think I can tell you that, Mr Huntley. Not without compromising the very promise I have made to you.'

'Well said, Miss Dobbs. Very well said.'

The black motor car came to a halt alongside Maisie's crimson MG. She opened the door and exited before the driver could assist her.

'Be in touch, Miss Dobbs.' The vehicle pulled away before Maisie could respond.

She hoped Billy was still at the office; her next stop was Fitzroy Square. It was time to find out if there was news in the search for Sandra.

EIGHTEEN

'Has Caldwell come up with anything?' Maisie had taken off her hat and now sat at her desk, with Billy seated opposite her as she leafed through messages and unopened post. 'What did he say this morning when you spoke to him?'

'Turns out this bloke that Sandra was on to is a right one – just like you said. He's reeled him in, along with Reg Martin, though apparently Reg is as scared as they come. It was protection, as I said – and it went wrong. That poor girl.'

'But does anyone have any idea where she is? She must be terrified – that's if Walling hasn't had her picked up somewhere and silenced.' She pushed the pile of paper to one side.

'Miss, you don't think—'

'I know, I'm not being very rational, am I? I'm terribly worried about her; I hope she's just gone to ground somewhere – but where?'

They were silent for a while. Maisie was concerned with all there was to be accomplished in just a short time. Tomorrow she would return to Ipswich, and afterwards – dependent upon the outcome of her business in Knowsley – straight back to Cambridge to find MacFarlane and Stratton.

'And there was another telephone call from that Miss Robinson at the Compton Corporation.'

Maisie looked up. 'Oh yes, I'm to collect a letter. It seems using a bag that goes back and forth to their offices in Toronto is now the best way for me to receive mail from James. I was supposed to get in touch with her at the beginning of the week, wasn't I? But I just didn't have the time – and I so wanted to pick up the letter. I wonder why they couldn't have simply had it brought over by messenger?'

'Might have a nice little present in it, eh? That aside, she wants to know when you can go over and pick it up.'

'Does she, now?' Maisie stood up. 'I'm just going along the corridor to splash some cold water on my face – would you mind giving her a telephone call, Billy? Tell her I will be over before half past six, if that's all right.'

'She did sound a bit anxious, as if it were burning a hole in the desk.'

Maisie laughed. 'It might well be doing just that!'

She returned to the office ten minutes later to be informed

by Billy that she was expected at the Compton Corporation, where Miss Robinson was awaiting her arrival. She looked at the clock. 'I'd better be off, then. I don't want to be late for the very efficient Miss Robinson, do I?'

Despite her recent doubts, Maisie realised that she had been missing James more than ever over the past few days. When he was at home with her, there was no echoing silence in the flat, and their excursions at the week's end – to Chelstone, or to Priscilla's country house – seemed to be filled with a heady blend of deep conversation and laughter. Yes, she looked forward to his homecoming.

'Miss Robinson, I'm sorry to keep you waiting,' said Maisie as she entered the secretary's fiefdom, a spacious anteroom to James' office. Since taking over the running of the Compton Corporation, James had embarked upon a programme of modernisation at the offices, and had started with his own. The walls had recently been painted in a creamy white, and the mahogany furniture was of a modern design, with smooth corners and chrome fittings. The decor reminded Maisie of a ship; she thought it might have seemed impersonal had it not been for the bouquet of flowers in a vase on the secretary's desk, and a large tapestry of geometric shapes mounted on the wall behind.

'I had trouble parking, what with one thing and another,' added Maisie. 'You must be dying to get home at this time on a Friday.'

The woman smiled, but there was something in her

expression that caused Maisie to wonder if all was well.

'Is everything all right? I mean, I am terribly sorry if you were meant to be somewhere. After all – I could have waited, and—'

Miss Robinson picked up the telephone as if to place a call that could not wait. She held out her hand towards the door that led to James' office.

'If you'd like to go in, Miss Dobbs, your letter is on the table.'

'Are you sure?' asked Maisie. 'I mean, I don't want to just charge into the office.'

'No, it's perfectly all right. On you go.' She waved in a way that made Maisie feel as if she were a schoolgirl who had just been dismissed by the headmistress.

Maisie placed her hand on the large chrome door handle, and as she pressed her weight against the door, she looked back at Miss Robinson, who was watching her, smiling. She waved her hand again. Maisie nodded and walked in.

Her shock at seeing James Compton coming towards her with his arms open almost caused her to faint. The table before her was covered with packages.

'James! James Compton, you rogue!' She was soon in his embrace. 'You have been here all the time!'

James kissed her, but she soon pushed back from him to speak. 'You sent that letter from here!' She laughed, knowing that once upon a time she would have been devastated by such subterfuge. 'Why didn't you tell me you were home? What are you up to? Apart from committing a crime in the eyes of the post office, that is.'

'A crime?' James laughed as he spoke. 'What crime?'

'You forged a postmark – that's a prison sentence. How did you pull that one off?'

'Oh, that was easy – I just had Miss Robinson talk nicely to a man at the post office, asking him to smudge a stamp to disguise the franking, and had the letter delivered by hand.'

'But why? Couldn't you just have let me know you were in London?'

'Ah, it was all part of my grand plan – as much as I wanted to call you the minute I disembarked at Southampton, I was trying to keep a secret, and I made sure anyone who knew I was here in London had sworn on their life not to let the cat out of the bag.'

'What cat? Oh, this doesn't make sense, James.'

'It will when you see your surprise.'

'I think this is all a surprise. Anything more would constitute a shock.' She allowed herself to be embraced again. 'And what about those?' She nodded towards the packages.

'Just a few things I thought you'd like, Maisie. Don't worry, nothing extravagant; a few bits and pieces to bring a smile to your face.' He looked at his watch. 'There was something else I wanted to show you, but I think it will have to wait until tomorrow morning now – too dark outside.'

'This sounds very suspicious.'

'Just a surprise. Now then, shall we load these up in the back of your motor car? We'll stop somewhere for supper, then deliver them to your flat. Do you still have the guest you wrote about?'

'No, I don't, and I'm worried about her – oh, James, so much has happened since you left.'

'And I suppose you can't tell me the half of it.' He gathered up the parcels, handing several smaller ones to Maisie to carry.

'I can tell you more about Sandra, but not about my other job.'

'Other job?'

'I shouldn't have said that much. It's an official secret.'

James wanted to linger over a long breakfast the following morning, but Maisie knew she had to leave for Ipswich at around midday if she was to pay another visit to Alice Thurlow.

'Can't we just sit here on your comfortable sofa, drink our tea, and enjoy the morning? I haven't even had so much as an egg yet, and you've only opened one or two of your presents.'

'Imagine what a surprise it will be when I come home – I can ration them out. In any case, I thought you were anxious to show me something.'

'Absolutely. I'll just be a tick. We'll be off by nine and I will let you go to your urgent appointment if you promise to come straight back afterwards.'

Maisie shook her head, then reached out to touch James' arm. 'I can't return immediately, but I'll be back at the end of the week. I have a contract I'm committed to, and to leave now would not be wise.'

James held his hand to his heart and gave an exaggerated sigh. Then he smiled and nodded towards the door. 'All right, let's go.'

When they reached the edge of Belgravia, James pulled over and stopped the motor car.

'Now, you have a choice,' said James.

'What sort of choice? You're being very strange, you know.'

'You can either close your eyes and cover them with your hands – or if you can't keep them closed, I'll have to blindfold you.'

'James, you do realise how very edgy this makes me feel, don't you?'

'You only need to keep them closed for a little while, then my secret can be revealed.'

'All right – but no blindfold. And I promise I won't look.' Maisie held her hands to her eyes as they set off again.

A few moments later, the motor car came to a standstill and Maisie breathed in the air around her. There was a faint loamy smell of fallen leaves, and a light rain on flagstones. There were just a few motor cars and not far away she could hear a horse and cart.

'Oh dear. Oh, it can't be. James, I know the smells here, I know, it's—'

'All right, you can look now.'

'Ebury Place!' Maisie all but shouted. 'Oh goodness, what are we doing here? Why did you—?'

And at that point, he turned her around to face number

15 Ebury Place, the house where she had come to work as a young girl, where she had struggled to study despite her duties as a domestic servant. The house had been mothballed when Lady Rowan announced that she did not want to come to London any more. Sheets covered the furniture, and the property appeared deserted – the last time Maisie drove past, she thought how lonely the house had looked, when it had once been so full of life. And now the mansion was half-shrouded in scaffolding and heavy canvas sheets, and a builder's van was parked outside. A man wearing white overalls and cleaning his hands on a cloth walked towards them.

'Good morning, sir.'

'Mr Judge, I thought we'd come and have a look at your progress. How's the job going? Did you have any luck with that door frame?'

'Yes, we did – took two men to pull it out, but we've solved the problem, and now we're going great guns.'

James turned to Maisie. 'Mind where you step now.'

The foreman led the way across the entrance hall and Maisie looked up at the sweeping staircase which led to the first floor. Scaffolding had been erected to enable men to reach the high ceilings and windows; it seemed the mansion was receiving complete refurbishment.

'When do you think the job will be finished?' James asked the foreman.

'You should be able to move in by Christmas, all being well.'

'Well done. Tell your men there will be a bonus for them if the work is completed by December 23rd.'

'I'll do that, sir, and I hope I'm not jeopardising that bonus when I tell you the men are pretty determined to get the job done anyway.'

Maisie and James exchanged glances, and James smiled. 'What do you mean, Mr Judge? Is everything all right?'

The man shrugged and reddened. 'It's not the sort of thing that would bother me, but some of the lads are a bit uneasy, what with the fact that you've got some haunting going on here.'

James laughed, yet Maisie moved closer to the foreman. 'What makes you think this house is haunted?'

'The noises. Creaking floorboards and all that. And things have gone missing. Ronnie said he could've sworn he had his sandwich box with him when he came in the other morning. He went back out to the van, came back in again, and what do you know – gone!'

James stepped forward. 'Oh, I'm sure there's a reasonable explanation. I lived in this house almost all my life, and I assure you, if a ghost had crossed paths with my mother, I know who would have been given a fright – and it wouldn't have been Lady Rowan Compton!'

'Tell me, Mr Judge, have you been up to the old servants' quarters yet?' asked Maisie. 'The attic rooms? There's a back staircase leading up there and a disguised door on every landing.'

'No, we won't get to that part of the house for at least another couple of weeks, and no one's been up there.'

At once Maisie was stepping quickly across the dust sheets, and then along the hallway until she reached a place where she pulled back another dust sheet and opened the door that many a visitor would not have noticed was there.

'Maisie, where are you going? Maisie! Maisie have you lost your senses?'

She could hear James' footsteps behind her, but now she was on the back stairs. Oh, how often she had gone up and down these stairs as a girl, a coal scuttle in hand, stopping on each floor to light the fires in the family's reception rooms. As she made her way up, it was as if she were on a stairway to the past, but now she had only one thing in mind. She was in pursuit of a ghost.

Almost out of breath by the time she reached the attic floors, she stopped at the room she had once shared with a girl named Enid. She stood outside the door, caught her breath, and knocked with a light hand. She stepped with care across the threshold. To the right was a dressing table, on top of which was the typewriter that had once been placed in the library for the use of guests visiting the mansion – of course, that's why the typeface on her letter from Sandra had seemed so familiar. She moved into the room and sat on the first of two cast-iron beds, reaching out to touch the young woman curled on her side with her eyes open, her cheeks red with the feverishness of so many shed tears.

'It's all right, Sandra. I've got you, you poor love. I've got you.' Maisie leant over and put her arms around the bony frame of Sandra Tapley. 'I should have known you would come here. This was your home when you met Eric; it was where you fell in love. I should have known.' She waited a while as the sobs ebbed, rubbing Sandra's back as if she were settling a baby for the night. 'It's over, Sandra. The police have got him – the man responsible for Eric's death is in custody. You won't be getting into trouble. There, there, it's all done now.'

And as she looked back towards the door, Maisie saw James Compton standing in the doorway.

'I can't leave her alone at the flat, James,' whispered Maisie. 'We must take her to Priscilla's. Could you . . .'

'Yes, I'll find a taxi – and I'll let Priscilla and Douglas know – the telephone's been reconnected downstairs. It's Sandra, isn't it?'

'Yes. Tell them we've found Sandra.'

Maisie did not trouble Sandra with questions. She could see the young woman was beyond exhaustion, physically and emotionally, and that her spirit had been battered as if it were a ship in a storm. Now, in the guest room at Priscilla's house, she helped Sandra into the bed and pulled up the sheets and counterpane, cocooning her so that she might sleep. She waited a moment, then tiptoed away, closing the door behind her. Priscilla was waiting for her on the landing.

'Maisie, you will stay for lunch, won't you? Sandra isn't the only one who looks as if she needs a rest – look at you, I bet you've been rushing about all over the place.'

'I've been busy, Pris. And I have to leave for Ipswich very soon.'

'Ipswich? Ips-bloody-wich! What are you going there for, and leaving that lovely man behind?'

Maisie put her finger to her mouth. 'Shhhh. You'll wake Sandra.'

They walked towards the staircase, but lingered there, still speaking in lowered voices.

'I tell you, Maisie, you'll lose him if you carry on like this. I mean, it's all very well to be working, if that's what you want to do, but for heaven's sake – that man adores you, and I know you feel the same way; you can't fool me, you know. Can't you stay just one day?'

Maisie could barely meet her friend's eyes, so filled with concern. 'I wish I could, but the sooner I go, the sooner I'll be back again. James understands.'

'I think you'll find there's a distinction between understanding and tolerance. I don't think he'll be that happy about it for much longer.'

'He'll surprise you, Pris.'

'I hope you're right, my friend. I do hope you're right.' They began making their way down the staircase. 'You'll stay for a quick lunch, then?'

'Yes, that would be nice.'

'We've some salmon in aspic, very nice with new potatoes and a salad. And cook made some freshly baked bread.'

'I could eat that – we didn't have a moment for a proper breakfast.'

Priscilla winked at her friend. 'Didn't we now?'

Maisie liked Priscilla's dining room. It could have been so much more formal, and indeed, when they were entertaining on a larger scale, the room appeared very grand. But at other times, there always seemed to be something to indicate that this was a house where children lived and were not only loved by their parents, but enjoyed. A cricket bat might have been left behind a door, or a rugger ball under a side table. She had once discovered a muddy sock by the French windows, and it seemed there was a model aeroplane or an abandoned toy motor car to be found in almost every room. At intervals Priscilla was known to announce, 'That's enough! All toys to your room!' But such discipline was soon lost with her desire to have fun with her boisterous sons – a sentiment that most of their friends found incomprehensible, if not alarming.

'So, Maisie, what did you discover about Sandra's foray into the world of cat burglary?' asked Priscilla.

'She didn't tiptoe over any tiles, yet I wouldn't have put it past her. But she *was* on the scent of the man who killed her husband, though he didn't touch him with his own hands.'

'What happened?'

'First of all, it was my assistant who did most of the legwork, as I've been concerned with an assignment on behalf of another client. Essentially, here's what happened. A man named William Walling – who appears respectable and businesslike enough but runs a fairly large criminal corporation and controls all sorts of rackets – had stepped up pressure on his people recently. Everything he's done has been under the cover of a legitimate business, but like many such men, he has a protection operation – shopkeepers and so on have to pay a certain amount to him, and if they don't go along with his "proposition", then he exerts some force. On the other hand, the business is protected from a similar approach by other men with the same intention, and of course from the attentions of smaller-time crooks.'

'I understand there's been an increase in this sort of thing, Maisie,' said Douglas Partridge.

'I had a similar case just recently,' added Maisie. 'Only the villain in that one was a loan shark who had expanded his business interests.'

'This is all making me very nervous, Maisie,' said James.

'Me too,' said Priscilla, turning to James. 'I've been telling Maisie for a long time that she should find something less threatening to do.'

'Oh, but that wouldn't be Maisie, would it, darling?' James leant across and squeezed Maisie's hand, while Maisie smiled at Priscilla, who rolled her eyes.

'Walling had acquired some motor cars needing repairs – likely all of them were stolen,' said Maisie. 'He asked – by which I mean he *told* – Reg Martin, Eric Tapley's employer, that he had the job, and was to complete the work in a very short time – or else. Reg and Eric were working flat out.'

'I would have thought that, on the contrary, they might have had time on their hands – aren't those sort of businesses having trouble at the moment?' said James.

Maisie shook her head. 'If you've decided not to buy a new motor car, you have to spend more on keeping the old one on the road, so Reg wasn't doing too badly, but he was worried about taking on another mechanic to help out, only to lay him off when this influx of work from Walling dried up. To cut the story short, Reg ran late with a job, he complained that it was more than they could take on, and Walling had equipment tampered with, just to scare Reg. But Walling's men obviously took things a bit too far, because Eric was killed. And Sandra was not going to let it go. She had been suspicious for a while, because she had been doing the books for Reg, then he had suddenly told her he didn't need her to do them any more. She realised what had transpired, and broke into Walling's offices – to go through his books – only to discover that he was sending money overseas. Of course, little of this came out when she was held at Vine Street. I asked Billy to speak to a Scotland Yard man we know, and apparently they've had their eyes on Walling for a while. He's increased his activities to enable him to send as much money as possible to relatives in Spain – his mother is Spanish. Surprisingly, it wasn't for reasons of criminal intent, though there are people in Spain who would think so. It was to help family members, people who had become dispossessed due to the political turbulence over there.'

'This is the sort of talk that rather scares me, to tell you the truth,' said Priscilla, extinguishing a cigarette, then placing another in the long holder, lighting it, and inhaling deeply.

At that moment, Douglas and Priscilla's sons came bounding into the dining room, and it seemed the four walls echoed with the sounds of childhood exuberance.

The three boys clustered around James Compton – the fact that he had been with the Royal Flying Corps during the war had made him a firm favourite with Priscilla's aeroplane-mad boys. Maisie looked at James as he pulled the youngest, Tarquin, onto his lap and fielded their questions. She turned her attention to Priscilla, who was seated next to her, and realised her eyes had filled with tears.

'I get so inexplicably scared at times, Maisie,' Priscilla whispered to her friend.

Maisie took her hand, knowing the memory of losing three beloved brothers in the war sometimes filled Priscilla with a dark dread of the future.

'Look at the time. I suppose you ought to be on your way, Maisie.' Priscilla stood up, squaring her shoulders as if she were prepared to take command of the world once more. 'Right, you three toads. I don't know what made you think you could return from the park and rush straight into the dining room without washing hands, or while grown-ups are talking. Elinor doubtless has your lunch ready in the kitchen – special treat while cook's out on Saturday errands.'

'We should leave now, James,' said Maisie.

'Don't worry, I'll ensure Sandra remains under our roof until you return,' said Priscilla. 'And I am sure that, if she gets bored, Douglas will have plenty of work for her to catch up on. Should we expect a visit from your friends at Scotland Yard?'

'I'll telephone Caldwell; he won't have you bothered unduly, though Sandra will have to make another statement.'

Priscilla kissed Maisie on both cheeks, then turned to James.

'For my sake, James – make an honest woman out of her. Her exploits are turning me grey.'

James laughed and shook hands with Douglas, then turned to Maisie and led the way to the MG – he had followed the taxi in Maisie's motor car.

'Still leaving me, are you?'

'I can be in Ipswich by half past four if I leave now. It's terribly important that I go now; sooner rather than later. And I have a memorial service to attend tomorrow. Don't worry, James. I promise I will be back soon.'

It was four by the time Maisie reached Ipswich, and half past the hour when she parked the MG alongside the cottage where Alice Thurlow lived with her family in the village of Knowsley. She leant her head forward and rubbed her neck. 'A little soft would be awfully welcome right about now,' she said aloud to herself.

Hearing voices coming from the back of the cottage, she followed a path leading around the side of the property to the back garden. The family were outside – the sky was overcast, though it had not started to rain. It seemed as if they had all spent Saturday afternoon tending vegetables and clearing leaves. Cups of tea had been passed around, and Ursula Thurlow was teasing her eldest son, who then pointed to his sister, Amber, and professed to know who she was in love with.

Ursula was the first to notice the visitor.

'Miss Dobbs. So lovely to see you again. Alice! Alice, your friend from Cambridge is here.'

Alice stood up; her cheeks reddened when she saw Maisie, but she approached as if she were indeed the friend her mother believed her to be.

'Miss Dobbs – Maisie – we've just had tea, but I can make another pot. And my sister made some quite delicious fruit cake today – mother dried the fruit last year so its very rich, and Amber added a little brandy.'

Maisie accepted the offering, and after properly greeting the family, she followed Alice into the kitchen.

'May I ask you some more questions, Alice?'

Alice rinsed out the brown teapot and took it to the stove, where she poured in a little of the water that had been kept at a simmer. She did not answer Maisie immediately, but instead used an iron handle to lift the hot-plate cover, then drew the kettle across so that it could be brought to a rolling boil. Maisie watched the young woman's deliberate movements, as if with each element of the task at hand she were slowing down time, buying herself a moment here, a moment there, while she anticipated the questions that had brought Maisie back to the cottage.

'Yes, of course. Would you like to sit down?' Rosemary glanced at Maisie, then fixed her attention back to the kettle while she waited for it to boil. A series of cloths were hanging on a line above the stove; she pulled at one, and was wiping her hands when she sat down opposite Maisie.

'Alice, did you see Dunstan or Robson Headley on the day Greville Liddicote was murdered?'

She nodded.

'Which one?'

'Both.'

'Did you speak to either one of them?'

Alice sighed. 'Mr Dunstan Headley.'

'Would you tell me what you spoke to him about?'

Alice looked back at the stove, and stood up. She grasped the kettle handle with the cloth, and poured boiling water into the pot. Setting the kettle back down again, she put the lid on the teapot, then placed it on the old pine table, which was almost white from years of scrubbing. She placed clean cups and saucers in front of herself and Maisie, stirred the tea once, and left it to brew for a few minutes. She sighed.

'I told him about my father, Miss Dobbs. I told him that he was a conscientious objector, that he had died in Wandsworth Prison, and that the book published under the name of Greville Liddicote was in fact written by my mother – as were others that he passed off as his own. I told Dunstan Headley that Liddicote did well out of those books – which is true, he did – and that my mother never saw a penny. I told him it was a woman's work that set the cat among the pigeons; a woman who wrote stories for her children, to help them to understand the war, and why their father could not hold with such a thing.'

'What made you tell him?'

Alice lifted the teapot lid again and stirred the tea. She did not ask Maisie how she liked her tea but poured milk into each cup, then the tea. She pulled a cosy over the teapot, and leant back to take up her tea and sip. She kept the cup in her hands.

'All right, you might as well know what I did.' She took

another sip, but this time returned the cup to its saucer. She crossed her arms. 'Miss Dobbs, I like to think I can tell a lot about people just by watching them.'

'That's very true.' Maisie crossed her own arms, and smiled. The crossed arms reminded her of a wooden plank pulled across to secure a drawbridge. She knew that while Alice Thurlow had declared that she would tell everything, there could well be details that she would keep locked inside.

'There was something about Dunstan Headley – I mean, there he was, with his son, two men rattling around together and no woman, unless you count the servants. Did you notice that he couldn't quite meet your eyes? I saw him talk to Dr Thomas, and to Delphine Lang, so I knew it wasn't just me – the man really didn't like women; I reckon he saw us as the root of everything that's bad in the world.'

Maisie nodded. 'So what made you approach him, if you knew he was prejudiced in such a way? Wasn't that asking for trouble?'

She smiled and shook her head, uncrossing her arms. 'I didn't really care by that time. I came to the college and applied for a job because I wanted to see Liddicote. I wanted to know if he recognised me – which he didn't – and I wanted to . . . I wanted to make him sorry. He caused my mother great distress, Miss Dobbs. He broke her heart, and she's a very good woman. She is the most wonderful, darling mother anyone could have, and she had to bring us up alone. After father was gone, and after Liddicote stole her work – and it *was* as good as theft – well, if it wasn't for

372

Aunt Rose, we would have starved. She was an angel, just an angel. So, I wanted to . . . I wanted him to hurt, just like we've all been hurt. I am sure it was the deep worry about everything that caused my mother to become so crippled.'

'How do you think you hurt Dr Liddicote?'

'I told Dunstan Headley everything – everything. I let him know that the book that caused his son to do what he did, and go in front of a firing squad, was written by a woman. I told him Greville Liddicote took the stories and claimed they were his. Then I let the truth do the work for me.'

'What did you think he might do?'

'I thought he might withdraw his money from the college. I thought he would have nothing to do with Liddicote ever again, so the college would fail – and then where would the famous, world-renowned author be? No college, no job, no reputation. No nothing.'

'What happened when you told him?'

'He was so angry, I thought the top of his head would just explode. He was furious, but the part that really must have caught in his craw was the fact that Liddicote had taken a woman's work to bolster his reputation and his coffers, and Martin Headley paid the price and was labelled a mutineer and a coward. And the cause of all this was a woman who wanted to excuse her coward husband's absence in a story – well, that's how he must have seen my father.'

'Then?'

She shrugged. 'He went flying off, his coat flapping,

with those bits of grey hair at the side of his head spiralling up in the air with the breeze. He went into Liddicote's office through the French doors – they were open – and I suppose that's when . . . well, that's when he killed Liddicote.'

Maisie nodded. 'And how do you feel about that?'

Alice turned her head to look out of the window at her family; Ursula was seated on her chair, her sketchbook in hand, watercolours on a small table at her side. The younger siblings were working in the garden, and her older brother was engaged in repairing a part of the fence. She looked back at Maisie.

'I went to the college wanting to kill Greville Liddicote and I found I couldn't do such a thing – it was a stupid, childish idea. But I burnt with hatred for him, if you can understand that. So, am I sorry? No, I can't say I am, entirely. But I am sorry about what came to pass in another way, Miss Dobbs.' She stopped talking as the words caught in her throat.

'Go on, Alice.' Maisie set down her cup.

'My father would have been so very disappointed in me. He would have been . . . so sad. He was a pacifist, you see. He did not care for killing. We hardly ever had meat on the table, not simply because there was rarely enough money, but because he couldn't bear the thought of animals being killed. He died because he did not believe that one person should take the life of another, so I am haunted by what I did. I might not have done whatever Dunstan Headley had to do to kill Dr Liddicote, but I am just as much to blame. As I said, part of me thinks, "Good riddance, you deserved it all." And the other thinks, "Oh, poor man."'

On the road back to Cambridge, Maisie wondered whether MacFarlane and Stratton were still at the Old Fenland Mill, or whether they had returned to Scotland Yard. For his part, Stratton hated being apart from his son. She hoped they had decided to remain in Cambridge until at least next week, for she wanted to see them both on a matter of some urgency.

NINETEEN

According to the landlord at the Old Fenland Mill, the gentlemen had returned to London, but were expected back in Cambridge on Monday – they had asked for their rooms to be held for another week. Maisie thanked the man and was about to leave when the aroma of cooking coming from the kitchen caught her senses; she decided to take supper at the inn and gather her thoughts. Having ordered a half-pint of cider and a plate of beef pie and potatoes, she took her drink over to a seat by the window, which was ajar. As she settled herself, she heard her name called.

'Miss Dobbs! Miss Dobbs! Would you care to join us?'

Maisie looked up in the direction of the voice, and saw her student Daniel, with a group from her second-year class. They raised their glasses in her direction, so she took up her drink and joined them, leaving her jacket on her chair so she could return to her seat to eat supper when it was served.

'Good evening, ladies and gentlemen – I won't squeal on you, but I know that at least one of your number shouldn't be in this hostelry. College rules are stricter than the laws of the land when it comes to pubs.' Maisie smiled as she seated herself on the chair Daniel had pulled up for her.

'We know you won't tell, Miss Dobbs. And we're doing nothing to give the college a bad name,' offered Daniel, raising his glass to his lips.

'Have you all made the most of your days off?' Maisie smiled again to let them know she was teasing – just a little. 'I'll be checking my pigeonhole tomorrow morning before the memorial service, and I do believe I should see a number of completed essays waiting for my attention.'

One of the students reddened, while another claimed he worked better at the last moment, so although his essay had not been delivered, it would be there in the morning. Maisie raised an eyebrow at the young man. 'On a Sunday morning? When I know very well there's a dance at the hall down the road this evening – I'm surprised you're not there already.'

'Just a quick one before we go down, Miss Dobbs,' said Daniel.

The others laughed, then went quiet. It appeared they did not know quite what to say with one of their teachers in their midst. It was Daniel, again, who broke the silence.

'Do you think the police will be at the college much longer, Miss Dobbs? They seem to have been there a long time, and done a lot of questioning.'

Maisie cleared her throat, knowing she had been put on the spot. 'A sudden heart attack always leaves questions, especially when it's someone who is well known, so it isn't unusual for a lingering enquiry. And I understand the policemen concerned have other business in the city.'

The students looked at each other, while another, Frederick Sanger, voiced his opinion. 'They're probably trying to find out who upset old Liddy so much that his heart just gave out.'

'Well, they don't have to go far for that, do they, Freddie?' said Daniel. 'We all know who was upset, and who did the upsetting.'

Maisie sipped her cider, not wanting to appear too interested. She set down her glass. 'Oh dear, being a lecturer means I am never privy to the real goings on that you students see – come on, put a poor teacher out of her misery and tell me who you're talking about.' She turned to Daniel. 'What's all this about people upsetting each other? The College of St Francis is supposed to be about peace.'

'And it is!' Another student, Rebecca Inglesson, looked at Daniel, then Frederick. '*We're* all having a wonderful time being peaceful together.'

Maisie laughed, now wondering whether the comment that had piqued her interest was made in jest, or whether there was substance to it. 'I take it that no one is really upset, then?'

Daniel reached for his beer and took another sip. 'Oh no, there was a huge upset on the day Liddy died, wasn't there, Fred?' He looked back at Maisie. 'We were walking along the corridor, you know, towards Liddy's office, when we saw the puppy dog coming bounding along from the opposite direction.'

'Puppy dog?' asked Maisie.

'Now you've done it, Danny,' said Rebecca, who had not touched her drink since Maisie had questioned the wisdom of one or two of their number being in the pub.

Daniel turned to Maisie. 'You know who I mean, Miss Dobbs.' He pulled a clump of his swept-back hair over his forehead and took a pair of spectacles from the nose of another student and put them on, executing what Maisie thought a very good impression. 'Puppy dog bounding to see the adored master.'

Maisie nodded. 'Oh, yes, of course – don't let any other member of staff see you do that or you will be hauled over the coals.'

'Oh, Dr Thomas is much better than I when it comes to mimicking the puppy dog – not a lot of love lost there!'

She raised an eyebrow again, then made another attempt at pressing Daniel to continue his story. 'So, what happened when you met in the corridor?'

He shook his head. 'Oh, we didn't meet, but we saw him listening at the door. He seemed very agitated, you know, flushed and angry – I really don't think he even saw us, he was so upset. He might have been alarmed because of the shouting – it's not what you want to hear at the college, is it? Not very peaceful, eh? Even I could hear it, and I was a few steps away – and that door is pretty heavy, but there was someone inside shouting about Ursula someone-or-other, and "fraud" this and "fake" that and – here's the bit that I thought was a bit thick, "killer by any other name – and just for the money!" Our puppy dog must have heard everything before the shouting stopped. Then he entered Dr Liddicote's room without knocking. Of course, we just went on our way, but from what I know about the time of Liddy's heart attack, that was what must have done it. Funny, we didn't see anyone come out, you know, before our pup went in with teeth bared.' Daniel pretended to growl, to much mirth among the students, then turned to Maisie. 'I say, Miss Dobbs, I do hope I haven't gone too far there – I'm terribly sorry if I offended you.'

Maisie smiled, though she found the expression difficult to maintain. 'Not at all – I pushed you to tell.' At that point, the landlord called out to her, and she stood up to leave the group; the young men also stood as a matter of courtesy. 'Now, you must all have a very good time at your dance – and, Rebecca, try to stick to something lighter than ale. I expect I'll see you all at the service tomorrow.'

The students nodded in agreement, and made ready to leave the inn. Maisie settled back into her place in the seat by the window. She checked the clock on the wall, picked up her plate, and approached the bar.

'Something wrong, Miss?'

'Oh, no, it looks lovely. Look, I have to nip out for a moment – could you put a plate over this and keep it warm for me? I'll be back in about ten minutes. I have to make an urgent telephone call.'

'Right you are, Miss. We'll put some fresh gravy on it as well – and I'll make sure you get the same seat by the window.'

Maisie thanked the landlord and hurried out of the inn and along the street to the telephone kiosk. She hoped MacFarlane was in situ – she had heard along the grapevine that the detective had several lady friends and was often not to be found at his home. She dialled the number for Scotland Yard and was put through to MacFarlane's department.

'He's not here, Miss Dobbs, but I know where to find him.'

'Don't tell me, The Cuillins of Skye.'

'Well, I shouldn't really say, but—'

'It's his favourite watering hole; I know that much about him. They have a telephone there – do you have the number, or do I have to waste time finding it out?'

'That's all right, Miss – here it is.'

Maisie jotted down the number, thanked the policeman, and placed a call to the pub where MacFarlane spent many an hour after the working day – which was always long for the detective chief superintendent. After a wait of several moments while the landlord went off to find MacFarlane, she soon heard his voice booming in the background, instructing his drinking partners to put their hands in their hole-ridden pockets and get another round in.

'MacFarlane! And it had better be good.'

'Good evening, Robbie.'

'What have you got for me, lass?'

'Greville Liddicote's murderer.'

MacFarlane and Stratton arrived by motor car before dawn the following morning. Maisie had made a special request for a private breakfast for three in the dining room before the other lodgers came down. The landlady had begun to complain, but was of a cheerier disposition when Maisie mentioned the fee she would pay for the trouble of providing for her colleagues.

'At least you don't try to sneak men home with you of a night, that's all I can say.'

MacFarlane asked Maisie to recount her findings that had led to their conversation the night before. 'The lads had finished off a couple of rounds before I took my seat again after that telephone call from you!' added MacFarlane, before Maisie repeated the account for Stratton. The three remained in the room for some time, with MacFarlane and Stratton going back to their notes taken during the investigation, and once again consulting the pathologist's report on Greville Liddicote's postmortem.

'Do you have any doubt, Maisie?' asked Stratton.

'I sometimes think there's always room for doubt. I

had almost made up my mind in another direction.'

'You shouldn't have been making up your mind either way, Maisie – you have another job to do.'

'And I'm doing it – I just happened to come across more than any of us bargained for.'

Stratton shook his head. 'We thought we'd interviewed everyone, yet we missed your student Daniel and a couple of others. For goodness sake, why didn't that Miss Hawthorne tell us that some of the students had gone off to London for a day or two?'

'In her defence, they sneaked off – they should have informed the office of their intentions; it's a college rule, and they are not children but responsible adults. They're supposed to register when they are in and out and when they are away from Cambridge, in case of emergencies.'

'They're being brought here for further questioning – I don't want to alert anyone over at the college before I'm ready.' MacFarlane sighed. 'What time does the memorial service start?'

'After Sunday services, so around noon, with a procession leaving the college for the church – Dr Roth thought it would be an appropriate honour to go to the service en masse, hand in hand, in memory of Liddicote's dearest wish that the peoples of the world are never put asunder again.'

'Well, there's going to be some asundering this afternoon.'

'When will you make the arrest?' asked Maisie.

'I hate these religious meetings, really I do.' MacFarlane

wiped his plate with the remaining wedge of fried bread. 'We'll wait until everyone has left the church afterwards, and then make our move.'

Maisie nodded.

'But you won't be there, Maisie,' he added.

'What do you mean, I—'

MacFarlane looked at Stratton. 'Would you see if that dear lady wouldn't mind making up a plate for our good man behind the wheel out there – I'll bet he's so hungry he could shake hands with his backbone.' Stratton looked from his superior to Maisie, and left the room. As soon as he heard the door close, MacFarlane continued. 'Orders from Huntley. Directly the service is over you will return to London. He wants to see you.'

'But—'

'But, *no*. You're playing a different game, Maisie. This is not your arrest, though we couldn't have done it without you. You're working for the funnies now, and once you've worked for them, they'll be keeping tabs on you. They want you out of the way while we do our job, then you come back to the college tomorrow afternoon clean as a whistle, though as far as I can see, you've done as much as you can here.'

'I think so – though there is a term to finish.'

MacFarlane threw his table napkin down, pushed back his chair, and stood up. 'You've done a good job, lass. I know how you must feel, but this is police work. Now, eat up that breakfast, or you'll waste away.'

* * *

Matthias Roth led the procession of staff and students to the church, with one of the students carrying the college flag high enough for all around to see. In rich colour and intricate embroidery, Saint Francis of Assisi was depicted with the face of a cherub and a bright halo above his head. His long, brown robe appeared on the flag as if made of silk, and he was surrounded by woodland animals, with a white dove at rest on his outstretched hand. Underneath the image of the saint for whom the college was named, the words *Make me an instrument of peace* had been woven into the fabric.

Roth was flanked by Alan Burnham and Dunstan Headley, and behind them walked Robson Headley along with other benefactors, followed by college staff. Francesca Thomas was as elegant as ever in a black dress with a matching jacket and black heeled shoes, while Delphine Lang, in a black dress of fine gauzy fabric over silk, seemed almost ethereal with her fair hair drawn back in a chignon. Maisie joined the other staff and students, and as they filed into the church, at the back she saw the Thurlow family seated in a pew, with Ursula alongside in her wheelchair. She smiled at Maisie and nodded, while Alice sat stone-faced.

Dunstan Headley eulogised Greville Liddicote, and spoke of his deep abiding love of humanity; the love that inspired him to write a simple children's book that touched the hearts of soldiers on both sides of war's divide. Then Matthias Roth stepped forward to read the Prayer of St Francis. Maisie looked around the congregation as words from the prayer filtered through.

. . . grant that I may not so much seek
to be consoled as to console;
to be understood as to understand;
to be loved as to love.
For it is in giving that we receive;
it is in pardoning that we are pardoned . . .

She was aware of some movement towards the back of
the church and turned to see that MacFarlane had arrived
alone. He did not seek out a place to be seated, but stood
with his head bowed and his hands clasping the hat he had
removed upon entering the church.

The vicar led the congregation in the Lord's Prayer, and,
following another hymn and a blessing for the deceased
and those who mourned him, the service came to an
end. Maisie filed out slowly among the column of people
who had admired, hated, loved, respected, and doubted
Greville Liddicote, and though she did not stop to speak
to MacFarlane, she acknowledged him with a brief nod,
which was met in kind. Once outside, she stopped to greet
the Thurlows, then walked across to the yew tree that
stood sentinel over the lych-gate. She lingered there under
the deep evergreen canopy, and watched those who had
paid their respects leave the church and go on their way.
Soon there were only a few stragglers, at which point two
policemen in uniform and one plainclothesman approached
the church. MacFarlane emerged with his hand holding
Matthias Roth's arm in a firm grasp, and as soon as they
were beyond the church door, the policemen approached

and Roth was handcuffed. It was obvious he was weeping as he was escorted to a police vehicle and helped aboard. MacFarlane gave instructions to a policeman before turning to beckon another motor car, which drew up alongside the lych-gate. Maisie stood back so that he did not see her; once he had departed, she stepped into the churchyard. The sun moved behind a cloud, and at once she was chilled by the events of the day.

'Miss Dobbs!'

Daniel, on the other side of the lych-gate, was astride his bicycle.

'Miss Dobbs – did you see that? I think the police have just arrested Dr Roth.'

Maisie made her way along the flagstones, securing the gate once she had stepped through onto the pavement.

'Yes, it seems so.'

'What do you think it's about – perhaps he murdered old Liddy.'

Maisie gave a half-smile. 'I really couldn't say, Daniel.'

'But what if he did, why do you think he'd do such a thing?'

Maisie could see the concern in the young man's countenance; he was filled with questions.

'Remember your myths. Go back to the legends, and perhaps those great philosophers we've been studying. See what they have to say about the despair that assails a man when he discovers his hero has feet of clay. And see if there is comfort for the man who learns that the words of one he has worshipped – words that inspired men to make a stand that would lead to their deaths – were not his, but stolen from another. Greville Liddicote was Dr Roth's hero. But he was just a man, not a god beyond doubt, and I believe Dr Roth wanted him to be something more.'

'I-I think I understand, Miss Dobbs.' The student looked down at the bicycle clips on his trouser legs. 'Might I ask if what I said to you yesterday had anything to do with Dr Roth's arrest? The policemen came to see me early this morning to ask questions.'

Maisie shook her head. 'No, it wasn't anything you said.' It was another lie, and Maisie wondered again at her ability to speak untruths without a telltale catch to her voice, or colour rising to her cheeks. 'I would imagine the policemen simply realised there were some outstanding interviews and they wanted to get them completed before the service. That your observations proved to be useful is, really, nothing you should concern yourself with. You could not have lied, after all.'

'I think I might have, if I thought my words would send Dr Roth to the gallows.'

Maisie sighed. 'I'd better be off, Daniel. I have to be on my way.'

'See you tomorrow afternoon, Miss Dobbs – oh, and I left my assignment for you in the office.'

Maisie walked back to the college, which was Sunday quiet; many of the congregants had returned to their lodgings for tea, and those remaining were in their rooms. A service of remembrance could dampen the enthusiasm of even the most exuberant student. Miss Hawthorne was in the office, trying to catch up, and they both commented on the lovely send-off given to Greville Liddicote by the staff and students of the college he'd loved. Maisie collected student homework from her pigeonhole, then walked out to her motor car, which she had left parked on the road a short distance from the entrance to the college. She placed her burden of books and papers on the passenger seat next to her, then left the MG and made her way back to the college and out to the grounds until she reached the path of St Francis. She began the meditative walk, her thoughts on Matthias Roth and the twist of fate that led him to take the life of a man he admired so much that he had changed the course of his own life.

On the day Dunstan Headley had marched through the French doors into Greville Liddicote's office, Roth was still struggling to persuade Liddicote to agree to the debate. He could not understand Liddicote's stance; they had both worked hard to underscore the integrity of the college so that the institution would be accepted as equal by the established colleges of the university. The debate represented the pinnacle of success Roth had worked towards, and would bring students together from so many countries – something he had set out to do since the war, when the book written by Liddicote had infused him with a desire to change the world of death he saw about him. He had gone to Liddicote's office at a fateful moment and overheard the heated argument between

Headley and Liddicote. Roth understood, upon listening to the none-too-quiet voice of Dunstan Headley, that Liddicote had taken the work of another – and done so for reasons of vanity and greed. Roth was beside himself with disappointment and grief – as Maisie had said to Daniel, his hero had revealed himself to have feet of clay. As soon as he heard Dunstan Headley depart by the open French doors, he entered the room and took leave of his temper.

Maisie suspected that as Dunstan Headley left his office, Liddicote had taken the photograph of Ursula Thurlow in his hand. With his thoughts on the woman who had given him so much, whom he had betrayed – and most likely, whom he had loved – Liddicote was overpowered by Roth; he was, after all, hard of hearing and likely unaware his assailant had entered. Roth had simply taken Liddicote's head in his hands and twisted his neck, killing him in an instant. Then he had left the room and began weaving a web of lies when he returned again, after the body had been discovered, to ask the college secretary known as Rosemary Linden whether Dr Liddicote could see him. Maisie wondered if at that point, Roth had not quite believed he had taken Liddicote's life, and simply wanted to see if it had all been a waking nightmare. She shook her head as it occurred to her that, if they were in France, the case of Matthias Roth would be tried as a *crime passionnel* – a crime of passion.

She realised that she had stopped walking. It was dusk, but as she turned to leave, she looked down at the words carved on a stone placed adjacent to the path. Kneeling, she ran her fingers across each letter, until she could read aloud the lines:

> . . . where there is darkness, light; and where there is sadness, joy . . .

Maisie did not return to London immediately, as instructed by MacFarlane. Instead, she telephoned Huntley at the number he had given her during their meeting at Scotland Yard. After engaging in another scripted conversation she had been charged with learning by heart – about the weather and a fictional Mrs Smith's ill health – she was put through to the man who expected her report.

'I thought I would remain here to take my classes this week and come back to London on Friday. The students are all a bit shaky after losing Liddicote and now Roth, and I feel I can be of service to them. Alan Burnham is now acting principal, so I am sure things will soon be on an even keel, but nevertheless, I wanted to stay.'

'Right you are, Miss Dobbs. In any case, despite the fact that our friends at Scotland Yard have found their man, your work continues; I wanted a report in the wake of the arrest.'

'We'll see what happens. The debate may well have caused feathers to be ruffled – I have an idea that Dunstan Headley might have his son removed from the influence of Delphine Lang, though I would say that wherever that young man goes, he will fall under the spell of someone who has a way with words. He's looking for an anchor, and political groups offer that sense of belonging, don't they?'

'But we're really not too worried about the Nazis, as I said – though I know you disagree.'

Maisie shook her head. 'I know why you wanted me here, Mr Huntley, and what I have to say bears repeating. Young people are always looking for that something new, aren't they? They are seeking passion in all quarters, and they are ripe for infiltration – and bearing in mind that many of those young people in a place such as Cambridge, or a college like St Francis, are related to powerful men, powerful families, they present both our future and our vulnerability.'

'We can't afford that vulnerability.'

'I know. But the College of St Francis is not our Achilles' heel.'

Huntley sighed. 'I expect to see you at my office on Friday afternoon. Usual precautions, Miss Dobbs.'

'Of course.'

There was a click on the line as Huntley ended the call, and a single dial tone issued from the receiver that was not quite like the tone one would normally hear; then it changed, and Maisie replaced the receiver. As usual, her conversation with Brian Huntley had been scrambled.

Maisie made one more telephone call before leaving the kiosk. It was to James Compton, at his club.

'I'll be back in London on Friday, James. I think I might get away early – there's a lecturer who owes me a favour, so I might get her to take my classes.'

'I wish I knew what was going on – all this business about teaching in Cambridge. It makes me feel quite unintelligent.'

Maisie laughed. 'Oh, that's how I feel when I stand up in front of my class of very acute students.' She paused. 'Have you spoken to Priscilla?'

'Yes – and do not worry, Sandra is still with her, and some fellow from Scotland Yard – Caldwell is his name – has been to see her. Priscilla said he was actually very kind, very gentle with Sandra, who is looking much better.'

'Any other news?'

'Priscilla had a message from Caldwell for you. He said to tell you it's just a bit of gossip, but thought you'd like to know.'

'I don't believe it – Caldwell wants to share gossip with me?'

James laughed. 'I wish I knew more about these men you fraternise with at Scotland Yard. Anyway, he said that someone called Stratton had resigned. He's left the Yard – apparently left the police entirely. Caldwell said you'd worked with him on several occasions and would like to know.'

'Stratton has left?'

'That's all I know – can't comment any more than that.'

'Well, that is a turn-up for the books.'

James laughed. 'And I have a message from Billy that came via Miss Robinson – just in case I spoke to you, he said, which made me laugh – the message is that your father telephoned.'

'Oh dear.'

'Is he all right, Maisie? I hope he hasn't been ill.'

Maisie smiled. 'No, as far as I know he's not ill, but he might be lovesick.'

'I beg your pardon?'

'James, though he tried to keep it from me, I have discovered my father is courting.'

James began to laugh again, and at once Maisie could not help herself – the tension of the previous days broke and she laughed along with him.

With another six weeks of teaching before her, Maisie began her final accounting while still employed at the college, though she had asked to be released from her contract as soon as another junior lecturer in philosophy could be found. With Alan Burnham as principal, Dr Francesca Thomas had been promoted to become deputy principal, and it was during a meeting at her office in Eaton Square on an autumn afternoon, with the sun now low in the sky and the first signs of a clinging winter smog beginning to envelop the city, that Maisie asked her how long she thought she might be at the College of St Francis.

'It's a good place for me, Maisie. I am a respected lecturer in a position of some responsibility, and I enjoy the work – though the naïveté of some of my students rather worries me. I wonder about them, what might happen to them when another war comes, if it comes. But as I said, I am well placed. And of course, given my position, I find myself invited to the drawing rooms of some very interesting people – and anyone interesting to me will be interesting to those I consider an enemy of my country.'

Maisie nodded.

Thomas looked at Maisie, her stare direct, her question equally so. 'And you, Maisie? I know who you have been working for over the past few months, and I know exactly what you do – whether reporting to dear Brian Huntley or your clients. But what will you do when you have completed your reports for Huntley?'

'Then it's back to my business – which is growing, I might add.'

Thomas smiled. 'They won't let you go, you know. And we will meet again, Maisie.' She paused. 'Let me tell you something that Greville said to me, during one of those "how are your classes progressing" conversations in his office. He said that in his estimation we do not pay enough attention to the past, and that one of his fears was that in 1914 we had become a reflection of history when we embarked upon what could be considered another European Thirty Years War. He wanted to do his part to nip that progression in the bud. It's an interesting theory, don't you think? We both understand that the war of words, of economics and underhand activity goes on. The front line is still there, though the trenches look a little different.'

Maisie felt a chill go through her, and touched the place on her neck, the constant reminder of the wounds of that past war, so long ago now, but remembered at times as if it were yesterday.

* * *

The Thurlow family had moved into the property left to Ursula by Rose Linden. The sons had constructed a wooden ramp to allow their mother's chair to be wheeled in and out with ease, and the family seemed to have already made the house their home, and had brought the garden back to its former glory. At Maisie's request, Andrew Dene saw Ursula at his new clinic in Harley Street, and thereafter arranged a series of tests to discover whether anything could be done about her condition. He spoke to Maisie before taking the news to Ursula's family.

'I'm sorry, Maisie, but not much is known about this disease. Sometimes it takes its time to have an effect and the patient seems to go from remission to a sort of attack. Sometimes they live full and productive lives without noticing anything more than tingling in the fingers, and some fatigue. Then there are the other cases where the decline is more rapid. I think Ursula is somewhere in the middle of those extremes. We've struggled to understand how it all goes wrong; how the brain's messages get misdirected.'

'How can the family help her – are there any medications?'

'I can prescribe medicine for pain, should it come – and it develops mainly from being bed- or chair-bound for so long; sores and so on. Otherwise, I would say that she must live a very balanced life – no surprises, no shocks, a good diet. Unlike many of my fellow doctors who think milk is the source of all solutions, I would suggest a limited intake of those kinds of foods. But I will be speaking to colleagues in France later this year – they've done a lot of research on this type of sclerosis.'

Maisie nodded and thanked Dene. 'Send me the bill, Andrew.'

He shook his head. 'No account – she's a dear lady and deserves to be helped, if help can be found.'

She visited Clarence Chen in Limehouse, and took tea with Jennifer Penhaligon at Somerville College, though they did not linger on the subject of her former student, Francesca Thomas. One by one, place by place, Maisie returned to the roots of her investigation, and watched, again, German citizens now living in London gathering at Cleveland Terrace for a meeting of the *Ortsgruppe*. She hoped Huntley and the men he advised would pay attention in time – though she was afraid time was slipping through their fingers while they looked elsewhere for threats to the realm.

Stratton met her at the café on Oxford Street where they had often lingered to discuss their shared cases. They had always described it as 'more *caff* than café.' They sat down at a table close to the window, each with a cup of strong tea and a round of buttered toast and jam.

'I can't believe you've decided to leave the police, Richard – so soon after moving to Special Branch.'

'I can hardly believe it myself, to tell you the truth. But MacFarlane is a difficult man to work with, and that brought other considerations to a head.'

'Your boy?'

'He was only three years old when his mother died, and the past few years have not been without problems – for both of us. My mother stepped in to help, and he goes to stay with his mother's parents for a couple of weeks each summer, but the time seems to be passing so quickly. I thought transferring to Special Branch from the Murder Squad might reduce the number of middle-of-the-night calls, but it didn't quite come off as planned – looking back, I cannot imagine why I thought it would. Wishful thinking, I suppose. And to be honest with you, the College of St Francis sort of made up my mind for me.'

Maisie nodded, understanding. 'He'll be gone all too soon.'

Stratton nodded. 'Yes. Another ten years and he'll be eighteen. My wife always wanted him to have the opportunity to go to university if he wanted; she left some money to pay for his education. I suppose I don't want to wave him off to university – or wherever it is he'll go – and think, "I hardly know the boy."'

'What will you do?'

'Don't laugh – but I've got a job already, starting in January. Until then, I will have time on my hands to spend with my son – seeing him off to school, taking him fishing on Saturdays, football practise in the evenings, whatever I want.' He sighed and took a sip of the still scalding urn-brewed tea. 'Before the war I had wanted to be a teacher, then after university I was more or less in uniform straightaway, and ended up in the military police – which of course led to Scotland Yard when the war was over. I'd been thinking about going into teaching for a long time, and I began applying for positions a few months ago now.'

'You kept that to yourself,' said Maisie.

'Can you imagine what MacFarlane would have said if he had known?'

Maisie laughed. 'Yes – I'm afraid I can.'

Stratton went on. 'I've been offered a position at a boys' boarding school in Sussex, teaching mathematics and physics. There's a cottage in the grounds that goes with the job, and a primary school nearby. My son will be able to attend the school where I teach when he turns eleven, and without fees. It works all around.'

'Will you miss the Yard?'

'Some of it, of course. But I have missed my boy so very much, and I want to spend more time with him.'

Maisie glanced out the window, at the melee of shoppers and people of commerce rushing back and forth, the taxi-cabs vying for road with horses and carts, the buses and the noise. She turned her attention back to Richard Stratton. 'You've done the best thing, Richard. I wish you well.'

'And I wish you well, too, Maisie.'

They held each other's gaze longer than either had intended, then Maisie cleared her throat. 'Well, this will never do. Time is marching on and I have work waiting for me. When do you leave the Yard?'

'At the end of the week.'

They made their way towards the door, then stood outside in the bustle of the street.

Maisie held out her hand, and as Richard Stratton took hers, he drew her towards him and kissed her cheek. She touched her face with her free hand. 'Take care, Richard. I am sure our paths will cross again.'

Stratton smiled. 'Yes, Maisie. Our paths will cross, of that I have no doubt.'

With that he raised his hat, and she turned to walk back towards Fitzroy Square. She looked over her shoulder once, but he was lost in the crowd. And as she made her way back to the office, she wondered, just for a moment, where, in time, she might see Richard Stratton.

Maisie stood outside Wandsworth Prison and pulled her scarf up around her neck against the cold smog that lingered above the brick building. From the centre, it spanned out into five wings, though it was only in 'E Wing' that men were sent to the gallows. She thought that prisons were probably all designed to resemble medieval forts, and she wondered how it felt when the doors clanged behind the condemned once they crossed the threshold. Matthias Roth had been transferred to Wandsworth from Cambridge. He would leave only to stand trial, for which the outcome was a foregone conclusion.

Having passed through several corridors, each with clanking iron gates and guards who checked her papers, she was led to a room where Roth awaited her.

He stood when Maisie entered. 'Miss Dobbs, how kind of you to come. I confess, I was surprised when I learnt I was to have a visitor.'

She took account of Roth's appearance. He wore plain overalls, his hair was shorter than it had been and could no longer flop into his eyes as if he were a boy. He had lost a considerable amount of weight, and his eyes seemed hollow.

'I thought you might like some books.' Maisie placed a parcel tied with string on the table. 'They went through them at the desk; fortunately, none were of much interest to the guards.'

Roth reached forward, unpicked the string and squinted at the titles. 'Ah, a very good mix, Miss Dobbs, though I have to request my spectacles each time I wish to read. My niece brought me in a similar package last week – I must say, her taste differs from mine.'

Maisie smiled. 'I won't ask how you're feeling, Dr Roth. This isn't the most convivial place, but if there's anything you need, please send word. I have contacts . . .'

'Yes, of course.' He rewrapped the books and sighed. 'I wish I could turn back time, Miss Dobbs. I have had time – an irony, of course – to consider time itself, and those small, almost inconsequential decisions that lead to something terrible, that change the path of one's life in a dreadful way. I have wondered why fate chose that particular moment for me to walk down to Greville's office so that we could discuss timetabling of classes when the new building gets under way.' He began to ramble, as if still trying to make sense of his decision. 'You see, it was clear that it would all be a bit chaotic if we didn't have a plan in place, and Greville was quite absentminded at times – the running of the college wasn't as interesting to him as the content of the classes, and understandably so. He was an avatar of hope, not a mere administrator. Which is why I wanted to talk about the debate too.' He shook his head. 'Had I not been there, I would not have heard the row. I would never have known the truth.' He looked up at the ceiling and bit his lip as tears welled up and ran down his cheeks.

Maisie said nothing, but reached out and placed her hand on his. He grasped hers in turn, as if for strength.

'I changed my whole life for Greville Liddicote. I saw men alter the course of their lives because they read his words – men died because they chose not to fight after reading his words. *His* words.' He shook his head. 'I gave him my life savings, and I believed in every word he said, but . . . but they were not his words after all. In that second outside his office, I realised that . . . that we'd all been had. Duped. I'd been taken for the fool I was. This man whom I revered had been no more than a liar, a cheat, a charlatan. He was no better than a common thief. I felt as if my heart would beat from my chest. There was this . . .' He pulled back his hand as if describing a funnel of emotion rising up through his body. 'This . . . emergence of something I cannot describe. I opened the door and I went straight to him and I took his head in my hands, and I killed him.'

Maisie felt the ache of despair emanating from the man before her. She had heard the guilty speak of their crimes before, but she, too, wished she could turn back time, could stop Roth walking along the corridor to Greville Liddicote's office.

'They taught some of us man-to-man combat in the war, you know. I learnt how to kill. But I never thought I would kill in such a way. When you go to war, you wield a rifle, but you hope you never have to look into the face of the man whose life you take. When I entered his room, Greville was sitting there, gazing at something – I believe it was a photograph – and the next moment, he was dead.' Roth stared into Maisie's eyes. 'Seven minutes later, I was back in my office, and I had hardly any recollection of what had happened. It was as if I had woken from a very bad dream and could claim back my real life. But I couldn't. I had killed a man of peace – and at a time when there is so much to fear.'

'So much to fear?'

'You know. You were at the debate. You saw Robson Headley – and my niece. I was shocked. And in that moment of clarity, when Headley stood before us with his misguided rhetoric and his arm raised, I knew what Greville had seen and I had not. I fear our efforts to bring a more widespread peace through the mutual experience of learning will be like David pitted against Goliath.'

'But David prevailed,' said Maisie.

'A single man is not an army, and a mere catapult is no match for a cannonade – for guns, bombs, tanks. Sadly, in this case it is the small man who has a great army at his disposal, and he will come to power, of that I am sure – look again at Headley and Delphine. Imagine so many dispossessed people following blindly, with misguided hope in their hearts.'

Some moments passed. Maisie and Matthias Roth sat in silence. A guard entered and informed Maisie that her visit had come to an end. She turned to Roth. 'You and Dr Liddicote created a place where young people could learn the true meaning of peace. Your work will continue, of that you can be sure.'

He stood up and held out his hand. 'Thank you, Miss Dobbs.'

She bid him goodbye and walked out of Wandsworth Prison and out into the bright, low, autumn sunshine. She closed her eyes and held her face to the warmth, then went on her way.

EPILOGUE

The telephone entered Maisie's dreams before the insistent ringing drew her to consciousness. She shook her head, heart in her mouth, and ran to the telephone; she always worried that a telephone call at nighttime meant that Frankie was ill.

'Hello, this is—'

'Miss!'

'Billy, whatever is the matter? Is everything all right?'

'Margaret Rose was born at midnight.'

'Oh, Billy – you've got a girl. How's Doreen? Is the baby well?'

'Mother and daughter are in the best of health, though Doreen is a bit tired.'

Maisie looked at the clock. It was past two in the morning. 'Where are you, Billy?'

'The hospital. Her doctor reckoned that, with her history – you know – and what she'd gone through last year, she shouldn't have the baby at home. I had to pace the floor a bit before they came and found me and told me we had a girl, and then after a while they let me in to see them, but then they wanted me out a bit sharpish. I'll go home now – Mum and the boys will want to know what's coming home with Doreen – I reckon the boys will be pleased it's another little sister.'

Maisie laughed. 'I'm so happy, Billy. So very happy for you.'

'And you know the best thing, Miss?'

'I think you have the best thing, Billy.'

He laughed, and Maisie heard him yawn. 'The best thing is that we'll be bringing our little girl back to her new home – and it'll be her really new home. And the other best thing is that I'll treat myself to a taxi-cab back there without the driver refusing to take me because he's scared he'll be set upon; that's how it was in Shoreditch.' He yawned again. 'I'd better be off, Miss. See you on Monday.'

'Night, Billy.'

Maisie set the telephone down and made her way back to the bedroom. She snuggled down under the covers – the nights were becoming colder already.

'Who was that?' asked James, his voice thick with sleep as he put an arm around her.

'Billy. They've had a daughter. Margaret Rose.'

'Isn't that the name of the King's granddaughter?'

Maisie began to fall asleep again. 'I believe she's her father's princess already.'

* * *

408

Despite his courtship with Mrs Bromley, her father still showed no interest in moving to the Dower House, and was perhaps even firmer in his intention to remain in the Groom's Cottage. James cautioned her not to press him further, advising that, 'Time will bring him around, though it may be quite a while.'

In the meantime, Maisie was occupied with seeing Sandra well again, and as gently as she could, encouraging the young woman to look to the future once more. She went with her to visit Birkbeck College, a place where many a student of more mature years was able to study in the evenings, so that they did not have to compromise a job to get on. And it was due to Douglas Partridge that Ursula Thurlow was introduced to his publisher. It was a connection that eventually bore fruit, with a subsequent introduction to a publisher of children's books, who thought her stories and illustrations excellent, and offered a contract to publish.

As she worked through to the end of term at the College of St Francis, Maisie spent the time from Friday to Monday in London, keeping up with her business and spending time with James. And each Saturday morning they went to 15 Ebury Place so that James could monitor progress on the house that would become his home once again. The decision to pass the property on to James sooner rather than later had been made by Lord Julian, who realised that he and Lady Rowan would not be likely to open up the house for their use again. As the years advanced, it was clear that they were too ensconced at their home in the

Kent countryside, and thought living at the club might be getting rather tiresome for James. It was time for him to have a London home of his own; the Ebury Place mansion was an obvious choice.

It was close to the end of November on a clear but cold morning, when the air was crisp but the brim of a hat was welcome shade for the eyes, that James, while conducting his usual tour of the rooms, put his arm around Maisie and pulled her to him.

'It's coming along so well, isn't it?'

'I can hardly recognise it – it's so much brighter,' said Maisie, looking around the large empty front bedroom, currently in the process of being painted in the palest shade of sea green.

'Carter will be coming up close to Christmas, to begin bringing in new staff for me – they'll be here in the New Year. It's a bit like launching a ship, getting everyone on board ready for the passengers to embark on the journey of a lifetime.'

'It seems a bit like that, though I've only crossed the Channel a few times, and all but one of those journeys was during the war.'

'Then I will have to arrange a much more enjoyable voyage.' James kissed her forehead and held her to him. 'Will you be my travelling companion, Maisie?'

Maisie swallowed deeply, feeling as if she had caught something in her throat. 'We're not talking about ships, are we, James?'

'No, not really.'

She nodded, framing her answer. 'Then, can I come along just one step at a time? Perhaps when you have the tickets, I'll be ready to jump aboard.'

Maisie could not miss his sigh, but was glad when he spoke again.

'And in the meantime, we'll just enjoy whatever the day brings and be happy with that.'

She smiled and kissed him. 'That suits me, James Compton. Now, perhaps you'd like to take me to lunch; I am quite famished.'

During her final week at the college, Maisie set to the task of packing up her belongings. She had acquired a good many new books since she started teaching, and it seemed that after each visit to Chelstone, she brought a few more from Maurice's library. As she looked through the folders of lesson plans, she considered all that had come to pass since September, when she had been followed by two men as she departed Chelstone. Much had been laid bare – a man's duplicity, a young soldier's question, another man's stand for peace, and a mutiny of enemies. There had been lies and secrets and a children's book that changed the course of so many lives, though it had seemed such an innocent story. She picked up her copy of *The Peaceful Little Warriors* and began to turn the pages. It was an easy read, as children's books are, with larger print and bold illustrations designed to catch a young imagination. And the ending was as she expected it to be:

. . . and they all lived happily ever after.

She wondered about *happily ever after*. Did it only exist in fairy tales, in stories for children? Or was there hope, really? Billy and Doreen had a new daughter, named after a princess; yet the pain of losing their dear Lizzie would never quite leave them. And Sandra, stepping forward into a life she had never imagined as a new bride, without the man she had loved so much. Frankie was, she knew, even friendlier with Mrs Bromley, but the slowly fading photograph of her mother, now more than twenty years gone, would never, she was sure, lose its place on his mantelpiece. And there she was, Maisie Dobbs, a woman who was loved, again. Was it that she did not trust happily ever after, that she was deliberately indifferent to the possibility? Or was happily ever after another one of time's secrets, waiting to be revealed on the journey? She smiled at the irony – the junior lecturer in philosophy struggling with a child's fairy-tale ending. Yes, time would give up her secrets. She just had to wait.

ACKNOWLEDGEMENTS

I would like to thank Dr Tammy M. Proctor, associate professor of history at Wittenberg University and author of the excellent book, *Female Intelligence: Women and Espionage in the First World War*, for so kindly providing me with additional information on the crucial role played by the great number of women who served in the intelligence services across Europe during the First World War, 1914-18.

My thanks to Amy Rennert, the best literary agent in the world and dear friend.

I am equally blessed to work with the enormously talented Jennifer Barth of HarperCollins, who in my estimation is the best editor in the world. My deepest gratitude to you, Jennifer.

Thanks must also go to Susie Dunlop and everyone at Allison and Busby in the UK, for the enthusiasm brought to publication of the Maisie Dobbs series.

If you enjoyed *A Lesson in Secrets*,
read on to find out about the previous book
in the Maisie Dobbs series . . .

To discover more great fiction and to
place an order visit our website at
www.allisonandbusby.com
or call us on
020 7580 1080

THE MAPPING OF LOVE AND DEATH

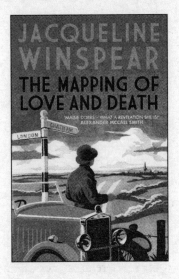

It is 1932 and the remains of a young American are found in a former battlefield in France. The autopsy proves the body is that of missing cartographer Michael Clifton, and when it's clear he was murdered, his wealthy parents hire Maisie to find the woman who wrote a series of love letters discovered among Michael's belongings. The lover identifies herself only as 'The English Nurse'.

While tracking down the elusive woman in an investigation that ventures from London's most exclusive drawing rooms to its most downtrodden neighbourhoods, Maisie must also wrestle with memories of serving as a nurse in the Great War – memories that she has tried so hard to conquer – and of the passionate wartime romance that ended in tragedy . . .